The Nine Day Queen

ELLA MARCH CHASE

EBURY
PRESS

1 3 5 7 9 10 8 6 4 2

First published in the USA in 2011 as *Three Maids for a Crown* by Broadway
Paperbacks, an imprint of the Crown Publishing Group,
a division of Random House, Inc., New York
First published in the UK in 2013 by Ebury Press,
an imprint of Ebury Publishing
A Random House Group Company

The Random House Group Limited Reg. No. 954009

Addresses for companies within the Random House Group can be found at
www.randomhouse.co.uk

A CIP catalogue record for this book is available from the British Library

The Random House Group Limited supports The Forest Stewardship
Council (FSC®), the leading international forest certification organisation.
Our books carrying the FSC label are printed on FSC® certified paper.
FSC is the only forest certification scheme endorsed by the leading
environmental organisations, including Greenpeace.
Our paper procurement policy can be found at:
www.randomhouse.co.uk/environment

Printed and bound by CPI Group (UK) Ltd, Croydon, CR0 4YY

ISBN 9780091947170

To buy books by your favourite authors and register for offers visit:
www.randomhouse.co.uk

In honor of perilous journeys to new worlds.
Samuel Benedict Bautch, born November 11, 2009.
Thank you for helping your gram remember joy when things felt darkest.
I will never forget the moment you grabbed onto my finger and held on tight.
I had been holding on to the promise of you from the day I heard
you were coming, my very own king of the Wild Things.
I can't wait to discover what adventures life holds in store for the two of us!

In memory of my mother, Shirley Ostrom.
She taught me even more about love, laughter, and courage of the spirit as
she battled cancer and Alzheimer's disease than she had in the precious years
before. Here's to smudged-up nail polish, giggling through pedicures, teaching
me to golf, and serving as "fashion police" to the Today show anchors in
your "Rianna pajamas" every morning. I miss you, Squeaky, every single day.
Be happy, Mama. Be you again. Remember everything, especially
how much I love you.

Loving farewells to Rose Tidei, Cindee Taylor, Puck Bautch, and little Emmet.
And hugs to those who said goodbye to loved ones when they didn't want to:
Maureen and Cal, Carl and Ammon, Trudy, Stephanie, Kate, Kevin, Bob,
Barb, Jim, Janie, Cindy, Beckee, Michael, Bethanee, and Garret.

❦ ❧

What have I to wager? Three maids for a crown.
I send them in turn, each to London Town.

❦ ❧

Lady Mary Grey
29 years old
1574

EOPLE TELL ME I WAS NOT ON TOWER GREEN TO SEE my sister die when I was nine years old. They claim my child-imagination twisted the memory as the devil's hand had my spine, or that I distorted the truth the way he dwarfed my frame. I confess there are times I even doubt myself. I am a most accomplished liar. That skill has kept me alive when far worthier souls died. It is no small feat, surviving the dark legacy of my Tudor blood. Just ask my royal great-uncle Henry's six wives. Ask my lord father, my lady mother, my two older sisters, Jane and Katherine. To make such inquiries you would need a sorcerer's art—for they are all dead now, moldering beneath chapel stones.

Yet if I was not within the Tower's confines, on that bleak February twelfth 1554 during Cousin Mary's reign, why can I remember every detail of the grim spectacle so vividly? The frost-sheened walls of the London fortress where three generations of my forebears had come to await their coronations; the vast courtyard that my eldest sister Jane entered in royal glory on a hot day the previous July, forced to become England's most reluctant queen.

Why do my lungs clot with the stink of perfumed bodies pressing close to the oak-hewn scaffold, the witnesses for the crown—a barrier of velvet and lace, doublets and gowns that tower above me, blocking my path as I scrabble to reach my sister?

Even now, twenty years later, I can feel my fingernails tear as I claw my way through the crowd. My cheeks burn, scoured raw by gold thread embroidery and scratched by the jewels stitched to the garments of Queen Mary's courtiers.

But no one in the crowd takes heed of a nine-year-old child—even if she is the traitor Duke of Suffolk's daughter. In the strange hush I am no more worthy of notice than the lieutenant's three-legged dog. Not even those who will profit from my sister's death indulge in an execution's usual fair-day mood. No banter fills the green, none of the vicious excitement that ever boiled about an execution day, be it a hanging at one of the crossroads or Protestants burning alive on fiery stakes at Smithfield. People cluster together, whispering, averting their eyes from one another, the Catholics finger ave beads at their waists, and those of the new religion touch the gold crosses at their throats.

I pause, trying to catch my breath in the suffocating throng, and overhear a spindly noblewoman in a Lincoln green cloak murmur to the man beside her. "The Lady Jane is but sixteen. She is no older than our Anne."

"No guiltier of treason, either, and everyone in England knows it. The Lady Jane was never more than a pawn. But pawns must be sacrificed. Queen Mary will do what she must to get herself a husband and an heir after all these years. She is far from young anymore."

It was true. On Cousin Mary's last birthday, when she was thirty-seven years old, I had given her the gift of a music box. She scarce looked at the trinket because she was so enchanted by the sight of her lady-in-waiting dandling a chubby babe. The queen's face flooded with yearning. For love. Even at eight years old, I understood her desperate craving, perhaps because that same need has lodged with a barbed hook in my own breast.

In my memory, the gentleman blocking my path lifts one shoulder. "The Spanish king demands Lady Jane's head as a wedding boon. They say he will not let Prince Philip sail for the wedding until Lady Jane Grey is dead. The bloody corpse of a highborn English maid is a fitting price to pay, since the king will be snatching the English throne for his son."

The green cloak ripples as its owner shudders. "Imagine what Lady Jane must feel. To be innocent. Executed by your own cousin."

Cousin. My stomach still clenches at the hollow death knell in that word. *Cousin.* My cousin. Jane's cousin. Mary Tudor, with her voice gruff as any man's, her eyes fierce and staring, and a face deep-pocked by sadness. King Henry's eldest daughter, scorned as a bastard, her will bludgeoned until it broke under her father's hand. Mary, who draped Jane's throat in pearls and rubies at Hunsdon House four Christmases before, who gave my pretty sister Kat the silky-eared spaniel she loved. Mary, who slowed her step to my uncertain gait, taking my hand when my impatient lady mother would have left me behind.

How could Cousin Mary have done what everyone said? Signed the death warrant that sent Jane to the block? In our bedchamber back at Dorset House, I had slapped Kat's tear-streaked face when she insisted it was so.

No, Cousin Mary would never carry out the dreaded sentence, no matter what the Spanish king demanded. She was only pretending to acquiesce to Philip's demand, to frighten Jane's supporters into obedience. I was certain a royal messenger would ride in at the last moment, waving a royal pardon at the executioner. Everyone would heave sighs of relief, and then Cousin Mary would let Jane retire to our family estate of Bradgate Hall in Leicestershire. There Jane would be able to read her beloved books and study as many languages as she pleased and perhaps even learn how to be wife to the beautiful, spoiled boy our parents had forced her to wed. After all, Her Majesty the Queen, my kind, beloved cousin, had promised me Jane would be spared.

An elbow jabs me in the cheek, but the splinter-thin woman does not even glance down. "Look you, Arthur! The prisoner comes."

Drums beat a dirge apace with my dread. My sister rises above the crowd as she mounts the stairs to the scaffold. If the messenger does not arrive at once, it will be too late. The winter-white coif of Brussels linen that our sister Kat stitched last Christmas bundles Jane's red-gold hair away from her heart-shaped face. Freckles spatter her ashen cheeks and nose like flecks of blood. The severe black gown Jane wore to her trial enfolds her like the wings of Father's falcon when it dives for the kill, Jane's frame so small she looks like a child playing execution in some macabre game. In her hands she clutches a prayer book. Her lips silently shape the holy words that have comforted her so often. They do not comfort me.

I try to call out to her, but terror and guilt stop up my throat. I will Jane to look at me, but my sister is already beyond my reach, determined to block out the crowd, inhabit her own world, her old defense against our parents' constant battering at her spirit. I wonder if she will finally know peace in heaven. But I do not want Jane in heaven. I want Jane here, where I can steal up silently and curl at her feet, rest my head against her knee. Sometimes, if she is deep in concentration, she does not mind it so very much.

Jane addresses the crowd, but I am too stricken to hear what she says. She presses her prayer book into the hands of the lieutenant of the Tower, Sir John Bridges. The man who was first her jailer, then her friend. His hands shake as he gives Jane a white silk cloth, and she ties it across her eyes, blotting out the last sunlight she will ever see. My sister kneels upon the straw, then reaches out with fingers spread, searching for the block. She cannot find the waxed oak surface. "Where is it?" she cries in distress, groping at nothing but air. "What am I to do?"

Jane, forever trying to be perfect, failing now when the most powerful nobles in England are watching. I know she can hear our lady mother's scathing voice in her head, damning her for shaming the noble house of Suffolk.

A kind hand reaches out to Jane, guides her. Dr. Feckenham, Queen Mary's own confessor, who tried to convert Jane from her Protestant beliefs. Hope fills me. Will he offer Jane the queen's pardon? No. He only guides Jane's fingers to the wooden block with its two half-moons carved out for her chin and shoulders, leaving a narrow, raised ridge in the center where her throat must rest. The hard surface that the ax blade will bite into after it cleaves my sister's neck. Jane grasps the wooden block and sighs in relief. I know she is picturing heaven. I am in hell. Kat was right—no messenger is coming to Jane's rescue. The queen has broken her promise, bent to the will of the powerful men around her. I crumple to the ground, weeping, too far away for Jane to hear me. Events of the past year whirl in my head.

"Forgive me." The words burn my throat as the ax slashes in a terrible arc.

I sob into air now thick and sweet, metallic-tasting with my sister's blood. "This is my fault, Jane. This is all my fault."

I believed it then. Believe it still. Yet in some ways Jane's destiny was forged the day the midwife laid her into the heavy-carved cradle with its royal crest, our parents scowling down at her with disappointment. Our destinies were sealed thus as well, Kat and I, each in our turn. Our lord father said so the night when I first sensed the darkness tightening its noose about our throats.

I should have believed him.

Chapter One

Mary
8 years old
Suffolk House, London
May 24, 1553

SPYING ON THE DEVIL WAS A DANGEROUS PROSPECT, BUT if the whispers were true, he had visited me before. I limped through Suffolk House like a gargoyle brought to life, clutching my dark bed gown under my chin so I might blend into shadow. At any moment the guards might demand to know why the youngest daughter of the Duke of Suffolk wandered alone past midnight. Yet I had learned early that people avoided looking at me if they could. They shrank away as if deformity could be catching, like sweating sickness or plague.

They were wise to be wary. I overheard more than anyone suspected, and I sensed what could not be seen, only felt in that ticklish place inside my head. Of late the voices in that secret spot shrilled that something wicked had come to steal my sister Jane away.

I peered around a corner, saw a guard stationed outside my destination. I ducked behind a heavy chest, but a moment later the man's soft snore sounded. I slipped past. Most of Suffolk House slept—exhausted from the preparations for the greatest wedding England had seen since the dead king Henry took the last of his six wives. Or so my mother claimed. But I could not rest. From the nursery window I had seen the devil ride through the gates, the bear and ragged staff on his banner visible in the light of the torches his guards carried. I knew where he was bound. I had heard my father ordering servants to lay his dice upon the gaming table in his privy chamber. I would hide in the chamber. Tonight I would see the devil's face.

I slipped through Father's door, then stole into the space between the wall and the tapestry of blind Saint Lucy holding her eyeballs upon a plate. I could see the table clearly from there, though I hoped no one would be able to see me. What would happen if my father discovered me? He would beat me. But I had to help Jane if I could.

The tramp of boots sounded in the hall, and I caught my breath. The guard must have wakened. My father did not reprimand him before entering with his guest.

The stranger sank into Father's best chair, his shoulders weighted with gold chains of office. Dark hair fell about a harsh face. His eyes seemed as if they could cut stone.

From the time I could remember, I heard people whispering that Satan had twisted me into a hunchbacked dwarf. Now he was coming to steal Jane away.

For two weeks my eldest sister wept into her bolster at night. Jane, only fifteen, who cried when her lessons were over and kind Dr. Aylmer sent her back to our parents. Jane, who loved me and never lied.

"They have sold me to the devil, Mary." Her words scraped into my memory. I trembled to think how dark the wickedness must be to make Jane defy our parents' will. I still winced every time I recalled the hiss of the willow branch as our mother cut bloody stripes into Jane's back. The beating had gone on until I feared it would kill Jane, and Kat, who could not bear cruelty of any kind, had flung herself at our sister, pleading. "Give way! You will have to do what they command in the end."

Mother boasted that her stern hand had bent Jane to her will. I knew better. Jane had given in because what Kat—at almost thirteen years old—said was true. Even the humblest of fathers had the right to beat a daughter until she followed his command. Our father, the great Duke of Suffolk, wished his eldest to marry the devil's son come morning. The lord chancellor of England was determined on the match too. As chancellor, John Dudley, Duke of Northumberland, held the reins of government instead of the boy king. Dudley was the most hated man in England. The devil . . .

Father leaned across the table, his voice low. "Our plans may come to nothing, Northumberland. Even you—the most powerful man in England—cannot hold back death. The wedding must be accomplished, and you must have time to convince His Majesty to—"

"Bow to the will of God?" Northumberland smiled. "It should not be difficult to convince His Majesty to resolve the situation as we wish—not with eternal damnation hanging over the boy's head. That is what he will face if he allows his Catholic sister to succeed him on the throne and lead England back to the evils of popery—the worshipping of saints' bones that are really pigs' knuckles and indulgences for sale by greedy priests, any sin forgiven if enough money is paid to the church. Worse still, servitude to Rome and a foreign pope who cares little for the welfare of this island. No. We cannot allow a return to that slavery. As to your fear that Edward will thwart our plans before all is prepared, do not underestimate my resourcefulness, Suffolk. I have certain assurances from the woman I have hired to see to His Majesty's comfort."

I chewed my lip. Edward . . . His Majesty . . . they were speaking of my cousin, the king. I had barely formed the thought when my father gave a snort of disgust.

"Comfort? Last we spoke, you said Edward coughs up blood. There is no telling how soon he may die."

"Careful!" Northumberland looked around the room. I held my breath, fearing he might see me with his demon powers. "It is treason to predict the death of a king."

"It may be, but I have seen enough consumption to know when the end is near." Father lifted a gilt ewer and poured two goblets of wine. Never had I seen my father perform such a lowly task for himself. Strange, not even Father's most trusted servant was near. "As for treason," Father said, offering a goblet to his guest, "there are many in this kingdom who would call the business we do tomorrow the work of traitors."

What business? I frowned. Tomorrow there could be no business at all. The day would be spent in celebration of two weddings. Jane's to Guilford Dudley, Northumberland's youngest son, and Kat's to the Earl of Pembroke's lad. My chest ached whenever I thought of it. Two sisters lost in one day. Me, left behind.

My musings were drowned out by Northumberland. "Ignorant crofters might object to what we do, but many Englishmen would say we pull the realm back from the brink of hell. If the Catholics regain power, what do you think will happen to those who took the chalices from their churches and turned abbeys into country manors? Men like you and me, Suffolk? It is our duty to protect England's simple people from their own ignorance. Your daughters will give us the power to see it done. First Jane and Katherine, then Mary."

At the sound of my name, I closed my hands into fists. My nails scraped the rough back of the tapestry. I held my breath in terror.

"Leave Mary out of it," Father said. "No nobleman will wed someone like her—even if she does carry the blood of the royal Tudors in her veins."

"I think you underestimate the power of ambition. We will gamble with her in addition to the others." Northumberland's smile chilled me. "So the game begins. What is your stake to be, Suffolk?"

Father grasped his ivory dice, then cast them upon the table. "I wager three maids for a crown."

Chapter Two

Jane
15 years old
Suffolk House, London
May 24, 1553

PERCHED ON THE EDGE OF MY STOOL AS IF THE SLIGHTEST sound could send me fleeing, my bed robe a ghostly pool on the rush-strewn floor. *There is nowhere on earth I can run to. No safe place to hide.* The words chased through my mind as I set the bright bead eyes of the poppet I was stitching. But no matter how many times I repeated the grim truth, it could not tamp down the panic that battered my self-control.

I drove my silver needle through the cloth, determined to finish the gift I had been working on through the sleepless nights that had hollowed bruised circles under my eyes.

The needle stuck my finger, but there was no one to hear my gasp of pain. It was my own choice, I reasoned. I had wanted to be alone. As long as I could remember, solitude had provided the sanctuary I loved best, walling my world apart from my parents' with concentration they could not penetrate. Solitude was the one gift my nurse, Mrs. Ellen, could grant me on this terrible night of waiting. A few hours of peace before the madness tomorrow. Time to pluck up my courage for what was to come.

The marriage vows, God's decree that Guilford Dudley should become my master, able to take away anything I treasured, command my every waking hour, force me into his bed whenever he wished to avail himself of my body. I shuddered.

Why had I been condemned to this fate? Once I had looked toward my wedding day as something far different. A hope that I might escape the prison of my parents' anger.

Your life will not always be like this, Bess of Hardwick, my mother's favorite lady-in-waiting, had promised after a blow bruised my cheek. *Be brave, Jane. One day you will leave the duke and duchess's care. Pray God will give you a kind husband. Imagine what it will be like to have someone who loves you and will tenderly care for you.*

My heart constricted with grief at Bess's words. I did not have to imagine such love. I had experienced it the year I turned ten and became maid of honor to the widow of King Henry VIII. Catherine Parr had bestowed all the caresses that my mother had never given me. The lady scholar had wed three old men out of duty but had finally married for love—Sir Thomas Seymour, who filled her house at Chelsea with excitement.

I could still feel the dowager queen's tender grasp as she pressed my palm to the swell where her babe grew. I closed my eyes, my mistress's voice preserved in my memory like honey put away for winter.

"Can you feel my little knave kick, Jane?" Catherine Parr's face shone. "I vow I love him already. But you look troubled, child. What is wrong?"

"What if the babe is a girl?" I dared asked. "Will you be disappointed?"

The dowager queen cradled my face between her palms, and for a moment Catherine Parr looked younger than her thirty-six years. "It is true my husband wants an heir, and it would bring me joy to give him one. But if I am blessed with a little maid half as bright and brave and loving as you, I will cherish her above all the boys in Christendom."

I remembered the lump in my throat, the guilt heavy in the pit of my stomach. "I wish you were my mother," I had confided.

The dowager queen enfolded my hand in hers. "I wish I were your mother too."

❦   ❦

A SOUND OUTSIDE THE DOOR STARTLED ME, AND I DROPPED MY sewing as the portal creaked open. Firelight shone on the familiar shape of my youngest sister. Tiny Mary's crooked back made her appear even more painfully dwarfed beneath the weight of a head that might have graced a normal-sized eight-year-old girl were it not for the mismatched eyes. Shadows made the thick, clumsily shaped bones in her face seem even more pronounced. Mary's reddish-brown hair reflected the firelight, and her uneven gait made her shadow jerk across the wall, her eyes as penetrating as some pagan spirit older than time.

"Mary, you gave me a fright!" I nudged the fallen poppet under my stool so the girl could not see it. "You should be in bed."

Mary shifted, her rumpled cloak blotted out by some object I could not identify. "Did you not guess I would come? You always slipped into my chamber to comfort me when I had a wicked dream."

"We are not dreaming, Mary."

"That is why I had to make a plan." Mary raised the object she grasped into the light, and I could discern a cloth bundle full of mysterious protrusions. "I even brought books, though it made the sack heavy to carry."

As I tried to puzzle out my sister's thoughts, Mary limped toward the trunks filled with bridal finery, everything I owned in readiness to be hauled away tomorrow.

"You cannot come with me once I am wed, Mary. Remember. I explained to you."

"I am not going with you. You are to come with me. We are running away."

The words echoed my own desperate instincts. Memories swirled in my mind from the day Mary was born. I could still taste my fear that my father might kill my broken sister the way he had drowned a crippled puppy that Kat's favorite spaniel had whelped.

I remembered braving my mother's lying-in chamber, scooping Mary from the cradle, the memory of the pup flailing against Father's grasp pouring resolve into my limbs.

Father dares not hurt the baby, I had told my mother. *Murder is a sin.*

My mother rose from the bed. I could see the wild light in her face, horror that she'd borne a babe so cursed. *How would you stop my lord if he did decide to destroy her? You, a girl just seven years old?*

I would take Mary, run away.

My mother's laugh still haunted my nightmares. *Where would you go? You're a princess of the blood. No one would dare take you in.*

That truth was even more certain now that I was a maid ripe to wed. There was no escape for me. Not tonight. Not ever. Shoving the memory back, I turned to my sister. "I cannot run away, Mary. It is impossible."

"Of course it is possible. That is the only way you can escape from that terrible man. I heard such things, Jane, with Father and the devil talking."

"The devil?" Gooseflesh prickled my nape.

"That man Northumberland."

"Mary, you must not call him that!"

"Why not? You called him the devil. He *is* evil, like you say. I went to Father's chamber to see for myself."

"Never say you spied upon Father and His Grace of Northumberland!"

"I hid behind Saint Lucy and listened. Father said he would wager you and Kat and me and some people might call it treason. The king is dying, and the wicked man is going to make him do something bad."

"Make who? Father?"

"No, the king. Cousin Edward has to do what Northumberland says, or else there'll be eternal damnation. The devil can do that, Jane."

I grasped Mary by the arms. Her bundle fell in a clatter. "You must never say such things again! No matter what happens. There are already dangerous rumors regarding the Dudleys. God knows what Northumberland might do if someone hears you."

"But it is the truth." Mary looked bewildered. "God wants me to tell the truth. Isn't that what you always tell me?"

"Yes, but sometimes the truth is too dangerous to speak aloud."

"That is why we have to run away!" Mary insisted. "We will go to Hanworth and find Edward Seymour. You promised to marry him before you even met that popinjay Guilford Dudley. Marry Edward instead."

Shame jabbed me. I pictured Edward in the horrible days after Northumberland seized power and trumped up charges to have his father, the Duke of Somerset, executed. What must it have been like for Edward? He had been part of the most powerful family in England—son of the lord protector, cousin to the king. Now he was fatherless, an outcast.

I could imagine Edward's humiliation when he received the message bearing my father's seal: the heir of a traitor was no fit husband for a princess of the blood. Lady Jane Grey was to marry the son of the man who condemned Edward's father. We were not a love match, Edward and me, to wound hearts, but that did not make the severing of the bond a painless one. I had not even written Edward a farewell or told him I had tried to fight my parents' will and honor our betrothal. In the end, what did it matter? The deed was done.

Mary dug her elbow into my side to get my attention. "Why can we not go to Edward? You liked him." It was true.

He had been kind to his adoring sisters those few times our families had been together and soberly applied himself to his studies, passionate about the reforms to aid the simple people that had earned his father the hatred of the self-serving Dudleys. "Besides," Mary insisted, "Edward's father did not have evil eyes. I know that for certain."

"How? You never met the Duke of Somerset."

"No. But Hettie Appleyard called him the Good Duke. Her sister got a cloth dipped in his blood to help make cures and things."

"He was beheaded, Mary."

Mary made a face. "I know he was beheaded. The devil duke is the one who made them do the chopping."

"Northumberland ordered the execution. A headsman swung the ax and our own lord father—" I spun away. Of course Henry Grey had allied himself with the powerful Dudleys. What boon had Northumberland dangled as a reward for such loyalty? I wish I knew. I drew a steadying breath, searching for a way to explain. "Mary, all the Seymours are in disgrace. Edward's father died a traitor. His lands were forfeit to the crown, his titles stripped. Edward is a pauper with his mother and sisters to care for, one step away from being thrown in the Tower himself. He could not help me even if he wanted to."

Something in my tone struck Mary. The child leaned against me. Never would she wrap her arms around anyone in an embrace. Like a wild creature, she did not trust affection, wary when I even drew close. We stayed there a long time, the only sound in the chamber emanating from the hearth—crackling apple wood being devoured by the flames.

"What do you think Father and the bad duke are going to do?" Mary asked at last.

I touched my throat, thinking of Edward's father. "I am too afraid to guess."

Mary considered. "Father had his dice out, and they were wagering. It is some kind of game. He is even going to play with me. Nobody ever plays with me except you. I do not mind so very much about Kat going away. But I will be lonely when you are gone."

I stroked Mary's hair. "I will miss you, too."

"Kat says you will be glad to be rid of me. I ask too many questions that make people itchy."

"Itchy?"

"She says I am like getting rubbed with nettles. I bother and bother, and I won't let people alone. Maybe you want to be alone now, since you will not run away with me."

I looked about the room, saw the jewel-encrusted bodices, the silver-tissue skirts, the ermine-trimmed capes, and the elegant headdresses still to be wrapped in Holland cloth and tucked in my chests. How jealously Kat had pored over the treasures, richer than her own bridal clothes.

Why can I not have the green damask ribbon? she had pleaded. *Jane only wants to wear gray or black.*

Such colors are fitting for a sober evangelical maid! I had protested. *Even the Lady Elizabeth dresses thus.*

What Jane wants is not important, our mother had insisted. *She must be dressed according to her station.*

Our stations are the same, Kat had argued. *Jane is only older by three years.*

We might as well have been separated by half the world. Kat loved pretty things and winsome animals and looked forward to her wedding night with delight. Perhaps Kat would be happy with the Earl of Pembroke's charming son Harry. I hoped so.

"Do you want me to leave now, Jane?" Mary's question shook me from my thoughts. "You sent everyone else away."

I gave Mary a wan smile. "I thought I wanted to be by myself, but I am glad you are here. Will you stay with me?"

"No one will ask me to stay when you are gone. This will be my very last chance."

"Your last chance for what, Mary?"

"Not to be alone."

I knew what Kat would say to such a wistful claim. *Suffolk House is bursting with people. Besides, soon you will be leaving London and going back to Bradgate Hall. Think how many people you will find there.* But few of them would be pleased to see the elfin child who saw sins they wished to hide.

In that instant, I decided. "Mary, I made something for you. I planned to give her to you tomorrow."

"I do not have anything for you."

"Never mind. It is present enough that you would help me escape this marriage if you could." I swept aside bits of the rushes on the floor with the toe of my slipper. "I stowed your gift beneath the stool to hide it. But I do not see it anywhere."

"There!" Mary dove to her knees to scoop up the little rag lady. "Look at her kirtle. You made her gown from the green cloth Kat loved." She smoothed the shimmering fabric back to expose the doll's face. Loops of russet yarn hair had been mussed in the doll's fall. The beads I had used to make eyes were stitched askew, I had been so distracted.

"Her eyes are like mine," Mary said softly. I was not certain if that pleased or disappointed the child.

"I could snip the threads and straighten the beads if you wish," I offered. "It would take but a moment. And, oh! I forgot to stitch her mouth."

"I like her this way," Mary said, as I boosted her onto the big bed where I had lain sleepless so many nights. "I shall call her Jennet. My lady will be like you, Jane."

I managed a faint smile. "I have a mouth, Mary. Unless it has gone missing."

"It is the words that are missing. The hard ones that hurt. You never say them aloud, so the sadness just stays in your eyes."

"If you asked our lady mother, she would tell you I say disagreeable things far too often."

"You argue about Martin Luther and the pope and whether Aristotle or Socrates was greater. Those things cannot make you hurt inside. But our lady mother is full of sharp edges. When she cuts you on purpose, you never say a thing."

"It is my duty to obey her. God's commandment says it is so."

"I hate duty." Mary cuddled her poppet close. "I would rather run away."

Would Mary ever know how much I wished I could do just that? But I strengthened my resolve as dawn spun dark night's shroud. At last a distant, faint rattle warned me that the servants were awake. Soon they would reach my bedchamber door and I would make the journey to Durham House, Northumberland's London residence. Once there I would be sacrificed to whatever ambition had put that frightening gleam in my parents' eyes. Afterward? I gazed down at the poppet squeezed tight in the crook of Mary's arm. Afterward I must find the strength to do my duty. Stay quiet through this wedding and the marriage to come—even though I would be screaming inside.

Chapter Three

Katherine
12 years old
Durham House, London
May 25, 1553

URHAM HOUSE GLITTERED LIKE THE TURRETS OF JOYOUS Garde, the walls iced with tapestries so new, the colors shone jewel-bright, every length of linenfold paneling and leaf of gilding polished to the sheen of a sun-struck lake. Most exciting of all, everything, from the banks of flowers bedecking the great hall, to the feast being prepared in the kitchens, to the jousts to be contested in the newly refurbished tiltyard, were in honor of *me*. Lady Katherine Grey, favorite daughter of the Duke of Suffolk, soon to be bride of the most handsome Lancelot in all England: Henry, Lord Herbert, the son of the Earl of Pembroke.

True, I had known him but a few weeks, and he was as young as I. But a lustiness about him promised a wedding night filled with the pleasure I had heard serving maids giggle about.

I remembered how Henry had lingered when he kissed my hand. *I am forever in my lord father's debt for finding me such a bride,* he had said. *You are the fairest maid I have ever seen. Are you half so eager to be wedded and bedded as I am?*

I looked at the floor, as befitted a proper maid, but my vision snagged on Henry's codpiece, a virile bulge of velvet in the breeches he wore.

It was thrilling to imagine becoming a woman grown. True,

I would miss my sisters, and Father, who pinched my chin and called me the comeliest wench in England. But I had things to look forward to as well. I would suffer no more tedious lessons in classrooms where Jane would always exceed me as scholar. I would not be plagued by Mary's penchant for making everyone uncomfortable. I would have no mother on hand to wound my feelings, though Mary insisted that "the duchess" was least inclined to unleash her temper on me.

Unfortunately, this was to be a double wedding, shared with Guilford and Jane, but once the festivities were over, I would be a wife in my husband's household. I could choose any dress I liked, even if it glittered with as much cloth of gold as the pope's own vestments, my garb finer than what Jane thought proper for a lady of the reformed faith. Even more exciting, I would be privy to all the secrets of a man's body—wise in ways no virgin could imagine. I pictured myself triumphant after my deflowering, feeling smug as I told my maids they could not possibly understand what I knew intimately. I would never admit that I found the prospect of the marriage bed a trifle nerve-racking as well, not knowing what to expect or what to do to please my husband, but hoping that he would find me appealing. Father would have laughed at my doubts.

Ah, my pretty Kat, he had teased when our mother embarrassed me by announcing I had started my courses. *No husband in the common way will do for you. I must find a man worthy of you lest you imitate Helen of Troy and run off with a handsome Paris.*

How serious Jane had looked at his allusion. *I would not wish to be likened to Helen,* she had insisted. Mother scolded her for being jealous of the compliment, and Jane said, *It is because Helen fled her rightful husband that all of Troy fell.* Later that night, when Jane caught me dreaming over my copy of the *Roman de la Rose* instead of the Cicero I was supposed to read, she leaned over to tuck the warming rug more snugly around my feet. I noticed the worried frown line between her brows as she spoke. *Kat, I know it sounds most appealing—tales like Helen of Troy and Guinevere and this.* She touched my beloved volume. *But in truth it would be quite dreadful to give way to such passion and hurt yourself and everyone around you.*

I kicked the rug free, feeling cross. *Can I not have a little pleasure? It is just a story!*

True, but there is danger in filling your head with too many tales such as these. Like when you eat too much marchpane and make yourself sick.

I am not like you, Jane. I like things to look pretty and taste sweet, and I cannot think God made marchpane and roses and— yes—love so beautiful if he did not wish us to take pleasure in them.

Jane had started to speak, but I pleaded, *Let me dream of Sir Lancelot even if I never win him.* I feigned a pout. *Now my feet are cold.*

With a sigh Jane retrieved the rug, placing it back over me. *Kat, sometimes I fear for you.*

I fear for you as well, I said, suddenly feeling sorry for my sister. *I fear that you will never see a single miracle, even if it is right beneath your nose.*

How long ago that conversation seemed. The night Father introduced me to Henry, I hugged Jane and told her she could put her fears to rest. I was in no danger of creating havoc in the name of love like Helen of Troy. I did not wish to run in any direction save into Henry Herbert's arms.

In truth, this bridal day would have been perfect, were it not for the somber figure being decked in wedding finery herself across the room. Jane's unhappiness burdened my every joy with a layer of frost. But I had no time to cajole her out of her mood and have a better day on the morrow. If she continued, the festivities would be spoiled, for me at least. "Jane, can you not be amiable for just one day? You are wedding the son of the most powerful nobleman in England!"

Jane only lifted her arms for Mrs. Ellen to tie the points of her silver tissue sleeves. "Perhaps I should ask him what his father is plotting. I wonder if he knows."

"There is no plot! You are fretting yourself sick for no reason. How many times has strain turned your stomach to acid and given you terrible headaches? And most times your fears came to nothing." I shifted to a wheedling tone. "Your marriage is a great honor. The most powerful nobles in the kingdom are come, and the king himself opened the royal wardrobe for our use—sent ermines and velvets and more jewels for us to choose from than I ever dreamed were in England. Never in our whole lives will we have a day like this, when we are the most important ladies in the land."

Mary chimed in, "Our cousin, Lady Mary, is more important than you are. She is to be queen if the king does not have a son. Besides, you like your husband, Kat. Jane does not."

"Jane is not thinking clearly! She should be grateful our father did not match her with some ancient widower with rotted teeth like Catherine Parr's first three husbands."

Jane's eyes sparked with indignation. "Her Majesty's fourth husband—the handsome man—is the one who broke her heart. Her majesty died of it."

Jane's anger stung. "Father says people do not die of love," I said.

"I was there, Kat." Jane's eyes grew haunted. "If Her Majesty's great love match came to that, what chance do I have with Guilford Dudley?"

My worry over Jane's misery deepened. What would I not give to see her happy just once, without the ghost of sadness shadowing her eyes? "You'll have no chance at all if you continue the marriage the way you have begun. No man likes to be rejected by his bride, even if that bride is a princess of the blood." I saw Jane's shoulders stiffen, and empathy slipped to impatience. "Why are you always determined to make things difficult?"

"Things are what they are."

"Father says that life is what you make it. If you would make an effort to be agreeable, matters would go so much better for you."

"I do not have your gift for smiling no matter what occurs."

"You make it sound deceitful."

"It is."

Hurt burned beneath my satin stomacher. I scooped up the puppy who was tugging on my hem with its teeth. Pressing the warm bundle against me, I wished it were as easy to pluck my sisters out of harm's way. But sisters could not be bundled into a closed stall to keep them out of mischief—even when you knew it would be for their own good. It was hard to watch them make mistakes I knew they would pay for. "I do not wish to argue, Jane," I said, setting the puppy down. "This is the last day we will be together, probably for a very long time. Tomorrow we will not just be sisters anymore. We will be wives, with lives far apart from each other. Who knows when we will see each other again?"

I saw Mary's sad face and noted the poppet crushed in the crook of her arm as a commotion sounded outside the door.

"Jane, you cannot be free of this marriage. Can you not postpone your melancholy for me? Just enjoy this day for what it is? I do not want to carry away the memory of you being unhappy."

"I am unhappy."

I reached out to squeeze Jane's arm as two figures swept in: first, our mother, the Duchess of Suffolk, her Tudor-red hair decked with emeralds from the royal wardrobe, and behind her, Anne Dudley, the Duchess of Northumberland. But my attempt to warn Jane did not matter. As ever, Jane's misery showed on her face.

Anne Dudley looked down her nose at Jane as if she had seen gold beneath a pile of offal and disliked the necessity of having to dig what was valuable out. "What have you to be unhappy about, I would like to know?" She regarded Jane's tear-swollen eyes and ghastly pale face with disgust. "My husband warned me you were a sullen, stubborn girl."

"All we Tudors are headstrong," my mother said. "It is part of our royal blood, which is, after all, the reason you sought my daughter for your son's wife. Once wed, she will be too busy doing her duty to indulge in such nonsense." Our mother dealt Jane a pinch so vicious that my arm ached in sympathy. "Until then the Lady Jane will not displease Her Grace of Northumberland or embarrass her father and me by displaying such distasteful emotions."

Bess of Hardwick entered the room in a swirl of rose satin, the pretty lady-in-waiting's cheeks flushed. "His Grace of Northumberland wishes you to hasten. He bids me remind you there are three weddings to achieve this day."

I remembered the third with surprise. One of Northumberland's daughters was to marry Lord Huntingdon's son in another ceremony this day. Mary had overheard Mrs. Ellen and Hettie Appleyard gossiping about how rare it was: three alliances struck in one day between England's most powerful families. It *was* strange, how quickly the events had been pushed forward. Not that anyone would suspect unseemly haste. The proud Suffolks and our cousin King Edward had made certain that the marriages of Kat and Jane—Henry VIII's great-nieces—were accompanied by the pomp and majesty a royal wedding deserved.

I nibbled my lower lip, not liking the twinge of uneasiness that pricked me. *Careful. The last thing you need is to have Jane's worry rub off. Or to have our lady mother's displeasure spill over onto you.* But Mary did not seem to care about the threat of our mother's anger. My little sister stole past the duchess to slip Jane a small embossed book.

"Mary!" our mother said. "Do not step on the train of your sister's dress! And what is that thing you are holding?"

"Jane's prayer book," Mary said, as Jane took the volume.

"She does not like to go anywhere without it." It was true. While our parents also adhered to evangelical beliefs—especially the one that claimed the riches of the church should be taken and distributed to loyal courtiers—Jane was different. She clung to her faith as a sailor might a floating barrel from a sinking ship. Perhaps it was all the time she had spent with Catherine Parr, who had been so devoted to the reformed faith that she had almost been arrested by her own husband.

"It is not the book I speak of, you quarrelsome child," Mother said. "What is that bundle of cloth tucked under your arm?"

Mary shifted the object, cradling it with a tenderness she rarely showed. "It is a poppet. Jane made it for me because I will miss her when she goes far away."

I felt something between jealousy and shame. I had not thought of giving anything to our little sister. Jane might have told me so we could share in giving her the gift.

"Get rid of it at once, Mary," our mother ordered. "You are too great a girl to be dragging a plaything where the king's whole Privy Council can see it."

Mary thrust out her bottom lip. "I want to show my doll to Cousin Mary. Even though she is quite old, she likes poppets. She told me so when we visited last Christmas."

I knew Mary Tudor had always shown Mary kindness. Perhaps it was because King Henry's eldest daughter had suffered a great deal herself, her alarming stare similar to our Mary's, her gruff, manlike voice startling when first one heard it.

"Lady Mary will not be attending the wedding, nor will Lady Elizabeth," Mother said.

"Why?" Jane asked, the worry lines deepening between her brows. I felt an answering tension in my own shoulders. "They are not ill?"

"Why do you care what the reason is?" I asked. "You do not even like them."

"But they are cousins. We have spent Christmastide with

Lady Mary and visited her often. I cannot think why they would not come to see us wed."

Our mother averted her eyes in a manner most unlike her usual forthrightness. "We did not invite them."

"What?" My shock was mirrored on my sisters' faces.

Jane washed a shade paler. "But that makes no sense."

There were few friends our mother deigned to be kind to, but she had always courted the Lady Mary's favor. Excluding the Lady Elizabeth might be no great matter—our mother regarded Anne Boleyn's bastard with barely veiled contempt. But Lady Mary had been our mother's playfellow, ridden on countless hunts, and gambled long into the night with the nobles that thronged Bradgate Hall. She had even stood as godmother to little Mary. I could see Jane's mind dark with suspicion. Of what?

Nothing. I brushed aside the nagging uncertainty in my own mind. Was this not one more thing to cast a pall over the wedding day?

As if sensing my thoughts, our mother regained her customary belligerence. "That is just like you, Jane, to kick up a fuss now!" Mother said. "You take no interest in your gown or any other wedding plans, then criticize the guest list."

"I only think it strange my royal cousins were not invited."

"It is largely on your account that the Lady Mary has been omitted. After your performance at Newhall, she is not nearly as fond of you as she once was."

"What performance?" the Duchess of Northumberland demanded.

"One of Lady Mary's maids-in-waiting curtsied to the Host when she passed it, and Jane debated theology with her, insisting the bread is but a symbol, not Christ's Body."

Color flooded back into Jane's cheeks, passion into her eyes. "You know I spoke rightly, my lady. The popish religion deceives people. It is not logical—"

"True or false, there is no reason to quarrel over matters of religion with your cousin. She has never felt quite the same about you since that outburst, and it is never wise to make an enemy of a king's daughter. As for her attending the wedding, the Lady Mary makes people uneasy with her clinging to the Catholic faith."

"The Lady Elizabeth is not Catholic." Mary scratched her nose.

Mother's lip curled. "It is hardly fitting to have the concubine's bastard honored at Durham House when Katherine of Aragon's daughter is not here."

"Parliament made Lady Mary a bastard also," Mary insisted. "My tutor said so."

I saw my mother's displeasure, a force as alarming as old King Henry's. "Troublesome child!" she said. "See what you have done, Jane? Infecting your sister with your quarrelsome nature?" Our mother turned back to my little sister, looming over Mary. "I cannot punish your sister for fostering your bad behavior. I will have to discipline you. You will ask no more questions, or you will spend the wedding feast locked in your room, mistress. Make a burden of yourself once more, and I will not even allow you to peep from the back of the chapel."

Jane started to step between them, but her silver tissue train caught upon something behind her. "Do not banish Mary. I beg of you."

Mother leveled Mary with the glare that always made me surrender. Mary did not flinch. "Nor do I want to see that doll in your hands all night. Do you understand what I expect of you?"

"You do not wish to see me, my lady."

It was true, I knew, but I could not bear Mary's wrenching up the tension in the chamber a moment longer. "Mary, why can you not do what our lady mother says? Just put the silly toy in your Thief's Coffer with the rest of the rubbish you steal!"

"Thief's Coffer?" the Duchess of Northumberland asked sharply. "My lady of Suffolk, my family is not accustomed to mingle with thieves."

I saw our mother's affront, but before she could speak Mary cut in: "It is not stealing if you only take things nobody else wants, Your Grace."

Anne Dudley sniffed. "Well, I had best not see you taking anything tonight."

"Never worry, Your Grace." Mary curtsied with a hint of smugness. "You will not see me at all." I watched my sister limp off and knew she was going to the battered wooden chest where she had secreted away her treasures since she was five years old.

I went after her, glad to leave behind the disagreeable women who were attending to Jane. "Mary," I called, catching her beside a window set with the Dudley coat of arms.

She stopped, clutching her poppet as if she feared I might snatch it away. "Jane gave this to me."

"Do not make that face at me!" I said. "I could not care less that Jane gave you a gift. Poppets are for babies, and our lord father bought me ever so many wedding clothes."

"Then what do you want?"

"I wished to ask you something." My cheeks burned. "I do not know exactly how to say it. You know I love you and—and Jane and I . . . everyone in Father's household is used to the way you stare at people and blurt out the things you do. But Henry is not. Please do not be—be mucking about him and . . ."

Something in Mary's face made me hesitate. I did not want to hurt my sister, yet the idea of being humiliated in front of my bridegroom was more distressing still. "A young man like Henry might . . ." *fear I will make a babe like you.* Even though I did not speak the words, they shamed me. But I had seen that fear in Henry's eyes, and it cut. "He might take what you say amiss. I want Henry to love me," I said, feeling raw inside.

"He does love you. I heard him talking to Guilford Dudley out in the gardens."

My pulse tripped. "What did Henry say?"

"That he got the beauty. Guilford whined that Jane is a tiresome prig, but at least he and Henry did not have to swive the royal toad." A rare vulnerability darted into her eyes, and I was struck by the difference between Mary and me, the bones in her face thick and off-kilter where mine were delicate and fine. "Did Guilford mean me, Kat?"

I felt a surge of dislike for Jane's betrothed. "Even if he did, Guilford should not have said that! Your blood is more noble than a Dudley's will ever be."

What would it be like, I wondered, if people shuddered when you drew near? Made nasty jokes about you? Despised you for things that were not your fault? Mary could not help being different. "Mary, I have something for you, too. A take-leave gift."

The child brightened. "You do?"

"Of course I do," I said. I just was not sure what that gift was yet.

❧ ❧

NEVER, IF I LIVED TO BE A HUNDRED, WOULD I FORGET THIS DAY. No, I thought with a delicious shiver. There was no Katherine Grey now. I was Lady Katherine Herbert, wife of the youth sitting beside me on the dais. His thigh crumpled my wedding dress as he pressed as close as he could get to me amidst the voluminous folds. His eyelids drooped, but not with an excess of drink like Guilford Dudley, who sat beside Jane, his broad shoulders slouching from all the toasts he had drunk with his scoundrel friends. Henry's eyes sparked eager as he and I stole kisses while the crowd applauded, and Mary looked out from her hiding place behind a pillar, practicing kissing on the back of her hand.

"You had best send my lord and lady Herbert to their bridal bed, Suffolk!" one of my father's hunting friends bellowed. "The groom chafes so, I doubt he has tasted a morsel of this splendid feast you have spread before us."

"I fear my new sons will need to be patient," Father called back. "His Grace of Northumberland and I have decided it will be best for the young people to get to know each other better before they bed together."

"What?" I paused with an almond cake halfway to my mouth, honey dripping on my fingers.

Henry grasped my wrist and licked the sticky golden drops. "Never worry, wife. Your father is jesting. It is the custom with a bridal couple. My lord of Suffolk, you must not tease when Guilford and I have been anticipating the wedding night with such enthusiasm. You will not get grandsons with patience. Surely you are not so cruel as to give us the slightest sample of sweetmeats, then snatch them away."

But Guilford Dudley looked as bored as ever, and Jane . . . I looked at my sister. Jane looked as if she had received a gallows pardon.

"Guilford, tell our new father how anxious we are to do our duty!" Henry kicked his friend under the table.

Guilford sucked the marrow from the peacock bone he was eating, then threw it aside. "I bow to the wisdom of my lady's father."

Anne Dudley fluttered her ring-laden hand. "Was there ever such a handsome, amiable youth as Guilford? My last babe, the child of my older years. You are a lucky bride, Lady Jane. Guilford is wise enough to be guided by his elders in all things."

Henry leaned over and murmured in my ear. "Perhaps Lady Dudley will observe her precious darling in the bedchamber to tell him how prettily he swives his wife."

I choked on a laugh.

Henry thumped me on the back. "You and I, sweetheart, will need no such encouragement. We shall find our own way together, shall we not?"

My cheeks burned, but I smiled. "You are my lord and master now."

Yet my father rose from the table and strode to Henry and me, gathering us in his embrace. "You hear this little beauty, everyone? Of the three, Katherine is most my daughter. Hot-blooded and ripe for her husband. Lord Herbert is a fortunate man to have such an eager bride." He turned to Henry. "She is worth waiting for, my lad. It is only the final act you are forbidden. There is much you can amuse yourselves with until then."

Henry was no longer smiling. He looked puzzled. "You are serious, Your Grace?"

"His Grace of Northumberland thinks it best. Wipe away those long faces, children. You are not the first bride and bridegroom to tarry before consummating the marriage."

"But there is no reason for the delay," Henry argued. "We are not babes who are too young, nor sick, nor too weak to do our duty."

"Nor too patient, from the sound of you," Father said. "It is a lesson that will serve you well, my boy. Now, let us drink another toast to the fine grandsons you will breed me when the time is right."

Stunned, I watched my father weave back to his seat beside my mother. He kissed her with a fierceness I had come to recognize over the years, hot passion never far beneath the surface between them.

I blinked back tears and looked at the nuptial ring Henry had slipped on my finger hours before. Why had our father insisted on this delay? It was Jane's fault that I was feeling so unsettled—all Jane's suspicions from earlier this morn. The urge to quarrel with my sister grew so strong, I drew Jane to a nook beneath a bank of flowers where we could be alone. "It is not fair," I said. "Why would Father deny us our wedding night?"

"I do not know, but it puzzles me even more." Jane's wide hazel eyes grew more troubled. "Three marriages on the same day binding the most powerful noble houses together. It is almost as if they are sealing some sort of pact."

My anger grew hotter because the dealings of the past day were every bit as strange as my sister said. "That is just like you, imagining conspiracies on our wedding day! You might as well be some fairy of doom spoiling everything."

Jane relented a little, pressing my hand. "I am sorry you are disappointed, Kat. If it makes you feel better, I do believe everything will turn out right for you in the end."

"Thank God that isn't the most enthusiastic wedding blessing I received today."

"For all my uneasiness about our lord father's motives, I cannot help believing he may be right in this matter: It may be better to postpone lying together, allow us to become accustomed to each other in small doses."

"You say it as if the nuptial bed were some kind of bad-tasting physic like the ones Mrs. Ellen used to give us."

"When I was in the dowager queen's household, Catherine Parr told me that marriage is like a glove you purchase without trying it on first. You cannot know how it will suit you until your hand is trapped in it forever. After she died, I had nightmares. Did you ever hear the tale of the French queen? Catherine de' Medici?"

"I do not need a history lesson! We are not in the schoolroom, praise God."

"People whisper that she murdered Jeanne of Navarre by giving her a pair of poisoned gloves." Jane touched the soft embroidered kid sheathing her own fingers. "I could not stop thinking about that after the dowager queen died. Did her husband poison her? Or was she poisoned by heartbreak when she found him with another woman?"

I knew what "woman" Jane spoke of, though she did not say the name aloud. Our cousin Elizabeth, with her concubine mother's sly, slanting eyes and lush bosom. What would I feel if I caught my Henry in another woman's arms? Might Henry, in his impatience tonight, go find some serving maid to relieve his passions since he was denied his wife?

"Kat?" Jane's voice tugged me back to the great hall, its crowds of people, the glitter of jewels, the subtleties of sugar and towers of almond cakes. "What if we have just slipped our hands into poisoned gloves and can never get them off?"

"For once it would have been nice to have a sister who could sympathize with me, without twisting everything around to make it so much worse! I am glad I am going to Pembroke House with Henry tomorrow! I will not have to listen to talk of poisoned gloves when all I want is to be happy!"

Jane touched my arm. "I am sorry."

"Do not be." I shook off Jane's hand. "I intend to be the happiest wife ever. Just you wait and see how perfect my marriage will be." Tears burned my eyes as I stomped back to the table where my husband was waiting.

❧ ❧

I PACED THE BEDCHAMBER THAT HIS GRACE OF NORTHUMBERLAND had assigned to me, but I could not bear to lie in the vast bed alone. Frustration gnawed at me, confusion bewildered me, my heart felt bruised beneath my breasts. It was as if Jane's mood had summoned dark clouds over my beautiful wedding day and the storm had finally broken.

I was a wife, and Henry was my husband before God, but our elders had banished us to separate rooms like children. More irritating still, I found myself missing my sisters in this strange house, this room empty of Mary's odd chatter and Jane's quiet presence. It was one thing to be torn away from everything I knew with Henry at my side. But to be trapped in this chamber alone, with nothing but my troubled thoughts for company, was misery.

You must admit it is strange, Mary's voice seemed to mingle with Jane's, *to order you to wait when our lord father was in such haste to get you wed*.

"It is Northumberland who is behind this delay," I muttered. "He is just exercising his power for the pleasure of it. Or perhaps he does not wish the embarrassment of his guests seeing Henry and I so happy on the morrow while his own son and daughter-in-law look as if they have suffered through a war instead of a wedding night." I thought of Jane when last I saw her. Stripped of her wedding finery, she perched on a stool near the fire, her nose thrust in yet another of her endless books. Her every muscle strained, her pale lips soundlessly forming words in Greek or Latin or Hebrew. I had not bothered to discern which. Postponing the wedding bed was the greatest gift Northumberland could have given Jane. I felt an urge to find my sister and pick at her until we quarreled again, to release the tension making me so edgy.

I remembered all the times we had stolen to each other's rooms once the rest of Bradgate Hall slept. But would I even be able to find Jane's chamber now without asking a servant the way? No doubt Mary could have drawn a map to Jane's chamber, I thought sourly. Imagining my younger sister's smug expression spurred me to action.

Smoothing the front of my silver-embroidered bed gown, I crossed to the door to quietly push it open. But the panel had barely swung a hand's breadth when it slammed to a halt, a low oath startling me from the other side.

A shriek of surprise rose in my throat, and then someone clapped a hand over my mouth. Panic surged, and I struggled, until I recognized the shadowy figure's tousled dark hair, his twinkling eyes.

"Hey ho, wife!" Henry said with a broad grin. "Not wed a day, and already you are trying to blacken my eye?"

"Henry!" I gasped the instant his hand fell away from my mouth. "What are you doing here?"

"I have come to claim my bride." He guided me back into my room as he kissed my cheek, my throat.

"But my father . . . he said we must not . . ."

"Only you can forbid me your bed." One large hand slid up to unfasten the laces at my throat. "Do you wish me to go, sweetheart?" Henry slid his hand into the cove of silk he had opened, his fingers finding satiny warm skin.

"No. I wish you to stay."

"That would be foolhardy." The gravelly voice sounded from the still-open door. Henry and I sprang apart. "My master forbade it."

"What the devil?" Henry exclaimed as one of Northumberland's serving men stepped from the shadows. The intruder's black livery blended with the night. He regarded us with keen eyes, his arms folded over his chest. Henry moved to shield me from the man's sight, but it was too late. I could feel him looking at my rumpled bed robe. I clutched the edges of cloth tight at my throat.

"Leave this chamber at once!" Henry ordered, but I could hear a sudden catch in his voice. "We are wed before God. There is no reason we should not bed together."

"His Grace will have something to say about that. Come along with me. He returned from some errand but a few minutes ago."

"An errand? In the middle of the night?" I could not help but ask.

The servant puffed up his chest. "His Grace is a very important man. The business of the kingdom does not come to a halt because a pretty little wench got herself wed."

The servant gestured, and we followed him through the grandly appointed chambers to the most exquisitely decorated of all. I felt that lump of dread so familiar from the times Jane and I had been brought before our mother for some infraction. But the Duke of Northumberland was far more daunting than our formidable mother had been. Even Henry's hand slicked with sweat where it grasped mine.

The servant knocked upon a door. A muffled voice bade us enter. I balked for a moment, fighting a childish urge to flee. But Henry held fast to my hand, his face pale, his chin high in defiance.

"My lord duke," the servant said as we entered. "It was just as you suspected. I caught Lord Herbert going into the Lady Katherine's bedchamber."

Outrage and dismay filled me as the duke flung off a dark cloak strangely simple for a man of his importance. "I thank you for your vigilance," Northumberland said to his servant. "It is a gift to be able to anticipate your opponent's next move. There is a streak of recklessness in this pair. Obviously I was wise not to trust them." With grave deliberation, the duke turned toward us. My stomach sank.

Henry cleared his throat, sounding younger than he ever had before. "Your Grace, the lady is my wife. We have the right to—"

"Lord Herbert, spare me the tedium of babbling lame excuses. You may think yourself the finest cock in the pit, but I hold your jesses, boy, and could snap your neck at a whim. If you ever challenge my authority again, you will see what happens when I am displeased."

Henry's Adam's apple bobbed. "Your Grace, I only wished to . . . I do not understand why we must delay."

"It is not for you to understand. It is for you to obey." Northumberland turned on me. "As for you, my lady, what have you to say for yourself?"

I tried to squeeze words through my throat, but I never knew what to say when I was in trouble. Jane would argue logic, Mary would pierce to the core of the matter, but I could only hang my head and blink back tears of remorse. I loathed my own helplessness. "Your Grace, I am sorry I displeased you." I sank into a low curtsy, but my knee caught upon Northumberland's cloak and tugged it from the stool he had tossed it upon.

The cloth slid to the floor, and a sudden, strange tinkling sound startled me. Glass? I froze in horror as a vial tumbled free and shattered against the stone. White powder spun a cloud over the shards. *Merciful heavens*, I thought in dismay. Glass was valuable, rare. Whatever Northumberland carried in it must be precious indeed. I dove to scoop up the pieces of glass, but he grabbed my arm and jerked me away so hard, I knew I would be bruised come morning. "Do not touch it, you stupid girl!"

I leaped back. Henry caught me in his arms. "Your Grace, it was an accident," he said.

"I am certain my lord father will replace your . . ." I faltered, trapped in eyes that burned with rage and something more, something sinister, terrifying.

The devil duke, Mary had named him. Mary, with her strange ability to see more than anyone.

"We will not disturb your father with tales of your disobedience. It would be most unfortunate for you should anyone hear of your *accident*." Northumberland drew out the word like a blade. "You understand my meaning?"

"We do, Your Grace," Henry said. Even he looked frightened.

"My man will see you out," Northumberland said.

The servant looked to the mess upon the floor. "Your Grace, let me sweep the glass so you will not cut—"

"By Christ's holy blood, do as you are told!"

The servant jumped, as startled as Henry and I were. "As you wish," he said with a bow.

I looked over my shoulder as we were hastened from

the room and saw something strange. The haughty Duke of Northumberland knelt beside the wreckage, scraping glass and powder up with a stiff sheet of parchment, careful to touch none of it. He had bound a Holland cloth over his nose and mouth. To protect himself? From what? I remembered tales I had heard of the duke's ruthlessness, how he had befriended purveyors of poison.

The duke paused in his task, looked up, and caught my eye. It was as if he could read my mind. I fled to my room, too afraid to set foot beyond my door even to find Jane. But what could I tell Jane even if I reached her? That I believed the Duke of Northumberland had a supply of poison? Could a powerful man use such a devious tool? If so, what pains might he go to in order to keep from being exposed?

Murder. I could almost hear Mary's voice. *Murder is usually what poison is used for.* I stopped up my ears, but I could not silence my fears. I crossed to the bed Henry and I had not shared. I huddled under the covers, straining to hear any tread of footsteps drawing near, any sliding of a wooden panel concealed in my room.

Do not be ridiculous, Katherine, I told myself. *Northumberland could hardly poison the daughter of the Duke of Suffolk even if he wanted to.* But what strange thing had Mary heard, wandering about last night? That some game of chance was being played— and that Jane, Mary, and I were the stake?

What if that were true? I hugged myself against the question that chilled me. If Northumberland's powder was poison, then who was it destined for?

Chapter Four

Mary
Bradgate Hall, Leicestershire
June 1553

KNOW LIGHTNING. WHEN IT WILL CRACK THE SKY WIDE
open and split oak trees with trunks so thick, five men
linked together could not circle them with their arms.
Where it will touch its finger to thatched roofs and set the straw
on fire. I feel it ready to strike when the crooked place in my
back aches. I know when lightning is building up inside my lady
mother too.

The storm crowding the sky over Bradgate should have been
over three weeks ago, but the duchess struck out with fists and
sharp words at anyone unlucky enough to cross her path. Even
Bess of Hardwick, my mother's favorite person in the world,
shook her head in confusion, saying she did not know what
could be amiss.

Upon our return from London, things here in Leicestershire
should have gone back to the merry, pleasure-rich life my parents
love. Hunting all day, lounging at the table until no one could
eat another bite, the whole Suffolk household gambling late into
the night.

So why did the air grow thicker as the days dragged by? Why
did my mother grow more on edge? And why did mud-spattered,
exhausted messengers from London still come and go at all hours
of the night and day? My parents' eyes grew hard and greedy

when they hid themselves away with whatever missives those messengers brought. They looked as if the letters were gold coins they were about to sweep into their purses.

Mistrusting the patch of blue sky beyond the window of my chamber, I tucked myself into my corner and cuddled my poppet close, but Jennet's black bead eyes could give me no answers to the questions that troubled me. No one noticed. Since the wedding it was as if I had disappeared, like Jane, like Kat. I was a ghost.

"I am beginning to fear one of the servants packed Lady Mary's tongue along with her sisters' bridal clothes." Hettie's voice poked into the shadows of my favorite corner in my chamber. She turned toward me, hands on hips. "Not a smidgen of gossip have you told me for weeks. Lonely, I wager. Best get used to it. From now on you will not have your sisters to cling to like a cocklebur. They are wives now. They have husbands and soon, God willing, children to occupy them. They will have no time for the likes of you."

"Hettie!" Bess chided. "There is no reason to be so hard."

"I am just telling the child the truth." Hettie tossed her head. "The world is hard, and it will be even harder for Lady Mary than most unless she learns to make herself more agreeable to those around her." She did not sound as if she held much hope of my doing so.

Bess reached out to touch me. I stared hard at her motherly hand, wondering what her fingers would feel like on my cheek. But my gaze built a fence around me. She let her arm fall back to her side. I tried not to mind. Kind as she was, Bess never warmed to me as she had my sisters, especially Jane. Still, her voice was gentler than most when she addressed me. "Mary, never mind what Hettie has told you about the bond between sisters. It can never be broken, no matter how far away fate sends them. I am sure Lady Jane and Lady Katherine are missing you as well."

Hettie made a dismissive sound. "Lady Katherine's head was awhirl with her lusty young husband even before she left London, while if all accounts are true the Lady Jane—"

Bess looked at her in a way Kat would have called formidable, hints of a steely will that made my pretty sister bow to Bess's every command. Hettie retreated from the field of battle with a "harrumph" of protest, and Bess swept out of the chamber, off, no doubt, to serve my lady mother. Hours passed while I played with Jennet and wondered if Hettie was right. What good would I be once my sisters had pretty babies? Sweet-faced babes with straight spines for Kat and Jane to love?

I jumped a little, startled, as a serving girl rushed through the paneled door, her palm pressed to her cheek. A handprint reddened the maid's skin.

"You would think Her Grace would be puffed like a peacock now, proud of those exorbitant weddings," the woman complained to Hettie Appleyard. "The whole court is still buzzing about it. Half a dozen of the messengers who have ridden through told how the king ordered treasures from the royal wardrobe be sent to adorn the brides. They recounted how many exalted guests graced the ceremony and mentioned that King Edward himself was disappointed because he was too unwell to attend. But instead of reveling in the triumph, Her Grace is more stinging than a beehive struck with a stick."

"Hush now!" Hettie nodded in my direction. "Mind the Lady Mary."

The servant blew her cherry-round nose on a fold of petticoat. "Little crouchback knows better than any of us. The duchess nigh knocked her across the room the other day."

Since then I had done my best to stay out of my lady mother's way.

"I am here to tell you matters just got worse, God save us. Her Grace is in her solar, shattering enough Italian glass to feed the village for a twelvemonth. Half-wild she is. The latest messenger brought tidings that sent her into a fury at Lady Jane."

Despite my mother's temper, excitement bubbled beneath the popinjay-blue sarcenet of my bodice. After all, Jane was far away where the duchess could not strike her. I came out of my corner. "Did my sister send a message to me?" I demanded. Twice Jane had included a note for me with the formal missives that duty compelled her to write to our parents. I kept the letters in my Thief's Coffer and read them until my eyes ached.

"I fear the Lady Jane is not well enough to hold a pen. Mrs. Ellen writes the poor thing is sick in mind and body. Your sister fears she is being poisoned."

My heart felt like a rock in my chest, but Hettie discounted her claim. "Who would want to poison the Lady Jane? A more quiet and devout girl never lived!"

"She has a stubborn side. She will scratch like a cat on questions of faith." The servant's voice dropped low. "Perhaps Northumberland seeks to rid his son of an unhappy bride. Gossip says the lady's hair is falling out and her fingernails and skin are peeling."

A picture flashed into my head—Jane's skin flayed away like the image of Saint Sebastian in the gallery while the devil duke looked on, his eyes glowing like a blacksmith's iron. I did not care how angry my mother was or how cruelly she might punish me. I scooped up my petticoats and went to find her.

My legs shook as I made my way down the gallery, still thronging with my parents' friends and acquaintances. Even they were gathered in nervous groups, whispering. I listened for the sounds of confusion, looked for my parents' gentlemen and ladies-in-waiting. I found them clustered together outside the solar door looking nervous. I knew my parents were in the room beyond the closed oak panel.

". . . dead any day . . ." I heard Bess whisper. Terror made my stomach coil.

Something heavy crashed against the door. I charged toward

the gentleman usher guarding it. "I will see my lord and lady now."

"My Lady Mary." He tugged at the collar of his doublet. "I cannot think it wise."

I gave him the look that made Owen, the stable boy, think I could make his fingers drop right off.

"I will ask if their graces will see you." The usher opened the door and began to announce, "The Lady Mary—"

I did not wait for their response. I went in. The chamber was awash in wreckage. Gold plate and bric-a-brac littered the stone floor. Father paced near the window, his cut-leather doublet half unlaced. His velvet cap had been torn from his balding pate, the white feathers trampled on the floor. A glass shard cut through the sole of my slipper, but I did not slow down, not even when my mother turned on me, her eyes filled with rage.

Her face was as red as the Tudor roses painted on the sideboard. "Get back to the nursery! I will have Hettie Appleyard whipped for letting you run amok!"

I clutched the edge of my mother's ivory inlaid gaming table, resolved that no one would drag me from the room before I had an answer. "Is Jane going to die?"

"Die?" Father echoed. "Of all the stupid questions."

"People outside—I could hear them whispering . . ."

"Your sister is not going to die," Father said, "though she makes me want to wring her neck of late. If she does anything to ruin the honor we have worked so hard to bring about, I will make her pay for it!"

"But the duke is poisoning her," I insisted. "I heard Jane's skin is peeling off—"

My mother grabbed my arms so tight, I thought the bones would snap. "Quiet, you idiot child! Your sister imagines things. Jane was always given to flights of sick fancy. Why would Northumberland poison the girl? He needs to keep her alive."

"Someone is dying. Lady Bess said so. If it is Jane, you must tell me." I fought to keep tears at bay. Tears were a weakness my mother could never forgive.

"They were speaking of the king." Relief that I would not lose Jane filled me as my father waved his hand. "Be it in a day, a week, a month. Let His Majesty die now. All is in readiness." His eyes glittered in a strange manner. But not even that could frighten me, as long as Jane was safe. Still, my curiosity stirred. "What is in readiness, my lord father?"

"You fool, Henry!" my mother said. "You know how tenacious the child is when her curiosity is roused." She shook me. Hard. "It is a sin to be eavesdropping around corners, and God will punish you for it. Say nothing of this to anyone, Mary. It is treason to foretell the death of a king. Do you want your father to have his head chopped off with an ax?"

"No." I put my hands up to cover my own stubby throat.

"I would take you to Tower Hill and make you watch the headsman do his work if your father died because of you. What do you think of that?"

"I would not like it." The insides of my stomach bubbled up, bitter on my tongue.

"Surely a girl who is responsible for such a terrible thing should have to watch the fruit of her wickedness."

Knocking sounded at the chamber door. The gentleman usher appeared strained as he shoved the panel open. "Your Graces, a thousand pardons—"

"Again you interrupt us!" my father exclaimed. "Did we not tell you we should not be disturbed?"

The usher appeared ready to duck should my mother fling a plate at his head. "But Your Grace, I was certain with such an exalted visitor, you would wish to be notified."

"Northumberland!" My father wheeled toward my mother.

She looked like a wolf about to feast. "No. His Grace would have to stay in London to secure matters there. Perhaps it is Pembroke."

Pembroke? I thought. Why would Kat's new father-in-law come to Bradgate?

"It is neither of those goodly lords, Your Grace," the gentleman usher said. "It is Lady Mary, the late king's own daughter."

My father swore. My mother looked more thunderous than before. I could not guess why. In the past my royal cousin's frequent visits had been greeted with excitement.

In spite of my parents' singular reaction, pleasure drove back the sick feeling in my stomach. Jane was not dying, and my kind cousin had arrived. Perhaps my mother would forget how wicked I was.

Father waved at the usher. The man bowed and backed out the door. "This bodes ill!" Sweat beaded Father's upper lip as the door shut behind the servant. "Do you think Lady Mary suspects something? If she discovers the truth, she might have time to rally supporters to her cause."

"She is not canny enough to unmask us. My cousin is as blindly trusting as a child, though considering the blows life has dealt her, I cannot tell you why." My mother's scorn for the relation I cared so much for pinched at me.

Father looked to her like one of his hounds waiting for their master to give them direction. "What shall we do?"

It was as if God jerked my lady mother's mouth with invisible purse strings into a smile. "We must keep her occupied until I can think."

"You had best be kind to her," I said. My parents started, as if they had forgotten I was there. I did not falter. "When King Edward dies, she will be queen." Everyone knew Cousin Mary was heir to the throne until Cousin Edward wed and had babies. If he were dying any day, there was no time for that.

My mother's voice grew as chill as ice slivers. "We must trust the succession is in God's hands."

"Or in the hands of His Grace of Northumberland," Father muttered.

I rubbed my crooked back, the lightning threat I sensed in my mother growing fiercer. Something dreadful was rumbling beneath the surface of my parents' smiles, I knew not what. Suddenly I wished my cousin were riding out of the manor's gates instead of waiting to be received in the great hall below.

"Daughter, get to the nursery," Father said. "We have enough to manage without a child getting in the way."

My lady mother looked at me. I did not trust the set of her mouth. "Mary shall accompany us to greet her cousin."

I blinked in surprise. "Will I?"

"Frances," Father said. "I do not think—"

"Do not attempt it, husband. That is what you have me for. My cousin has always been fond of our Mary. Is that not true, daughter?"

I felt as if I were treading on rotted boards, ready to fall through. "She is very kind."

"Yes, and you are most bereft without your sisters, are you not? I am certain Cousin Mary will give a good deal of attention to easing your loneliness. She experienced much painful solitude when she was a girl. Do you not see the solution to our dilemma, Henry? If the girl is about, Lady Mary can scarce pursue more troubling questions."

Father kissed my mother on the cheek. "You are a wonder, Frances. Wily as Machiavelli himself. It was a fair day when I wed you."

My mother straightened my headdress, her nails scraping my temples. The scratches burned. "Mary, you look a fright, but I know you cannot help it," she said, trying to right the kirtle and petticoats that had come askew when she shook me. "Be a good girl now, and you will have a sweetmeat."

After smoothing her own rumpled garments and replacing Father's cap, she went to the door and summoned the usher. "Before a quarter hour has passed, I want this chamber to sparkle as if naught had happened here. Not a trinket out of place. Do you hear me?"

The usher bowed in assent.

My mother offered her arm, and Father linked his through it. "We shall see this through," he said. "In six months' time we will laugh over how raw our nerves were on the princess's final visit."

Her final visit? What could that mean? Would she not come to Bradgate once she was queen? That would be sad indeed. As the three of us descended to the great hall to greet our visitor and her retinue, my parents' smiles turned as slick and sweet as sun-melted butter. Cousin Mary stood in shadow, her auburn hair caught beneath a cloth of silver headdress sparkling with amethysts, her thrice-piled velvet gown the deep, rich purple she favored. A table-diamond as big as my fist hung from a gold chain that circled her neck. Sparkling rings piled on her fingers until her hands looked too heavy to lift. She had been pretty once, I had overheard our lady mother tell Kat some time ago. It was hard to imagine because of the sadness deep-drawn on Lady Mary's face. Kat said the sadness was because they had taken the princess away from her mother for four long years and had not even let her see Queen Katherine when that good lady lay dying. Of course, their suffering was not our uncle King Henry's fault. It had been that witch Anne Boleyn's doing, the royal whore trying to protect her bastard Elizabeth. Or so Kat had assured me.

In Lady Mary's presence my father tried to act his usual hearty self, only a spot of color on each cheek hinting at his strange mood. But my mother made the skin at the nape of my neck crawl. She raced forward and grasped Cousin Mary's hands, pretending to be overjoyed.

"So you have come to Bradgate, cousin!" my mother exclaimed. "How did you know I was pining for the sight of your face?"

"And I yours." The princess's voice quavered just a little.

She looked uncertain and even sadder than when last I had seen her. Her pale hazel eyes—overlarge and shortsighted—stared so fiercely, they made most people wish to step back from her in alarm. "I pray I am not inconveniencing you by arriving unexpectedly." She gave a weak smile. "I found I could no longer keep away."

"You are most welcome, as always, cousin. Look, our own Mary is delighted to see you again." My mother reached around and dragged me from behind her.

The princess's gaze found me and warmed. Her rosebud lips tipped into an expression I had never seen on my mother's face despite the fact that she and Cousin Mary both had mouths exactly like the one Uncle Henry wore in the portrait in Bradgate's gallery. The princess stooped in a rustle of sandalwood-scented petticoats and caressed the place where my lady mother had scratched. Lady Mary's fingers felt overwarm but soft. "Greetings, my little friend. I see you have a new poppet since I visited last."

I clutched Jennet tighter in my arms, certain my lady mother would snatch the doll away, perhaps even thrust Jennet in the fire, as she had threatened to do last time I carried the poppet in company.

"Daughter, let us not forget our manners," my lady mother bade me. "Make your curtsy to the Lady Mary, and show your cousin your doll." The joints in my knees felt rusted. I could not make them bend. Was this some kind of trick? I thrust Jennet behind my back.

"Mary." My father's voice cut sharp edges. "Do as your lady mother bids you."

My cousin rushed to intervene. "Do not scold the child, Your Grace. We will look at your doll later, Mary. Will we not?"

My mother jabbed me in the back, and I nodded, then dropped into an awkward curtsy. I knew my mother would have Hettie make me practice the curtsy until my joints swelled up.

"Come and break your fast after your long journey, cousin," my mother urged.

"Yes, do," Father said with a heartiness that sounded strained. "Then as soon as you are well fed, we shall have some fine sport in the deer park. It will be a pleasure to have the company of another lady who loves the hunt as much as my wife does! My master of the hounds spotted a magnificent stag while we were in London three weeks past."

"Yes, London," the princess echoed, and I could see hurt in her eyes. "I had heard something of your stay there."

She was thinking of the weddings, I knew. My parents knew as well. My mother stiffened just a little, and my father's eye twitched as he rushed to cover his blunder. "Few ladies sit a horse with the skill you do, Lady Mary, save Frances. Is that not so?"

"It is," Mother said. "But do give our cousin time to refresh herself before you sweep her off to your precious park. She must be very tired."

"I am. Tired and sick at heart and in need of my oldest friends. I have heard that His Majesty, my brother, is very ill. His Grace of Northumberland wrote to tell me that Edward's doctors fear it will tire him too much to see me. But it causes me pain to stay away. Frances, you, of all people, know how much I love the boy. Remember when his mother died?" Lady Mary's eyes misted. "Queen Jane Seymour, the kindest of stepmothers, who restored me to my father's favor after all the evil Anne Boleyn did me."

Cousin Mary had once shown me the ring her father had given her to remind her of Queen Jane's kindness to her and the importance of being obedient to one's father. In Latin it said: *Obedience leads to unity, unity to constancy and a quiet mind, and these are treasures of inestimable worth.*

The princess continued. "At Queen Jane's deathbed I vowed to repay her kindness by loving Edward like my own son. It is cruel of Northumberland to keep me away."

I dared a sidelong look at my mother, waiting for her

temper to rear up, as it did anytime Jane criticized the devil duke. But to my surprise, my lady mother today seemed eager to smooth rough waters that she usually liked to stir to tempests. I wondered why.

"The king needs to preserve his strength so he might get well," she said.

I felt puzzled. In the solar had not my lord father said "let the king die," as if he might even be glad when Edward did? But when I thought of asking about it, my imagination filled with sharp-bladed axes and headsmen in leather hoods. *It is treason to foretell the death of a king*, my mother's warning echoed in my head.

My mother laid her hand on the gold lions embroidered on Lady Mary's sleeve. "No doubt His Grace of Northumberland is only doing what is best for the kingdom."

"Perhaps." My cousin's cheeks reddened, and her mouth pursed smaller still. "Yet I would give much to mend the rift that his interference regarding my faith has caused between my brother and me before it is too late."

"I am certain that Northumberland will see to it that you are summoned to Edward's bedside when the time is right."

"I am not so sure. The duke and I clashed mightily over my celebrating the Catholic mass in spite of the royal edicts that forbade it. He is not a man to forget such defiance. I am convinced there is only one way I might overcome this obstacle. He might consider my cause more seriously if I could find a trusted advocate who has Northumberland's ear. You came to mind."

I wished I could warn her to keep the pleading tone from her voice. My mother held such weakness in contempt. Cousin Mary would do better to bark commands and stomp about and say it was not wise to anger a future queen. "Will you use your influence with him on my behalf?" the princess asked.

My mother surprised me again, smiling with something that

might have been tenderness in any other woman. "How can you ever doubt we would help you? Have not our families been joined since my father and mother stood against Anne Boleyn? Since before, when my own father stood as your godfather? Have you not been my most cherished friend since we were girls together? We are family. You must never think our new loyalties would overtake bonds of blood. There is no service I would not do for you."

"Pray God it is so," the princess said. "I fear I will need friends in the days to come more than I ever have in all my life."

I could not unravel what she meant by that. Surely once she was queen, she would have all the friends she could want. Those who were unkind to her, she could send to the Tower, where the headsman lived. I envied her that power. So why did I see uneasiness in her face? As if somewhere in her bones she suspected something was amiss? She wanted to believe my mother's words. I could feel just how much. But in that place inside me where lightning whispered, I knew the truth.

Whoever Lady Mary's friends might be today or in the weeks to come, my lady mother and lord father would not be among them.

❧ ❧

THE NEXT DAY, WHEN I WAS SUMMONED AWAY FROM MY LESSONS to spend the time with my mother and Cousin Mary, the knot of unease in the pit of my stomach tightened. I felt pulled two ways like a thread that might snap—glad of time with my kind cousin, but wary of being more in the presence of my lady mother than I could ever remember.

It was strange to be allowed into the richly appointed chamber, where sharp-eyed Bess kept the other ladies-in-waiting at their task of untangling skeins of silk, to be used in the cloths that my mother and the princess were stitching on the other side of the room. Lady Mary and my mother sat on cushions beside the arched window where they could talk as if they were alone.

Alone, except for me. While the ladies were distracted, I had squeezed myself underneath a table, close enough to touch the soft, bright cloth of Lady Mary's skirts when no one was looking, but far enough to be out of my lady mother's reach should she regain her senses and wish to strike me for my forwardness in eavesdropping on my elders.

After a long silence Lady Mary sighed. My mother looked up from her own work, with a sharp, measuring expression in her eyes that she quickly hid away. "Is something not to your liking, cousin?" she asked. "We would do anything in our power to secure your comfort."

I fastened the tiny new doll cap that the princess had made for me onto Jennet's head and listened as the princess spoke. "You and Henry have been fine hosts, as always. There is nothing you can do to rectify what ails me but turn back the hands of time. Bradgate does not seem the same without the girls here. You must miss them terribly. I remember how it pained me when my mother and I were parted. I waited for her letters as a drowning person waits for breath."

That was how I felt when I waited for a missive from Jane. But not a word had come to me in over a week. Had Jane forgotten me?

"I heard Jane and Katherine had a splendid wedding." Cousin Mary looked down at the altar cloth she was stitching, and I could hear the hurt in her words.

"I wish you could have been there," my mother replied. "I cannot tell you the sleepless nights Henry and I spent mourning your absence. But if we invited you, we would have had to invite Elizabeth." Mother looked as if she smelled fouled linen. "I could not invite one sister and fail to invite the other without the whole court noticing and asking questions."

"The difference between your relationship with Elizabeth and your bond with me is that we have been friends since we were children," Lady Mary reproached.

"True." My mother looked uncomfortable. "But there was the king to consider. His Majesty intended to honor the ceremony with his presence. Relations between you and your brother have been strained over religious questions for so long, and the king has been so ill, we dared not risk upsetting him. I hesitate to mention it, not wishing to vex you, but when you last met, His Majesty became overwrought. We thought it dangerous to bring you together."

"One who loves the king as much as I, a danger to him?" Lady Mary said. "It twists my heart to think so. I wish I had not caused him one moment's unease."

"But your stubbornness on the question of faith raised delicate questions . . ."

Mary gave a strained laugh. "*Delicate* is not a word I should choose to describe my disagreement with His Majesty. I cling to the old faith, my brother the new. My greatest hope has been that once Edward reached his majority, the rift between us might mend. Perhaps when he was not under Northumberland's thumb, we could begin again. But as things now stand . . ." Her eyes glistened, and I knew she was thinking that Edward would never grow up at all. "I know Northumberland is Jane's father-in-law, yet I cannot like him, Frances. Was it at his behest that my name was stricken from the list of guests?"

My mother pressed my cousin's hand. "Would you hate me if it were so?"

"I could never hate you. And yet while I understand your reasoning, it would have served our friendship more justly if you had explained your reservations to me but given me the chance to decide whether to attend or no. Compared to the humiliation of not being invited at all . . ."

I squirmed, remembering how I felt when the maids of honor asked Kat to play skittles or hoodman blind in the garden, leaving me behind. I pretended I did not care, not wanting to give them the satisfaction of knowing they hurt my feelings. But Lady Mary concealed nothing. The wound was raw on her face.

Even my lady mother had the grace to look ashamed. Was she really? I could not tell.

But Lady Mary believed her. The princess's voice softened. "One can forgive much of a friend like you," she said. "May God punish me if I ever forget your family's loyalty to my mother in her travail. I must remember that even brave Charles Brandon had to kneel to Anne Boleyn when she was in power. Only after her hold on the king began to crumble was your father able to show where his true loyalties lay."

"Surely you cannot question my loyalty to you." I watched my mother press her hand to her heart. "Cousin, I vow—" My mother's breath caught, as if with emotion so deep she could not speak. Only I seemed to notice she had not vowed anything at all.

Lady Mary held my mother's other hand and squeezed it. "Forgive me for surrendering to my insecurities. I try to overcome them, but I have seen much that makes me mistrust . . . not you, Frances," she rushed to amend. "It is just that the world we live in is full of shifting sands. More than once fate has come close to sucking me under."

A sound at the door made me turn to see the most handsome of Father's gentlemen entering the room. The maid of honor who had been Kat's favorite giggled, but Bess shushed her, reminding her to maintain her dignity.

"A thousand pardons, Your Grace," he addressed my mother, "but I bring a message from your lord husband." The gentleman bowed. "His Grace begs you to wait upon him in his chamber. There is a matter regarding the new cistern he wishes your advice on."

"I am attending to my cousin, as His Grace is well aware." My mother pretended to take offense, but she had been watching the door from beneath her lashes for the last half hour or so as if she had been expecting Father to summon her and was growing impatient.

"Go, Frances," Lady Mary urged. "I am an ungrateful guest. Henry mentioned there are important matters the two of you must discuss today, and here I am keeping you stitched to my side. Your husband will become most vexed with me."

"Husbands can be demanding at times," my mother said.

"I can only imagine." Yearning shadowed Lady Mary's face.

"Pray you will soon be wed and able to complain as Bess and I do," my mother said.

"It is my dearest wish, though so far God has denied me the comfort of married life."

Kat said the princess had been betrothed to one man after another since she was practically in the cradle. Yet time after time something had broken the alliance, be it a political snarl or the fact that Uncle Henry had ordered Parliament to declare Cousin Mary a bastard just as he had Elizabeth. Now he was dead, it seemed they would be bastards forever.

Last Christmas at Cousin Mary's house at Hunsdon, Kat had shuddered at the princess's fate. *How terrible it must be to be a thirty-seven-year-old woman with little chance at ever winning a husband at all, let alone his love. They say King Edward will not give her in marriage because she clings to the old faith. He does not want to breed up enemies to the new religion.*

Mother's voice broke through my thoughts as she addressed the Lady Mary. "I must attend to my lord, but Bess and the other ladies could take you for a walk on the grounds. I know that you often have pain with your monthly courses that walking eases."

"Indeed it does, but much as I admire your very capable Bess, I am not in the mood for ladies' chatter. I prefer to take my walk with only little Mary to accompany me."

My mother's eyes rounded in surprise and a hint of unease. "You wish Mary to go?"

The princess turned to me. She squinted, and I knew she was trying to see me better. "Would that please you, Mary?"

I started to nod but knew my mother would be vexed if I did not answer aloud. "I would like it very much. I could show you the oak trees that are twelve soldiers."

My cousin rewarded me with a smile. "Then it is settled."

"Bess? Hettie?" My lady mother called, and the two rose from the cluster of ladies and hastened toward us. "You will accompany Lady Mary and my daughter as far as the stone bench and remain there in case they have need of a cloak or a draught of wine. Keep a watchful eye on them, and make certain the child does not try my cousin's patience. At the first sign of vexation in our guest, I expect you to send my daughter off to the nursery."

"That is hardly necessary," Lady Mary said. "Mary could never vex me."

"I trust not. Even so, Hettie will be watching just in case."

Hettie curtsied, and I could see some sort of silent understanding pass between her and my mother. I knew something of what it meant. Mother wanted Hettie to make certain I did not tell Cousin Mary how unhappy my parents were to learn that she had come to Bradgate. I had overheard Hettie tattle to Mother about other matters from time to time. She was almost as keen-eared as me.

Afraid my lady mother might forbid my outing with the princess altogether, I started to slip toward the door, but Mother pinched me under the guise of straightening my sleeve. I knew better than to betray the pain by even a blink of an eyelash. "You will remember what I told you and behave as befits a daughter of the house of Suffolk, will you not, Mary? You know what happens to wicked little girls."

She wanted me to think of the headsman's ax. I imagined it, all curved and sharp and shining. "I will be good like Jane," I said, thinking of the best person I knew.

But Mother did not look pleased as she left to see Father, and the Lady Mary could not hide her distaste for my sister. It made me sad that the princess did not like Jane as she once did. Kat said she did not understand why people could not believe what they liked about religion and stay quiet about it, but Jane always had to speak up about Martin Luther and the evils of the pope.

My discomfort must have shown, for Lady Mary wiped away the sour expression and said, "You love your sister very much, do you not?" I nodded. "That is a gift you should thank God for. Not all sisters are so fortunate. My own sister and I were close once."

"Why did you stop liking the Lady Elizabeth?"

Hettie nudged me in an effort to get me to be quiet about matters that could only upset our guest, but the Lady Mary explained.

"You have heard of the great wrongs Anne Boleyn did my mother and me? The older Elizabeth grew, the more she became like her mother in manner and appearance." I prayed Cousin Mary would never look on me with such a chill. "The Lady Elizabeth is a crafty young woman with an ambassador's gift for telling people what they wish to hear while truly committing to nothing. It is a sly manner of dishonesty, and I cannot bear dissembling of any kind."

My thoughts turned from the wicked Elizabeth. I felt guilty on my own account. No doubt Lady Mary would stop liking me if she knew how often I sidestepped the truth. She took my hand, and I curled my stiff-jointed fingers to hold on.

Yet even once we reached the gardens, I could feel Hettie watching us, sensed she was ready to leap up and interrupt us should she see anything suspicious.

As the princess and I walked, Lady Mary shortened her steps so I did not have to struggle to keep up and my breath did not catch in gasps when I spoke.

I led her along the road where the great oaks towered above us and told her how Kat and Jane and I had once made up tales about them, that the trees were the Greek hero Achilles' army the Myrmidons, who would come to life to defend us if ever we were in peril. "When you were a girl, who would defend you, my lady?" I asked.

"I fear not even the Myrmidons would have dared," she said, looking so sad I wished I had not asked her. But suddenly the cloud of unhappiness lifted and Lady Mary's face brightened as a splash of yellow, blue, and bright red sailed across the sky. "Look, child. Is it not beautiful?"

The creature swept past us on wings that shone. When it circled back to land on a low-growing holly bush nearby, we stood still. I held my breath, admiring its red underside, snowy cheeks ringed with thin black lines and jaunty cap of blue feathers.

"I wonder what it must be like to be so beautiful," Lady Mary murmured. I could hear the awe in her voice, sensed what she was feeling as the bird fluttered its iridescent wings and gazed at us with black-pearl eyes. Did it wonder how it felt for us to be so ugly? I expected it to fly away. Instead it hopped toward us and cocked its head, absorbed in examining us as Jane did her texts.

At that instant a smear of red pelt and bushy tail dived through the undergrowth toward the unsuspecting bird. Jaws studded with pointed teeth flashed wide. I sprang toward the creature, shouting a warning, but my slipper caught on a twist of root, and I hurtled, face-first, toward the ground. Pain scoured my left cheek as I skidded across the path, but through the stinging haze I saw the fox miss its quarry, catching only a tail feather as the bird took flight. I grabbed the small plume from the fox's mouth, unwilling to surrender even that much of the bird's loveliness to its enemy.

The stunned fox vanished into the wood, leaving me in possession of the feather. I clutched it tight as a wave of purple petticoats washed over me, hands catching me about my waist. The whalebone that shaped my stays bit into my hips and chest as Lady Mary lifted me into her arms, heedless of the warm blood trickling down my chin.

"Child, are you hurt? Your poor face is all scraped up."

My scrape stung even more. "Hettie would say it cannot make me look any worse than I usually do."

The princess frowned. "Hettie is very wrong to say such a thing. The wounds look raw. We must make certain they are washed out so they do not grow putrid." Her voice softened. "That was a brave thing you did, Mary, but perhaps not a very wise one."

"The bird liked us, even though it was beautiful and we are not. I could not let that awful fox eat it."

"Even though it might have bitten you?"

"Even then."

Mary regarded me a long moment. "The bird is lucky to have a loyal friend to warn it of danger. Do you know what I wish, little Mary?" The princess's eyes gleamed with tears.

"What, my lady?" As a drop fell free, I touched the end of the feather to her cheek, soaking up the moisture.

"In the days to come I would think myself the most fortunate of women if I could count just one friend as brave and loyal as you."

"You may count me, my lady," I vowed with all my heart.

I heard footsteps running closer, saw Bess and Hettie drawing near us. "Child, take care!" Hettie scolded me. "You will get blood all over the Lady Mary's gown."

"I would not mind the stains after what little Mary just accomplished," the princess said. "She saved a life."

Something curious flickered on Hettie's face. "A life, Your Grace?"

The princess balanced me atop the rim of her farthingale. "Little Mary saved a bird from a fox, and this was her reward."

She held my wrist, displaying the bright blue plume I still clutched. "Perhaps Hettie might stitch it onto one of your caps," she suggested.

"No. I wish to put my feather someplace else," I said, determined to tuck it into my Thief's Coffer so I could remember this day. Perhaps if I could draw Cousin Mary away from my lady mother tomorrow, I would even dare to show her my other treasures.

❦   ❦

WHEN MORNING CAME, I WOKE TO A COMMOTION IN THE courtyard. I donned my clothes so hastily, Hettie had barely finished tying my laces before I hastened down to see what was happening. Lady Mary's retinue bustled about hitching horses to carts, loading them with trunks filled with her gowns and linens and jewels. Was she leaving before I even had a chance to tell her farewell?

"What's happened?" I asked the nearest servant as I pressed through the throng.

"The Lady Mary must leave at once," Owen the stable boy told me, his eyes big with fear. "Sweating sickness has broken out in the servants' quarters." I went cold all over. The sweat was a terrible thing. One could be eating heartily and two hours later lie dead.

I searched for the green rooftop of the princess's coach above the crowd, then made my way toward it. As I drew near, I heard Lady Mary plead. "Frances, I beg you, let me take Mary with me to Hunsdon House. I will get her away from the contagion." My heart leaped at the prospect of going with my cousin, escaping both the frightening illness and my parents.

But my mother waved her hand in dismissal. "There is no time to gather Mary's things. I am far more worried about you. You are heir to the throne. You must hasten to safety before you catch the sweat."

The princess's face showed very real pain as she looked about her. I knew she was searching for me. I tried to push my way toward her, hoping for rescue, but I was too small to be seen in the crowd, and the servants rushing about their business were too frightened to make way for me. Not that my lady mother would have let me go with the princess in any case. Her jaw was set unyielding as stone.

I climbed up onto one of the wooden barrels stacked beside a pillar and watched until the last cart rumbled down the road flanked with oaks. I wondered if Lady Mary was looking at the Myrmidons. But even they could not protect someone from the sweat.

Much later I was able to get close enough to my mother to speak to her. Not a line marked her face with worry. "Who is sick?" I asked.

"Sick?" she echoed.

"With the sweat. Owen said we were all in danger. That was what made Lady Mary go away."

"There is no danger anymore, not with Lady Mary gone. I will stake my life and your lord father's on it. Your sister Jane's as well." Something frightening lurked under her smile. I puzzled over what my mother had said, though I had no chance to ask her. She was far too busy to be bothered with me.

I spent two long days with Hettie in the nursery, then another messenger rode in, the Duke of Northumberland's livery crusted with mud. The man stumbled to his knees when he dismounted from his horse.

I tucked Jennet under my arm and slipped off to find my parents, certain that something momentous was happening. They were near the fireplace that spanned the great hall, their ladies and gentlemen at a distance, restless as hounds about to give chase.

My father thrust a piece of parchment into the flames. I watched a gobbet of sealing wax melt like blood. "We must away to London," he said, his eyes bright as if he had drunk too much wine.

My mother clutched his sleeve. "Our plans bear fruit?"

"God willing, our daughters will bear fruit as well. Northumberland ordered his son to bed Jane to seal the union between our families. She and Guilford are to join us when the time is ripe at Syon House."

My mother's face grew as hard as the princess's table diamond. "Then when next we see Jane . . ." Her words trailed off. I could not guess what she meant, but Father knew.

"Not yet, wife, but soon. Northumberland sends word that there is a last task that only I can be trusted to discharge for him."

"You are not Northumberland's manservant!" My mother puffed up with pride. "You are the father of the new—"

"After we get Jane securely in place, there will be time enough to make Northumberland and all of England feel our importance. Now hasten. We must join our daughter."

I did not question the contents of the message. I only felt relief and hope that my logical sister could put my intangible fears to rest. "Am I going to see Jane?" I asked as I drew near my parents.

My father started in surprise. "By God's blood, you slide about the room, silent as a cat! Your sister will have more important matters to attend to in the future than listening to your prattle, Mary."

"But I want to show her my feather."

"Show her what you wish once all is accomplished," Mother answered.

"What needs to be accomplished?" I squeezed Jennet tight.

"It is none of your concern. Your only task is to stay out of everyone's way. I would leave you here were it not for the chance . . ." She looked at Father. "The Lady Mary seems more attached to the child than ever. If things go awry, little Mary might prove useful."

"For what?" I asked. Neither of my parents even looked at me.

"It will not come to that," Father insisted.

"Best to be prepared in any case." She turned to me. "Well, Mary. Do you wish to see Jane, or shall we leave without you?"

I went to my chamber and flung Jennet into my Thief's Coffer. Clutching the wooden chest in my arms, I staggered down the gallery, into the great hall, then to the courtyard where the Suffolk retinue was gathering—not in the confusion I expected but rather as if they had been poised and waiting to spring into action.

Everything was so strange, I thought as the train of coaches and carts rumbled down the road, the Myrmidons standing guard. But perhaps that strangeness did not matter. Nothing mattered except that I was going to see my sister. Soon I would be with Jane, and she would make sense of all that confused me. I would curl up at her feet, lean my head against her knee, and drink in the peace that always surrounded her.

How could I know that peace would never again touch my sister? Or that when next I saw Bradgate, my whole world would lie in shatters around me?

Chapter Five

Jane Dudley
15 years old
The former abbey at Sheen, Surrey
Late June 1553

T IS SAID THAT THE MONKS KING HENRY DROVE FROM England could concoct poisons that ate at your sanity and carved the flesh from your bones until you were nothing but a skeleton rattling in a sheath of skin. But I was not being poisoned. Not by some phantom monk, not by His Grace of Northumberland. Or so my lady mother raged at me during those terrible days when she came to Sheen to demand I get well.

Even in my weakest moments, I believed that her redoubtable will might have the power to order death's retreat. Or was it my own fear of her that drove me to squeeze down more spoonfuls of gruel? Take a few more steps so I could gain enough strength that she would leave me in peace?

I must resist the dark thoughts born of the fever that held me in its fist. That was what Mrs. Ellen told me when I awakened in the middle of the night soaked with sweat—from nightmares now, not illness. I cannot say which is worse. In the flickering light from her candle, I watched rose petals drown in the bowl of cool water she brought to bathe my face. I was drowning as well. Drowning in this strange twilight world, in this place that was once an abbey. I was a wife who was no wife, my lord husband as blessedly absent as the monks who once lived here. My wedding seemed like an evil dream, or was it something more menacing now? Had my obvious repugnance toward Guilford made my marriage a mistake that Northumberland intended to rectify by using the powder in the vial that Kat saw?

It made no sense to poison me when Northumberland could just annul the union, reason argued. But logic had been burned away by fever and fear.

Mrs. Ellen tasted any morsel that touched my lips. She ran bare fingers over my books, my chemises, and my slippers. "Look, sweet lamb. These cannot be poisoned. Am I not still hale and hearty?"

True though her claim was, I would have given much to have my sister Mary's keen ears and strange intuitions to unravel this encroaching sense of doom. Mary—so young and yet somehow older than the standing stones—as if she sneaked through a crack that linked the distant pagan past with the present.

What a sinful thing to think about my own sister. It was the kind of thing others might gossip about, but I knew Mary better than anyone in the world. I should have been her champion, her shield. Yet here in this place I could not seem to leash my bleak imaginings or wall them out with books. I could not even *read*, God help me, my mind not able to string two thoughts together save the sense that Northumberland was determined to destroy me.

Was I losing my reason? I stared into the polished silver looking glass that I seldom bothered with in the past. The face that stared back at me was sharp with bone and splotchy where patches of skin peeled away. My hair, once thick and shining was so thin in places that glimpses of white scalp showed through. One morn I even caught my lady mother looking dismayed as she brushed a handful of the lost strands from my pillow.

I could not quell the twinge that I felt over my new appearance. I was never a beauty like Kat, but neither was

I unpleasant to look at, until now. Mary's image rose in my mind again. I could almost hear her comfort me. *You would grow accustomed to being ugly in time. But you will not look so forever.*

"Thank God," I whispered, then cringed as if my little sister had heard me. I picked at a loose thread on my claret-colored bed gown with fingernails so ragged I snagged the fabric. I pressed my folded arms against my stomach. To think such unchristian thoughts made me determined that today would be different.

Though Mrs. Ellen had urged me to go out into the gardens for days now, I had refused—only creeping about the old abbey's chambers since my fever began. I had been gaining a little strength. Perhaps today we could venture to the end of the garden. Only once I was well enough to travel could I leave this haunted place. Spurred by that thought, I went in search of Mrs. Ellen.

An hour earlier, I had left her in the next room, dozing by the fire after so many sleepless nights watching over me. I knew I was selfish to wake her, but I could not bear to remain in the night-shaded corridors of my own mind.

"Mrs. Ellen," I began as I went through the open door. "I wish to go walk—"

Her favorite chair was abandoned. The tambour she had been stitching on before she fell asleep had been dumped in a hasty tangle onto a table. Strange that she would leave without telling me while I was in such a fragile condition.

I looked farther, my steps a bit steadier than they had been the day before. When my flustered nurse came rushing around the corner, I was so startled I nearly lost my footing. "My lady, your lord husband awaits your pleasure below stairs."

My stomach pitched like a storm-tossed wherry, carrying me back to the worst hours of my illness. For a moment I felt as if I might vomit again. "My husband?" I echoed, stalling in an effort to gather my scattered wits.

Mrs. Ellen nodded so hard, her drawn work coif nearly slipped off her head. "Lord Guilford Dudley comes on important business from the Duke of Northumberland."

My hands shook as the duke's image rose in my mind, his eyes as piercing as hot irons, ruthlessness seeming to scream from every angle in his face. Perhaps Mary had been right to call him the devil duke, for he seemed invincible, his will impossible to resist. Despite my lady mother's protests to the contrary, I feared I had already experienced what he would do to one who defied him.

"I must see Lord Guilford." It was no question. Rather, a summoning up of my courage. Far better to face the cub than the lion. "What kind of business did His Grace of Northumberland send Lord Guilford here about?"

Mrs. Ellen gave a nervous shake of her head. "I do not know, but your lord's face is set as if it will be unpleasant and he is downing a quantity of wine."

Dread tightened around my middle. I wanted to flee back to my bed, burrow beneath the coverlets, and pretend I was racked with fever again. Surely if Guilford believed he would be in danger of catching my illness, he would eschew the abbey and me. But I squared my shoulders, taught by hard experience to face troublesome news with at least an appearance of calm. When I entered the hall, I found Guilford sprawled in a chair that was formed in two bog-oak sections crossed like an X. His sword and buckler had been tossed upon the table before him. A loaf of manchet bread sat on a board, a dagger buried in its crusty belly. A ewer I surmised had held the wine Mrs. Ellen claimed he had drunk lay on its side, while Guilford scowled moodily into his empty goblet.

Features Kat would have called handsome seemed anything but that to me. Straw-colored hair tumbled over his forehead, his green velvet doublet dusty and crumpled from travel. It was impossible that this man was my husband, some part of my mind insisted wildly. I did not know him. What little I did know, I did not like.

Still, I forced myself to move toward him. "My lord," I said, dropping into a curtsy. "This visit is most unexpected."

"I notice you do not call it a pleasure. No sense lying, eh, Jane?"

I stepped into the light from a nearby window and could tell when his eyes truly focused on me. "You are even ghastlier pale than you were at the wedding."

My cheeks burned. I stared at a crown worked into the wooden panel behind his head. The wood was much lighter there, new marked since King Henry had seized the abbeys. "I have been ill," I said.

"I heard something of it from my father. I have never seen him in such a temper."

"Because I did not die?" *from the poison he gave me,* I added to myself.

"No. He seemed most irate at the thought that I might become a widower so soon."

What sense would that make if he were truly attempting to kill me? My temples throbbed as I tried to unravel that mystery.

"Fortunately," Guilford continued, "His Grace assures me you are no longer in danger of the malaise."

"God willing."

"It is my lord father I am more concerned with at present. He has set our duty before us and says we cannot delay."

My stomach quivered as I guessed what that "duty" must be. My eyes slid closed for a moment. *Please, God,* I begged silently, *let it not be so.*

"We are to bed, wife," Guilford said, "though from your expression you dislike the idea as much as I do. Let us get the thing over with." He gave an unpleasant laugh.

My cheeks felt afire. "What is so amusing?"

"I was just thinking that if Henry Herbert and I had been

gambling the day of our marriages, there is no doubt who won this hand. If His Grace unlocked their bedchamber door along with ours, that beautiful sister of yours will be capering with joy."

Had the duke done so? I wondered. Kat *would* be happy if Northumberland had given them leave to bed together. The youth she had bound herself to looked at her as if she had painted the heavens blue, while my husband looked as revolted as I felt at the idea of his drawing near me.

"You know Herbert and your sister attempted to sneak into bed together at Durham House though my father forbade it."

I remembered Kat's stricken face next morning, her whispered caution. *I saw the duke with some kind of white powder in a glass vial. I broke it, and he acted so strangely. Tied a cloth over his face and swept the powder up with parchment so he would not touch it. Jane, I think it was poison.* What else could it be?

"Eager little filly, your sister." Guilford's voice brought me back to the present. "Ripe for the mounting, damn Henry Herbert's hide. You were nothing like her before and now." He surveyed me up and down. I could feel every patch of raw skin, the hot, dark bruises under my fever-hollowed eyes. "I would wager you were relieved by the reprieve on our wedding night, wife. But God is not rescuing us a second time. He and my father decree it is time to consummate our marriage. We must endure it the best we can." He pushed himself to his feet.

"Please, my lord. You can see I am not strong enough for—for—"

"You would not be any better equipped for bed sport if you slept for a hundred years. The best luck we can hope for is that I get you with child at once. Produce a son, and I can seek my pleasures in fairer harbors, while you can go back to being a drab little nun."

Outrage poured strength into my feeble limbs. "How dare you compare me to those superstitious Catholic—"

"Just accompany me to the bedchamber and submit like a godly wife. We must get heirs with the Dudley name."

"But why now? What harm can it do to wait until tomorrow?"

His eyes took on an implacable gleam. "I do not *wish* to wait until tomorrow. My father does not *wish* us to wait until tomorrow."

"My lord, I—" I scrambled to think of some reply, some way to drive that alarming expression from his face.

"*Your* wishes are of no consequence, Jane. Did your precious tutor neglect to teach you that in your infernal books?" He closed the gap between us and seized my arm, forcing me to the chamber I had left a short while ago. Once in the room, he shut the door, closing off escape.

I cried out as he dragged me full against him, his mouth crushing mine so hard I tasted blood—his or mine, I could not tell. He pushed me backward until my legs collided with the side of the bed. I cried out as the hard wooden edge bruised me. Guilford tumbled me backward, bearing his body down on mine, his hands fumbling at my breast. I tried to push him away, but he grabbed my wrists and pinned them above my head. "Lie still. You are only making things worse for yourself. I'll bind you to the bedposts to make you submit if I must."

The idea of being humiliated thus was more than I could bear. I crushed my eyes shut as he wrenched up my nightgown and forced my legs apart.

Something hard and blunt jabbed at me, tearing fragile skin on either side of its target. I tried not to cry out, but my misery only moved Guilford to frenzy. He drove inside me, shoving and groping and grunting. It hurt. It hurt. It hurt. Tears poured down my cheeks, and I prayed it would be over. Suddenly he gave one last, savage thrust, and arched back his head with a guttural cry. He collapsed atop me, so heavy I could not breathe.

I pushed at his shoulders, and he rolled off me. Cold air

struck my naked limbs, chilled the disgusting wetness between my thighs.

Bruised inside my body and deeper still in my soul, I slid from the bed, dragging the sheet with me. He did not bother to protest. He sprawled on his back and flung one arm across his eyes. In the hours that followed, I watched him snore, slack-mouthed and half-drunk. Hated him. At length he woke, pushed himself upright. For just an instant some emotion darted in his eyes as he noticed me, huddled in misery, wrapped up in a bloodstained sheet. Regret? Embarrassment? Or simply distaste? I would never know. Naked, he rose from the bed. That part of him that had caused me so much pain shriveled. I wanted to retch into the chamber pot. My skin felt soiled by our coupling, as if filth had been ground into me, down to my very bones.

He found his trunk hose, put them on. "My lord father sends you one more message. You are to be ready to depart for London at a moment's notice."

"I am too ill to travel." I felt as if I might never be well again.

"Just do as you are told, Jane!" he said in frustration. "It is time you learned to obey His Grace like the rest of England. If the king himself heeds my father's counsel, it should be good enough for you."

The king—had he not been under Northumberland's power for years now? I cannot say why, but a tale I had heard sprang into my head. All of England knew how Northumberland had manipulated the king into executing first one royal uncle, then the other. He struck first at the lord admiral, my kind Catherine Parr's wayward husband, then later at the Duke of Somerset, Edward Seymour's father. Northumberland had inflamed Thomas Seymour's outrage that his brother, Somerset, had all the power as lord protector—for was not Thomas Seymour as much the king's uncle and equally deserving? When the lord admiral attempted to "rescue" the king by force, Northumberland and the Privy Council deemed it treason. They forced Somerset's hand, making him order his brother's execution or lose the support of the council. But afterward those same men turned that act against him. It was easy to manufacture evidence damning a man guilty of fratricide.

Not long after, Kat heard a story that young King Edward had taken a pet hawk and carried it before his tutors. He had pulled out every feather one by one, then ripped the poor naked bird into four parts, saying: "This is how my advisers have plucked and rent me. But soon I shall be the one plucking them and tearing them to bits." Horrified as I had been at the tale, I could not help but wonder if my poor, sick cousin hated Northumberland half as much as I did. *His Grace forced the king to condemn men he loved in spite of crown and throne*, I thought, helpless. What horror did the devil duke have in store for me?

Chapter Six

Mary
Syon House, Isleworth, Middlesex
July 6, 1553

HE DAY WE ARRIVED AT NORTHUMBERLAND'S RESIDENCE of Syon House, the sky hailed blood: red and frozen, stones big as my thumb pelted London from a sky night-dark hours before its time. Hettie buried her face in her apron and prayed aloud, afraid it was the end of the world. It was, in a way, though we did not know it yet.

I could not tear my eyes away as blades of lightning carved up heaven, thunder shaking the sky until it seemed as if the very stars should shatter and rain down on our heads in shards like broken glass.

". . . *an omen* . . . ," I heard one of the ladies-in-waiting say. My lady mother grew restless, her fingers plucking at her skirts.

Some said this was not the first time Syon had been racked by an angry God. The Holy Maid of Kent had lived here and got letters written in gold and delivered by angels. She had fits and claimed that if King Henry divorced Queen Katherine of Aragon, he would die a villain's death, and Katherine's daughter would wear his crown. It was taking longer than the Holy Maid expected, but soon her prediction about Cousin Mary would come true. Another lady who got executed also stayed here. Catherine Howard, who married the old king when she was Jane's age, was locked up here before they chopped off her head. This place was full of ghosts. I was glad Jane was not sick anymore. She would not be one of them.

For three days I had been wondering what Jane would have to say about the bleeding hail. Jane was not at Syon House, but Father said she soon would be. Strange, it seemed everyone here was waiting for her. Important men talked of things like ships leaving harbor to guard the coast. Cannons at Whitehall and the Tower's many guns were all mustered out and at the ready. The noblemen talked late into the night and pulled their beards and scowled at maps while Father and His Grace of Northumberland paced like the Tower lion, waiting to spring.

I wondered who they were afraid of. The French king? The Spanish? Catholics beyond our shores had been angry at the way Cousin Mary was treated because she refused to convert to her father's religion. But soon there would be nothing for the Catholics to be mad about anymore. When Cousin Mary was queen, she could hear mass five times a day if she wanted to. Not even Father and Northumberland would be able to stop her.

It was strange, thinking of all the people Syon House had protected. A nunnery first, where daughters nobody wanted had been locked away from the outside world. Girls like me. But perhaps it was a good thing to live with a whole batch of women you called sisters, for I missed my sisters more than anything.

The Duke of Somerset, Edward Seymour's father, had taken this place right out from under the nuns. He turned it into a country house with the grounds all green and the Thames tickling the riverbank, a cool blue-gray ribbon where barges and wherries and sailing skiffs could glide about on hot summer days. Northumberland took Syon House next, after he cut off Somerset's head and made Edward no fit match for Jane anymore. It seemed a great lot of snatching and grabbing. But who knew? Maybe someday Edward Seymour would be able to take it back. He could not take Jane back, though, since she was Guilford

Dudley's wife. Some things you cannot take back, even if you wish you could.

Still, I had somehow to while away the time until Jane came, and there were so many new people to spy upon. The Earl of Pembroke, Kat's father-in-law, was here. So were the Marquess of Northampton, who was Catherine Parr's brother, Arundel and Huntingdon and Bishop Latimer, Nicholas Throckmorton, and the king's secretary, William Cecil.

I noticed my father and Northumberland striding toward the door, their foreheads wrinkled beneath their velvet caps, their faces stern as if something important were happening. I caught up the ball I was playing with and followed them into the garden. Hedges of holly grew thick along the pathway they took. I rolled my ball toward them, pretending it had escaped me so I could chase it close enough to hear.

"The crone I had attending Edward will not be troubling us anymore," said Northumberland. "We could not risk her going about London claiming she fed the king of England arsenic at my command."

Surely I could not have heard right. I rubbed my ears as Father spoke. "The poison was only to keep the king alive until all was in readiness for the succession, Dudley!"

I felt dizzy inside. No wonder the king was sick, if they were feeding him arsenic. Careful to stay out of view, I retrieved my ball and shrank closer to the nearest holly bush. The pointed leaves pricked me, but I did not dare move. Who knew what Father and the devil duke might do to a girl who heard them talking about such secrets?

"Oh, yes, Suffolk. My enemies would be so eager to believe me when I explained I only had the boy dosed with the stuff for England's higher good. What is even more dangerous, the arsenic left its mark on Edward's body for anyone who looks in his coffin to see. Now that the king is dead, he must lie in state."

The king was dead? I froze, stunned. Why was no one else

talking about it? All these noblemen should be planning his funeral ceremony, dressing in mourning, the bells tolling while preachers announced his death from every pulpit.

"What are we to do?" My father blotted sweat from his face.

"You need not look so stricken. No one knows the king is dead save you and me and a few others I trust. There is time to put my plan into action. My son Robert has found a baker's apprentice who looks much like the king. When the time is right, we will ambush him and replace Edward's body with the apprentice's. Few will know the difference."

Sour liquid rose in my throat. I once saw a cat that had eaten nightshade. It swelled until its body burst. Is that what had happened to Cousin Edward because of the arsenic? What would happen to the baker's boy? I did not want to think about someone killing him to replace the body of the dead king. For the first time I could remember, I did not want to know a secret at all. I started to move away, but Northumberland blocked my escape. Trapped, I went still, praying they would walk away without noticing me.

He continued. "As for the question of lying in state—we will give out that His Majesty did not wish it. He had been ill for so long, he wished to maintain his dignity."

"He had little enough of that at the end, poor lad."

"Do you think I enjoyed poisoning the boy? I raised him like my own son. Cared for him, and he cared for me. Not that anyone will believe that if the truth ever comes out. Half of London is already predicting the end of the world after that infernal storm."

Father rubbed his brow. "You were as shaken by what happened as the rest of us. Hail like blood—on the very day Edward died! It was as if King Henry were rising from his grave in a rage because we overturned his decision about who should wear the crown." I had heard of my great-uncle Henry's temper. It had made people around him lose their heads.

"Let Great Harry throw all the tantrums he wishes from heaven or hell," Northumberland said. "Earth is our dominion, and I will let no one ruin our plans. I just sent a summons to the former king's daughters at Hunsdon and Hatfield. No doubt they will come rushing to London thinking they come to their brother's deathbed to say farewell. They cannot know it is too late."

Why would Northumberland want to play such a mean trick on the princesses? The Lady Mary and the Lady Elizabeth would be very angry when they found out the truth. I kicked my ball a little closer to my father.

"Will they come, do you think? Lady Elizabeth is as cunning as her witch of a mother was, while Lady Mary has more friends than is good for us. God knows the trouble those two women could cause were they left running loose."

"Never fear, Suffolk. Those who might betray us are as deep in this conspiracy as we are. Before the week is out, the ladybirds will fly into the snare we have set for them. Our most pressing question will be how to dispose of them once we have them in hand."

"Elizabeth is easy to deal with—no one disputes that she is a bastard. Lady Mary is more complicated. The king's true-born daughter treated so cruelly as a girl. I tell you, Northumberland, there are many who would support her claim to the throne, Catholic or no."

"That is why we have to strike ruthlessly. I have dispatched my son Robert with four hundred horsemen to intercept her. Once she is in custody, we must twist our courage to the sticking place, Suffolk. If our plan is to succeed, the Lady Mary must die."

Horrified, I tripped over the ball and fell upon the hard stone path, but Father and Northumberland were so lost in concentration, they did not notice. My mind filled with another day, another fall, Lady Mary lifting me up into her arms.

I knew enough about court to know that people fell in and

out of favor, that Lady Mary might be snubbed by my parents in favor of someone more powerful. But this . . . this was too much. Surely Father would turn blustery with outrage, tell Northumberland that Lady Mary was my mother's cousin and our friend. He would never consent to her death.

But Father only looked more thoughtful. "We would need solid evidence of treason to send her to the block. It would take time to gather enough to make a case against her. Every day we wait will give our enemies another day to muster forces against us."

"Everyone knows the Lady Mary has never been in the best health since King Henry separated her from her mother. She would not be the first prisoner to fall ill in the Tower. However we accomplish it, we will see her buried before the month is out."

Father and the devil duke smiled, with a look in their eyes that reminded me of bloody hail and the Holy Maid's fits and heads rolling across bloody straw. There was so much I did not understand. But I knew one thing for certain. The message they had sent to Cousin Mary about Edward was a lie to catch her in their trap. Father and the devil duke meant to kill the cousin I loved. My memory filled with the image of a bright blue bird, the fox's sharp teeth, and the tail feather Lady Mary had presented to me as if it were a badge of honor.

I wish I could count one friend as brave and loyal as you.

I went to my chamber, dragged my Thief's Coffer from beneath my bed. I opened it, dug among the treasures there. Jane's letters fell out, and I looked at the words in clear black ink. If Jane were here, she would know what to do. But I dared not wait for my sister.

I wished I had an angel like the Holy Maid of Kent to deliver Cousin Mary a letter in gold, but no angel would ever appear to the likes of me. Even if I was able to smuggle a note out of Syon House, it was a long way to Hunsdon. Not even the most trusted messenger could deliver this news. Even if they wanted to be loyal to Cousin Mary, would they not carry the letter to the devil duke out of fear? If Northumberland did not mind giving a king arsenic or killing a princess who should be queen, he would not hesitate to poison me.

I bit my fingernail until it bled. Maybe I was not brave enough to send a warning someone might read, but there was another way. I gathered the small jewels I had hoarded: a bent gold ring I'd found in Bradgate's garden, a silver chain, and three pearls I had secretly snipped off Bess of Hardwick's gown. Pressing the iridescent feather to my breast, I ran to find Owen in the stables below.

As I returned to the house, I passed one of King Edward's secretaries, a man named William Cecil. I had noticed him before. He had three large warts on his nose and a face that looked quiet, but I could sense thoughts were racing through him like the water in the brook at Bradgate when it flooded during spring.

Now he looked as if those thoughts were going to burst out of their banks. Was he one of the men Northumberland had spoken of? The ones who knew the king was dead? Or was Cecil just suspicious like me, trying to find out what was afoot?

His face was shadowed beneath his black coif, his forked gray beard looking as if he had rumpled it with nervous hands. What was he doing, staring at me like that? Had he guessed what I had done? I tried not to tremble as I passed him, the one person at Syon House with eyes that saw as much as mine.

Chapter Seven

Jane Dudley
Chelsea Palace, London
July 9, 1553

NLY SIX MORE STEPS TO ETERNAL DAMNATION, I THOUGHT as I moved toward the coiling serpent of the Thames. It would be so easy to succumb to temptation. Just wade into the river. I could picture my skirts floating like the petals of a velvet lily, the water soaking into them, weighing them down as I walked deeper into the channel. I would not fight the river's pull. I would lie back and watch the sun dissolve from watery ripples into darkness.

"Lady Jane!" Mrs. Ellen's worried voice pulled me back from the bank as she had so many times during our stay in the old palace at Chelsea. I watched her hasten down the path to catch up with me. She had scarcely left my side in the two weeks since we had arrived here at what had once been Catherine Parr's widow's portion.

See, lamb, my nurse had said as our coach rumbled up to the red brick manor with its fairy-tale turrets and gardens of roses. *Remember how happy we were here five years ago? The air at the abbey did not agree with you. I feared if we stayed at Sheen any longer, you might never recover. Is that not what I wrote your lady mother? But you will get well walking in the dowager queen's gardens. Forget your troubles.*

Kind, simple Mrs. Ellen. My marriage to a Dudley would

follow me wherever I went.

I shivered as Mrs. Ellen closed the gap between us. If I had possessed the will to feel anything beyond my own pain, I would have suffered guilt. Keeping vigil over me had carved deep lines into my nurse's face, kept her red-rimmed eyes busy with worry and helplessness. If I died, at least Mrs. Ellen might get some sleep.

"My lady," she said, breathless, "you were so lost in thought, I feared you would stumble into the water! Look at you out here without your shawl. I know it is July, but the air is chill near the river. Come away from here before you catch your death." She looped one arm around me as if she feared I might resist, then guided me back toward the gardens.

"I would not really do it, you know," I whispered.

"Do what, you silly child?"

I raised my eyes to hers. "It would be a mortal sin."

She misunderstood me on purpose. "You wish to look up some reference to mortal sin? Sit here under this tree, and I will fetch your prayer book. Promise you will not stray from this bench. It would be unkind to make me search for you. My bunion is aching."

"Where would I go?" It was true, I thought as I watched Mrs. Ellen walk away. There was no place on earth to find succor. Nowhere in heaven. For the first time in my life the scriptures offered no refuge. Even Martin Luther, the German monk who condemned the corruption of the Catholic Church, claimed that women should bear their husbands' children in pain until they died of it because we shared Eve's guilt for original sin.

Not even the most tenderhearted would deny that Guilford Dudley was free to use my body as often he wished. Death was my only hope of escape. My death or his.

I leaned my head back and noticed an oak tree nearby—two knots in its trunk bulging like eyes. A split in the wood's growth formed a kind of mouth. My chest ached with missing my sisters. A memory of Mary flooded back to me, the day she named the trees lining the drive to Bradgate Hall's gatehouse after Achilles' Myrmidons.

"Perhaps this tree is one of the Sidhe," she had enthused to Kat and me. "Hettie told me about them when my back ached too badly to sleep one night. When Ireland was attacked by the evil Fir Bolg, the Sidhe melted into the hills and rivers and trees so their enemies could not find them. If I were a tree, the bumps on my back would not matter."

Would what Guilford did to me in that big bed still matter if I had armor of bark to wall him out, or a cloak of moss to cover my nakedness? I wondered as I wandered toward the boat landing. I felt exposed all the time, as if anyone with eyes could see my humiliation. Scenes from that night played in my head until I could not endure the feel of my own skin. Is that what had happened to Catherine Parr when she had wandered through this garden years ago?

Had the lady who had given me a taste of mother-love suffered anguish deep as mine? Torturous images of her husband coupling, yes. But the arms twined around Thomas Seymour were not her own. They were those of the Lady Elizabeth, the princess whom the dowager queen had loved as her own daughter.

Even now, five years later, I could not fathom why Elizabeth had hurt her stepmother that way. A *whore's daughter turning whore should shock no one*, my lady mother said when the truth about the affair between Princess Elizabeth and Thomas Seymour came out. Maybe Mother was right and Anne Boleyn's wantonness tainted Elizabeth Tudor's blood. In the end, the dowager queen had died of heartbreak. Or of poison her husband slipped to her to clear the way so he might wed his red-haired lover.

Unlike my beloved dowager queen, I would find no blessed escape. I was going to live. Sometimes I feared that most of all. *We must get heirs with the Dudley name*, Guilford had told me. If I gave him a son, would he be satisfied? More important, would his father the duke have gotten everything he wanted of me: royal

Tudor blood grafted into the upstart Dudley line? If only they would leave me alone, then perhaps I could endure—

I heard a rustle of skirts as Mrs. Ellen returned too quickly to have retrieved my prayer book. "My lady, look to the river," she said. "Is that His Grace of Northumberland's barge approaching?"

I felt as if I might splinter like a yew-bow strung too tight. My gaze locked onto the banners rippling above the vessel. The Dudleys' device of the bear and ragged staff mocked me on its ground of silk. I pressed my fists to my stomach so hard, the gems on my stomacher cut into my knuckles.

"Is it my lord husband?" I choked out. *Do not let it be*, I pleaded. *Please, God.*

Mrs. Ellen shielded her eyes against the sun. "The passenger is neither Lord Guilford nor His Grace. It is a woman."

"The Duchess of Northumberland?" The prospect was nearly as daunting as the appearance of the duke would have been. In the almost six weeks since the wedding, Guilford's mother had come to hate me as much as she doted on her son. She had even dragged me to Durham House at one point, insisting my place was with my husband. She had thrust me away from Guilford quick enough when I grew ill in her care.

Mrs. Ellen tried to soothe me. "Perhaps they are sending you a physic to help you gain strength, or oranges to tempt your appetite. It may be no more than that."

It was always "more than that" when it came to Northumberland. He did nothing without calculating his advantage. The Dudley family was so ruthless, they reminded me of dogs scrabbling over carrion. I knew enough to fear anything they might have in store.

The oars along the side of the barge stroked the water with ominous rhythm, the gilt-painted prow nearing the landing. In unison, the oars pointed skyward, and men scrambled to tether the boat.

One passenger rose from her nest of cushions amidst a cluster of ladies-in-waiting. I recognized Guilford's sister, Lady Mary Sidney. While I could not be pleased to see any of the Dudleys, she was less unnerving than her parents. For a moment I hoped she had come, as Mrs. Ellen suggested, with some gift or a posset, though why the daughter of the house of Northumberland would be sent on such a dispatch I could not imagine. Perhaps to see with her own eyes how her sister-in-law fared, then carry the news back to her parents—but as Lady Mary Sidney sprang onto solid ground, something about her kindled my alarm.

"Good morrow, sister." She swept me a curtsy, her eyes almost frantic with some strange eagerness.

"Good morrow," I replied. "I cannot think what I have done to merit a visit."

"I am come to bring you to Syon House in all haste. You are to join your parents and my father and, of course, your lord husband."

I would rather have faced the Inquisition. "Please offer my apologies. I am too ill to travel." It was true. I suddenly felt as if I had bled out every drop of strength I had gained.

"His Grace of Northumberland insists it is imperative you accompany me immediately. You are to have Mrs. Ellen follow later with your belongings."

My heart sank even farther. Not only was I to be dragged away from the comfort of Chelsea, I was even to be stripped of the solace of my nurse and trapped with the people I feared most. My knees went weak. What would my sister-in-law do if I collapsed in a heap? Have the oarsmen haul me bodily onto the barge to follow her father's orders? She would not dare disappoint Northumberland, of that I was certain.

I had no choice but to obey the duke's summons. "Mrs. Ellen, promise you will hurry," I implored, hating how pathetic my voice sounded.

My nurse pressed my hand. The dowager queen had done the same the last time I saw her alive. Lost in her big bed at

Sudeley Castle, she had been weak from childbirth though her feverish ravings were over, granting her a brief reprieve. *You must not be afraid, Jane. God willing, I shall watch over you, even from heaven.*

Clinging to her love for me, I paused at one of the rose bushes that my great uncle Henry had planted as a love-gift to Queen Jane Seymour when Chelsea Palace was hers. Plucking one bloodred blossom, I tucked it close to my heart.

I boarded the vessel, the weightless feeling of the water beneath the oak hull making my balance feel askew. I settled myself as far away from the others as possible and angled my body away from Lady Mary Sidney and her waiting women in an effort to beg silence—not that I had much hope Guilford's sister would give it to me. In the past Lady Mary Sidney had seemed haughty, but this time she was different.

"Jane . . ." Lady Mary Sidney plucked at her sleeve, as if she might find the perfect words somewhere in the damask folds. "In spite of the difficulties between you and my parents, they wish only for what is proper for you and Guilford. Perhaps our families might begin again and understand each other better this time. I know that His Grace, my father, desires that peace be struck between us as much as Guilford does."

Peace. I tried to imagine such a feeling between my husband, my father-in-law, and me. I averted my eyes, but Guilford's sister touched my arm. "I beg you to remember the friendship I have extended when you receive what the king has ordered."

This mysterious summons had something to do with Cousin Edward? We had been friends as children, before the dowager queen died. At least, as close to friends as it was possible to be with a boy who held himself so aloof. *I get frostbite every time I make my curtsy to His Majesty,* Kat had complained. Mrs. Ellen had hushed her with a scolding: *Poor motherless boy! And now the king his father dead, too! All he needs is a worthy, devout, accomplished wife like our Jane to make him happy.*

Yet Edward had been sick for so long now, I could not imagine what his behest might be. Perhaps I was to inherit an estate that the Dudleys wished to use to advance their power. At least I could not imagine anything too terrible coming from my ailing cousin.

As the trip along the river commenced, I could only surmise I looked even weaker than I imagined. Lady Mary Sidney anticipated my every need during the two hours we traveled, offering cups of mulled wine to hearten my fever-thinned blood, piling cushions behind my back, having one of her ladies adjust an awning to protect my eyes from the sun, until her relentless fussing drove me half mad. At last I feigned sleep, yet with every stroke of the oars I could sense Guilford's sister's eyes upon me, feel her small, restless movements between the thump of the drum beating a rhythm for the oarsmen. At last the hollow clunking of the barge against the landing at Syon House warned there was no avoiding my encounter with Northumberland and my parents and, God forbid, my husband any longer.

Liveried servants helped us disembark, then escorted us up the path to Syon House. I hesitated, but pride would not allow me to show my fear. We entered the building, all light momentarily blotted away. I blinked to clear my eyes as Lady Mary Sidney turned to the nearest servant. "Please tell my lord father that the Lady Jane has arrived," she said.

The man bowed so low to me, it was unseemly. "Welcome to Syon House, my lady. You are to await His Grace in the great hall. He will attend you when all is ready." What must be made ready? I wondered. It was as easy to order me about here as anywhere.

After a moment I heard footsteps approaching. I looked to the door and saw His Grace of Northumberland entering, the rest of the Privy Council close behind. What business did the most powerful men in the kingdom have here? With me?

Dr. Aylmer taught you not to leap to conclusions, I chided myself. *How foolish you will feel if their presence has nothing to do with you.*

Perhaps the king was nearby. By definition the king's Privy Council should be in the same proximity as His Majesty, should they not? I had seen these men gather numerous times—at my wedding and during those periods when I had visited court. They had even accompanied Cousin Edward to Bradgate when he came to hunt the Leicestershire deer parks. Then why did this encounter feel so different? I searched the crowd for my parents, hoping for some shelter from the strangeness that unbalanced me. Yet I could not find them, and none of the council addressed me. The men scattered in small groups about the vast chamber, speaking to one another in hushed voices and darting an occasional look my way. I clasped my hands together. They felt suddenly too large, and the ruby and pearl ring that Cousin Mary had given me one Christmas bit into my finger.

I strained to hear what the council was saying, but that only confused me more. Not a word that anyone could call remarkable passed their lips, and yet a sense of something momentous hung over the chamber.

The thought of an impending storm made me shudder, as I remembered the tempest that had hailed scarlet wrath from the sky. I might have thought what happened that night was a fever-bred delusion, but Mrs. Ellen had been as shaken by the strange red hail as I was. If only someone could guess what the storm might mean. My sisters would have opinions, of that I was certain. I longed to draw close to the bedchamber fire and talk with them late into the night.

After a moment I saw a familiar face, and my heart gave a tiny surge of hope. My lord the Earl of Pembroke, Kat's father-in-law, stood in conversation with the Earl of Huntingdon. Was it possible Kat was near? Even if she and her husband were still at Baynard's Castle, I might get news of my sister. As if he read my mind, Pembroke approached me with Huntingdon a half-step behind. Before I could address him, Kat's father-in-law knelt and kissed my hand.

Words dried on my tongue and I stared at him, confused as Huntingdon repeated the action. Someone murmured "our sovereign lady." Surely I could not have heard right, unless Cousin Mary was near. My stomach tightened at the notion. How affronted she must be after the slight of being excluded from the wedding.

I looked to Pembroke. "My lord, I am most eager to see my family. Can you tell me who is about?"

"Your sister Katherine will not join us until the morrow. She is lost in mighty preparations for the great event to come."

"What event might that be? Is it possible that she might already hope for a babe?"

"No, I am quite sure she cannot," Pembroke said, so sharply it startled me. Then he smiled in a way that only accented his strange haste. "There will be plenty of time for babes once all we have worked for is accomplished, will there not?"

"What is accomplished?"

"Suffice it to say that my family will arrive tomorrow. You will have your sister at your side before you know it."

"Have you seen anything of my youngest sister?"

"She was vexing your father not an hour ago."

So Mary was here. "I would like to see my sister at once. I fell ill during the six weeks since I last saw her. I know she must be worrying."

"We all rejoice in your recovery," Northumberland cut in. "I regret that any private reunion with your sister must be delayed, though she could well be in the company that awaits you." My pulse lurched at the unaccustomed subservience in the duke's tone. "At present there are important matters that claim your attention. Duty calls. You must obey."

Northumberland's mouth stretched in a grin, the rest of the council drawing close. A memory stirred in my mind. I was in

Bradgate's stable yard. One of the orphaned lambs Kat loved to adopt froze in the midst of nosing spilled oats. Six dogs, shaggy and avid, circled the tiny creature, trying to decide whether to guard it or rend it to bits.

"My dearest daughter." Northumberland offered his arm. "Allow me to escort you hence." I started to draw back, hoping for my parents to appear, but the lamb's fate still haunted. *Do not move . . . do nothing to encourage an attack . . .*

There was nothing to do but lay my fingertips upon the duke's sleeve. My skin crawled at the contact as the whole council fell into procession behind us. He led me through rooms dripping with tapestries. A vast gold plate upon a sideboard trapped my image as I passed, distorting my reflected face in a kind of scream. When we reached the duke's own presence chamber, what lay within startled me even more. A company of nobles filled the room, many of the great and powerful of the land lined up in order of precedence. They fell like hay culled by a farmer's scythe, bowing low, curtsying deep.

I caught sight of two familiar figures among them, but my parents did not engender the feeling of comfort I had hoped for. My lady mother swept into her place of prominence like a galleon at full sail, her face flushed with pride. Father swaggered forward, his fists planted on his hips, chest thrust out in the attitude I had seen in portraits of King Henry. Both parents were garbed in their finest, their clothes glittering with jewels, but neither emerald nor diamond nor sapphire could match the brittle, bright gleam in their eyes.

Whatever honor Cousin Edward had in store for me, they were well pleased with it. In fact, I had never seen them happier in my life. Trepidation fluttered in my chest. It deepened as I saw my small sister peeking around my mother's skirts. Then Mary's face fell into shadow as another figure stepped into my sight and accorded me a fawning bow. Guilford. He beamed, his outward show of devotion chilling me. Even his mother, standing near her beloved son, shone with satisfaction. She curtsied to me—that proud woman who loathed me. A curtsy deep and reverent.

My gaze locked on a shimmery canopy of gold cloth embroidered with the royal coat of arms. What stood beneath that cloth of estate was so terrifying, my whole body shook as Northumberland urged me toward it. A throne.

Chapter Eight

Jane
Syon House

ORTHUMBERLAND'S VOICE BOOMED OUT, DEVASTATING as cannon fire, obliterating forever the world I knew. "As president of the council, I do now declare the death of his most blessed and gracious majesty, King Edward VI."

Exclamations of surprise rang out from some of those assembled. Others nodded, smug in their foreknowledge of this momentous news. A number scattered through the crowd stiffened and appeared as uncomfortable as I felt.

Edward was dead. The magnitude of the news reverberated through me, thickening the air. His suffering was over. Yet what had he left behind? An England torn between Catholic and Protestant. His heir—a sister who would hasten to draw England back to the corruption and superstition of what she saw as the "true faith." A future so uncertain, we teetered on the brink of disaster.

"As we bid farewell to our king," Northumberland continued, "let us take comfort that he prayed to God to defend his kingdom from the popish faith and deliver it from the rule of his evil illegitimate half-sisters."

I saw my little sister tense at Northumberland's condemnation. I could not blame her. Evil . . . to judge Cousin Mary evil . . . Lady Elizabeth evil . . . had Edward truly believed it was so? They were misguided perhaps. Reckless. Superstitious or stubborn. But evil? That was the realm of the nobleman standing before me. Northumberland turned to face me, and I felt as if the very foundation of the building were crumbling beneath me. Or perhaps the foundation of my world. The events of the past six weeks slid into place as Northumberland's power-drunk gaze bored into mine.

"His Majesty has named Your Grace as the heir to the crown of England."

Mary gave a distressed cry. I watched in horror as each man in the chamber dropped to his knees. Vows tolled like death bells in a city full of churches, the voices unique, certain phrases painfully clear. "I do swear . . . shed blood for Queen Jane."

"No," I whispered, staring into my sister's stricken face. "God save me . . ." Northumberland grasped my arm to urge me forward. My gaze locked on the throne that I feared would be my downfall. Above the throne hung the cloth of estate boasting the royal arms of England.

The wood and gilt throne beneath the canopy seemed to grow like the mythical Kraken until it swallowed me whole. My world went black.

How long I lay there, facedown, I would never know. I came awake in aching moments, creeping back toward consciousness through a tunnel of ice and fire. Mary was clutching at me. I could hear her frantic voice calling my name, could feel her fingers being peeled away from my arm. My temple throbbed, something sticky matting my hair where my headdress had dug into the tender skin. The gold cross at my throat caught beneath me, twisting its chain so tight, the links had rasped away skin.

I slid my hands underneath my shoulders, the stone floor's roughness digging into my palms. It felt as if I were underwater in one of Bradgate's chill lakes. It took every scrap of strength I possessed to fight my way up to the surface.

Bewildered, I forced my eyes open. Ever so slowly the things filling the room took on shape, substance. My little sister was gone. Hauled away by some servant? I could only guess. A wide expanse of floor lay between me and the sea of rich gowns, elegant trunk hose, and fine cloaks that surrounded me in a ragged circle. Voices murmured, and I pushed myself upright, the cold from the stones seeping into my buttocks even through the layers of kirtle.

Through burning eyes I saw them all—the lords and ladies, Northumberland, my husband, even, God help me, my mother and father. They had told me I was queen, but now their faces angled away from me as if I were a child who had flung itself to the floor in a tantrum and, if they ignored it, might come to its senses.

I touched the small cut on my temple. My fingers came away stained crimson. Surely someone had seen I was bleeding, but the whole company had allowed me to lie there, hurt, unconscious. No one but Mary had stirred to help me. It was as if the flesh-and-blood Jane did not exist in the eyes of this assembly. I was a cold, carved ivory chess piece whose emotions were an inconvenience that was spoiling their pleasure in the game.

Completely and terrifyingly abandoned, I sank back to the floor and buried my face in my arms, sobbing. They would break me to their will, these powerful nobles. They would use me for their own ends, and there was nothing I could do to stop them.

Or was there? Bracing myself, I wiped my face with my sleeve, the embroidery and seed pearls leaving burning trails on my cheeks where the salt of my tears still clung. Though half-trapped by my skirts, I somehow managed to climb to my feet.

Dozens of faces turned toward me, marked with relief that my unseemly display was over. I knew what they expected. I was to be an obedient maid and walk to the throne. Had not Northumberland forced me to become his pawn? Had not my parents beaten me into becoming Guilford Dudley's wife? But there was no force on earth that would impel me to do what I knew to be wrong. No, not wrong. Treason.

The world seemed to roll beneath me like a stone sea, but I fought for balance, fought for my very soul. I spoke, my voice strange yet clear. "My lords and ladies, the crown is not my right. My cousin, the Lady Mary, is King Edward's rightful heir."

How had I expected them to react? Not with the almost indulgent silence that greeted my pronouncement. I spoke louder, the walls flinging my words back at me in a hollow echo. "I tell you the crown is not my right."

"You do wrong His Majesty and the house of Suffolk," Northumberland said. "Moreover, you question the will of God."

I wanted to dismiss Northumberland's assertion out of hand, yet to do so was not as simple as it should have been. Was there a divine hand in this, or was this alteration in the succession merely the result of human ambition? How could I tell which? Scripture rose in my mind: *Ask and the answer will be given.* I fell to my knees and clasped my hands so tight my knuckles seemed like to split.

"Heavenly Father, give me some sign if it is your will that I accept the crown." Broken pleas, fragments of prayer came from my lips, a desperate search for even a splinter of guidance. But it seemed even God had deserted me.

What would happen to England under Mary Tudor if I refused to take the crown? I closed my eyes, remembering my cousin's face the day her servant and I had clashed over the Host at Hunsdon House.

Why do you kneel?

I kneel to Him who made us all . . .

How many times had I heard how Lady Mary defied her brother Edward and the reformed faith he championed, insisting on hearing mass even when it might cost her life. What would she do if she gained the throne?

All England would be forced to bend its knee to baker's bread. Icons and false images would fill the churches again. The English translation of the Bible would be torn from people's hands. Would she bring Rome's wrath down upon us? The Inquisition itself?

"God, if you would only tell me what to do." But no whisper sounded in my ear, no sense of certainty flowed through me. Did I surrender out of devotion? Out of habit or fear? Or merely because I did not know what else to do?

I only know that I stood in the midst of that staring crowd and—may God forgive me—mounted the stairs to the dais and sat upon England's throne.

The archbishop stepped from the shadows and moved toward me in a whisper of jeweled robes, something in his grasp gleaming. His sleeve concealed part of what he held, making the metallic segment appear sharp as a curved blade. He righted the object, and it broadened before my eyes into the shining circlet of a crown.

"We must see how well this fits Your Majesty," he cajoled, as my mother divested me of my headdress. I winced with pain as the archbishop settled the crown in its place, the rim pressing against my wound. The crown felt heavy, cold, and final as death. Which queens had worn it before me? I wondered. Katherine of Aragon? Anne Boleyn? Catherine Howard, or my own beloved mistress Catherine Parr?

Had any of them felt this panic at the weight of it? Now that I had let them put the crown on my head, there could be no going back. I could see that hard truth in Northumberland's eyes as the archbishop continued.

"Our own Queen Jane, all England will rejoice at the handsome sight you and your husband make once we order a matching crown for Lord Guilford's head."

I looked at Guilford, his face that of a boy who had pilfered every bit of marchpane from the subtleties kitchen. He believed he would be king. That had been Northumberland's goal all along. I was a conveyance to raise the duke's poppet of a son to the throne. Then I was to be swept out of the way while Northumberland and my father ruled. Guilford would be easy for the two men to manage—merely distract him with pleasurable pursuits, and he would leave the tedious weight of governing to others. As for me, our fathers doubtless imagined I was of little account. A woman could easily be shifted aside: Guilford and I would be sent off to bed like inconvenient children when conversation got interesting.

I remembered what Mary had said about Father and Northumberland wagering us three maids in a gamble. The two dukes must be so smug, certain they had won. Defiance streamed, thick and hot, through my veins. For the first time since I understood the councilors meant me to sit upon the throne, I felt the steady flame of something I had not known I possessed. Strength.

"There is no need to fit Lord Guilford with a crown," I announced clearly. "I will not name him king."

Gasps rippled around me, and I heard Guilford's angry protest. Northumberland's tone grew even more obsequious. "Being raised so high has come as a great shock to Your Majesty. Once you have time to consider, you will trust the council of your advisers. We have England's best interests at heart."

Astonishing how often England's best interests match with your private ones, I thought, recounting the dissolved abbeys, the confiscated wealth, the titles and rich appointments that Northumberland had claimed for himself or showered upon his allies.

Had the duke read my eyes? "It is a queen's sacred duty to think of her country before all," he said. "Wisdom agrees it is disaster to place the reins of government in a woman's hands. The law is too complicated for even the cleverest female mind to grasp."

"Not so," I said, remembering the day Dr. Aylmer told my parents I surpassed even my brilliant cousins Edward and Elizabeth as scholar. It was a trespass Cousin Elizabeth had never forgiven me. "I know that only a parliamentary decree can legally name a king." *Or queen*, a warning whispered in my head. Edward could not have gone before Parliament to change the succession—such momentous news would have leaked out if he had.

But I could not worry about that complication now. I must shore up my resolve against the siege to come. "If God has seen fit to make me queen, I must accept that role, however reluctantly. But I will not make Lord Guilford king. I will grant my husband the title of duke."

"Duke?" Guilford appealed to his parents as if I had stolen his last sweet. His mother looked as if she would happily murder me if she only had a dagger to hand. Even my own father was blustering disapproval, while the vein on Mother's temple pulsed in warning. But none of them could unleash that fury before the nobles. No one dared shout at a queen.

I could see the cogs of Northumberland's mind whirring, his strategy adjusting to the unexpected. "This day's events have overwhelmed Your Majesty," he placated. "You are a pious, God-fearing woman. Once you have time to think on Our Lord's will, you will see the wisdom of the natural order He has set for the world. Scripture commands that a woman must be obedient to her husband, for he is fashioned by God to have a finer mind as well as stronger morals, while women are frail vessels. Once you give the subject further consideration, you will elevate your husband to his proper place as king."

"A queen cannot rule alone!" my father said. "What do you know of affairs of state?"

"I will depend on my Privy Council to help me navigate those strange waters. But—" I paused, enunciating each word clearly. "I will make the final decisions as to what is best for my realm on my own."

Fear still haunted me—the fates of my cousins Mary and Elizabeth troubled my conscience—but never again could anyone force me to do what I knew to be wrong. If I were patient, I might even bring Northumberland down. Had not Father and Northumberland destroyed Edward Seymour's father when Somerset was lord protector? Perhaps in the midst of mastering all the things that frightened me, I might be able to make England better for the people I would rule.

"Your Majesty, my lords," the Earl of Pembroke interjected, "let us not waste this night squabbling over details. There will be opportunity enough to debate later. Tonight should be a time for celebration. We have prepared a banquet in honor of Queen Jane's ascent to the throne." Kat's father-in-law turned to me with a courtly bow. "If it pleases Your Majesty, we might repair to the feast."

I doubted I would be able to eat, yet it would be better to have a table between me and the nobles than sit here arguing with them. This banquet would give me time to think.

As I looked at Pembroke, a thought of surprising sweetness occurred to me. My sisters. Because I was queen, I could keep Kat and Mary with me, and no one could separate us.

"I will have my sister Lady Mary join the celebration," I commanded.

"I fear she has been banished to her chambers after her outburst a short while ago."

"You speak of her attempt to come to my aid when the rest of you did not?"

"Your Majesty must forgive us. The shock of your collapse was overwhelming."

"I am recovered now." I infused my voice with the calm command that I had heard so often in the dowager queen. "I command you to fetch my sister to the banquet. Also, I would have you bring my sister Katherine Herbert to me the moment she arrives."

Northumberland bowed. "Majesty, I cannot think it wise to indulge a child of Lady Mary's age at this time. Personal matters will only distract you from your duty."

"My lord of Northumberland, I have never shirked my duty. Now I am queen, I will be even more scrupulous meeting the responsibilities God gave me. But it is my right to decide what will affect me for ill or good. If I am to be trusted with the care of a nation, personal decisions must be left to my judgment as well." His lips tightened. I turned away from him and took my lord father's arm. "I pray you take me to the banqueting hall."

I could almost feel Father puff up with pride. "It would be my pleasure, Your Majesty," he said. "You had best eat heartily to bolster your strength," he added in a low voice. "You are only just recovered, and tomorrow we must travel to the Tower of London to await your coronation. That ceremony is heavy work and you dare not falter."

I had been present at Cousin Edward's coronation when we were nine. The procession had been grueling, with Edward swathed in the heavy weight of his coronation robes. Once his party reached Winchester Cathedral, the archbishop handed the spindly new king the ball and scepter. The two symbols of his reign were so heavy, my father and my uncle, Henry Brandon, had been needed to help Edward support the gold objects. In spite of that complication, Edward had two huge advantages over me: he was male, and he was King Henry's legitimate son. No one would ever question whether he had the right to the throne.

Already I felt how grimly the responsibilities of monarch would weigh on me. Father was right—I must not falter. "What about Cousin Mary?" I asked quietly as Father led me to the banquet.

He lifted one shoulder then let it fall in dismissal. "I am certain Lord Robert Dudley has taken her prisoner already. Northumberland dispatched four hundred horsemen to do so three days ago. The contingent is to intercept her as she rides to Edward's deathbed to say farewell to her brother."

"But he is already dead."

"We have taken care so she does not know it."

I imagined Robert Dudley's soldiers surrounding the princess, her grief over her brother's impending death giving way to fear as she realized Dudley had her in his power. I touched my pearl ring with my thumb. "I do not want my lady cousin to be harmed."

"You must cultivate a strong stomach when it comes to such matters," Father said. "She will be a danger to you while she lives."

They meant to kill her? Despite the vast differences between us, I could not help remembering the suffering etched in Lady Mary's features. I had grown up hearing tales of her father's hard-heartedness. Four years she had been separated from her beloved mother and endured the humiliation of having to wait upon the infant princess Elizabeth, who had replaced her as legitimate heir and her father's beloved child. King Henry had broken Cousin Mary's will during the time Jane Seymour was queen, vowing to let her return to court once Mary signed a testimony that her parents' marriage was never legal. Mary had never forgiven herself for betraying her mother that way.

Anguish welled up inside me at the thought of condemning a kinswoman I had known since childhood. I pushed the sensation down. Northumberland, Father, and my Privy Council could not harm my cousin without royal consent—*my* consent—and I would not give it. My father must have mistaken my expression as fear for myself.

"You must not fret, daughter. His Grace of Northumberland has all the armament in the Tower at the ready. The military is in place and the fleet on alert lest she try to escape by sea. I have even heard rumors that the Spanish ambassador has orders from her cousin the Holy Roman Emperor to urge her to surrender her claim to the throne and retreat to the continent. Mary

Tudor is a frail, friendless woman. She is no danger to you."

Thoughts of my cousin's peril receded when I saw another Mary being led into the hall by Bess of Hardwick. My sister's face was red where someone had scrubbed away the tears she had shed in the presence chamber. She looked so subdued, I knew threats had been leveled to secure her good behavior. I wished I could go to her or seat her near me, but the rules of precedence forbade her from joining us at the queen's table. I gave orders she was to be situated as close to me as possible, hoping she would take comfort in that.

But my sister was beyond being soothed as her gaze fixed on my crown. Fear deepened the grooves and hollows of her face. Did she understand the import of the fate that had befallen me? Could she sense the danger, with that fey skill that had marked her from birth? I wanted to gather her close, promise all would be well. But Mary would never have allowed me to do such a thing, and besides, I could not make promises about the future. God alone knew how this would end.

Four hours later I heard a commotion, and the gentleman usher hastened to where I sat with Guilford and our four parents. The servant leaned close to Northumberland, whispered in his ear. I caught only snips of their conversation: "Messenger nigh rode his horse to death." The usher handed Northumberland a crumpled missive. I shivered at the way the duke's features went still.

"What news?" I demanded.

The duke and my father drew near, Northumberland snapping the wax seal. I saw Father lean over the duke's shoulder to read handwriting that sprawled across the page, jagged with agitation. "The Lady Mary has escaped," Northumberland said.

My father swore. "That son of yours made a muck of things! How hard a task could capturing a lone woman be? What kind of lack-spittle fool is that boy?"

The duchess's temper flared. "Do not dare malign Robert!"

"Robert Dudley's ineptitude will cost us dear. Your son bungled the whole scheme. Because of him, we will have God knows how much trouble setting the country in order."

It was not Father's outburst or even my mother-in-law's fury that frightened me most. It was the terrible stillness on Northumberland's face. "We have more urgent matters to attend to than assigning blame," he said. "Robert's letter says that the lady was riding to London at breakneck speed, just as we planned. At Hoddesdon she suddenly turned around and fled north to the stronghold of the Duke of Norfolk and bastion of Catholics. There is but one reason Mary Tudor would do such a thing."

"Someone warned her," I said.

"Indeed." Northumberland's eyes swept the company. "We have a traitor in our midst. But never fear, Your Majesty. We will turn this to our advantage. We will root the villain out and make him pay the price for betraying you. I swear by all that is holy, I will make this traitor an example no Englishman will ever forget."

Chapter Nine

Katherine Herbert
Baynard's Castle, London
July 10, 1553

ANE—QUEEN OF ENGLAND. NO MATTER HOW MANY TIMES I repeated the news my father-in-law had brought to the Herberts' grim family seat at Baynard's Castle, I could not make the ascent feel real.

When our wedding finery had been brought from the royal wardrobe, Jane had cringed at the richness of gowns and jewels. Perhaps she recoiled because they had belonged to the Duke of Somerset before he was beheaded, one of my maids had suggested. Was Lady Jane not once betrothed to his son? But it had less to do with Somerset's fate than with Jane's strict rules as to what became a sober Protestant maid. Now she would have every gem in the treasury to eschew.

The Pembroke coach lurched, and I banged my knee hard against the ivory inlaid box that Henry's sister Maud had insisted on squeezing into what little space remained between her and Henry and me as we jounced toward Westminster, where Jane would be waiting.

Everything would be different between us. I rubbed my bruise. It would hurt when I had to kneel to Jane. I would have to obey her every command. Even Father would favor her now. I turned my face to the window to hide the tears that were turning Cheapside to a blur.

It seemed I had spent the past three days avoiding people's eyes. My goal: to conceal the restlessness that gripped me since the earl had appeared, travel-stained but triumphant, and summoned the family to his privy chamber.

I remember my shock at Pembroke's news, as if the dank stone floor had collapsed beneath my feet. Moments later it shored itself up again, and envy soured my tongue. I could hear Dr. Thomas Harding's stern voice, Father's chaplain, upbraiding Mary, Jane, and me with the commandment: *It is a sin to covet thy neighbor's ox.*

How much more damning was the sin of coveting a sister's throne? my conscience demanded. *Would you change places with Jane? Be forced to wed a man you loathed, join a family you fear?* It was true that Henry's father had a reputation as a warrior, and was not as educated or civilized as my own, but he had lavished me with praise and gifts and provided me with every kind of delight in the six weeks since Henry and I had wed.

Jane had grown so unhappy, she became ill. I remembered Northumberland's face when I broke the vial, its burden of white powder spilling on the floor. Northumberland would spread poison in the same manner through the life of anyone who stood in the way of his ambition. Surely Jane was safe, I assured myself. Through her the Dudleys would hold on to the power they had gained during Edward's reign—disinheriting Cousin Mary, even though she was the rightful heir, according to her father's will.

Poor Mary. She had never been pretty, had no husband, no children to love her. Now she would not even be queen. But if King Edward thought Jane better suited to rule England, the crown was his to bestow on whomever he wished.

Even in light of that conclusion, I could not silence the other question that rose in my mind. "What of our lady mother?" I had asked my lord of Pembroke. "It is God's natural order that she come before Jane in the succession."

My father-in-law's eyes had turned fierce. For the first time

I felt uneasy in his presence. A ridiculous reaction, born, no doubt of my shaken nerves. "Her Grace of Suffolk has agreed to relinquish her claim in Jane's favor," the earl informed me. "Do you understand what that means, daughter? As of this moment, you are Queen Jane's heir. Should your sister perish or fail to produce a son, you will inherit."

Jane's suspicions had been right, as had Mary's warnings. Dudley and Father and, yes, even the Earl of Pembroke *were* using us as pawns in some sort of gamble. But even with all my flights of fancy, I had never guessed the prize they sought was the crown!

I spread my fingers against the embroidered fabric of my stomacher, imagining what it would mean to be raised to a station even greater than to which we had ascended when Father became a duke. The Grey family would grow wealthier as lands and lordships poured in, offices bestowed on us with all their attendant power.

I imagined being swathed in the richest furs that the royal wardrobe could supply, a crown atop my head. Suddenly I stopped myself, sickened to realize what dire events would have to occur for such a thing to be. I did not wish my sister dead, but if it was God's will that Jane be childless . . . That thought was wicked also. Even cuddling my spaniels failed to soothe my shame.

Later that night after the earl had dismissed us, I could no longer bear being alone with my misgivings. I went to Henry's sister Maud's bedchamber, where she blunted my worries with her delight. "Of course, it is only right we mourn our dead king," Maud had said. "But after—oh Katherine, just think! A coronation, tournaments. We must have new gowns—and jewels." She had bustled to her treasure-casket, retrieving something that gleamed between her fingers. She pressed the lumpy objects into my hand. I stared down at my palm where green stones glittered against gold settings.

"These earbobs belonged to my mother, a gift from her sister,

Queen Catherine Parr. My mother often said the emeralds were the exact color of Henry's eyes."

"They are." I remembered running my thumb over the gems.

"You love Henry so much," Maud said. "Mother would want you to have them."

The ugly knot of envy that had remained despite my best efforts melted away. Be jealous of Jane? She probably envied me! I was wed to my Henry, so handsome, as wild in love with me as I was with him. I had a powerful new family who pampered and adored me. Even Henry's fierce father treated me as if I were his own best-beloved daughter. True, I had heard disturbing stories about the earl, but people loved to imagine the worst, and tales grew more fantastical as they were passed from plowman to merchant to butcher. What else had they save gossip to enliven their dreary existence?

My life would be so much more exciting. As sister to the queen, I would be admired by everyone at court, my fashions copied, my beauty lauded, my favor sought. But I would not have to suffer the quarrelsome council meetings or appointments with tedious ambassadors that Jane would be required to endure—all of that unpleasantness made worse by the Duke of Northumberland hanging over her every moment.

I remembered the presents we sisters received on Twelfth Night. I had always compared them with a critical eye, my feelings hurt when Jane's seemed the greater prize. This time I had won the most precious gift, and it was one I would treasure for the rest of my life. My sister Mary had often said I was the luckiest girl in the world. She was right.

I had hugged Maud, moved by her kindness. It was good to have her to confide in while my sisters were far away. Strange how the absence of someone could leave a hollow place, even the absence of someone you had never met. I missed the presence of Henry's mother. I think the whole household did when they contrasted the accomplished, elegant Anne Parr against the rough manners of the earl. "I will cherish your gift always and wear these the day Jane is crowned," I told Maud.

She grinned. "Just promise to pass the earrings on to your own daughter when you and Henry have one."

"*If* we ever have one. Sometimes I wonder if we will ever be allowed to be together. It is cruel to still be forbidden my husband's bed."

"I am sure the ban will be lifted soon. They say the Duke of Northumberland never acts without considering every purpose or possible result tenfold. His motive in arranging the marriage between you and Henry is to secure powerful allies to your sister's throne. A babe will solidify the bond between Suffolk, Pembroke, and Northumberland, something all three families' desire. I would wager every jewel in my box that the night your sister is crowned, you and my brother will share a bridal bed."

I smiled, grateful that I would share Henry's bed instead of wear a crown won me by a Dudley. My voice dropped low. "Maud, I have never been to a coronation."

It had been a sore point with me—I had been left behind with baby Mary when Edward was crowned. Jane had described the festivities to me as best she could, but she had little imagination when it came to such things. When Father was in an expansive mood, his tales proved more satisfactory. He would draw me onto his knee and tell how he had attended Anne Boleyn on her triumphant procession to Westminster Abbey. She had been garbed in virginal white, her hair loose like a maid's even though her belly bulged with child. Father had become a knight of the bath on the eve of her coronation, keeping vigil the whole night through. But Jane's coronation would be my first chance to be part of so grand a celebration where all eyes would be upon my family, the crowds cheering and tossing caps full of coins in the air while fireworks burst in the sky to welcome a new reign.

I must ask Jane to make Henry a knight of the bath. How delighted he and my lord of Pembroke would be! How they would thank me! Jane would be queen, but she could never please people as I did. She was too caught up in her scholarly pursuits to care. Perhaps Londoners would come to love me as much as they did her. Maybe better.

A blast of trumpets shook me from my musings, and I felt Henry come awake where he had been drowsing beside me. The coach slowed, shouts ringing out from the earl's servants as they attempted to clear our way. I peered past the Pembroke banners unfurling like ribbons on the wind. A crowd thronged about St. Paul's, Cheapside. The center of their attention: the great stone cross that soared above their heads, a symbol that remained from the old, superstitious Catholic days. Since then wooden risers had been built to seat crowds that came to the cross to hear the important sermons and momentous announcements that were made there.

Today heralds in royal livery stood at attention on either side of the cross. More trumpets sounded. The crowd strained forward as a cleric draped in ecclesiastical robes mounted the platform in the shadow of the stone cross. The people knew something important was about to happen. All England had bruited about rumors of the king's failing health. Were they anticipating a celebration? Father said the fountains had run with wine when Uncle Henry died and Edward was proclaimed king.

Henry looped one arm around me, his voice still tinged with sleep as he murmured in my ear, "Look, wife. England is about to change forever."

Our lives as well, I thought, as I imagined awakening every day to that same husky voice. Surely the dukes would allow Henry and me to consummate our marriage now.

"Hear this, one and all!" the cleric's voice boomed out from beside the cross. "Our good and pious King Edward is dead. God save Queen Jane!"

I leaned out the window to wave to the throng, anticipating my first taste of being sister of the queen, intending to savor the crowd's shouts of joy. Instead, a strange silence muted the crossroads. Long moments dragged by. A few people echoed the cleric's words, but even those cries seemed blunted by confusion.

A lad a little older than Henry elbowed his way forward, his thatch of straw-colored hair framing a face crumpled with outrage. "Queen Jane?" he bellowed. "Who is Queen Jane? It is Great Harry's girl should be heir to her father's crown!"

I stiffened, affronted. The insolent pup! How dare he question the will of his king! I waited for someone to cuff him or reprimand him. Instead, other voices joined his protest.

"Indeed! It is true! We want the Lady Mary!" Who spoke I could not say. Only the youth's identity was clear. I saw a man grasp him by his leather jerkin. The youth's master, perhaps? Red-faced, the older man said something to his charge that I could not hear.

A brace of royal heralds plunged toward the two, but the lad yanked free and bolted through the crowd. He should have been easily caught, but a pathway seemed to open, then close behind him, foiling the pursuit. More unnerving still were the movements of the crowd—heads nodded, quiet signals that they agreed with what the apprentice had said.

"Beware!" a stout merchant cried out, gesturing in our direction. "Look to the crest on that coach! That is the Earl of Pembroke's device!"

"His son is wed to Suffolk's daughter," a woman cautioned. "Mind what Pembroke and Northumberland did in the North counties!"

Her words conjured memories that frightened me. I remembered the terrifying summer in 1549 when the new English prayer book had been put into the churches at the king's orders. What a fuss there had been over nothing but a book! Wicked, disobedient people had turned the countryside to a battleground. Fields had erupted in flames, and peasants had invaded the peers' parklands, tearing down fences, setting torches to the houses.

Pembroke had ridden against the rioters, hacking them to pieces with his own sword. What else was he to do? Those bad people had started the trouble.

At Bradgate we had hidden behind stout walls, Father sending a messenger on a desperate ride to fetch our military uncle, Sir Thomas Grey, so he could aid our defense. But the king could not spare him. With Bradgate under siege and no rescue to come, I had insisted the men who kept Father's hounds bring all my pets in from the stable, the rabbits, the spaniel puppies, the squirrel I liked to lead about on a thin gold chain. I was afraid the peasants would eat them.

Little Mary observed that Father looked as if he feared the rebels might eat us instead. Father had been sore relieved once the king set loose Lord John Dudley, his most ruthless soldier, upon the rebels. So had the rest of my family.

In the weeks that followed, the man who would become Duke of Northumberland had taught the miscreants their place. He proved even more energetic in defense of the lords' property than Pembroke had been. Dudley's army swept across the North like a flaming scourge, crushing the Catholic rebels. Five thousand five hundred of them had died before it was over. He had drawn and quartered the leaders, then hung a man from every village that had joined the uprising. That part had been unpleasant to think about. It had taken a long while to put it out of my mind. But what else could the king and his councilors do to quell such riotous behavior?

No one with the slightest sense could have expected the crown to behave any other way. But now the crowd was looking at me as if I were a monster who had fixed the nooses around the rebels' necks. Hurt stung me at the injustice. I wanted to tell them I had nothing to do with Pembroke or Northumberland's actions. It was unfair to blame me. But there was no point in defending myself. They were already fleeing as best they were able.

I could feel their alarm as they hastened on their way. Faces angled away from us, veils drawn over women's faces, the men pulling hoods up or dragging caps down, to obscure their identities.

I tilted up my chin, determined to show them that I did not care what they thought of me, but I caught flashes of sullen glares and dark frowns as the crowd bustled past us. Henry pulled me deeper into the coach and swung the leather curtain down between us and the world beyond.

"Do not worry, sweetheart," he said, taking my hand. "My father and His Grace of Northumberland will know what to do about such an outcry. They have hunted down malcontents before. They will find out who that troublemaker is and make him rue the day he dared speak against his queen."

I should have been glad that the lad who had shouted defiance would be taken to task for his outburst. Yet . . . had he not spoken aloud a question that had troubled me as well? I could not help but cringe inwardly. I knew rebellion must be stomped out before such kindling scattered to set the countryside aflame. Edward Seymour's father, the Good Duke of Somerset, had proved how dangerous mercy could be. He had nearly allowed civil war to erupt over the prayer book because he cast pardons to rebels too freely. But what would be the young apprentice's fate if Northumberland got him in his grip?

"Henry, what will happen to that lad?" Maud asked.

"They will pillory him, then cleave off his ears," my husband said calmly, as if he were discussing a cook plucking the feathers from a grouse.

Maud nodded with a satisfaction that made me uncomfortable. I could hear my mother's complaint: *Katherine, how are you to survive if you cannot even bear to see a horse suffer the lash?*

The horses had seldom committed any crime worthy of such punishment, but the rebellious boy had done so. I should not have minded so very much.

I remembered the hunted sensation that gripped me on my wedding night when Northumberland had looked at me across the poison-strewn floor. Part of me could not help hoping the blunt-tongued peasant boy would be swifter than the men determined to run him to ground.

"Come, love," Henry coaxed. "Put this unpleasantness out of your mind. I want my wife glowing with happiness when we reach court. Think of the coronation, the masques and banquets and balls. You, as the queen's own sister, will be the most admired of all." Creases formed between Henry's brows. How unhappy it made him to see me upset!

I made a valiant effort to curve my lips, but no matter how hard I tried to join in the talk of the delights awaiting us, I could not share Maud and Henry's pleasure. My day was ruined. I was not even sure all my new gowns and the promise of marchpane subtleties and champions clashing in the joust would be worth this journey, now that everything was layered with images of sullen faces and echoes of fear from the prayer book rebellion.

If only Henry could order the coachman to turn around, take us back home. Everything had been happy then, and pretty and bright, where not even the forbidding stone walls of Baynard's Castle could cast shadows over my joy. But the lad who had cried out for Queen Mary had overlaid the Grey family's ascent to the highest rank in the land with an image different from Jane being queen. I was haunted by the punishment that awaited him—the white hot blade slicing away the shell of his ear, letting it fall to the straw as he screamed in pain.

I burrowed into Henry's arms, and he stroked my hair with his warm, rough fingers. *Try to forget, Kat,* I told myself as the coach lumbered toward Westminster Palace. *Whatever ill* consequences fate deals to people like that boy, it cannot touch you. You will always be just what little Mary claims: the luckiest girl in the world.

Chapter Ten

Jane
July 10, 1553

HE ROYAL BARGE DROVE AGAINST THE CURRENT OF the Thames like a gilt arrow, its target the Tower of London, the domes of its White Tower pointing heavenward, reminding me to keep my eyes fixed on God. My mother, father, and husband clustered as near my seat beneath the cloth of estate as was allowed, the bright-hued costumes of my ladies-in-waiting a fantastical whirl of color before my eyes. Even the crowds that lined the riverbank to glimpse their new ruler seemed fashioned by some strange dream.

My face nearly cracked from the effort it took to seal a smile on my face. The glare from the summer sun on water burned my weary eyes. How long had it been since I had slept? I wondered. Would I ever sleep soundly again?

I had spent my first night in the royal bed curled in the smallest space I could, relieved my queenship gave me the power to banish my husband to another room but wishing I dared summon my sister Mary to keep vigil with me. Yet I dreaded the questions she might ask about that other Mary, her favorite cousin who was now fleeing before Robert Dudley's troops. In the past, I had rarely sought to avoid Mary's blunt probing. But now I was queen. I could not bring myself to betray emotions anyone might interpret as a sign of doubt or fear. Not even to myself.

In that elegantly appointed bedchamber I discovered an unexpected truth about my new situation. I had always cherished quiet time, safe with my books. But now I was alone in a way I never had been before. I would remain isolated forever, in spite of the fawning courtiers who would rush to satisfy my slightest whim.

I had seen the havoc a crown could wreak upon its wearer. My mistress Catherine Parr had struggled under its weight when she realized Thomas Seymour's love for her rank was greater than his affection for her person. My cousin Edward had been swallowed up in a sea of people grabbing for favors—the most avaricious of all his own uncles. My family would be more ruthless still. I must determine how to keep them at bay.

I would have no quiet interlude to sort out my new life, the way I liked to pick apart the knots of confusion in my mind. I sensed this new journey would be that of a leaf being whisked down a spring-gorged stream. I could only hope not to drown.

Even Kat's much-wished-for presence failed to ease my nervousness. Since she joined me at Westminster this morning, she had seemed withdrawn, the barrier between us more prominent than ever before. Even as she took up her duties as lady of the bedchamber, her hands were like those of a stranger. When she helped me don the gown that the keeper of the royal wardrobe had spread out upon the vast gold-paneled bed, Kat should have been entranced by the beauty of the dress, sneaking touches to test the softness of the lush green velvet when no one was looking, tracing the pattern of gold printed upon my skirts. Ever drawn to anything that sparkled, my magpie sister should have found my clothes irresistible, bathed as they were in the wan trickle of morning sunlight from the window.

But Kat had barely seemed aware of the velvet sleeves that swept nearly to the floor, giving way to a train that would prove as heavy as it was rich. Even the jeweled headdress that glowed pearly white beside it could not tempt her. When Mrs. Ellen, who knew of Kat's passion for clothes, offered her the honor of putting the gleaming crescent in place, Kat said she would likely get it crooked and went to fold my recently shed garments away.

Kat's response made my head ache even before I felt the weight that the French hood would cause in my temples. But there was no avoiding the discomfort, especially as a queen. The raiment I must wear in the days to follow was set out as precisely as the cuts in the linenfold paneling that decked the chamber.

In truth, all that would befall me until my coronation had been ruled in specific instructions by my great-grandmother, Margaret Beaufort, in her book *Liber regalis*, which she had written to document the pageantry that must attend the crowning of a Tudor monarch.

I explained it to my littlest sister when she joined Kat and me this morning. "See, Mary. I must board the royal barge and process before all my subjects until I reach the Tower of London, just as all Tudor queens did before their coronation."

Indeed, Uncle Henry's queens went there to put crowns on their heads—or to have their heads taken off their shoulders.

I had heard enough of Mary's pronouncements to guess what she might say. But she only pressed white lips together, looking so afraid it startled me. Mary—forever the boldest of we three—had barely spoken to me since the banquet when Northumberland had warned that someone had betrayed me.

I had made an effort to soothe her. "You must not worry about what the duke said last night. The traitor will be discovered and thrown in the Tower where he belongs." I laid my hand on Mary's shoulder. It was a mistake. She rarely liked to be touched. This time she sprang away from me as if my hand were a poker just drawn from the flames.

I fought sharp pain at her rejection, admitting to myself that the caress would have provided me with as much comfort as I had hoped it would give Mary.

I looked at where my sisters had drawn together upon boarding the barge. The two sat as far away from me as possible, yet so close to each other on their pile of cushions that their shoulders brushed. Had I slighted them somehow to drive them away? I was sure Kat would feel a stab of jealousy at my rise to the throne. Yet surely not Mary . . .

I had been longing for my sisters since we parted at Durham House. Now I wondered if it would be harder to have them close by, yet unreachable.

I wish this part were over—all the pageantry, the ceremony, the celebration.

I did not like the feel of so many gazes trained upon me, could not shake the familiar dread that I might reveal some flaw in my speech, my appearance, my actions, display one of the traits that my lady mother abhorred, expose my lack of fitness as a queen before, not only my attendants, but people who were now my subjects.

I peered at the blur of faces and wondered if my own painfully concealed awkwardness had been caught by these onlookers, a contagion like the plague. They seemed more subdued than I remembered when Edward inherited the throne.

Little wonder they had rejoiced then, I reasoned. King Henry had been aged and ill and waxed cruel in his declining years, while Edward had been young, full of promise to all of the evangelical faith, a Josiah who would found a New Jerusalem.

Or perhaps these people felt the same way as the malcontent at the crossroads by St. Paul's cross in the incident Bishop Ridley had reported witnessing. The youth who had cried out for Lady Mary.

My smile faltered, and it took all my effort not to rub where my jaw ached. I could imagine Lady Mary's face when she learned her throne had been usurped. The lines a lifetime of betrayal had etched in her features would carve deeper still. Where was my cousin now? Fleeing across the northern counties, searching for haven among the papists who dwelled there? I must not let pity make me fail to do what must be done to prevent England's return to the evils of Catholicism.

That was what my rise to the throne was destined to prevent. Eagerness flickered to life, then took hold in me, and I could not help but be glad to be named queen. I would have the chance to put my years of study to use for England's betterment. Almost from the cradle my parents, and later Queen Catherine Parr, had schooled me to be a worthy consort to my cousin Edward. But now I would be queen, the bearer of royal Tudor blood.

Was it possible for a woman to rule with her own wit and abilities? Most would say it was inconceivable. Even my beloved Dr. Aylmer, even the dowager queen, would have claimed that a woman ruling in her own right would be rebellion against God's natural order. Yet I knew in my heart I must do it, or the Dudleys would rule in my stead.

I squared my shoulders as the barge neared Tower Wharf, the gates of the golden-hued fortress looming above me. The entrance to my new life, one in which I would hold the power to direct England in the way it should go.

The bargemen bustled about, mooring the craft. Beyond them I could see peers lined up in order of precedence, banners unfurling in Tudor green and white. This palace was mine now. I looked at Kat, remembering when she was small and would play at being a lady in Mrs. Ellen's old finery. That was how I felt now.

I paused a moment to secure my balance—the tall platforms of cork chopines strapped to my shoes lent me height so the onlookers could see me. With great care I disembarked, four attendants bearing the cloth of estate over my head on poles. I saw my mother move behind me to bear my train. How odd it felt. I had spent my whole life trailing behind her. This was the first time proud Frances Brandon Grey, daughter to a French queen, entered a chamber where she was below me in rank.

She would never proceed before me again.

The weight of my gown bore down on my shoulders as I approached the lieutenant of the Tower, his soldiers lined at attention before him, the peers of my realm gathered near to honor this moment. Every man or woman who labored within these walls had mustered out to see this moment, one they would tell their grandchildren of in years to come: the day Queen Jane took possession of the Tower.

I caught sight of a mother boosting her gap-toothed girl up where she could see me. The child regarded me with her thumb tucked firmly in a rosy mouth. A confidence shone in that small, round face that I had never felt. For a moment, I envied them.

My chopine caught ever so slightly on a stone, and I turned my attention to reaching the dais that had been erected for the occasion so that I might speak to the crowd. Draped with green and white satin and streaming with pennons, the platform rose up before me, the royal coat of arms picked out in gilt, Tudor roses of red and white painted upon spires of wood for this festive day.

As I mounted the dais, I swept my gaze over the lords who were now my vassals, waiting in a place of honor. I noticed a certain emptiness among them. For an instant I felt troubled, a need to mark who was missing as if they were a puzzle I must fit together. Was this an ill omen? I wondered, then calmed myself. Events since Edward's death had happened very fast. Perhaps the absent peers had not been able to reach London in time.

The lieutenant approached me and knelt. "I am Sir John Bridges, Your Majesty, lieutenant of the Tower. May I have the honor of welcoming you to your most noble palace." He presented a huge iron key on his outstretched palms. The key to the Tower of London. To the throne itself. For a moment I forgot it was intended for me.

I took the length of iron in my hand, felt the heft of it. In the next instant His Grace of Northumberland swept the key from me. I could sense a stiffening of shoulders, disapproval among some of the lords. Even the woman with the little girl now frowned. Perhaps Northumberland felt the undercurrent in the mood of the crowd as well.

"Your Majesty, allow me to relieve you of this burden while you address your subjects," he said smoothly, but I was not fooled—nor, from the look of it, was the crowd.

It is the last time you will take anything from me, Your Grace, I vowed in silence. It might take time, but I would pry his greedy fingers from what was mine by right. I would not be afraid, even of him.

A herald trumpeted, a booming voice announcing: "Jane, by God's grace, queen of England. God save the queen!"

Had the evidence of Northumberland's power-grabbing ways muted their echoing cries? Or did I imagine it? My father's shout, my mother's seemed to pound against the very stones, but even my sisters' voices seemed strained. Mary, small and silent, looked ill.

I remembered all that Catherine Parr had taught me. Her dread that she would end in the Tower as so many other people had before her: Anne Askew, Anne Boleyn, Catherine Howard. In the end the dowager queen's beloved Thomas Seymour had been imprisoned there and was executed too, before his brother, the Duke of Somerset, died.

One thing was likely . . . before this was done, Mary Tudor, and perhaps Elizabeth as well, would join that grim roster. But today was supposed to be a celebration. I must try to remember to smile. I held my voice steady as I thanked the people for their loyalty, vowed with God's help to be a just and wise queen, then entered the fortress.

❧ ❧

THE BANQUET SEEMED to go on for hours. Even pleasure-loving Kat seemed wilted on her bench nearby, while Mary looked as if her back were aching more than usual. When my ladies and I were about to retire from the great hall for the night, the duke and my father approached me. I saw both my sisters strain to listen. "We bring happy news," Northumberland said. "The ambassador from Emperor Charles has just come to bring the emperor's good wishes for your reign. Chapuys informs us that his master is encouraging Lady Mary to allow the transfer of power to occur peacefully. She is to submit to King Edward's decision as an obedient subject should."

I blinked, heartened, yet surprised. Friendship from Lady Mary's own cousin? The man the pope himself calls the Holy Roman Emperor? I would have expected him to mount an armed campaign against me in hopes of restoring Catholicism to England. "I had not imagined I would secure his friendship."

"Now that we have his support, the rest of the world is sure to follow," Northumberland said.

"I am glad of it."

A smug expression curled his lips. It chafed me. "In truth," I said, "I am so pleased, I would hear such news from the ambassador myself in the future."

"Forgive my concern on Your Majesty's behalf. Of course I will bring Chapuys to you whenever I judge his news is important enough to trouble you." Northumberland bowed with feigned obsequiousness. "I feared it would tire Your Majesty after such a long day."

"It should never weary a queen to hear of an ally's loyalty. Now we must be assured that the rest of the country shares the emperor's view."

"I doubt many in London will dare voice dissent." Northumberland waved his hand in dismissal. "We have silenced one Gilbert Potter, apprentice to the master gunner at the Tower. The youth stirred discontent by calling out for the Lady Mary at St. Paul's cross."

I saw Kat stiffen.

"He was locked in the pillory and his ears were struck off,"

Father said with satisfaction. Kat looked as if she might retch. Little Mary clapped her hands over her ears. I wanted to recoil as well, but I knew I must harden my nerves. I would not have my advisers citing this moment as one of the reasons I must abdicate power to a consort because a ruler must have a stronger stomach.

I lifted my chin. "We do what we must to retain order." I looked at Kat, hoping she would heed my words. "Now, if there is nothing further, I would retire to my chambers."

Northumberland bowed. "I will endeavor not to trouble Your Majesty any further. Allow me to send your husband to wait upon you."

"Not tonight." A sense of power I had never felt flowed through me, knowing that the formidable Duke of Northumberland must obey my command. As for my husband, I could not forbid him my bed for the rest of our marriage, but I could choose the timing of our encounters. I would not be completely helpless against his lust.

"Have a light repast brought to my privy chamber for the Lady Katherine, Lady Mary, and me," I told Northumberland. "It has been weeks since I have enjoyed my sisters' company." But from the drawn looks of Kat and Mary, I doubted either one of them would be able to eat.

"I am certain your lady mother will wish to join you."

Tension knotted between my shoulders, fear of my mother's temper still pressed like a handprint into my muscle and bone. I could not speak freely to Kat and Mary if she was there. I might not have another chance to make things right between my sisters and me for a very long time. "Her Grace of Suffolk may attend us when we have been alone an hour. See that she joins us then."

I turned aside, dismissing Northumberland as pointedly as I dared. From the corner of my eye, I saw the duke's lids narrow just a fraction. He bowed to me again, though I made certain not to seem as if I noticed, as he summoned other attendants to do my bidding.

Once in my chambers, my ladies stripped me of the heavy state gown and swathed me in simpler garb. When they finished, they carried the day's finery to be brushed and aired and returned to the royal wardrobe. I motioned Kat and Mary to join me in my privy chamber. The gentleman usher closed the doors behind us, secluding us together, as we had been so many times before.

My gaze fixed on the tapestry depicting a scene from the Greek myth of Demeter, goddess of the harvest, her arms outstretched to her daughter Persephone, swept to the kingdom of Hades, already beyond her reach.

The bond between Kat, Mary, and me could not be as natural and heedless as it had been. I knew that in the rational part of my brain. Still, my heart had to believe I could reach through the barrier to our childhoods.

"I am so relieved to be away from all those people," I confessed, trying to recapture the ease of earlier confidences. "Now it can be just the three of us, at least for a little while."

Neither sister said anything for a long moment. Then Kat spoke: "If it pleases Your Majesty." Her reply pinched, so lacking in its usual warmth. Wistful, I remembered other times when we had been reunited after a spell apart: her eager chatter and abundant hugs had been bestowed with the generosity and charm that only she, of the three of us, possessed.

But my hurt faded as I turned to face her and recognized the expression I had seen whenever she had witnessed cruelty or violence, as if, merely by beholding it, she had suffered the same crippling blow. I knew what had wounded her this night.

"I can see you are troubled, Kat," I said gently. She started to protest, but I cut her off. "Do not bother trying to deny it. I know you too well. It is the tale Northumberland told about the apprentice Gilbert Potter."

Kat pressed her knuckles to her mouth.

"I am sorry if Northumberland upset you, but you understand, there was nothing else to be done. We cannot have rebels drawn to Cousin Mary's cause by allowing public defiance. Making an example of this boy is more merciful in the end than allowing his poison to spread to others who would also have to suffer."

I saw Kat's throat work. She nodded.

"I wish I could wipe it from your mind. Since I cannot, tell me something happy. How have you passed the time with your Henry? When I received the message from His Grace of Northumberland ordering me to the marriage bed, my greatest comfort was imagining you must be receiving the same command. How happy you must have been to get the chance to welcome Henry to your bed."

I expected to draw a smile from Kat—trusting the quicksilver shift of her emotions. She had always preferred happy thoughts to sad ones, turning to joy as naturally as flowers turn to sun. But my sister regarded me, bewildered. "The marriage bed? We received no such message from His Grace. When did you receive the duke's permission?"

I could not conceal my astonishment, or unease. "Northumberland sent word weeks ago, when I was at the old abbey."

"Perhaps the devil duke was too busy making Jane queen to send a message to you, Kat," Mary suggested.

"That is not the case. I cannot count the number of messengers that came and went between the Herberts and London in the past weeks."

"Then why would Northumberland not send word to bid you and Henry consummate your marriage?" I posed the question, more thinking aloud than searching for an answer. "Surely the duke would want to seal all the unions he made between powerful families at the same time. Northumberland's goal in wedding you to Pembroke's son was to consolidate support behind my throne. It would be in the duke's best interest to make that alliance unbreakable. He would not want Pembroke to be able to change sides if anything went awry. The question is: who stands to benefit by keeping you and Henry from becoming in truth man and wife? The Earl of Pembroke?"

I could see Kat's resistance to the words. No Tudor was more stubborn than she when her romantic notions were in danger of being smashed. "You are wrong in this, Jane. My father-in-law knows how eager Henry and I are to love each other properly. He even commiserated with me, saying he can guess how painful it must be for us to remain apart."

I paced nearer the fire, rubbing my arms. When had the room grown so cold? The food that the servants had brought for us lay on the table untouched; the fat on the roast duck had congealed on the gold platter and left it cloudy, obscured like Pembroke's motives. I thought of the earl's face, its cast cruder than most courtiers', his expression sly.

"I do not like it here," Mary said in a small voice. "I want to go home."

"You cannot go home," Kat said sharply. "None of us can. At least not before Jane is crowned."

"Jane is queen. She can make them let me go."

I started to touch Mary's shoulder, then remembered her reaction the last time and let my hand fall to my side. "It is too dangerous for you to go right now. There are soldiers on the road trying to find Cousin Mary and people confused like Gilbert Potter was."

"I do not care! I want to go to Bradgate, where I can talk to Jennet and make her not be afraid."

"Jennet?" I puzzled, too distracted to remember who that might be.

"The poppet you made me. Hettie said I cannot even hold Jennet while I am with you, but I hid her in my petticoats."

For once my patience wore thin, unraveled by my own uncertainty and confusion. But I tried to master myself before I dealt a stinging reply: *What good can a doll do, pitted against the wickedness of a man like Northumberland?* Instead, I kept my voice level.

"Court manners can be difficult at first. I know it feels strange right now, all the changes going on. But it will get easier, I promise. Do you not want to stay with me?"

"No!"

I was stunned to see the truth in her eyes. I felt my throat close. How had this happened? Instead of easing the distance between us, I had made it wider. Kat paced about, fidgeting with one of her earrings until I feared she might tear her lobe, and I could almost see the cogs wheeling in her mind as she wrestled with Pembroke's subterfuge.

Mary clutched at a lump beneath her petticoat. I was certain her doll lay beneath. I was tempted to tell her to take Jennet out, but certain dignities were expected. We were not at Bradgate anymore. Even there Mary would not have been allowed to carry a doll in the presence of Father's retainers. How much less could she parade about a queen's court with one?

"You may take Jennet out when you are in your own quarters," I said.

"Jennet is not scared then! It is when all the council is about, and Father, and the devil. Even you."

Pain knifed my heart. "Mary, you are not afraid of me?"

"I am afraid—" Her voice broke. "You do not look like my Jane anymore, and there are too many people around, and they cut off the ears of people they do not like here, or poison them like they did the king."

My heart plunged. "Poisoned the king? Mary, I know there have been rumors, but—"

"Rumor means it is not true. But I know this time it is."

"You do not!" Kat cried.

"I do. I heard Father and Northumberland in the garden. They had to keep Cousin Edward alive until Jane could be made queen, so an old woman gave him the poison. Once they could let Edward die, they killed her to keep her from telling about it all over London."

"Quiet!" Panic leaped in my chest.

Kat gasped, white-faced. "That is what the vial of powder I saw the night of our weddings held. Jane, if that were ever revealed, would everyone think you knew?"

I reeled. Would people believe I had been party to regicide to gain Edward's crown? If so, no punishment in the nation would be too dire to use against me.

Kat must have read the horror on my face. She grabbed Mary by the arm. "You must never speak of this to anyone. You always liked snooping about. Now you discovered something that could get Jane killed. Maybe all of us, if Cousin Mary ever gains power."

Mary's lower lip trembled. "I do not like secrets anymore." She fumbled with her kirtle, dragging out her doll. She crushed it to her. "I did not mean to do a bad thing."

I felt tears bubble up. I could not bear to be alone with such dark terrors, but I dared not break down. Not when my mother would be descending upon us.

"How long have we been alone?" I startled Kat with the abrupt question.

"Alone?" she echoed.

"The time." I looked at a nearby clock. "I did not notice when the other ladies left."

"Nor did I. Does it matter?"

"It will if our mother enters the room while these secrets are writ on our faces. She cannot press me, but you know she will do anything to batter the truth out of you or Mary. We must compose ourselves. Think what to do."

"You could plead a headache," Kat suggested.

"Then she would only go to your chambers and insist on your telling her what transpired while we were alone. If you did not break, she would turn on Mary. Better we three stay together, do our best to pretend we have just had a sisterly rift, some jealousy, or—surely we have had enough of those over the years we can make our lady mother believe it." I chafed my bottom lip with my teeth.

"Stop that, Jane," Kat said. "You will make yourself bleed."

I pressed my fingertips to the burning place on my lips to cool them. "This is just what I fear. If Mother walked in and caught us by surprise, she would guess . . ." I hesitated, then made a decision. "Better to know when the others will join us. At least we can prepare ourselves if I summon my ladies. I will have some sense of control."

Kat nibbled at a fingernail. "I suppose that is true."

"Mary, you will have to put Jennet out of sight again before they arrive. I would not have her taken from you."

"If you were a brave queen, you would not let them. Cousin Mary would make them let me keep Jennet," Mary asserted, but after a moment she bundled the poppet back into its hiding place in the folds of her petticoat.

Once we had all steadied ourselves, I went to the door and told the usher to summon my mother and the other ladies. Perhaps Kat, Mary, and I could hide our emotions in a crowd, let them dilute whatever pain we felt, three drops of wine disappearing in a river. I hoped so.

Three hours later we were all gathered near the fire, stitching, when my father burst in, Northumberland in his wake. I knew the instant I fixed my eyes on them that something terrible had happened.

I set my tambour aside and rose to my feet. My knees trembled. "What is it?"

Northumberland betrayed the first hint of alarm I had ever seen in him. "The Lady Mary raised her standard at Framlingham. She has declared herself queen."

I heard my ladies gasp and saw Mary cower back, hiding behind Kat's chair. My own sick dread echoed hers. Everything seemed to fade except the discourse raging in my mind.

How had I imagined that Mary Tudor would surrender her birthright with no resistance? Had she not defied even her father, refusing to say her mother was not Henry's true wife even when the head of his dearest friend, Sir Thomas More, was rolling across the straw?

Later, when Edward and his advisers made it a crime to hear Catholic mass, did she not continue to practice her faith, no matter what threats Northumberland leveled against her? People claimed she would have died rather than forsake her faith. I believed them.

I swallowed hard, knowing that in my Catholic cousin I faced a will as strong as my lady mother's own. I could see the fear that Mary Tudor spawned in those who surrounded me. If she could inspire this much trepidation in men like Father and Northumberland, the threat must be dire indeed. How fearful might other lords be? Ones whose fate was not tied so closely to the houses of Suffolk and Northumberland? I pictured the opposing pieces on a chessboard. In the end who would gather in the most powerful chessmen?

One thing was certain, I thought, as my surroundings spun slowly back into existence. I must give those who would be loyal to me a secure mooring to anchor themselves to in the coming storm. Even if a true war never broke out—may God make it so—my actions now would be the warp and weft that would bind my subjects to me.

If I was to be queen, let me be a brave one.

I turned to my ladies, determined to calm them. "The Lady Mary's defiance is futile. Even her cousin, the Emperor Charles, has acknowledged my claim."

"But it seems there are those in the North who do not," Northumberland said. "Yeomen and peasants are flocking to her standard. I fear that even the loyalty of those peers absent from today's ceremony must be called into question. The Howards, for example."

I remembered the sinking feeling I had experienced. The puzzle of why those lords were missing was solved. A sound I could not remember having heard before sent shivers down my back: my mother, weeping. Guilford's mother sobbed as well, the two duchesses who had seemed so intimidating weeks before brought low. Fear pressed hard.

It was no surprise that Mary had sought out the infamous Howards, the most powerful of Catholic nobles. They would doubtless do all they could to see her triumph. It would be easy enough to draw their vassals and others like them to Mary's cause.

In their northern stronghold people loathed Northumberland even more than they loathed Kat's father-in-law; they blamed those two men above all others for corpses at the crossroads, the hanging, drawing, and quartering of the rebellion's leaders.

How many Norfolk lads had Pembroke and Northumberland killed? Boys wielding scythes, passionate in their misguided loyalty to the old faith. They had hoped they might realize the promise Edward Seymour's father gave them and get a fairer share of the profit their labor produced. Girded with such ideals, even simple folk could be formidable foes indeed. I had to lead England against them.

I squared my shoulders. "If Lady Mary has followers who would oppose us, we must deal with her rebellion swiftly. Muster more troops to fight against them."

The Earl of Pembroke and his shadow, Lord Huntingdon, strode in. I saw my sister regard her father-in-law with hurt eyes. How had Kat managed, beneath our parents' rule, to still be so surprised when someone she loved wounded her?

"The rest of the council is convening," the earl said. "I told them the news. We are to meet them as soon as we are able and determine what action to take."

I saw Father's fingers tighten against the russet satin of his doublet. "Queen Jane has already ordered us to muster troops in her name," Father informed him.

"Good," Pembroke said. "The sooner we can confront the rebels, the less chance they will have to prepare. Who does Her Majesty choose to command these troops?"

I remembered he had denied Kat and Henry the joy of bedding together. He would not be riding off with the troops no matter how fine a soldier he was. I dared not allow him to go where I could not watch him.

Father stepped forward. "Let me take this command, Your Majesty. No one will fight more fiercely in your name."

"I know." Whatever our differences in the past, Father was proud of me, now I was queen. I recalled what my little sister had claimed. Had Father actually plotted with Northumberland to feed the king poison? If that was true, he would do anything to see that the crown would not slip from my grasp. With a pang I thought how precious my father's loyalty would have been to me, had I not suspected Mary's tale was well founded. "It will be as the Duke of Suffolk wishes," I said.

"Majesty," Pembroke cut in, "I must speak where others will not." He turned to my father. "Tell Her Majesty the true state of your health, Your Grace. You will do your daughter no good if you cannot sit a horse, no matter how determined you are."

"Are you a surgeon to physic me, Pembroke?"

"Anyone can see you are ailing. You cannot even straighten up." Pembroke gestured to where Father's hand clamped to his middle. I had noticed his lips compressed in a tight line now and again at the banquet, but I thought it due to some misstep in my decorum.

"This paltry discomfort is nothing, Jane—Your Majesty." Conviction hammered his words, but there was no masking the pain. I felt another jab of fear. He might not have loved me as I wished, but he was my only shield against more ruthless opportunists.

I let tenderness color my tone. "You are not well. Father, I dare not risk you."

"When it comes to waging war, the Duke of Northumberland is without match in all England," Pembroke said. It was true. Northumberland might be the most dangerous man in my realm, but no one would fight harder to crush a rebellion that threatened to dash his wolf-pack of a family away from the throne. Besides, his absence could ease his grasp on the reins of my council.

I nodded. "It is only just that I give the Dudley family a chance to redeem their name, since it was Lord Robert who allowed our cousin to escape at Hoddesdon." I saw Northumberland's jaw harden. "I will place my army under His Grace of Northumberland's very able command." My steadiness heartened the others.

"Majesty," Northumberland began, "do you think it wise . . ."

I saw Mary's frightened face, a pale half moon in the flickering candlelight. I considered Kat, dragged into the chamber at Durham House, the white powder from the broken vial swirled on the stones beneath her feet. Most recent of all, I remembered the sensation of Northumberland snatching away the Tower key.

"My lord father will guard our interests here," I said. "You, Your Grace of Northumberland, will carry our standard afield. It is an honor you richly deserve."

Even fearsome Northumberland seemed to gather strength from my orders. "Your traitor cousin will be crushed, of that I am certain," he said. "Many cities have already declared for you. They closed their gates to her while she was in flight."

"Then I do not doubt that all will be well. It is in God's hands."

"We fight His battle against the Roman whore," my father said. "We will deal with these fools once and for all."

I turned to my ladies, their noses reddened as they still wept. "Do you not hear what His Grace says?" I chided. "You must all calm yourselves."

"But with Lady Mary gathering troops, we cannot know what may happen." Tears started in my mother's eyes despite her efforts to control them.

I thought of all she had seen. The fall of her mother's dear friend, Katherine of Aragon. The rise of Anne Boleyn, purchased by the blood of her uncle's greatest friends. Cromwell's fall, and the execution of Catherine Howard. Somerset and the leaders of the Pilgrimage of Grace. Fates that could shift between one heartbeat and the next.

"Come, now, my lady mother. There is always unrest at the passing of a crown," I said with unfamiliar tenderness. "I can list scores of examples throughout my history books. Are we not safe in this fortress? The rebels cannot get in unless we open the gates, and that will never happen."

Northumberland turned to reassure me. "This fortress is armed and ready against any attack, Your Majesty. There is nothing to fear. No army can breach these walls, and your royal navy stands sentry in the channel to cut off your traitor cousin's escape. The Lady Mary is a stupid, stubborn woman like her mother. But her defiance will serve no purpose. She will find herself locked in a cell."

"No cell will be safe enough to hold her," Father said. "King Henry's bastard has pushed us too far, as I expected. She leaves us no room for mercy. The Lady Mary will end her days on a scaffold upon Tower Green. Until that day, we cannot be sure of peace."

I paced to the window, peered out into the courtyard. Already I could see men wrestling cannons into position. Doubtless Northumberland had given orders to further secure the Tower even before he came to tell me Cousin Mary had declared herself queen.

Father had said we could not be sure of peace until Mary lay dead on Tower Green.

I did not want to imagine my cousin facing such a grisly fate, and yet did I have any choice but to condemn her to the ax?

I touched my neck, remembering the ruby necklace she had fastened around my throat one Christmastide much to my dismay. As a Protestant maid, I had no use for such gaudy trinkets.

Had the gift of bloodred stones been harbingers of the conflict we would wage among us? For now that she had raised her standard and openly challenged my claim to the crown, how could either of us lay down our sword? My victory or hers would determine which of the warring faiths we loved would survive upon English soil.

Chapter Eleven

Kat
Tower of London

ENRY. I NEEDED TO FIND HENRY. THAT WAS ALL I could think of as everything I had learned in Jane's chamber churned inside me: Cousin Mary starting a war, the Duke of Northumberland poisoning kings, and the Earl of Pembroke scheming to keep Henry and me stranded in this excruciating limbo between chastity and becoming true man and wife.

Of all that upset me, the last disturbed me most. Jane had always worked herself into tempests, searching for hidden motives, infecting everyone around her with doubts. Her determination to see the worst in every situation often made me want to pull her hair as I had when we were children, running in the parklands at Bradgate.

Yet she had been right to suspect some plot was afoot at our weddings. Was it possible she was right about my father-in-law's motives as well?

No, the earl had shown me nothing but honor and affection. Perhaps he had sought my marriage to Henry in hopes that Jane would be queen, but he loved me for myself now. I was certain that was so. Once Henry confirmed that Jane was crying doom over nothing, I would tell my sister just how foolish she had been.

You will not, a voice whispered in my head. *Now Jane is queen, you will never be able to scold her for her dreary outlook again.*

That thought plagued me as I suffered through the endless ceremony of putting the queen to bed. Even after Jane's other ladies and I finally bowed our way out of the room, I could not hasten to the men's quarters in search of my husband. My little sister clung to me like a cocklebur. "Go find Hettie, and take that doll out from under your kirtle. It looks ridiculous!" I told Mary in an effort to shake her off.

"I do not want Hettie." Mary's eyes reminded me of a bird trapped behind a pane of glass, trying to batter its way outside. My own doubts beat against my ribs all the harder.

"Can you not leave me alone?" Even that did not detach Mary from my side. *Why must she always force me to be harsh with her?* I thought with a pang. Yet nothing gentler would dislodge her. "I have a husband to tend to and important things to talk to him about. A child like you could never understand." She stood there, clutching the lump where her doll was hidden as I hastened away. But at least she did not follow me.

Hoping to find Henry, I waded through pools of torchlight, wound through the shadowy corridors to where Guilford's men were lodged. My prayers were answered when I saw Henry within a knot of young men talking war, eager as Father's pack of hunting dogs just before his master of the hounds loosed them from their leads.

Northumberland's older sons were among the most vehement, gesturing as their servants bustled about fetching swords and armor. A little ways apart from them, Lord Huntingdon's son stood with his arms folded across his chest, his expression surly. Henry appeared grim as well, almost embarrassed when I hastened up to him.

"Heigh ho, Henry Herbert!" the youngest of the Dudley brothers called. "Fortunate for you that your wife has arrived.

You might as well go off with the women and leave the fighting to us men! You have nothing better to do."

Henry's face darkened as I tried to catch hold of his hand. He pulled away. I had never seen such an expression on his face—as if I had humiliated him on purpose. Hurt spilled through me.

"I do whatever the queen commands," Henry told his critic. "I do not have to like it."

"It is obvious your bride is as unhappy as you are." Dudley bowed to me, swirling his sable-edged cape over one shoulder. "You had best tend to her at once. It would be tragedy indeed for a nose as pretty as Lady Katherine's to grow red from weeping."

Henry looked at me, and I knew he was aware he had hurt my feelings. Storm clouds in his eyes receded. He gestured toward a chamber where we could speak in private.

The moment we were alone, he turned all contrition. "I did not mean to snap at you. Those Dudleys have been tilting at me with such insults ever since we heard what mischief your cousin Mary was about. Northumberland's whelps grow bolder every day until even I—son of their great ally—would give much to cut that arrogance out from under them."

"It is no wonder so many people dislike them. Now the enemies the Dudleys have made will be riding to join Lady Mary." The tears that had been threatening since my tangle with Jane threatened to burst free. Henry must have seen my lips trembling, for he gathered me close.

"Do not fret," he murmured into my hair. "It is bad news, your cousin making trouble in the North. But Father said we must not worry. We have crushed Catholic upstarts before."

"Will you have to fight?"

"I will not ride out with the others to hunt down the rebels, if that is what you are asking. That is the reason the Dudley upstart was tormenting me. Father is to remain here to help guard the Tower, and I will stay with him, though I cannot guess why he is not to fight alongside Northumberland. Father has fought in many battles—"

"I do not care about battles, Henry!" I cried. His eyes widened in astonishment.

"I learned something today that I do not understand. Something that has nothing to do with Cousin Mary or rebels or Jane being queen. It vexes me terribly."

"What has so distressed you, love?"

"Do you remember how often your father has told us he is sorry to keep us from joining as man and wife?"

"I believe he regrets the delay nearly as much as we do, but we are all bound by Northumberland's will. Perhaps now your sister is on the throne, the duke will see fit to give his blessing to finishing the business begun at our weddings."

"Jane told me that Northumberland ordered her marriage to Guilford consummated weeks ago, when she was at Syon House."

Henry was as surprised as I was. "I would say your sister and her husband were fortunate, then, save the fact that they dislike each other so. It seems unfair that they should be released from constraints on the marital bed while we are not. If we were given such a chance at loving each other, we would not waste it." His gaze dipped to where the tops of my breasts swelled above the gold-lace edging on my bodice.

"Jane believes Northumberland intended we consummate our marriage as well."

"If that were true, we would still be abed." Henry's features were so clear of doubt, I almost let the matter go. But something inside me would not allow it.

"Jane says the duke needs his alliance with your father to be unbreakable, now she is on the throne. She says the only one who could benefit from delaying our union is your father."

"She has been living around the Dudleys, my love, and a more scheming family never lived. It is only natural she would suspect others of the same ravening ambition. Perhaps in the beginning our union was for political advantage, but since then all has changed. My father adores you nearly as much as I do, and nothing could dislodge his affection."

I felt as if a stone had rolled off my chest. Jane would have cautioned me that to feel relief over something as trivial as a family misunderstanding was foolhardy when the country was on the brink of civil war. I did not care about that nearly as much as I did about the possibility that someone I loved might have been plotting against me.

I vowed to stitch my father-in-law a pair of velvet slippers to make up for the fact that I had doubted him. I would ask Maud what Pembroke's favorite color was.

"Katherine," Henry said, "you must be wary of gossip now we are at court. People will be stirring up trouble, vying for your favor while attempting to undercut anyone they see as a rival. You cannot always trust people's motives. Not even your sister's."

I had been upset with Jane myself, but for some reason Henry's words sparked me to come to her defense. "Jane imagines trouble everywhere, but she would not stir discord between us on purpose."

"She accused my father of scheming against us when I am sure he would not," Henry said hotly. "I know there are tales of his ruthlessness, but when it comes to his own family, he would do no harm. I would wager my life on it." Did Henry's gaze shift away from mine for just a moment? I must have imagined it.

Muted laughter penetrated the door from the crowd beyond. Henry seemed almost relieved at the sound. "Peace, wife." His voice softened. "If your sister is innocent as you claim, and my father is without blame, this discord must be the Dudleys' doing. God knows Guilford was jealous of the affection we share. If he hoped to divide the house of Pembroke, it almost worked."

"I do not trust any of the Dudleys." Cousin Edward's pinched features rose in my memory. Had the pallor that people had whispered about been caused by Northumberland's doses of arsenic just as my sister Mary claimed? "You should hear the awful things I heard," I confided.

"Lies like the one about my father?"

"Not all lies."

"Then tell me, my love: what is this horrible thing you believe? Let me ease your fears and relieve whatever burdens you bear."

I wavered between spilling out Mary's tale and keeping the secret. The poisoning of a king was so dangerous that instinct stopped me. "I cannot tell even you. What matters is this: if Northumberland allowed Jane and Guilford to consummate their marriage, and if your father is eager for us to become husband and wife, there is no reason to deny what we both want." Passion flared in Henry's eyes.

"Father has not given us his leave."

"Perhaps in the flurry over going to war against Mary, your father forgot to give us the news we could bed together. Or maybe Northumberland meant to send a messenger, but in the confusion he forgot."

Henry's gaze turned cold. "The duke has never forgotten anything of importance save perhaps the dangers of hell. In spite of that, I wish I could get Father to let me ride out with Northumberland's army on the morrow. There is so much I could learn from the duke about soldiering. But Father will not hear of it."

Why would he not stop talking of stupid things when we had something more important to settle between us? "Henry, do you love me?"

"You know that I do," he said, impatience edging his voice.

"Then let us seize this chance to bed together. No one even has to know. Later, when all this madness has calmed and they remember to give us their blessing, we can pretend it is our first time. Even if they discovered we made love, no one could truly blame us." I kissed a bare place on his throat. I felt his pulse race beneath my lips.

But instead of melting into my embrace, Henry grew stiff and cold. "I will not shame my father. Not even for you. He has the right to expect his son and daughter-in-law to obey him. Even if that daughter-in-law is of royal blood."

My cheeks fired hot, but I would not be deterred. My fingers trembled as they sought his cheek, his hair, his mouth. "Henry, I cannot bear to be kept apart from you. What if something happens and we never are able to be together in that way? You are my husband. I only want to be your wife." My voice cracked, and Henry turned tender. But not so tender as to break through his resolve.

"Hush, sweeting. You are imagining disaster where there is none. Before you know it, you will be wearied of my lovemaking as all the other husbands say their wives are. You will be making excuses to avoid my caresses."

"Never!"

"Wait and see. When we are grizzle-haired and looking out across a table filled with our grandchildren, I will remind you of this day, and you will laugh at these fears of yours."

Something akin to alarm fluttered in my breast. Where it came from I could not guess. "Promise, Henry? Promise me."

"Did I not promise before God and all the peers in England to be your husband? Nothing but death will sever those vows."

How could I not believe him? Henry crushed me against him, and I could feel his love for me. How fortunate I was, I was Henry Herbert's wife. Daughter-in-law of the powerful Earl of Pembroke. A cherished member of my new family.

I remembered the worry that had turned Jane even sadder than I had seen her before. Times were perilous, as Jane said. But no matter what happened with the insufferable Dudleys or Cousin Mary's inconvenient rebellion, Henry and his family loved me. That was the thing that mattered most.

I wrapped myself in that certainty as if it were the warmest cloak in London.

Chapter Twelve

Jane
Tower of London
July 14, 1553

FAR AWAY IN THE NORTH PIKES AND SWORDS WERE SLASHING, hails of arrows falling, rich Norfolk farmland slick with blood and strewn with the dead or dying. It was alarming to realize that the army belonged to me. Yet if I reigned as many years as my great-uncle Henry, I would never forget the feeling of pain and power as I watched my troops set out for Bury St. Edmunds—the place where Northumberland hoped to stem the flow of supporters now flocking to Mary in Suffolk.

I wondered how many of the men who had swarmed about in preparations for war would return, their bodies maimed, or more terrible still, would die, their children orphaned, their futures stolen away forever. How many of them had wives or sweethearts who wept? Even in victory, what would become of those who were left behind?

You are responsible for the losses they will incur, Jane. They go at your command. You could keep them here, safe.

But that would only make the task of the men who defended my crown more difficult. It would give my cousin Mary more time to entrench herself more deeply, mount a more effective attack against me.

Mary's quest was a hopeless one. For three long days I had clung to my father's reassurance that it was so, and to

Northumberland's certainty that he would deliver me victory. Members of my Privy Council reminded me how Mary's cousin the emperor bade her surrender her claim to the crown. Even if she had some small support among the common people, the rest of the world had abandoned her cause. No empire would launch a navy with supplies or troops to place her on the throne.

I remembered Northumberland as he rallied the army "For England and Queen Jane," his face carved white and hard, as if the muscles might snap. Was he imagining what would happen if we should lose?

But we would not. Everyone was certain of that. So why were some members of my council avoiding my eyes? Why did I see them whispering in clumps of shadow?

It was only natural they should talk amongst themselves, I reassured myself. Their futures hung in the balance, as certainly as mine did. In their hearts they must be as on edge as me.

I paced across the privy chamber and peered out the mullioned window, trying to disguise my anguish at not knowing what might befall those brave soldiers. Befall my family. Befall me.

Our fates were being decided even as I went through the motions of my royal day: greeting ambassadors, reading dispatches, meeting with what members of my royal council remained behind: Pembroke with his calculating gaze, and Huntingdon, whom I caught appraising me as a wherry man might a carrack that he was not sure was seaworthy. Arundel was another who disturbed me, his thick white hair framing a face marked with wistfulness for the church of his youth, as did Cobham, who had returned from his meetings with ambassadors Scheyfve and Renard exhibiting a restlessness that fed my own unease.

What had unnerved him? I asked upon discovering Cobham in earnest discussion with Arundel. The earl had insisted it was nothing save a complaint of the stomach, an ailment I could sympathize with since my own insides resembled a bark on a pitching sea.

But my discomfort was nothing compared to that of my father, who seemed to grow more ill with colic as days bled with agonizing slowness into sleepless nights.

Three days had passed since the Duke of Northumberland led my army off to the North. I peered out the window overlooking the courtyard, remembering the rumble of heavy carts, the sounds of horses, and the shouts of soldiers as they disappeared through the Tower gates in a deadly ribbon that filled the roads. Lined with people, those roads were, my subjects watching my army set forth to meet the pretender.

What had I hoped for now that the first shock of my succession was past? Cries of Godspeed to send my forces on their way? But when I begged a description from those who had gone into the streets to watch the army ride away, my ladies had stammered excuses.

Today I was desperate enough to summon the one person who had as much to lose in this gamble as I did. Guilford had ridden a fair way with his father and brothers before returning to the Tower. He would be able to ease my sense of blindness.

I sent a gentleman usher in search, saying I wished to speak in private with my husband. I waited for the sensation I had experienced so often when seeing the man who had violated me. Surprisingly, I felt only its shadow as Guilford strode into the room.

He swept his white velvet hat from his dark blond hair and bowed, the fabric pulled through the ornamental slits in his doublet the color of blood. "Imagine my surprise when told that Your Majesty wished to see me. I am delighted to wait upon you."

"Neither of us wishes to wait upon the other. Let us at least be honest in that."

Guilford arched one brow. "I find myself baffled. You do not wish me to wait upon you, but you require some service?"

"Others are too determined to paint bright skies over the landscape no matter what the true temper of the weather might be. You rode beyond the Tower walls with your father and brothers. Followed them until they left the city walls."

"I did."

"What was the mood of our subjects when the army marched north?" I inquired of him. "I ask you not as a queen whose ears are to be filled with pretty inventions, but as a wife who seeks the truth."

"You have not been a true wife save once at the abbey, Your Majesty."

A sliver of old pain slipped past my guard. I cooled the sting by turning my voice icy. "You were no husband to me then. Not in the way God intends."

"How lovely that God has revealed his motivations to you." Guilford's cheekbones darkened, but not before I saw a flicker of fear. It was harder to intimidate a queen than a helpless girl. I looked him in the eye, shedding the last remains of the girl who had lain crumpled and bruised upon the abbey floor.

"I did not bring you here to argue about old wounds. Rather, I would know what people beyond this fortress's walls are feeling about the battle that your father of Northumberland has joined with the rebels."

"London has declared for you. So has most of East Anglia."

"That was before the Lady Mary declared herself queen at Framlingham. Since then people have been riding to her standard even from those places who immediately declared me their queen."

"It is a damned nuisance that Robert let Mary Tudor slip away. If she were locked in a cell as Father planned, she could cause no trouble."

"It does no good to rake over what might have been. What lies ahead is of more importance. I would hear whatever rumors are being bruited about."

"The Spanish fear my father will make some secret pact with the French. The French do not trust him. The rest of the world believes he will strike whatever bargain he can to place one of his blood on the throne. Father says the day the house of Northumberland cares what such knaves think will be the day the world ends."

"Do not tell me what your father says. What do the townsfolk of London say?"

"Their rumblings hardly matter."

I compressed my lips. "I would know my people's opinions. What did you hear from the crowd on the day the army set out for Buckinghamshire?"

"They had little more to say than when first we came to the Tower. Many came out of their houses to watch the army pass. Robert grumbled that they were silent as stones."

I could not help but think of times the sky over Bradgate became clotted with blackened clouds. "Do you not think it strange? Such silence?"

"They would not dare speak dissent after what happened to that vile apprentice Gilbert Potter for his outcry against you. Father vowed he would pile severed ears as high as the cross at St. Paul's if that is what it takes to silence Mary's supporters."

I surprised myself by sharing my thoughts aloud. "Will such harsh treatment make those misguided men more apt to be loyal to me?"

"Better they should be afraid of you. You must hold your realm in a glove of iron."

I thought of the poisoned glove of marriage that the dowager queen had spoken of. The gauntlet of rule was already mine. It was too late to draw either garment from my hands.

"Do not fear your cousin," Guilford said. "She is weak."

"She may seem pitiful, used harshly by her father and other powerful men. But she is the daughter of Katherine of Aragon, who defeated the Scots on Flodden Field. She is the granddaughter of Isabella of Castile, who drove the moors from Spanish soil. It would be foolhardy to underestimate her."

I plucked a torn place on my fingernail. It began to bleed.

"We must not risk more people fleeing the city for Buckinghamshire. Go to Arundel and Pembroke and tell them I would place the city under a curfew. Have the city gates locked from eight at night until five in the morning. You will see to it."

"As you wish." He looked a trifle puzzled at the new strength in me, and a little intrigued by it as well. I dismissed him, his boots thudding against the floor as he left the room.

Softer footsteps approached, far too soon to be my ministers. I looked in the direction of the sound and saw my small sister.

"Mary, you must not creep up and listen to the secrets of a queen." But my heart was not in the reproach.

"I was not listening on purpose. Kat sent me in when she saw Guilford leave. She is still angry at you, but she did not want you alone if he upset you."

It was painful and unexpected, the way Kat held tight to her anger. Sister Mary held grudges, while I remained determined to prove I was right. But Kat . . . "I am surprised you would come even when she bade you. You do not seem to wish to be around me of late."

"You do not seem like my Jane anymore." Mary fidgeted with the pomander dangling from a gold chain at her waist. It rattled strangely. Not long ago it would have been so natural to ask what Mary had placed inside the filigreed ball, since she had so obviously cast away whatever spices Hettie bought from an apothecary to ward off plague.

"Did the crown that the archbishop put on you suck your brains out of your head? Kat says that is why you were saying bad things about her new family. She likes the Herberts better than us."

"Tell Kat next time she wishes to know what I am thinking, she should have the courage to come herself instead of sending you."

"She will not like that." Mary looked up through sparse

lashes. "You are queen, and Kat belongs to the Herberts. I am the only one who wants to be a sister anymore."

"It is not that simple. I wish—" The strength in me was so new I dared not test it by giving way to feelings that might leave me vulnerable once more. The moment passed, and I knew I had missed this chance to comfort my sister. Perhaps now that I was queen, we would always be on opposite sides of a great divide.

"Jane, what does a queen wish for?" Mary asked in a small voice. "You always say 'I wish,' and I used to know what you were wishing for. Now I cannot tell."

My dreams of quiet rooms to study in and an endless supply of books seemed to belong to some other Jane a world ago. What did I wish for now?

"I wish that the people would rejoice at my succeeding to the crown. That I would be accepted by them." My voice grew softer. "Loved by them."

"It will not make people love you if you lock the city gates. Remember when I tried to grab the sparkles on the water at Bradgate?"

"I remember."

"I heard Guilford say queens must rule with iron gauntlets. I do not think it matters if you wear gloves of iron or pretty, embroidered ones, like the wedding glove you gave me. You cannot make water or people stay in your hands if they want to slide away."

Mary was right. Once I had wanted my lady mother's love so desperately, I thought I might die of it. But the more I had tried to capture that regard, the more distant she grew.

"Mary, I cannot stand by and let people like that Gilbert Potter run about loose saying I am not the rightful heir. What would people think?"

"I do not know. But you cannot stop them from thinking it, no matter how many ears you cut off or gates you lock."

Her words made me afraid as no reports of rival queens ever could. Another headache sank talons into my skull. Anger and frustration welled up.

"Can you not see I have weighty matters on my mind? I did not summon you here. You should not come unless I do." It was a cruel thing to say, no matter how much my sister vexed me. I saw the hurt fill Mary's eyes, but she said nothing.

Silence . . . I was sick to death of silence. Why did no messenger come from Northumberland? Why was I no longer sure if I could trust those closest to me?

Perhaps capturing people's love or loyalty was as difficult as trying to grasp water in your hands. But I had no choice now but to try to hold on.

Chapter Thirteen

Jane
Tower of London
July 15, 1553

EVER HAD I SEEN MY PARENTS SO AFRAID. BUT HOUR by hour, day by day, cracks spread in spidery webs through the wall of arrogance that had defined Henry and Frances Grey as long as I could remember: the pride of royal blood that filled my mother's eyes, the almost casual sense that victory was my father's due. In spite of the fact I was now queen, I would have welcomed the painful slaps and criticisms that bared my imperfections, familiar wounds that could conceal the terrifying truth from me.

My parents' world—*my* world—was threatening to crumble apart.

Since yesterday when I spoke with my little sister, I could not banish the image Mary had evoked in my mind: water dripping through clenched fingers. Seven days since I had been made queen, I knew control was slipping from my grasp. The news of the rebellion—when news came—grew grimmer by the hour.

"They have declared Mary Tudor queen in Buckingham-shire." Pembroke had shared the information this morning, news an exhausted yeoman had ridden all night to deliver to us.

"People flock to her standard," Huntingdon added, the two

unnerving me with their watchful eyes. I had barely had enough time to digest that information when Northumberland's own messenger had entered, the bear and ragged staff of the Dudleys on his livery.

"Is it true, the tales we hear?" I asked him. "Is Lady Mary gaining support?"

The man wiped sweat from his brow, grime from the road leaving a smear on his skin. "His Grace of Northumberland tries to stanch the flow of rebels, but if he stops one hemorrhage, another vein bursts," he told those assembled—Father and Mother, the Duchess of Northumberland, Guilford, Lord Pembroke, Huntingdon, Lord Cobham, and me.

I could see tension affect my councilors. Cobham twisted a ring on his finger, Pembroke's hand clasped and unclasped on the hilt of his sword. Huntingdon's brows seemed to meld into one. Guilford inserted a finger between his collar and throat, while his mother, eyes still swollen from weeping, tried to hide her despair behind her fan.

My own father doffed his hat, wringing the jaunty plume that decorated it into a crumpled wreck. "The Lady Mary is a papist, declared a bastard by her own father."

"Something is drawing these people to Lady Mary's cause," I said. "What power does she hold?"

"They say Lady Mary rode to review her troops and dismounted before the simple folk who would do battle for her," the messenger said. "She walked among them, spoke to them, encouraged them, thanked them for their loyalty with such humility, some were moved to tears."

"She always did have her mother's gift with the common people," Cobham said.

My father clamped his hand over his stomach. I watched him, my own heart pounding. Twice in the past three days he had fainted dead away, lying on the stones, insensible as his retainers tried to rouse him. But though the pallor of illness still bleached his face, he seemed in no danger of collapsing again—at least for now.

"Damn the woman!" he said. "Three more lords have gotten word from their estates that their own crofters are refusing to work their land as long as those lords support Queen Jane. The knaves will live to regret it! We will string them up at the crossroads once this is over."

"Mary Tudor stirs trouble with the same spoon her mother did," Pembroke mused. "It is a miracle the peasants did not rise up to dethrone the Boleyn whore and restore Katherine as Henry's wife. If Queen Katherine had given the tiniest sign to the peasants, every man of them would have risen up in her defense. Two things saved Henry: his ruthlessness, and the fact that Katherine of Aragon considered him her husband in spite of the annulment. She believed a godly wife should never defy her lord and master."

My mother paced near the window, her hair straggling from beneath her headdress, her eyes reminding me of a rat in a corner with a terrier drawing near. Time and again she twisted the gold chain at her throat until I wanted to shriek at her to leave off.

But somehow I sensed if I gave way to that impulse, the cracks in her, in Father, perhaps in my whole court would give way, and everything would lay in shatters at my feet.

I must keep my head and guard my tongue. I must be strong enough to brace their courage. At that moment a commotion sounded beyond the chamber. Whatever had happened was important, I knew by instinct. *Please, God, let this dispatch be in our favor.*

"Majesty," the gentleman usher announced, a little breathless. "There is news from the coast. The seaman who brings it is half-dead."

The navy. At least nothing could go awry there. Northumberland had assured me he had stationed ships off the coast to make certain my cousin could not escape. "Bid the seaman enter." My voice held steady. "I would hear what news he brings."

I retreated to my throne, as if the cloth of estate spread above it could shield me as a canopy over a litter might have fended off the rain. But the embroidered velvet suspended upon its four carved poles could not protect any of us from the fresh disaster.

"I bring bad tidings." The portly sailor's leathery face sagged with exhaustion and despair. "Your Majesty, five ships set to guard against Lady Mary's escape have mutinied. The scoundrels belowdecks forced their captains to declare the Lady Mary rightful queen."

My mother burst into tears, and the Duchess of Northumberland started to sob. The simple folk on land declaring for Mary had been frightening enough. But now ships that should have been cut off from news of Mary's rise were turning against me? The very forces Northumberland had sent to capture Mary should she flee now cut off any hope that I might have of escape, should we lose this gamble.

And I might lose. How could I hold a country when the common people would not have me? When I could not count on the loyalty of my own navy?

"Majesty, there is more. I stopped to change horses, and the hostler said he had heard a fine lord was riding toward the north. A man all cloaked in black, looking furtive. Though the hostler did not see him with his own eyes, he did see the brooch that fastened the lord's cloak. Dropped it, the lord did, in his haste to be gone."

"Who did the brooch belong to?" I asked.

"It was embossed with the crest of the Earl of Arundel."

"I cannot believe it was dropped by Arundel himself," Pembroke said. "I spoke to Arundel's man before I came to wait upon Your Majesty. They were waiting for his lordship's physician to arrive."

"His physician?"

"It seems Arundel is afflicted with the same ague my daughter Maud suffers from."

Just that morning Kat, her husband, and her sister-in-law had left for Baynard's Castle so that Maud Herbert could convalesce in the comfort of familiar surroundings and—pray God—save us from contagion. Pembroke had requested that Kat and Henry be allowed to accompany her. I had acceded to his plea. Part of me was actually grateful for the chance to rid myself of Kat's reproachful glances. Perhaps a little time away would give her time to get over her anger that I had dared to question her father-in-law's motives.

But a number of people had been claiming illness as a reason to quit my court. And the more tidings arrived in Cousin Mary's favor, the more such claims increased. Suspicion made my pulse thrum hard in my throat. "I would speak with the earl myself in spite of his malaise. My lord of Pembroke, you will go to him at once. Tell Arundel that his queen has need of his wise counsel and must, regretfully, rouse him from his sickbed."

Did Kat's father-in-law look uneasy? He bowed before I could tell. I signaled my wish for silence while Pembroke was gone, then turned my attention to some dispatches that Northumberland's secretary, William Cecil, had brought earlier. I did not wish to discuss this fresh calamity with those who surrounded me. Already they looked like a flock of sheep when the wolf drew near. Time crawled. The people in the chamber were like water droplets spattered on a hot iron kettle, skittering restlessly on the surface.

"Arundel hates your father and ever loved Mary best in secret," I heard Guilford's mother say to him. "If Arundel betrays us, who else will?"

Indeed. Who? Other Catholic lords and ladies would join Arundel's defection, the more timid among them growing braver as the ranks of Mary's army swelled with peers.

Voices clamored around me, distress and outrage, anger and fear—a chaotic poison.

I wanted to drive them all from the chamber. I wanted to flee to the chapel to pray. I wanted all these people to go away, to leave me alone, to stop looking at me as if they expected me to be wiser than I was, stronger than I knew, steadier than I could be.

I was only a girl of fifteen. They had lived at court far longer. They had navigated those treacherous waters through the years King Henry had turned dangerous, through divorces, annulments, beheadings. They had held on to their station through the reign of a boy-king who had executed his two uncles, disowned his sisters, and made me queen in their stead.

They had felt the heaves and shifts of power before and managed to survive when others had been tossed to cruel fates. What did I know about moving through this uncertain landscape? My hands started to tremble. I folded them in my lap, determined not to show my own dread.

At last the Earl of Pembroke returned, his features sharper than when he had left, as if someone had whittled away both his flesh and his resolve. I clenched my fingers so tight, the nails cut into my palms as he approached.

"Majesty," he said, sweeping me a bow that concealed his face for too long, "I regret to inform you that the Earl of Arundel is not in his chambers as was supposed. When pressed, his servant confessed that it is likely the hostler was correct. The earl rode out sometime yesterday evening."

I could see fear and a concern for self-preservation seeping into my councilors' features. Moments before, I had been wishing to be alone. Now the prospect terrified me. I must find some way to keep these men here beside me, their fates bound up so tightly with my own that they dared not follow Arundel's lead.

But how could I keep them from slipping away? I had only

one way to hold their loyalty. I would have to make it as difficult as possible for the important men of this realm to leave the Tower. If the fortress walls were formidable enough to keep an army out, they would also serve to barricade people inside.

Clasped within the circle of these walls, the remains of my council could not slip away as neatly as Arundel had done. As long as they were trapped beside me, my cousin Mary would not think they were sympathetic to her cause.

I stood, the crown of my head near enough the cloth of estate that the edge of velvet hid at least some of my expression.

"I would see the lieutenant of the Tower at once," I said with a calm I did not feel.

"You wish to reinforce the Tower defenses?" someone asked.

Though Pembroke repeated the question, I did not answer him. A queen had no obligation to answer those who served her. The conversation around me seemed to vary and change until at last the lieutenant of the Tower strode in.

Sir John Bridges's face was long and solemn, reminding me of Thomas Cranmer, the Archbishop of Canterbury, the holy man who had served the Reformation so well. Bridges straightened his doublet before he dared approach me. Despite the confusion all around me, I found a strange sense of peace when I met the man's eyes.

Bridges bowed low, and I remembered all I had heard about his sense of honor. "I am at your service, Your Majesty," he declared. I wondered if he would be thus only as long as it remained likely I was going to emerge victorious. But there was empathy in his face.

I regarded him with a measure of trust in spite of the wolves now circling around me. "Sir John, I give you orders, directly from my mouth to your own loyal ears."

"I will serve you as best as I am able, Majesty."

"I am glad of it. At eight o'clock this night you will mount a strong guard and lock all seven gates leading out of the Tower."

Gasps, whispers filled the chamber. My father nodded approval, and my mother looked a trifle hopeful. But more than one of my other advisers seemed to look at the door. Was it a portent of the future? I wondered. Or merely an instinctive reaction born of the knowledge that such portals might soon be closed to them?

Sir John bowed again. "I will see to it myself, Your Majesty."

"The moment all is secure, Sir John, you will deliver the key to me."

"I will put it in your hand myself."

"I trust that you will." It was true—who else in this chamber could I trust half so well? My husband? I doubted Guilford was fashioned of strong enough stuff to withstand much pressure. Like iron tempered by a clumsy apprentice, he would most likely break. Pembroke and Huntingdon? They were unpredictable at best. Perhaps the marriages Northumberland had struck were alliances strong enough to hold. But the others? The threat of papist rule would inspire them only so far.

"Majesty?" The Earl of Pembroke interrupted my thoughts. "I feel compelled to make a request of you. I would be easier in my mind if I could visit my daughter, see with my own eyes how she fares. I could bring your sister back when I return."

"That would please me greatly." Why, I could not guess. Kat was too flighty to depend upon for anything of practical use in such a dire situation—even if she were not away at Baynard's Castle. Besides, Kat was Henry Herbert's wife. Some might say her first loyalty should belong to him. But surely of all ties blood was the strongest.

Yes. I could depend on that much at least. I looked to my parents, pushing back my growing unease. Perhaps my mother was afraid. Perhaps the future my father had hoped for was crumbling. But they would stand with me. I was certain. The Greys of Suffolk would rise or fall together.

July 18, 1553

How could it be that the day trudged on as if it were any other? Rising and having my hair combed and braided and bound beneath my headdress. My linen shift drifted down by my ladies' hands to cover my shivering body, no longer warm from its nest of coverlets in my bed. I broke my fast, directed my servants, met with those of my council who remained. But I knew the loyalty they had shown when my reign began just eight days ago was changeable now, ephemeral as the wisps of mist clinging to the spires of the White Tower.

As I sat beneath my cloth of estate signing dispatches, I paused to peer out the streaked window, looking toward the gate that opens in the direction of Baynard's Castle. I willed Kat to appear and ride through the stone portal, her red-gold hair shining, her face turned up to the sun. She would be searching for me. Surely she would have had time enough to get over our earlier discord. I would draw her off alone, tell her I was sorry I upset her. I wanted her to be happy. I wanted it more than almost anything. Anything except for this day to be over.

A day of celebration, it was supposed to be. A new queen asked to be godmother to a babe. I had sent one of my ladies to stand in my place at the font in St. Peter ad Vincula, the chapel in the courtyard below. It was hard to pay attention to the sacred when my generals were betraying me and no one—not even the chaplain—would meet my eyes.

I might have given way to panic, were it not for tiny, mundane tasks. I attended to each one as if my life depended on it—the sharpening of a quill, the pressing of my royal seal into melted wax. The wax shone, thick, oozing like blood.

I suppressed a shudder, my attention tugged to the chapel again. St. Peter in Chains, to translate the Latin name properly. Thomas Seymour, who my beloved mistress the dowager queen loved so well, is buried beneath those stones. Edward Seymour's father lies there as well. Anne Boleyn and Catherine Howard, once queens, lie headless for eternity.

Would that be my final resting place?

No. I must not give up, some place inside me—still faith-filled, believing in miracles—insisted. How many times had I told Mary and Kat tales from the Bible? Daniel in the lion's den, Jonah in the belly of the whale, Esther and Deborah and all those whose cause God favored. He saved them just when it seemed certain all was lost. Was that not what made for a thrilling tale?

If you believe faithfully enough, your head filled with nothing but God's will, He could part seas and calm storms and drain floodwaters away. He would save me if He chose. He could carry Kat through that gate and calm all our fears if I believed strongly enough. If I were not afraid.

I dipped my quill in ink, then wrote as Dr. Aylmer taught me: bold strokes that must not waver. *Jana Regina. Jane the Queen.*

I am believing with all my might, God, I prayed silently. *Why do you not make Kat come here to me?*

Chapter Fourteen

Kat
Baynard's Castle, London

OW MANY TIMES DURING THE DAYS AT JANE'S COURT did I wish Henry and I could return to Baynard's Castle. We had been so happy there, stealing rose-scented kisses along the garden path, our fingers stroking whatever bare skin we could reach beneath the barriers of our clothes as we spoke in eager whispers of what pleasures we planned to give each other once we could share our bed.

But the new home and family I had come to love more than my old one had changed like the beggar woman in the old tales Hettie liked to tell. But instead of transforming from hag to a fairy queen, the love-spun magic of this place had vanished, stripped down to reality harsh as pitted stone.

Though Maud did lie abed, no physician ever came to examine her, no apothecary dosed her to cure her malaise. She started every time I came in the room, and when I asked about the flood of horsemen and carts flowing in and out of the castle gates, it was as if some invisible thorn had driven beneath her skin.

Even Henry behaved more strangely by the hour, closeted with his father and the parade of important visitors now attending on the Earl of Pembroke. A lump of ice seemed lodged in my belly, a certainty that all was not as innocent as they would have me believe.

Finally I concealed myself in the shadow of a sideboard and lay in wait for my husband, watching the door to the earl's presence chamber, hoping to catch Henry so I could draw him off alone to speak.

It seemed forever that I waited, listening to snips of conversation, studying faces, badges of office, livery that identified those having audience with Pembroke. At last my husband emerged. The expression on his face deepened my fear.

I faced Henry, my heart hurting, betrayal stinging. "What is happening? I saw the mayor of London and a group of aldermen gathering in the courtyard below."

"The situation is bad, Kat. When Lord Cobham and the Earl of Arundel went to the Spanish ambassador's, Scheyfve told them Northumberland was attempting to make a deal with the French to put the little Queen of Scots on the throne instead of Jane. England would be swallowed up by France—"

"That is ridiculous! Northumberland wants his son to be king. It makes no sense that he would plot to take Jane off the throne!"

"The rest of the council believes it could be true. In any case, it does not matter if it is true or false. The people will not have Jane as queen."

The ice in my belly swelled until it ached. "The people? It is not their decision to make. King Edward named Jane queen. Mary is Catholic. Her father named her a bastard."

"The people have never forgotten the torment she suffered. They loved her mother, and they love Mary. They hate your sister."

I stumbled at the ferocity in his words. "They do not know Jane. In time they will become accustomed—"

"I am heartily sorry to say it, Kat, but Jane is a Dudley now. People know Jane is Northumberland's creature, and that is enough reason to reject her."

"Jane is no one's creature! She loathes Northumberland! My parents had to beat her to force her to marry a Dudley."

"So you told me, but that does not change the fact that she is under Northumberland's control. The duke chose your sister because he could easily turn her to his own wishes. Everyone knows that."

"Then everyone is wrong!" I cried. "Jane will be a good queen. She works so hard to get things perfect. She will wear herself to a shred trying to be a perfect queen as well. From the time we were little girls, everyone said what a remarkable queen Jane would make. Even Catherine Parr and all her ladies made such a fuss over her that Father sent her to be fostered in the dowager queen's household. Many people thought Jane would be a perfect match for King Edward—that if he chose Jane, he would not have to wed a foreigner. Catherine Parr and Thomas Seymour were supposed to arrange the match. All I have ever heard was—"

"The simple folk have barely heard of Jane at all. But Northumberland scourged the North, enclosed the common land, and dissolved the abbeys. Grabbed everything to fill his pockets while others starved. Father says—"

"Your father was stealing and burning right at Northumberland's side!"

"Your father took his share of the spoils as well, even though he did not wield a sword. That is what powerful men do. They do not win riches and lands in battle, then distribute the spoils to the poor! Unless you're Edward Seymour's father Somerset. It got him killed by Northumberland and your father and mine! Sacrifices must be made."

"Who is to be sacrificed now? My sister?"

"We cannot save her. We can only try to save ourselves."

"How? You will tell me!"

"Father and the mayor and the aldermen are to gather below within the hour. They ride to St. Paul's cross to declare Lady Mary the rightful queen."

"They said they would die for Jane. Swore fealty to her. An oath before God." I could see how torn Henry was. I did not care.

"Men have changed loyalty before," he insisted. "It is necessary."

"Are you forswearing yourself, Henry? Abandoning my sister?"

"I have no other choice for the sake of my family."

"Jane is your family now. I am your family!" I cried bitterly. "Or is it as easy to cast aside a wife as it is a queen?"

Henry pulled me into his embrace, but I twisted free. "Katherine, I will not abandon you! I swear it on my life! But I have to stand with my father. We have got into a tangle, and every man has to free himself as best he can."

Sick with betrayal, I recoiled from him.

"You think your family is made of finer stuff than the Herberts?" he said. "Your father would sacrifice the house of Pembroke as easily as he draws breath if it meant the queen's pardon."

"Jane *is* queen," I insisted.

"She is not! It is over, Katherine, and we must shift as we can to survive."

"Do as you will, then. Follow your father to St. Paul's. I am going to my sister." I spun away from him, intending to fling a few belongings into a chest and leave Baynard's Castle behind me as soon as I was able. But Henry caught my arm. "Let go! I am going to my sister! Summon a cart to take me back to the Tower."

"You are going to ride through streets full of people who see your sister as a traitor? Who loathe Northumberland and your father? Do you want them to drag you off your horse and murder you in the streets?"

"They would not dare!"

"Remember the crowd we encountered at the crossroads the day Jane was declared queen? Their mood was dark enough then.

Next morning Northumberland set their hatred afire when he had Gilbert Potter pilloried, his ears sliced off."

"Stop it, Henry! I do not like to hear—"

"There are things you would like even less, I would wager." Pembroke's voice cleaved between Henry and me like a knife.

"My lord," Henry said as we sprang apart. My breath caught. My father-in-law's expression was brutish, that of the man who had hacked rebel crofters with his own sword.

"Lady Katherine Grey, I have made a study these past weeks as to your likes and dislikes. And I can assure you that, should you be so rash as to bolt in the direction of the Tower of London, you would dislike what is happening beyond these gates."

"I am going back to my sister!"

"Would she be pleased if you arrived lighter by the weight of your ears? It is possible that our true queen's supporters would consider it fair judgment to take your pretty ears in payment for Potter's suffering."

I recoiled in horror at the image.

"I could not spare a single man to guard you," Pembroke continued. "We must make as great a show as possible if we are to have any hope of Queen Mary's forgiveness."

"There is no Queen Mary! No country can have two queens."

"That is so. At least not for very long. Until this inconvenience is sorted out, you will stay here at Baynard's Castle while my son and I try to salvage what we may—our estates, our rank. Maybe even our heads. Mary's supporters will be eager for a crop of traitors to replace the corpses that marked the prayer book rebellion."

My stomach lurched at the thought of Henry dying such a terrible death. Pembroke was right. Heads would roll. I thought of Jane, my father.

"I can only thank God I had the foresight to ignore

Northumberland's order that you and Henry consummate your marriage," Pembroke said.

"You were the one keeping us apart?" I choked out. "Jane was right all along!"

Henry confronted his father, betrayal in his eyes. "You swore it was not your doing!"

"How else was I to protect you, boy? Let Northumberland and Suffolk go to hell. I can wrest you out of this disaster of a marriage, Henry."

My knees went weak, but Henry was already beside me, shoring me up. "You are wrong, my lord. My wife and I met in secret. I swived her." He was lying, knowing that if we had consummated the marriage, even Pembroke could not sever the bond.

But the earl would not be so easily fooled. "You did no such thing. You are far too obedient of a son to defy me. Even if you had been so foolish, I would force you to swear on the Bible that the girl is a virgin. The troubadours may sing of the romance of dying for love, but it is a far grislier fate than most imagine. You are my son. In the end you will bow to my will."

I saw Henry's fists knot, his throat constrict. He looked at me. I had seen that expression on a different face. Memory carried me back to Bradgate Hall. Jane, lying upon the stone floor, her back torn and bleeding from the bundle of willow switches my mother had used to whip her. On her ashen face I had recognized just what I saw in my husband's face now. Heartbreak. Defeat. The moment before surrender.

Jane
Tower of London
July 19, 1553

O ONE TROUBLED THEMSELVES TO TALK TO ME NOW. My sister Mary was nowhere in sight. I had not the energy to find her. My mother had worn herself out. My ladies drooped like storm-battered roses, stabbing halfheartedly at their stitching.

They had not been sleeping any better than I had, each woman wondering what would happen to the husband, father, or brother who had placed her in my service. These men were now fugitives, running from the retaliation of the Tudor whom they had tormented through the years of Edward's kingship, the woman whose crown they had stolen for me.

Now the question was this: though my cousin had loved her mother, Henry's cast-off queen, would she prove her father's daughter when it came to vengeance?

Surely many of the women were wondering the same thing, but I could not voice my fear. It seemed as if the sound of a voice might shatter people like glass. I loved quiet once, but silence in this room seemed foreign now. I had spent nine days with everyone around me scurrying to grant my every command, anticipate my needs. They had even quarreled over who would win the honor of distracting me from my cares.

Now the lute they plucked to please me stayed silent, the

deck of cards fanned out across the table in disarray. A red queen had fallen to the floor sometime during the day, her printed eyes staring up at the cloth of estate over my head.

Even that mark of my queenship seemed a mockery. We had lost. Northumberland had quit the field, fled before Mary Tudor's army. It was only a matter of time before the crest of that inexorable wave crashed over us all. Guilford himself had brought the news just this morning in my privy chamber. How strange this tenuous truce between us felt. When he entered the room, I was almost grateful to see him.

"Has Pembroke returned?" I had asked.

"He has not."

"I would see my sister as soon as I am able."

"It is hard not knowing how they fare beyond the Tower's walls."

His face carried an uncertainty that echoed my own. A dependence that neither of us wanted had been forged between us.

"I wish I was with my brothers," Guilford said. "At least then I would know what was happening." All the Dudley sons save him were out where blood flowed.

My gaze met his, and real regret filled his eyes. I remembered that he had not wanted our marriage any more than I—even if he had coveted the crown I might bring him.

Guilford drew in a steadying breath. "Katherine will not be returning to the Tower, Jane. Pembroke joined Arundel, Cobham, and the other ministers in supporting Mary."

Part of me had expected it. That did not make the lonely ache for my sister any less.

"The traitors rode out from Baynard's Castle. The crowds that gathered to watch the humbling of the lords were so thick, the horses could barely get through." Guilford made a sound of disgust. "The cowardly bastards put on quite a masque, weeping with shame for betraying Mary. Pembroke even filled his cap with gold coins and threw them into the air for the simple folk to squabble over. Doubtless he hoped gold could buy the people's good will and tears secure him Mary Tudor's forgiveness."

Was it possible to secure my cousin's mercy, at any price? Perhaps some could. Even Pembroke might manage it, despite his son's marriage to Kat.

Poor Kat. If Pembroke extricated himself from this tangle, he would cast his son's unfortunate Grey bride off with no more thought than a mare who had gone lame.

It pained me to imagine my sister so cruelly used. How often had I felt impatient at Kat's too-open heart? What could she expect but to end up bruised? I had often thought. I had even hoped that she might learn to be more careful in the future.

But now I only wished the world were half as good as my sister believed it was.

The faces of the men who had betrayed me rose in my mind. Of all those who had knelt before me at Syon House, swearing to live and die for me, only two remained loyal—my father and Guilford. But then, their fates were hitched firmly to my own.

I looked across the room to where Guilford sat, stiff in his chair. His mother perched near him, but he did not look to her for the reassurance that no one could really give him: that all might come right in the end. All would not end well. The only mystery was how brutal the ending would be. In the hours since Guilford's revelation, I had much time to think on that.

Fear slid cold blades under my skin, but I concealed it as best I could. The tambour, forgotten on my lap, began to fall, and instinctively I grabbed for it. My knuckles struck something beside me.

I heard a small, startled gasp, then saw something skitter across the floor as if it had been flung: Mary's poppet, its cloth arms and legs splayed out. How vulnerable, how fragile it looked.

Its black bead eyes seemed to plead with me. It seemed a hundred years since I had stitched them onto that cloth face.

My little sister pressed her finger to her lips, begging me not to reveal her hiding place as she grabbed her doll and snatched it back into the shadows.

In the days since I learned Mary Tudor had evaded Robert Dudley's attempt to capture her, my youngest sister had been barely visible in my life. Mary—just disappearing around a corner, ducking behind a tapestry, withdrawing to the darkest place in any chamber. But then, Mary had always been a shadow.

When had my little sister stolen beneath the cloth of estate and concealed herself behind the fall of my skirts? It tugged at my heart to think of how often she had hidden herself just so at home. The fact that my mother had not noticed Mary's trespass and chased her away from me told me just how locked she was in her own misery.

Now Mary tugged my skirts. "I want Kat. She promised she would come back."

"Kat will not be coming back for a while. Be patient until things settle out."

I could see that my sister was wise enough not to believe me. Then footsteps approached, and my ladies jumped to awareness. Every muscle in my body tensed. My gaze leaped from my mother to Guilford and the Duchess of Northumberland. I felt sympathy even for my daunting mother-in-law. Her face had aged since we received news of Northumberland's flight. Now it contorted as if waiting for a blow. Guilford stood. I sat erect, gripping the arms of my throne.

Were they coming to warn me that the new queen's forces were outside the walls?

The final confrontation must come. Soon the council troops would break through into the courtyard. I surveyed the room, the last remnant of my court. A court I had never wanted. Yet to lose it this way—was I sorrowful or relieved?

Before I could decide, my father strode through the door. Illness and strain had gouged lines in his face. The man who had swaggered about Bradgate and raced at the hunt was gone. He had shrunk, somehow. I knew I should never be afraid of him again.

"The council's troops have arrived," he said. "I told your soldiers to lay down their weapons." His voice rasped. "Daughter, I come to tell you that you are queen no more."

He strode to the cloth of estate. He gripped the velvet in his fist and ripped the canopy down. The poles it had been mounted on almost struck Mary. She leaped up, and I felt her press against my leg as the staves clattered to the floor, sounding like breaking bones.

"God save Queen Mary!" Father decried.

I was not sure what I should say. I decided to speak the truth. "I am much relieved the crown is gone, Father. You know I did not want it. I would not have taken it if you had not insisted." I gave him an uncertain smile. "Can we go back home to Bradgate now?"

He turned away. "There are horses waiting outside to carry your mother, sister, and me. Katherine will reach us as soon as she is able."

"I am glad of it. I long to see her. I can leave whenever you are ready. I want to take nothing from this place but my books."

"You will not be leaving with us."

I pressed my hand to my chest, unable to breathe. "What? But I did not want the crown. You know that. Everyone knows that. It is not fair—"

"The council soldiers are charged to hold you in the name of the queen. Of course you will be moved to different quarters until Her Majesty arrives."

"I am under arrest. That is what you mean, is it not?"

"What can you expect? You took the crown."

"I did not want it!"

"Do you think anyone will believe that? Even if they did, it would not matter now!" He turned to my mother. "Frances, Mary—make haste."

Mary rushed from her hiding place. "I will not leave Jane!" She clung to me, tight.

"You will, or I will drag you out," Father threatened.

"You must go, Mary," I urged, wishing it were not so.

"They cannot make me leave you."

"You have to." I searched for some way to convince her to go to safety. "There is something important you must do for me. Something I cannot trust to anyone else. You must tell Kat how sorry I am that we argued. Will you do that for me?"

"Are you afraid?" she asked.

I almost lied, wishing to spare her feelings, but Mary was so wise that if I did so, she would not believe it. I did not want to say goodbye to her now with a lie between us.

"I am afraid. I do not know what will happen once you are gone. But still you must go. I need to know you are away from here and safe, even if I cannot be."

"Will they lock you in chains and put you where rats live like they do the other prisoners I saw in their cells?" When had she seen such miserable wretches? Had she gone burrowing about where she was not supposed to? Witnessed horrors she could not understand? I had no time to question her now.

My throat closed, but I squeezed out a reassurance. "They do not put princesses of the blood in chains, sweeting. I do not know where they will lodge me, but I am certain it will be comfortable enough. Anyway, you know how I am once I begin reading. I would not notice if there were a whole army of rats." I could only pray that that much was true. "I will tell you all about it in nice long letters."

"I will keep them in my Thief's Coffer with the other letters you wrote me."

"By God, we have no time for this nonsense!" Father swore.

"We must be off before the queen changes her mind and decides to keep us all imprisoned."

Panic struck me as he stalked toward us to drag my sister away. "Mary, write to me. Promise." She nodded, her lower lip quivering. "You cannot know how much it will mean to me." My voice cracked as Father's hand clamped on her arm. She tried to wrench free.

"Do not make me leave Jane! I want to stay with Jane!" she wailed, thrashing against Father's grasp. Her poppet, still crushed beneath her arm, seemed to flail against him as well, but its cloth arms were no more effective than my heartbroken little sister's.

Father struck Mary in the face. The blow spun her around, her elbow slamming square into his blue velvet codpiece. He doubled over with a hoarse oath, letting her free. I wondered at my sister's courage and her love for me as she threw herself against my skirts.

I scooped her up in a hug, wishing that I could press some of her courage into me. "I know it is hard, but you must go with Father," I told her, watching out of the corner of my eye as my mother flew to him and helped him right himself. "He will see you safe home."

"I hate Father!"

"You must not say that, or even think it. It is a sin." But the possibility of being caught out in a sin had never frightened Mary the way it did me.

"I will not leave you! They cannot make me leave you!"

I buried my face against her small shoulder, one of Jennet's black bead eyes cutting into my cheek. My salt tears stung. I grasped onto the one chance I might have to soothe Mary. I forced a smile. "You must be a good mother to Jennet. I am sure she is even more frightened than we are. She will be very glad to see the Myrmidons when you get back to Bradgate. Our magic oaks will keep you both safe."

Mary looked at her doll, its gown bedraggled from loving.

I could sense a battle raging in my sister. "Jennet wants to stay with you." She pressed her doll into my arms.

"No, Mary!" My chest felt as if it might crack. "I could not take your poppet."

But as swiftly as she had evaded my father, Mary now eluded me. She limped toward the door. It was as if she had loosed a stiff wind upon fallen leaves.

In a flurry my maids scattered to gather their belongings, find their own ways out of the Tower, and return to country estates where they might avoid Mary Tudor's wrath, or at least postpone it until it had a chance to cool. One maid looked toward the Duchess of Northumberland. "You must hasten. I am certain there is a cart that will take you to Warwick."

"I will not leave my son here alone!" She turned to glare at my mother, who was even now hastening toward the door without me. I envied Guilford his mother in that moment.

Outside I could hear the commotion of riders. I ran to the window and searched the courtyard below until I saw my mother and father and their servants pour outside.

So this is what defeat looks like, I thought as they clambered into carts and litters. I strained to find Mary in the crowd. There she was—a blur of russet velvet, caught up in Hettie's arms. The Thief's Coffer was clutched between my sister and her nurse. I feared what trinkets Mary was taking from the Tower. Could one store heartbreak in a wooden box? Horror of defeat? The great sacrifice she had made in leaving her doll with me?

I wept, realizing it would not matter if I cried forever now. The reign I had never wanted was over. My mother and father and sisters were gone. I hugged Jennet tight. Even with Guilford and his mother in the room, I was alone.

Chapter Sixteen

Mary
Bradgate Hall, Leicestershire
August 1553

I DID NOT THINK IT WAS RIGHT FOR MY MOTHER TO BE happy, not with Jane in prison, condemned to a traitor's death. But to look at Mother's face, you would never guess that Jane and Guilford had joined Northumberland and the rest of the Dudleys—Robert and Henry and Ambrose and the other boy I can never remember—in being condemned to the worst punishment anyone in England could suffer.

This was how they killed traitors: hung them by their necks until they near choked, then cut them down and threw water on them to make sure they were wide awake while the executioner used a knife and cut open the traitor's middle so he could take the inside bits out to burn them right in front of the prisoner's face. That was the last thing they would see, Hettie said—their insides burning. It does not often happen that someone nobly born suffers the full sentence, but that depended upon the queen. Her mercy was the only thing standing between Jane and having her belly cut open.

I felt like my insides were burning too, every time I thought of Jane walking away from her trial through the mob of angry people, the sharp edge of the executioner's blade turned toward her instead of away.

If the ax faced the other direction, it would say that she

was innocent. If God were fair at all, he would have bent down from heaven and twisted that ax around to show everyone Jane should not be blamed for what had happened. That was not the way God worked, Father's chaplain told me. But if God could split a whole Red Sea in two so Moses could help innocent people get away from Ramses, why could God not help Jane?

I was scared of what would happen if no one helped my imprisoned sister. Bad dreams woke me up at night, and I was crying. I would not let anyone hold me. I was too wicked to touch.

"Cousin Mary cannot kill Jane!"

"All your caterwauling will not keep it from happening," Hettie scolded when I woke her too many times with my weeping. "There cannot be two queens. Hard as it is, one of them must die. There is one person who will benefit, though. Whoever warned your cousin to flee Robert Dudley will earn rewards aplenty in the new reign. Without their help, Mary Tudor would now be locked up and awaiting execution instead of your sister."

It was my fault that Jane's head would be cut off or that she would burn up in a fire. Executioners did not cut noble ladies apart the way they did other traitors. Hettie said I should remember that from when she taught me about Anne Boleyn. The witch queen had had six fingers, the mark of the devil just like my twisted back. After all that had happened since I sent Cousin Mary that feather, I knew I was even wickeder than people thought I was. But I could not tell anyone what I had done, not even Kat, who had come back to Bradgate three weeks ago without her wedding ring or her husband and had to go back to being a Grey again when she would rather be a Herbert.

Kat would be of no use anyway. She still wrote letters to Henry—pages and pages of them. And she wept every time she wore the emerald earrings that were the color of Henry's eyes. I had to steal them and hide them away in my Thief's Coffer to make her stop.

Stop crying, and stop hoping that one of the letters she smuggled out to Henry would bring an answer. I thought if she did not have the earrings to remind her of losing her husband, it would not hurt so much.

I did not think Jane would have minded losing her husband at all, but even in prison she could not be rid of him—he was locked up in the Tower as well. Hettie said his head would get cut off. I wondered if Jane would be glad.

I did not think anything could happen to make things worse—until our lady mother brought some news. She summoned Kat and me to her privy chamber. Her eyes seemed almost hot, she was so excited. "I have just received such news! Thank God! Oh, thank God!"

"Did they let Jane go?" I asked, my spirits soaring. What else could have filled my mother with such joy?

She looked as if she had just bitten into the rotten spot of a peach. "Of course not! How could they?" She gave a huff of disgust. "I have far better news than that!"

What it might be, I could not imagine.

"You and Katherine are to return to court. Our cousin has requested you be raised up as her ladies-in-waiting."

"You cannot make me wait upon Cousin Mary. I want to wait upon Jane," I insisted, but no one—not Mother or Kat or Hettie—would countenance it.

"You will wait upon your cousin and be glad of it!" my mother scolded me, with every jolt of the litter that took us back to London. Not to the Tower or Westminster or any of the palaces where Jane had been queen, but to Greenwich. There Hettie scrubbed my skin raw and stuffed me into a black dress so tight I could barely draw breath. When I complained, my mother said she wanted me to look as bad as I possibly could—maybe even a little ragged—to gain Cousin Mary's sympathy. She said I certainly looked miserable enough.

Greenwich Palace
August 1553

Being the sister of a traitor is far different from being the sister of the queen. As Kat, Mother, and I made our way to the presence chamber, women drew back their skirts and men held pomanders to their noses as if they could smell some kind of stink on us and did not want to get any on them.

The way they acted hurt Kat worst of all. Even Maud Herbert did not like her now. Kat was not used to people not liking her. She tried not to show how their meanness pinched, but once I saw her chin quiver.

The gentleman usher announced in his booming voice: "The Lady Frances Grey, Duchess of Suffolk, Lady Katherine Grey, and Lady Mary Grey."

A rumble of whispers went through the crowd of people who were waiting upon the queen and hoping to press her for favors. Everyone craned their necks to look at us. Kat's chin bumped up a notch. As the wall of courtiers moved to make a path for us to reach the queen, I saw the cloth of estate on its four poles. I could still feel the sting of one of them falling on me, when Jane had been the one sitting beneath the velvet canopy.

Now Cousin Mary held court. I could not look at her. Would she tell that I had sent her the feather? She must know it could only have come from me. Hettie claimed the new queen would reward whoever had sent the warning that saved her. What if she singled me out in that way? Kat would hate me for ruining her marriage to Henry. Jane would not blame me for getting her in prison—she would try to make me feel better. That would be worse than anything, even whatever my parents would do once they got me alone.

"Your Grace of Suffolk, Lady Katherine, Lady Mary, come forward," our cousin said in a voice I had not heard before—one stronger, surer, more regal. She had beaten all the important men who tried to take her throne. I wished I could be glad.

We obeyed. Once we reached the edge of the cloth of estate, Mother fell to her knees. Kat followed. I hung back, so if Cousin Mary told my secret I could run. Mother yanked me down, banging my knees hard against the stone floor. I tried not to yelp in pain.

"Gentle, Frances. Gentle," the queen cautioned. "Have we not all been bruised enough these past weeks by events?"

"Forgive me," my mother said. "I am just so ashamed of my family's part in your troubles, Majesty, that I cannot allow my own child to show you disrespect."

"I cannot imagine Mary would ever do such a thing," the queen said, so kindly it hurt.

Please do not tell them what I did! I begged in my head, as if it could build a wall to hold those damning words at bay.

"Little cousin, I have been expecting you. You need not be afraid. Look at me."

I did not want to do it. Still, I had to raise my eyes. Cousin Mary's small frame and sad, lined face stood out, stark and familiar against the dark wood, but there was something new in her eyes that showed she was very sure of something she had not been before. Dark blue velvet fanned out to form her kirtle, every fold of the rich cloth sparkling with silver thread or jewels, as if the frost had come early and drawn patterns on her gown.

Suddenly I noticed something in her hand. Light from the nearby window chased shimmers of color up the length of the blue feather. I feared I would retch all over the queen's slippers.

"Has your lady mother told you that I wish you and your

sister to wait upon me?"

"Both my sisters?" I dared. "Jane would be better at being a lady-in-waiting than I."

"Mary!" Katherine hissed, and my mother jabbed me with her elbow.

"It is true!" I insisted. "Jane does everything right, and I get things wrong, even when I am trying my hardest to do something good." I looked at the feather. My eyes burned.

"Your Majesty," Mother said, "I beg you forgive the child's forwardness. She does not know she offends you."

"Mary and I have always been honest with each other, have we not, little cousin?" The queen looked wistful. "Lady Mary loves her sister. It is something to be envied, not to be punished over."

A measure of alarm drained from Kat's face. "Thank you, Your Majesty, for understanding. It is very hard for Mary, having Jane under arrest."

"As for you, Cousin Katherine, you are much thinner than I remember. I can see it is hard for you to be separated from your husband since the annulment Lord Pembroke requested has gone through. I was not invited to your wedding to see it for myself, but I have been told you are quite in love with Henry Herbert."

"Yes."

"You are very young, and you have the pretty face and charming manners that make love easy to come by. Your heart will heal in time." Kat stiffened, but she did not argue even though she wanted to. "I have never been in love. My hopes for a husband and children seemed faint for a very long time. Now I hope to fill that sad void in my life. It is a pity that you, who found love so young, should lose it because of politics, but that is reality. "

"So I have told the Lady Katherine," my mother said. "Sometimes a woman must bear the consequences for the mistakes of men."

"It must be challenging, helping a daughter make wise choices of the heart while maintaining the dignity of her station. But there are some things even the best mother cannot teach." She looked away. Deep sorrow etched in her face. "I wish my mother could see me now, and know that her struggles were not in vain. She endured much for my sake."

"I am certain she is looking down upon you from heaven, rejoicing," Mother said.

"I have bought many masses for her soul to make certain that that is so. But which heaven does she inhabit, cousin?" Cousin Mary asked a little sharply. "You and your husband made it clear that you scorned a Catholic paradise."

Mother started to grovel, but Cousin Mary quieted her with a wave of one hand. "Enough arguing about religion. I have brought you to court not to punish you, but to attempt to reconcile. God bids us be merciful."

"Your Majesty, we are not worthy."

"It is a new beginning for me and for England. I choose to extend the same opportunity to your family." She looked stern for a moment. "I pray the Greys will not give me reason to regret my leniency."

"Jane is family." It took all my courage to say it.

"Mary!" Mother warned. "Do not be difficult! Do you wish to anger Her Majesty?"

But the queen did not seem angry. "Mary is my goddaughter, and as such has a special claim on my heart. Perhaps you would withdraw along with the rest of court so that Mary and I can have some private conversation about the matter that concerns her."

"Your Majesty is kind to indulge my youngest, but—"

"Mary and I have always shared a unique understanding, have we not, little friend?"

"We once did, but I cannot be a friend to someone who will cut off my sister's head."

Shocked whispers welled up around me. The queen's favorites were outraged. I held my breath, knowing how reckless I had been, but I would not take the words back. After a moment the new queen spoke.

"Cousin Frances, Lady Katherine, all the rest of you— away, as I commanded." The queen clapped her hands, and the waves of skirts and colorful doublets receded, leaving a wide space between the two of us and the rest of the people. I could tell they wanted to hear what we were saying, but they could not without being noticed by the queen. When you are grown up, it is harder to hide behind tapestries or slip under tables unseen.

"Little Mary, will you not rise from your knees?" the queen asked in a voice gentle in spite of its gruff timbre. "They must ache after the blow they struck against the stone."

I pushed myself up to my feet. My knees wobbled, but not from pain.

My cousin drew the feather against her palm. "I remember when we were together at Bradgate. You snatched a feather like this one from the jaws of a fox. It was very brave."

I hung my head, unable to meet her eyes.

"Now you see what has happened because the fox's prey escaped. Perhaps you regret you gave warning."

So I had caused this disaster. It was all my fault.

The queen seemed to sense my distress. "What have people told you about Jane and me? Be honest."

"You can cut off Jane's head whenever you like. That is what the judges said."

"Yes. But I will tell you something, just between the two of us. To cut off your sister's head, I would have to sign a death warrant. I will not sign."

I lifted my head so I could look at her, and I saw her smile. "You will not?"

"I promise you. What your sister did was very wrong."

"It was not Jane's fault! She did not want the crown! Northumberland made her—"

"The duke has been condemned for his crimes, and he will pay for separating me from my brother, costing the poor boy his very soul. Northumberland has jeopardized the soul of England with his heretical ideas. He will die on the block. What say you to that?"

"My tutor said that when your father King Henry had Cromwell's head chopped off, the executioner missed and had to strike three times before it was done. I would not care if the headsman chopped Northumberland a hundred times after the bad things he did to you. But I think Northumberland hurt my sister Jane most of all."

"That does not change the fact that she took what God intended to be mine. Yet all is righted now. Northumberland will sate the peoples' need for retribution. You and your parents are once again beloved family."

"It is Jane I care about."

"Yes, Jane." Cousin Mary's lips looked prim, and I remembered how Jane had made her angry over bowing to the Host. Maybe Kat was right, and Jane should not have made a scene. "People only need to forget your sister's part in this affair. In time I will release Jane from her cell and she can return to Bradgate. She will not be able to stay at court, but she will be free. Will you like that, little friend?"

"More than anything. You would really do that?"

"The bird you saved would be very ungrateful indeed if it hurt someone you loved."

I wanted to embrace her, as Kat would have. But I was not my sister.

The corners of Cousin Mary's mouth turned down. "I had hoped to wipe all of the worry from your face. You look as if something is still troubling you. What is it?"

"I am afraid someone will tell Jane and Kat that I sent the

feather and they will not love me. I know my parents would not, and I do not mind that so very much, but my sisters . . ."

"No one but you and I know the truth. I will not tell our secret. You can trust me."

I did not trust easily. I had overheard too many lies from my hiding places in the shadows, had suffered too many cruelties from those who could taunt me. I had even worked my own acts of wickedness with headstrong abandon—stolen trinkets for my little hoard and spun falsehoods just for the excitement of deceiving the rest of the world. But when I looked into the queen's pale eyes that day, I believed Mary Tudor with my whole heart.

Jane was safe. The ax that had filled my nightmares would not cleave off her head. She would not even spend the rest of her life locked in a cell with rats, like the prisoners the jailer's son had shown me after I paid him with a small seed pearl from my coffer.

Jane would walk out of the Tower's terrible gates one day and wander among the Myrmidons again. She would sit on a tussock of moss by the stream and read by the light of a candle in her chamber until Mrs. Ellen scolded that she would study herself blind.

"Cousin Ma—" I began, then realized my mistake. "Your Majesty, I promise I will be a good lady-in-waiting. I will take care of you the way you will take care of Jane." I hesitated, then said in a breathless rush: "I will love you."

How often had I heard other children fling out that promise, heedless as butterflies in hot summer sun? But to me it felt as if I had flung myself from a precipice.

My cousin must have sensed what courage it took to speak my love for her aloud. She cupped my cheek with her palm. The warmth washed through me. "Little Mary, neither of us has been happy for a long time. Let us try to find joy in our new life. Who knows? Perhaps a year or two from now time will wipe all memory of the Tower from your sister's mind, and I will be wed to a husband and have a child of my own on the way."

"I will pray for it every day," I said, with a fervor I had never known.

Contrary God. Of all my awkward childhood prayers, why was that the one he chose to answer?

Chapter Seventeen

Kat
Greenwich Palace
November 1553

S SEPTEMBER PASSED, THEN OCTOBER, I THOUGHT that I would die of losing Henry. Come fall, pain stalked my new life at court until I pined like heroines in the tales of chivalry that Jane chided me for loving too much. The humiliation burned almost worse than the heartache. The whispers and mocking glances the other ladies cast me when the queen was not watching tormented me nearly as much as the shock of seeing Henry again.

Six times in the months since our marriage was severed, I had turned a corner and stumbled upon him. I had had to look into his green eyes, see his face—so familiar, and yet so changed from the bold youth I had married just a few months ago. Trapped in the queen's pavilion with her other ladies-in-waiting, I watched Henry ride in a tournament without asking for my favor, then perform the role of King David in a biblical masque. Through leaden days that dragged on forever, I tried to live with the shame of the annulment and the stain of my family's treason—forgiven though it was.

But the incident that seared itself most deeply into my heart came during the queen's coronation, with all its pageantry and glory. That was the last time that I hoped. For what? Courage from the man who had been my husband but had never dared to be my lover? Regret from the father-in-law who had cast me away like a soiled slipper? Hope that the rise in my standing with the new queen might spark a change of heart in the Earl of Pembroke, so he would allow Henry and me to be together again?

What made that chill November day when Mary Tudor processed through the streets of London so different from the others? All the nobles attended the queen in order of importance, and the ladies nearest Her Majesty ranked highest in all the land. The queen traveled first in her white-draped litter, next Anne of Cleves and the Lady Elizabeth.

Behind those two ladies I rode, swathed in a red velvet gown finer than any I had ever owned. I felt some measure of pride returning, as the queen signaled to all the country that she loved me and valued me, as she often said, like a daughter.

It was inevitable at such an assemblage that I would encounter the other person, besides my parents, who had claimed to love me in that way—my former father-in-law, who had once spoiled me, then kicked me aside.

Pembroke made his bow to me with grave attention as we waited to enter the banqueting hall for the coronation feast. He betrayed only for a moment that smile I now hated—so knowing, as if he had kept count of every tear I had shed over his treachery.

"Lady Katherine," he said, making a show of kissing my hand, "you are as beautiful as ever, I see. How fares your family?"

I wanted to scratch the smugness from his face. "My sister Mary and my parents are somewhere in the company where you can ask them yourself. As for the Lady Jane, she has not left the Tower except for her trial, as well you know. You attended the proceedings where she was condemned, I was told."

"I am flattered that you cared to keep track of my whereabouts." Pembroke straightened the gold lace edging his cuff. "It has been a busy season for trials—and for executions—

most notably the traitor Northumberland."

I was glad the devil duke was dead. He could never again poison lives with ambition, which was far more lethal than his vials of white powder. The one question that remained was whether the dose that his plotting had fed Jane would prove fatal. I shivered, making ready to excuse myself and vanish back into the crowd.

Pembroke stepped in front of me. "I was there when Northumberland died. A witness for the crown. He was a most dangerous traitor."

"I remember when you were his ally."

"Both the Herbert and the Grey families must be grateful for the queen's understanding. But when there is upheaval like this, the simple folk's bloodlust must be satisfied. Ten thousand people came to see Northumberland die. Had not the queen's halberdiers held them at bay, I believe the crowd would have ripped him to shreds with their bare hands. I suppose Queen Mary wished His Grace to reach purgatory in one piece— Dudley being a devout Catholic when he met his end. It was quite a triumph for England's papists, his conversion to the true faith."

"I wonder if the act was worth it to the duke in the end. It did not save his life."

Turning traitor to his faith had not won Northumberland a pardon from the queen, but it *had* destroyed his reputation among the reformers in England, all of whom now regarded Northumberland with disgust.

"His Grace had much to answer for," Pembroke intoned. "Did you hear what he said on the scaffold? 'I have deserved a thousand deaths.'"

"Unfortunately, England will have to satisfy itself with only one," I said, thinking of Jane still imprisoned in a cold Tower cell. "Would he could suffer them all instead of leaving the prospect of one to my sister."

Pembroke chuckled. "I had forgotten how amusing you could be. Doubtless you have bewitched many a young man since your return to court. You entranced my son during your stay at Baynard's Castle, but the lad has learned much about court during the months since the queen took her throne. He is warier now. You remember Henry, I trust?"

"I was his wife!" I snapped, thinking he was trying to make a fool of me. "Of course I remember—" At that moment I realized he had actually summoned Henry to approach us.

Reluctance slowed Henry's long-legged stride as he came forward and bowed. He did not look as handsome as I remembered: his mouth was a little less decided, his jaw a trifle softer, his eyes thinner of emotion, like a pool of rain upon a hollowed stone.

"My lady." Henry pressed one hand to his blue gallant doublet. I remembered how that hand had caressed my cheek. His voice caught, and I felt an answering jolt in my own chest. Was Henry thinking of the times he had touched me? Kissed me? Had he yearned for me in the time we had been parted?

I was certain he must have. He wanted a stolen moment with me as much as I wanted one with him, but how could he approach me with his father always so near? Perhaps he was just waiting for his chance to catch me alone. Surely in the midst of a coronation crowd, he would be able to leave Pembroke's side.

My heart nearly hammered its way out of my chest as I pictured the meeting to come. Henry would draw me into the shadows and kiss me. We would speak of our hopes for the future, our desolation at losing each other. We would say the farewells Pembroke had denied us when he swept me from his household in such haste.

Henry and I could pledge our love and vow to be faithful until the favor of God or the favor of the queen smiled on our union. As long as we two were of one mind and heart, Pembroke could separate our bodies, but he could not break the bond forged between us.

That hope was what I lived for. Through the early dawns, the queen's tiresome routines, the praying and popish rites, the dispatches and granting of charity that made up our everyday life, I had wished this moment between Henry and me into being. As I moved through the festivities of the coronation, I was certain he was thinking the same thing.

I waited for the tiniest signal all through the feasting and dancing, through tournaments and masques, taking care to be alone as much as possible where Henry could see me. When I could bear the suspense no longer, I begged my little sister to tell him I wished to speak to him in private, but when Mary approached Henry, he looked more awkward than before, then moved deeper into his crowd of friends.

The snickers of Henry's companions made my stomach queasy. I wished the floor would gulp me down, but God was not disposed to be that merciful. I tried to keep tears at bay as I watched my sister move toward me with her odd gait.

She regarded me solemnly. "Henry says he does not have time for frivolous concerns and cannot imagine that changing in the future. I did not know Henry was such a blockhead." Mary's brow wrinkled. "Hettie knows how to put something in a man's drink so his bowels turn to water. Do you wish me to give some to Henry? It is hard to be so pompous when you are constantly running to the closest stool."

At least I no longer waited for a moment that would never come. There would be no tender words, no kisses stolen from beneath the watchful gaze of Pembroke. Grief welled afresh at the death of hope.

I wished to put all thoughts of marriage behind me, but that was impossible in my cousin's court. Everyone from the lowliest scullery maid to the queen herself was consumed with the question: "Who will Her Majesty marry?"

The decision Mary Tudor made would rock the foundations of her kingdom and cost my sisters and me more than we could bear.

Chapter Eighteen

Jane
Tower of London

THE QUEEN MAY KILL ME WHEN SHE WISHES—SO SAY the tribunal of lords who presided over my trial. How many of my judges had vowed to shed blood for me at Sheen such a short time ago when I was queen! Now I am condemned to be consumed by flames that will eat their way up my body, or to face a quicker yet no less gruesome death by the blow of an ax to the back of my neck.

I touch the place with my fingertips, feel bumps of spine pushing against the thin covering of skin. Some part of me cannot believe that I will die. I am still young, my birthday, spent in this grim place, just a month ago. Is it possible not to hope for life when one is only sixteen? Especially when the death overshadowing you is such a brutal one?

People carry tales of headsmen who miss their mark, making a painful business of executions. Is that not why crowds of onlookers come to watch? I have too much time to think on it and wonder how soon I will be summoned to Tower Green to meet my end.

Will the ladies who combed my hair and laced my bodice and tied the points of my sleeves come to watch me die? They are Queen Mary's servants now, all save Mrs. Ellen and two other ladies who chose to stay with me. Grateful as I am for that, they are not my sisters, not my parents.

I have heard nothing from my family since Mary thrust her poppet into my arms. I know she will be safe from the new queen's retribution. Our cousin would not make war on children, and she has always been fond of my little sister. Mother and Father are courtiers born and bred, with skills that might help them weather this blast. Even though they embroiled me in the midst of all this trouble, I pray they will escape punishment as well. If they do not, I comfort myself by remembering that they joined Northumberland's schemes of their own free will.

But as weeks have passed, and I am still cut off from what is happening beyond these fortress walls, my fear for Kat grows deeper and darker. What is happening to my sweet-tempered sister? Pembroke survived the new queen's ascent—I saw him at my trial, looking down his nose in condemnation, smug and safe and free. What measures did he take to lift himself out of the morass? I can imagine little that he would not do to save himself. Like my parents . . .

If Kat has Henry to comfort her, she will survive no matter what transpires with the rest of our family. He loves her—that was evident in my brother-in-law's eyes. But does he have the courage to match? I do not want to imagine my sister stripped of that love.

I rub my arms to chafe warmth into them, the chill of my cell seeping into my bones. Not that I am being treated harshly anymore. The guards were cruel when they knew our cause was lost, moving us to cruder quarters, taunting me and Guilford and his mother.

But the place I am quartered now at the queen's order is comfortable enough. If only I were not left so alone. Kat would laugh out loud at my complaint. I have spent most of my life wishing to be left alone. I did not expect silence to be so loud—hammering at my concentration.

❧❧ ❧❧

At length I heard a sound at my door, and the jailer, Mr. Partridge, opened it. "My lady, you are to make ready for an audience with the queen."

My stomach plunged, cold sweat dampening my palms. I dreaded facing her, so shamed by what I had done. I feared what she would say: that she was loath to sign my death warrant but must do so to protect her throne. Exactly the words I might have said to her, if Robert Dudley had captured her as the conspirators planned. "When are we to leave?" I asked Partridge.

"The barge will carry you to Winchester after you break your fast, my lady." I could see he feared for me. Kindness moved me nearly to tears now.

"I am not hungry, Mr. Partridge," I said, wishing my encounter with Cousin Mary over. "I will be ready as soon as I am able."

Still, time dragged like boots caught in fresh mud as Mrs. Ellen laced me into the simple black gown I had worn to my trial. Partridge himself escorted me to the water gate, where a barge sat, moored and waiting.

From the time my conveyance landed at Winchester to the moment I was ushered into the queen's presence chamber, every person I passed stared at me with a macabre curiosity—condemnation, wary empathy, and in many cases relief that I was the one in such straits. Many of my observers had gambled on Northumberland's coup, as my family had. Were it not for good fortune and God's grace, they could have been facing the same grim future I was.

When I reached the presence chamber, my hands were trembling. It took all my will to remain calm. My cousin sat on the throne. Her crimson gown, with popinjay-blue silk drawn through the slashes, was dripping in gold lace and spattered with sapphires. A great gold chain about her throat displayed a table pendant painted with Saint Catherine being broken on the wheel. A set of old, priceless beads hung from her waist. Most startling of all, though, was the sight of her attendants—my sisters stood flanking each side, their garb lovely. I gasped aloud in relief.

"You may approach," she said. As always, her voice startled me, but I did as she commanded. She waved one hand to the other courtiers assembled. "The rest of you will leave us. Lady Katherine and Lady Mary, you will await my pleasure just beyond the door."

Kat gave me a pleading look, begging me to keep rein on my tongue, while Mary dragged her feet, loath to leave me. But after much bowing and scraping, the rest of the crowd exited with visible reluctance. It was like watching a bear baiting, I imagined, but just when the hounds would have torn out the bear's throat, these spectators were banished from ringside.

The moment the last person vanished behind the closed door, my cousin motioned me forward. This cousin, with whom I had been at crossed swords for so long, appeared both stern and triumphant. "Come forward, Lady Jane. I would examine you more closely."

"I am too ashamed. Majesty, I pray you believe I am sorry for the grief I caused you."

"It was considerable." She laid one finger alongside her cheek. Her ring of state sparkled—I had worn it a short time ago. "What have you to say for yourself?"

"I did not seek the crown, tried to refuse it, but it was pressed upon me by my lord father-in-law and by the order of succession signed by King Edward, may God rest his soul."

"The order was not legal without an act of Parliament." The queen's voice turned harder than the diamond decorating her brooch.

"I know that now. I had no time to unravel the truth before. Northumberland insisting I must take the crown threw me into such a state of shock, I could not sort it out."

"Your sisters claim you did not wish to wed Northumberland's son. Your parents forced you to do so, then made you accept the crown."

I hesitated, fearing to make my parents' situation worse by some blunder. But by hedging the truth, I might hurt my own cause or damage my sisters' standing with the queen. "It is true my parents compelled me, Majesty. But I believe they were fearful of Northumberland as well."

"Many people were. But it is harder to intimidate people when one is lighter by the weight of his head." I fought the urge to touch my own neck. "You say nothing?"

"He was a traitor, deserving of punishment."

"As are you, according to many."

"I am certain that is so." My voice cracked. I looked at the hem of the queen's gown.

"Cousin." The queen's voice grew suddenly gentler. "I see the truth in your eyes. You would never have challenged me of your own free will. I know what it is like to be forced by one's parent to obey. I did so many years ago, when my own father demanded a terrible price to enable me to return to court. I signed a document that I knew was a lie. I loathed myself for it. I have spent many hours on my knees, praying for God's forgiveness."

I remembered the tale. Tenderhearted Jane Seymour had convinced King Henry to forgive Mary if she signed a document declaring that her parents' marriage had been rightfully annulled, that Queen Katherine of Aragon had lied to her husband and the church and had not been a virgin when she had come to Henry Tudor's bed. To reconcile with the only parent she had left, Mary had signed. In that one stroke of her pen, Mary surrendered all that her proud mother had suffered for six years to preserve for her: legitimate birth, her claim to the crown. Only when no more sons were born after Edward had Henry reinstated both his daughters into the succession. He had never removed the stain of bastardy that tainted the girls, but it had mattered little in Mary's case. The English people had never accepted the annulment of the king's first marriage. To them, Mary was their princess, daughter of the queen whom the witch Anne Boleyn had betrayed.

The queen pursed her lips. "There are many things you and I do not agree on, cousin. But let us agree that it is painful when parents, who are supposed to protect us, force us to do what we know is wrong."

"Yes, Your Majesty."

"Also, there are those who love you who are especially dear to me. For their sake if not your own, I am disposed to be merciful to you."

I caught my breath. "Majesty—"

"You have been tried and condemned—by many of the same men who pressed you to take the crown, I am certain. No matter. To fulfill the sentence they laid down for you, I would have to sign the death warrant. That I will never do."

I fell to my knees at the queen's feet and kissed her ring of state, weeping. "Majesty, I beg you believe me, I never sought to displace you."

She stroked my hair, a little awkwardly, but with real empathy. "There, now. When the time is right, I will set you free. You can live quietly in the country where your sisters can visit you when I can spare them. They are ladies of the bedchamber now."

I smiled at the queen through my tears. "Lady Katherine would love that above all."

"She is quite the most elegant and gifted among my ladies. As for Mary—she is devoted both to you and to me, Cousin Jane. It is hard for her, I think."

"I thank you, Your Majesty, for your many kindnesses to my sisters and to me. I swear you will never have a more loyal subject than I will be. I will give you no more cause to worry."

"Not even should we debate religion? Ah, well. God will see those issues resolved in His own time."

"Majesty, my sister Mary does not give her affections easily, but when she does, she is fiercely loyal. I am grateful she has found another person she can trust."

"I will keep her close to me. Safe. As for your sister Katherine, she knows how to make herself agreeable—as do your parents." Her eyes narrowed. "It is a trait you could benefit from learning, Lady Jane."

"My parents—Your Majesty, forgive me for asking—but I have had no news of what has befallen them."

She regarded me strangely. "They are family. They were kind to me when the rest of the world scorned me. I owe them a debt. Now it is paid. I intend to pardon Suffolk, return all his property, and reinstate his dukedom. So, cousin, it appears the Grey family has survived this tumult with little damage, well earned though harsh reprisals would be."

"No one could doubt it is so."

"Indeed. Do not try my patience further."

"No, Majesty. I will try to deserve your mercy."

"Whether you will is up to God to decide." The queen smiled. "God did decide in the battle between us, cousin. In my favor."

The words stung. I started to speak but remembered Kat's wordless plea and bit the inside of my lip. The queen obviously observed it. "So you have learned a little wisdom in your time as guest of Mr. Partridge. That is good. I will allow you a few moments of private conversation with your sisters. You may join them and withdraw to a privy chamber."

I curtsied, then backed out of the room to where my sisters were waiting. My guard followed us to a closet, a tiny room with a small fire burning. The instant he closed the door leaving us alone, Kat hugged me so tight, she squeezed the breath from my lungs. I could feel her bones, sharper through the material of her gown.

It was one of those she had worn for the wedding festivities when she had been round-limbed and blooming. Now it hung on her much-thinner frame, the roses bleached from her cheeks, her eyes smudged with heartache. Had she worried herself into such a state over me? Or had Pembroke done what I feared and annulled her marriage to Henry?

"Jane! Did all go well?" she asked. "I was so afraid you would do something foolhardy, like arguing religion with the queen!"

"I managed to avoid it, but it took effort. It was hard enough to be so rejected by the English people. Even from the Tower I could hear the cheers and see the bonfires dotting the city, and my guards took great glee in recounting tales of the celebrations at Mary's coronation. To hear from her that God cast me aside was even more painful. I know it is not true. The faithful must always endure great tribulations before winning salvation."

"This is not about salvation, Jane! It is about survival. What did the queen say?"

"She has promised that someday she will set me free."

Mary piped up. "I knew Cousin Mary would. She promised because of the feather."

I was too relieved to question Mary's queer pronouncement. "I cannot fathom why she has done it. To promise to spare me the ax is one thing. But to release me? I feared the best fate I could ever hope for was to spend the rest of my life a prisoner, as Edward Courtenay would have, if Mary had never come to the throne."

Called the last sprig of the white rose of Lancaster, Courtenay had been jailed by Henry VIII because he was a danger to the Tudor dynasty. He had been released along with Catholic Bishop Gardiner the moment Mary Tudor was named queen.

"To be set free seems unimaginable." I felt a twinge, remembering the talk I had had with Father the night I first learned I was to be queen. I would not have been so merciful to my cousin—or so reckless. But there could be little danger to the queen now. People, both Catholic and reformed faith, had wanted her to wear the crown.

"I am so glad you are all right. Being in the Tower will not be so terrible, now I know I will walk free someday."

"Now there is nothing more to fear. We are all safe. Mother was even given precedence over Lady Elizabeth in a procession. You should have seen her face! We have survived, Jane. You have the queen's word she will release you from that terrible place. All will be well."

"All except for Henry Herbert being a cowardly knave," Mary said.

"Mary!"

"Well, it is true. He has made Kat cry."

Kat held up her hand, bare of its nuptial ring. "You were right, Jane. As always."

"I am sorry for it." I could have said that she would heal, love again. With such a warm heart, she could not help it. But I knew Kat would not appreciate her pain being discounted. She would be happy again in her own time. My guard returned, and I bade my sisters goodbye. Kat with a warm hug, Mary a briefer, fiercer one.

I did not think, until the bargemen were rowing me back to the Tower, about the family I had not seen. My mother, who was so much in the queen's favor that she had taken precedence even over Lady Elizabeth, could have seen me if she wished.

Still, my mother had not come.

Chapter Nineteen

Kat
Winchester Palace
December 1553

AMBASSADORS FROM FRANCE AND THE HOLY ROMAN Empire paraded through our days, using every opportunity to put forth the matches for Queen Mary that would benefit their own countries most.

Bishop Gardiner and the Frenchman de Noailles nattered on about the importance of wedding an Englishman. The man they most favored was Edward Courtenay. Even after fifteen years imprisoned in the Tower he looked the romantic hero—young and pretty, with royal blood flowing in his veins. To link the houses of Lancaster and Tudor could only strengthen England— or so Courtenay's most devoted patron, Bishop Gardiner, claimed.

The union might have been perfect were it not for the tales that the Spanish ambassador carried of Courtenay's revelry in Southwark's brothels. Such stories repelled Queen Mary, and I could not blame her, though at times I wondered what such women did that men found so fascinating—and whether Henry had ever sampled such pleasures.

Renard, ambassador for the Holy Roman Empire, spent every moment in the queen's company maligning Courtenay for weakness and vice while extolling the virtues of Prince Philip of Spain, a widower of sober temperament and proven responsibility. He was even the son of the queen's cousin, Charles V, who had threatened Northumberland with war should the princess be harmed. But to wed a foreigner was to give another empire a foothold on English shores—a prospect that terrified any right-thinking Englishman.

Queen Mary shifted from one inclination to the next. I could scarce blame her. The kingdom seemed caught in some strange twilight between the old world and the new: the Catholic faith, which was still outlawed, pitted against reformers, whom the queen had forbidden to preach; her life as neglected spinster changing to that of a woman sought after as wife.

Even as distressed as I was over my own concerns, I felt ire at the injustice dealt her. It did not seem fair that she was unable to enjoy the attention men now paid her. The warmer the queen became toward Prince Philip's suit, the louder the rumbles of discontent grew, until Spanish emissaries were pelted with snowballs by angry apprentices. The queen's fury at the insult only increased the unrest.

Gossip caught fire, people fearing that England would become a mere vassal of Spain and that the Inquisition would be carried to English shores along with Philip's nuptial ring.

The threat of Catholic retribution was no small matter since the queen's patience with reformers was running out. Many claimed it was only a matter of time until the fires of Smithfield consumed the flesh of heretics once more. I tried to quell my terror that, in spite of Queen Mary's promise, Jane might be one of the first to die. If not for accepting the crown, then for championing beliefs the queen deplored.

My little sister insisted the queen would not sign Jane's death warrant. I wanted to believe her. The queen loved us, after all, at least little Mary and me. As for Jane . . . Jane had spent her time writing to her reformer friends in Switzerland about the evils of popery when she might have put her efforts to better use being pleasant to the queen, more docile, more contrite. Less stubborn, less determined. Less . . . herself.

But it was hard to stay angry over Jane's recalcitrance when I was so sad and weary and it took all my energy to appear cheerful to my royal cousin as she simpered over her favorite suitor like any Cupid-struck maid.

"Is Prince Philip not the most handsome man you have ever seen, Cousin Katherine?" The queen drew me to the portrait that had arrived toward the end of November. Painted by the great Titian himself, it hung in a place of honor. A stiff-looking man of twenty-six with pale hair and cold blue eyes peered from the canvas, his jaw thrusting out so far, it seemed almost as if the artist made a mistake. But even that blemish was not as disturbing to me as the hint of a suspicious nature in the prince's expression.

"It is good you find the prince appealing," I said, trying not to offend her should she choose this man to be her husband. "The other ladies have commented on how well he looks." I was not in agreement. I wondered if the queen was able to read my thoughts.

She gave a self-deprecating chuckle. "Beautiful as you are, I am sure you have had many comely youths court you, but I am thirty-eight years old and have never felt the first pangs of love." I tried not to wince at how desperate she seemed, but she saw and must have imagined I was thinking of Henry.

"Forgive me, sweet cousin. The fact that you are pretty does not save you from suffering pain. I know Pembroke's son is often in your mind. When the youth comes to court, I have seen the way you still look at him. Even as much as I favor you, Pembroke refuses to reinstate the match between you. The earl believes you will drive a wedge between him and his son as punishment because he insisted on the annulment. Nothing I can say will convince him otherwise. You must let his son go."

"What passed between Pembroke and me matters less than the fact that Henry would not fight for me. Should not a person be willing to fight for someone they love so much?"

"Obedience is a woman's lot and a man's duty. There will be another lover devoted to you someday. But for me . . ." She looked at the portrait as if she had drunk the strongest love potion ever brewed. "This is my last chance for conjugal happiness. Some of my ladies warn that the difference in our ages and in our faces and forms will build barriers between us. I feared the same. But Prince Philip writes that he would sooner have a Godly wife than a woman who has only her youth to recommend her."

She pressed her hand to her breast. The faraway look in her eyes only made the queen look foolish. I felt embarrassed for her, but what could I say? "Do you think me ridiculous, Katherine?" she asked.

I looked away. "Unless you take that risk, you can never hope to win the prize."

"Well and wisely spoken. I wish my sister, the Lady Elizabeth, had some measure of your grace. I have seen her examining the portrait of my betrothed with a speculative air that irritates me greatly. I know she is measuring herself against Philip and imagining she is more suited to match him in face and form. She fancies that once my Spanish bridegroom arrives, he will regret which sister he will be marrying."

I scoffed at the very idea: "No prince of royal blood would want to mix his lineage with that of a bastard." Once Cousin Mary had been easy to wound on this subject, but there was no danger in speaking bluntly now. Although her father had drafted an act to declare her illegitimate, no one else had ever considered Mary Tudor a bastard. Unless you counted his queens who would benefit from her disinheritance, and ministers like Northumberland who hated the Catholic faith. Mary had gone to Parliament and legally erased even that slight stain from her name.

But anyone with eyes could see the scars that the comparison with Elizabeth had left her. Bastard though Elizabeth was, she was also young and pretty. She wielded an appeal to men that

Mary never had. The queen's insecurities were reflected in her eyes. I groped for words to soothe her. "When my sister was at Chelsea with the dowager queen, she said the Lady Elizabeth acted in a way most unseemly with Thomas Seymour."

I mentioned my sister whenever I could to raise her in the queen's good graces. Often I had felt a softening in Queen Mary when I did so. Today the queen grew restless.

"It will be a good thing for the kingdom once I am safely wed and brought to bed of a Catholic prince. Any question of the Lady Elizabeth inheriting will then be quashed. The true religion will be restored in England again. People will see for themselves what a good thing this Spanish marriage is for the country. They will thank me for it."

"I hope so, Majesty." No one could mistake the temper of the land. It grew more hostile to a wedding between England and Spain every day. Bishop Gardiner had even dared to serve the queen with a petition signed by members of both the Lords and the Commons begging her to eschew a foreign prince in favor of an English marriage. There was even talk of rebellion. So dangerous had feelings against the Spanish become that the queen, in an effort to silence public outcry, had issued a proclamation forbidding unlawful assemblies and lewd words.

I feared how swiftly people's loyalty could change. The queen's kindness to me in the past months made me dread the disillusionment that would afflict her as people withdrew their love. "Majesty, I hope that you are right and people accept the marriage you desire—"

She cut in with a sternness that startled me, "My subjects must bow to my will. It is my divine right to choose."

"Your Majesty, sometimes even if it is your right to choose, it is best to be . . . gentle." The queen frowned, but I rushed on. "This matter with the Spanish reminds me of taming a horse to the bridle. No one disputes the animal must go where the rider tells it to, but if you rein it in a way so hasty it hurts its mouth, the horse will fight you."

"A queen cannot afford to appear weak. The spirit of unrest is making the Spanish nervous. They are not certain I can hold the loyalty of my own country, keep it under control, and force the people to accept my marriage. They are wrong."

"I am certain they are."

"I am glad to hear it. The Spanish fear your sister, even though she is safely captive in the Tower. Perhaps they are right to do so if—as you so aptly put it—the horse intends to fight the bridle."

I cringed, seeing the danger of my warning too late. "Jane would never betray Your Majesty. Did she not swear it herself at the audience you allowed her? Your leniency touched her deeply. She had a belly full of the crown. You must know that you can trust her. She wants only to go home."

Chapter Twenty

Jane
Tower of London
February 3, 1554

SOMETHING IS TERRIBLY WRONG. FOR WEEKS I HAVE NOT received a letter from Mary or Kat or been allowed to walk in the garden. Locked inside my chamber, the walls press down upon me until I think I shall go mad. I spend long days carving words into the stone.

I hope for light after darkness . . .

Darkness is all around me now. I cannot eat, cannot sleep. I get only whispered news from a guard who befriended Mrs. Ellen: a mailbag intercepted, revolt against the queen. Men who will not suffer a Spaniard becoming England's king. How to prevent Queen Mary from wedding the man of her choice? They are coming for me: my father, Carew, a knight named Sir Thomas Wyatt. Four armies to march on London, to set me free.

Now I can hear a spattering of gunfire from across the river. From my window I can see the confusion of the Tower troops, dragging out cannons, mounting them on the walls. Memory stirs. This is the same measured chaos as when I was preparing to hold off my cousin as the ranks of her army swelled. Was the same thing happening now?

I bit my fingernails, not even sure what I hoped for. I had promised my cousin I would be loyal to her. She had spared my life. Yet she had not pardoned me as she had vowed she would.

She had broken her vow, just as I would in claiming the crown that would be offered me if Wyatt was victorious.

What was happening? The suspense drove me mad. Was it possible that God had intervened so I might win His cause at last? If that was so, I must embrace the opportunity He offered. But if the armies got close, Cousin Mary could sign my death warrant, have me dispatched with the flash of a headsman's blade. Might that blade claim other lives as well? With me dead, Kat would become the figurehead for men such as Wyatt. Might the queen not decide then to obliterate Kat as a threat? No matter what happened in the conflict playing out in the city streets, I would not be able to protect my sister.

Torn with helplessness and confusion, I crossed to my carvings in the stone and tried to comfort myself by tracing my fingers over the curves and lines I had etched with painstaking care:

> While God assists us, envy bites in vain,
> If God forsake us, fruitless all our pain—
> I hope for light after the darkness.

Pray God the dawn would break for me and He would swing my prison door open wide.

Kat Whitehall Palace
February 3, 1554

Wyatt's army was coming to set Jane free. With each blast of gunfire outside Whitehall's walls, the knowledge terrified me, thrilled me, left me so confused I could not think. Chaos reigned—not only among the queen's ladies but in London as well. Citizens tore down London Bridge to cut off the rebels' path to the city. But their desperate act would only slow

Wyatt's men, not stop them forever. There were other bridges across the Thames, and the Londoners could not destroy them all. Wyatt had only to turn and march back upriver to cross one.

How desperate the Londoners must be, to sever the main artery that supplied their trade. Did the English hate the prospect of the Spanish marriage so much that Wyatt might actually win?

Since December the queen had been bombarded with news that grew more alarming with every passing day. My sister Mary and I had gleaned it in snips and shards, piecing it together: one of Bishop Gardiner's spies had intercepted a mailbag containing letters about rebellion fomenting in Suffolk. When Gardiner confronted Courtenay, the coward had confessed to his part of the scheme, betraying the rest of the conspirators. Sir Thomas Wyatt, Peter Carew, and—God save him—our father were to gather troops from the four corners of England, then march on London. Once there, they would sweep Catholic Mary from the throne, destroying her plan for a Spanish marriage and her intent to restore England to the pope.

Courtenay had cast their plans into disarray. Only Wyatt had remained steadfast, gathering four thousand men in Kent and laying siege to the city.

"The traitor's daughters," the queen's most loyal ladies now called Mary and me. "Her Majesty should never have spared your father's life, or your sister's. But this time you haughty Greys will get what you deserve."

What would happen to us now? If Wyatt lost, would we be imprisoned in the Tower like Jane? Or would the queen seek a more permanent solution? King Henry had executed every member of the de la Pole family within his reach, because they were a threat to his reign. He had even killed a little boy.

History was littered with the deaths of those whom monarchs regarded as a threat, no matter their age or innocence: perhaps the most famous among them were the princes in the Tower, whom evil Richard III had ordered to be murdered.

If Richard had killed his nephews just because they were too close to the throne, could not this queen easily execute her cousins, whose family had been involved in two rebellions against her? Even my little sister was afraid.

"The queen does not like us anymore," Mary had said, watching the other ladies attend our cousin on the far side of the room. I might have hushed her, but I doubted they would hear us, preoccupied as they were with the happenings beyond the castle walls.

"Her Majesty is much occupied at present with rousing the people to join her fight against the rebels."

"She gave a speech in the streets that I heard people talking about. She said she loves the people as her children. They are to think of her as if she is our mother."

"It was very brave." I had seen the queen ride out, a slender figure astride her horse, the embattled princess trying once more to capture the imagination of her subjects. "The people rallied around her once. She hoped to inspire them to do so again."

Mary tugged fretfully at her bottom lip. "I do not want Cousin Mary to be like our mother. Hettie says the people are angry with the queen because she wants to marry the Spanish prince. She says they tore down London Bridge, Kat. I do not believe Hettie."

"It is true. The Londoners did so to halt Wyatt's army in Southwark."

"All those cunning little houses that span the road across the river! How will the people cross the Thames with their sheep and carts full of goods?"

"It was a futile effort. A messenger says Wyatt's army is marching to Knightsbridge to cross. Even the queen cannot tear down every bridge over the Thames."

"Is Father with the rebels?"

"I do not believe so." I answered even more softly. "I heard the queen's councilors talking. Three of the four armies that were raised against the queen were broken up before the revolt could begin. I imagine Father is off hiding somewhere, awaiting the outcome." Or had he ridden for London to join Wyatt? We had no way to know for certain. I looked toward the queen, relieved to see her busy with some dispatch. "Maybe Father will run away to France. That is what Peter Carew did."

"Jane cannot run away from the Tower. It is a good thing the queen will not hurt Jane. Her Majesty promised." I did not have the heart to tell her how little that promise would mean after this conflict was over.

"There is one happy thought, Kat," Mary said. "If the rebels win and Jane is queen, you can have Henry again. She can order Pembroke to let him marry you."

Strange to realize, I did not want Henry nearly as much as I wanted Jane. I had begged the queen to let me go to my sister, even though I knew I might never leave the Tower again, but Her Majesty had refused. When we retreated to Whitehall, the queen was the only one calm.

A rebel's arrow had flown over the palace wall. Women had wailed, and soldiers cried out that all was lost. But Her Majesty had turned to us, her voice almost serene: "Do not waste your energies weeping. Pray, ladies."

But what was I supposed to pray for? Even now I did not know.

"What do the rebels want?" Mary asked.

"Wyatt demands that the queen surrender herself and the Tower into his keeping."

Mary's eyes grew wide. "Are these the same people who threw the dog through the queen's window?"

Six months ago someone had heaved the strangled animal into the queen's very chamber, the dog's head shaved in monk's tonsure, a noose around its neck. The memory still gave me nightmares.

A blast of cannon made me nearly leap out of my skin. I hugged Mary tight. "They cannot cross London Bridge," I said.

Mary shoved against me, hard, shouting, "I do not care about London Bridge! I want to go to Jane! The cannons are going to hurt her!"

From across the chamber, the queen heard her. Mary Tudor wheeled on us, her eyes blazing. "It would be well for England if the cannon shot obliterated the Tower your traitor sister lodges in!" Never had I heard the queen speak to Mary so harshly. "Do you know what that traitor father of yours is about? Men from Suffolk have told me right enough! He may not have been able to join with Wyatt, but Henry Grey wished to put your sister back on the throne! It is only by the grace of God that I was not foolish enough to let the Lady Jane go free!"

"You promised you would!" Mary protested. "You gave me the feather!"

But the queen would not be swayed by Mary's strange protest. "The Spanish are right," the queen said. "I will never be safe while she lives." A battle was raging in Mary Tudor's heart, a war even fiercer than the one being fought just outside these fortress walls. But she did not want Jane's blood on her hands, of that I was certain.

"I will not do it," she muttered to herself. "I am queen. Nothing can force my hand."

❧ ❧

BY FEBRUARY 7 THE REBELLION WAS QUELLED, THE CANNONS silenced. In the days that followed the rebels—including Wyatt and my father—marched, dejectedly into the Tower as prisoners. It was then that the Spanish devils brought to bear the one negotiation Queen Mary could not withstand.

I stood, attending her, as the ambassador from Charles V

entered her presence chamber to relay his master's message: "The Emperor Charles cannot in good conscience send his son into certain danger. Prince Philip will not sail from Spain until Lady Jane Grey is dead."

Chapter Twenty-one

Jane
Tower of London
February 12, 1554

Y FATHER HAS KILLED ME—OR MIGHT AS WELL have done. We will die in a macabre cluster of executions—my father, Guilford, and me—like nosegays strewn upon a grave. Wyatt's guns are silenced, his army shattered.

I watched from my window as the Earl of Pembroke marched the rebel leader and his followers into the Tower walls, where they would be held until they were paraded out again to face traitors' deaths. Soon crossroads all over England will be decked with their corpses, grim warnings to any who might consider such defiance in the future.

No man's downfall has brought more delight to Queen Mary's supporters than that of the haughty Duke of Suffolk. My guards informed me that my shivering, wet father was dragged from a hollow tree in his deer park. There he had hidden like one of the pathetic animals he loved to hunt—Father run to ground. His former ally, Lord Huntingdon, placed him under arrest.

Whatever Wyatt's purpose was—to stop Cousin Mary from wedding a Spaniard; to place Lady Elizabeth on the throne; or to reinstate me as queen—it did not matter. My father cried out for Queen Jane, so I must die as well, either that or damn my soul to hell. It is a devil's bargain Cousin Mary offers. If I recant my faith and turn Catholic, she will let me live—so says Dr. Feckenham, her own confessor and the emissary she has sent to tempt me. Would God I could loathe the priest as I should. But he has been too kind, too wise, too much a friend. The ruddy-faced clergyman disproves many things I was so sure of regarding the popish church and those who serve it. I am torn between wanting to spite him and wanting to bury my face in his lap and cry.

Sixteen is too young to die. I know I should surrender my life gladly, but it is hard, especially while Dr. Feckenham pleads with me, fatherly tears glittering in his eyes. He displays a tenderness I never witnessed from my own parents.

In spite of my stubborn clinging to my faith, the priest has promised not to leave me as my parents did. He will take that last long walk with me to the gallows. He will stay with me until the very end. I believe him, and it comforts me a little.

In the days after the rebellion, I waited. I no longer hoped for a pardon, not anymore. But I would give much for a letter, a visit, a basket of comforts from my mother, my sisters. I imagined my father in another cell, humiliated, his pride stripped away. In spite of the peril he placed me in, I would give all I own to see him or my mother or sisters.

Do Kat and Mary know I am to be executed? They must by now. What happened to them in the aftermath of Wyatt's ill-fated rebellion? Are they still waiting upon the queen, or are they banished somewhere, loathed and despised as daughters of a man condemned as a traitor two times over? What are they thinking? Feeling? Has Father's recklessness hurled them back into danger?

I imagine the queen's ladies sniping at Kat. Those loyal servants would delight in punishing Suffolk's daughters, to pay for the terror the rebels had put them through. But I cannot help my sisters now.

As Dr. Feckenham enters the room, I go to the table and

take up the small hoard of objects there, the last gifts I have to bestow on those I love. "Will you see that Kat gets my Greek Testament?" I ask him. "I wrote her a letter and placed it inside. This is for Mary." I pass him the doll I made in a time when I could not have imagined all that has come to pass. Mary's Jennet—she has been a silent witness to betrayal, hope, and despair ever since my little sister thrust her into my hands the last few moments I was queen. "You must tell Mary how much this poppet has comforted me these past weeks. Now it will comfort her."

Dr. Feckenham nods.

I hear footsteps beyond the door, know my time is here. Fear thrusts to my very marrow. I think of the crowd waiting just outside to see me die, imagine them watching my severed head roll across the straw. Then they will go about their lives, drink wine and eat meat pies and quarrel with their sisters. I will never see mine again.

Trying to hide my fear, I turn to the priest. "Dr. Feckenham?" My voice sounds high, tight. Even to my own ears it quavers. "You will not leave me?"

"No, child." His sorrowful eyes meet mine. "We will see this through together."

I take up my prayer book, square my shoulders. As I pace out into the sunshine for the last time, I try to focus on my prayers, but memories steal through. Bradgate's stream, Mary struggling to catch up while Kat races ahead to catch a gauze-winged butterfly. Me, forever caught between them. I will not be there to soften the places where their spirits chafe each other.

I fight to hide my trembling as I move toward the scaffold— step by step, wishing to hear their voices, my sisters, the two people who truly love me. I dare not think on what is to happen, the severing blow that Guilford faced earlier this morning. Dare not remember the sight of him walking to Tower Hill, his blond hair gleaming. I hated him after that night in the abbey, but in the months that followed I saw that he was a victim of his father's ambition as much as I was. I saw the fear in him. Yet when his father betrayed the reformed faith and fled back to Catholicism, Guilford held firm, even though it cost him his life. There is honor in that, and courage. Perhaps we could have learned to deal more amiably with each other after all, given time and distance from our families.

Pity for this stranger who was my husband filled me when the cart bearing Guilford's body returned to the Tower and made its way to St. Peter ad Vincula, his corpse swathed in bloody cloths, his head bundled separately and tossed in beside his body.

Soon my fate will be the same. My gorge rises, and I fight to keep my terror from showing, shaming me. I am a princess of the blood. I must meet my fate with dignity, or my lady mother will be angry. A wild laugh threatens to break free as I imagine what my sister Mary would say to that. She loves the tale of the Countess of Shrewsbury, who claimed she was not guilty of treason and ran from King Henry's headsman. The man hacked her to death in a series of clumsy blows. Dear God, why must I think of such a thing now?

"Jane!"

Through the crowd's rumble I hear a faint cry. No, imagine it. Mary's voice. She cannot be here, on Tower Green. But I cling to the sound. "Forgive me!" she pleads.

What is this? Some cruel torture? A demon sent to distract, not comfort? Or am I hearing my little sister's pain from across the miles? Her grief over the strangeness between us since that first meeting after I became queen? Barriers I felt in every letter since I was in the Tower? Poor little sister. She will worry over it in secret now with no one to coax it from her.

Whatever burdens her spirit, I pray she will realize another truth in time.

There is nothing in this world or the next I would not forgive my sisters.

My feet grow steady as I make my way across the scaffold where the wooden block awaits.

Mary
February 16, 1554

So much blood. Rivers of it, choking me. I could not scrub the sight of it off my mind. Jane's mouth still moved as the executioner grasped her head by its long auburn hair and raised it high. His voice boomed: "Thus die all traitors. God save Queen Mary."

What was Jane saying? In the moment between life and death, had angels told her what I had done? I could see her lips form the sorrowful words: *Mary, how could you?*

I moaned as I tossed and turned in a strange bed, far from my old room with the other maids. Where was I? I did not know, nor how I got here. I remember Jane, the ax, the blood, then falling, never wanting to wake.

I remember the queen's own doctor pressing some bitter brew to my lips. The sound of hushed voices, but none familiar enough to cling to in this nightmare. Even Hettie was gone. A stranger kept vigil over me now, dribbled watered wine down my throat, and sopped up the sweat and tears that made my hair cling to my cheeks.

More than I wanted Hettie, I wanted Kat. But she had been crying for days, even before I ran away to the Tower. Crying, not just for Jane, but for Father. He was to stand trial soon, but everyone knew what the judges would decide. They would cut off his head too. How long had it been since the world had gone all black and swirly in the crowd that watched my sister die? Kat would know. If only I could see Kat.

No! Panic filled me. I never wanted to see Kat again, have to look in her eyes. She might see that I was the one who warned Cousin Mary to escape Robert Dudley's men, and she would hate me. I had trusted my cousin, my friend, and she had killed the only person who ever really loved me.

I whimpered into the bolster. I was the devil child that people had named me. Even Kat would think so now. I would burn in hell. I deserved it. If only I were not so scared of fire.

I heard a scratching on the door. My guardian startled awake.

"Her Majesty, the queen," the gentleman usher said, in a voice so low I could barely make it out. I burrowed under the covers as the door opened. I did not want people gawking at me, especially the ladies who waited on the queen. They would be glad to tell everyone how wicked I was. They did not like Kat and me anymore.

When I did not hear the rustling of numerous skirts or the whispering of gossip being exchanged, I peeked from beneath the coverlet. The attendants that usually surrounded my cousin were nowhere in sight.

A cloth bundle was tucked in the crook of the queen's arm. The single taper illuminating the room cast it in shadow as she motioned for my attendant to leave us. The door thudded closed behind the woman, leaving the queen and me alone. She drew near me, and I pulled the covers back over my head.

"I would see with my own eyes that you are unharmed, as the guard who carried you back to the palace claimed," she said. "Come out from your sanctuary, cousin." I did as she ordered, but the instant I uncovered my face, I turned it away from her. I knew it was unforgivable to treat a queen thus. I would be punished for it. I wanted to be punished.

"You did a very dangerous thing, running off to Tower Green," she said sternly. "A child as small as you, Suffolk's daughter—there are many who would rejoice at the chance to do you harm. It would have grieved me if something terrible had happened to you."

I could not keep a sound of pain from rising in my throat.

This time the queen looked away. "You are right," she said,

twisting the heavy ring of state around on her finger. "Something terrible did happen. I know it will be hard for you to believe, but Jane's death was horrible for me as well. It is worse still to know I broke my vow to you, when you were so brave and loyal on my behalf."

I clenched my teeth so hard my jaw ached.

"When you are quite grown to be a lady, you will understand better. Sometimes we must do things we do not wish to do."

Her words pried loose the other question that had been lodged in my head ever since that fearful day when Wyatt had stormed nearly to the palace gates. "People say you should kill Kat and me, as well. I heard them."

I knew the queen had heard those people too. "I would never do such a thing. You and Lady Katherine are safe under my care."

I did not dare say she had promised that Jane was safe from harm as well.

She must have seen reproach in my eyes. "All will be well once your father is beyond his traitorous plotting."

"He is . . . he is still alive?" I knew he was in his cell in the Tower.

"He will be tried tomorrow."

"The day after Jane . . ."

"It is February seventeenth tomorrow, child. It has been four days since your misadventure."

Only four days. Such a short time, like the nine days Jane had been queen.

"I do not mean to distress you, Mary, merely to reassure you that the wild talk of doing you and Katherine harm will fade. Spanish fears will be calmed once the prince and I are wed, and courtiers who scorn you now will find some fresh scandal to feed upon. I am sure of it."

But I was no longer sure of anything except that Kat must not see what I had seen. "Majesty, I do not care if you kill Father. At least not so very much. It was his fault that they hurt my Jane. Even our mother says so. But Kat cares. She is Father's favorite."

"I remember the duke was very fond of her."

"I do not want Kat to go to Tower Hill with him, to see all that blood. It would break something inside her, like the crystal mother shattered in a temper. If Kat breaks like that, no one will ever be able to put her back together. You can make sure she does not break."

"It is good of you to think of your sister, though you have had such a shock. I will do what I can, but I could not protect you, could I?" I shook my head. "Even so, I would do the best I can by my cousins. You must aid me in a matter of great import to me."

"What is so important, Majesty?"

"*Your* feelings, Mary." Her words startled me. Jane was the only person who had ever asked what I was feeling. "Now I must ask you a question, child, and you must tell me the truth, no matter how hard it is. As queen, I command it. As your cousin, I ask humbly."

Silence fell, and I realized the queen was waiting for my answer. She looked so sad, almost afraid. It made my throat tighter. I nodded, agreeing to her terms.

"Can you bear to serve me after the wrong I have done you? Or shall I send you away? I will do it if you wish me to"—her voice dropped low—"though I will miss you sorely if you are gone."

I thought for a long time, knowing what I should say. After what Cousin Mary had done to Jane, I should go as far from court as I was able. But where would the queen send me? I was selfish enough to wonder. Would I go to my lady mother? She did not love me. At least there was tenderness in my cousin's eyes. I was betraying Jane all over again, but I could not help it. I did not want to be alone. I sucked in a deep breath and looked into my cousin's sad, squinty eyes. "I will stay with you."

The queen's shoulders sagged, and she released her breath in a shuddery sigh. "I am glad of it. There is one thing more, Mary. You know my confessor, Dr. Feckenham?"

I could picture the man who had guided Jane to the block when the kerchief was wrapped about her eyes. Dr. Feckenham was kind to Jane at the last.

"Your sister gave him charge of some of her belongings to deliver as keepsakes to those she loved most. This one is for you." Cousin Mary extended the soft-wrapped parcel.

For a moment, I could not take it. It seemed forbidding, like the secrets festering inside me.

"Come, child. It is a gift from your sister, not a curse." Her eyes brightened with tears. "I know you feel you wronged your sister, as I did my mother long ago. I am sure you have heard of my betrayal. Sometimes I still feel as if it is painted across my brow."

The queen laid the parcel on the coverlet, unwrapped it with her own hands. There, pillowed in the folds of cloth, lay Jennet. My poppet, her silk-thread hair no longer disheveled from my loving, a new gown laced about her cloth body. But it was Jennet's face I stared at, unable to look away.

Suddenly I was back at Suffolk House the night before Jane's wedding. Still frightened from overhearing Father and the devil duke, I had lugged a bundle, heavy with books, to Jane's chamber, bent on urging my sister to run away. Why had Jane not run away?

I made something for you, she had said, so solemn, then dismayed as she stared at the pale linen face. *I forgot to stitch her mouth.*

I had begged Jane not to, for it reminded me of her—how hard it was for her to say how my parents wounded her heart. They had not wanted to know what Jane was thinking, not even when she was in the Tower cell waiting to go to the block. They had not cared what Jane felt, what she wanted to say.

But my sister had managed to say something to me without using one word.

On Jennet's face she had stitched the soft curve of a red-silk smile.

Chapter Twenty-two

Kat
April 1554

ATHER WAS DEAD, AND I HAD NOT THE COURAGE OF MY little sister. Even knowing he had loved me best, knowing he would die alone on the scaffold on Tower Hill, I could not summon the courage to go to him. I tried to comfort myself by saying the queen herself had thwarted me, but that was not true. She warned against a trip to Tower Hill but said she had encountered the Grey family stubbornness before, and if I was determined to make the journey, she would send me in a coach with a full set of royal guards.

But stalwart as the guards might be, they could not protect me from the knowledge of my own cowardice. Or the certainty that even little Mary was far braver than me.

Nights were most fearful of all. I dared not sleep for fear of the nightmares—Father on the scaffold begging the headsman wait until he could find his "pretty maid" in the crowd, people sopping up Jane's blood with kerchiefs, martyr's blood for healing and good luck.

Worst still were the tales Mary sobbed out in the weeks since one of the queen's guards carried her into the palace. I tried with all my might to blot the sight of her from my memory—dirt-smudged, half delirious, the horrific scene of Jane's beheading burned into the backs of her eyes.

How had Mary escaped from the palace that day? Traveled all the way to the Tower? Gained entry past the guards? The queen herself had put those questions to me, yet neither of us could unravel the mystery; nor would Mary confide in us. Best to keep the matter secret, the queen bade us few who knew of Mary's flight.

It would not do to allow enemies of the crown to learn that security about the palace had been so lax. Her hand, with its ring of state, had trembled as it touched my sleeping sister's cheek. I suspected she was fearful for her Spanish betrothed, for many still wished the Catholic Prince Philip ill.

I could see the guilt in the queen's gaze, sensed that Mary's misadventure had shattered the barriers that the Spanish had erected between us, transformed Mary and me once again into the beloved little cousins she had spent Christmastide with for so many years. She knew what it was to be young and helpless, at the mercy of a parent's folly.

A new depth of tenderness wreathed Her Majesty's face when she laid eyes upon either of us. But as preparations for the royal nuptials set the court awhirl, I could not be grateful for her regard. How could I forget the bride-price the Spaniards had exacted? Jane was dead, yet come July, Mary and I would be expected to delight at the queen's wedding.

Even so, a mere three weeks after my father's execution on Friday, February 23, I had another wedding to reckon with. I would not soon forget the day in March when my mother visited me, daring to come to court despite our family's disgrace. "There is some news you must hear from me before you learn it from someone less kindly disposed on your behalf. I am wed."

I staggered back a step. "But Father—"

"Your father got his head cut off. No great loss since he refused to put his brains to good use when it was attached."

Hurt sliced through me. "You must not say that!"

"It is the truth. This is what his schemes have come to: Jane dead, you and Mary servants to the woman he tried to dethrone. Me, stripped of lands, wealth, husband."

"How can you be so cold?"

"I must be to survive. The queen is not best pleased by my marriage." My mother actually smiled. "My new husband is Sir Adrian Stokes."

"Your master of the horse?"

"Is that not the rank Edmund Tudor held when he wedded Henry VII's mother? They founded our whole dynasty. My own father, Charles Brandon, was not the equal of my mother. Sir Adrian will make me a lusty husband. He pleases me well."

"But it is only three weeks since Father died! I believed you loved him!"

"My *great love* can do us no good from the grave. But our fortunes will turn again. I intend to make certain you use the chance that you have been given to the most advantage."

"What chance is that?"

"Her Majesty has become guardian to you and Mary. Your father is dead, a traitor, your sister executed, your mother disgraced. You are every bit as vulnerable as the queen herself was at your age. Her Majesty has great affection for you and Mary and is coming to loathe her half-sister more with each passing day."

It was true that the queen's patience with the Lady Elizabeth was thin. When the storm of Wyatt's rebellion gathered, she had sent for her sister. Elizabeth pleaded illness, but the queen had not believed her. She sent her own doctors to drag her sister to court even if the girl was on her deathbed. When the doctors brought Elizabeth to London by litter, the clever princess fastened its curtains open so people could see her limbs and face swollen with dropsy. It was said the princess fainted four times on the way to the litter.

With Prince Philip's arrival slated for July, the queen had grown ever more suspicious of the sister who would inherit, should Mary fail to bear a child.

My mother's face looked as it did on the rent days when she counted up profits. "The reformers are already rallying about the Lady Elizabeth, and the queen would embrace any excuse to deal her Jane's fate."

"You would wish the Lady Elizabeth condemned to what Jane suffered?"

"Jane was innocent—she wanted none of your father's schemes. Elizabeth is more calculating than anyone else at court, born with her parents' thirst for plotting and power. There is something unnatural in that woman—little wonder, with her mother a witch. The queen does not forget it, nor all she and her mother suffered in Elizabeth's name."

"That is no surprise." I would never forget what Jane suffered and why.

"Now there is the most wonderful news. The Lady Elizabeth is arrested, suspected of conspiring with Sir Thomas Wyatt and his rebels. She is being taken to the Tower."

"I cannot be glad of it, no matter how much I dislike her."

"You stupid girl! You never did have Jane's wit. Do you not see what this means for us? Lady Elizabeth must be condemned and executed—everyone knows she was neck deep in Wyatt's plots. As soon as the queen's councilors present Her Majesty with proof, the queen can rid herself of Boleyn's bastard once and for all."

"Queen Mary execute her own sister? The guilt would eat her alive."

"Let it. Once Elizabeth is dead, you will be heir to the crown."

For a moment I could not speak. "The queen is to wed. She hopes to bear a child to follow her to the throne."

"From the time Mary's courses began, they have been a

misery for her, while of all the children Katherine of Aragon bore, only Mary survived. Mary is old to have a first babe. Think what happened to Catherine Parr. No, Katherine. Mary Tudor is not made of the stuff to bear strong sons for England. You are."

My heart thudded hard against my rib cage.

"You will ingratiate yourself into Her Majesty's favor. Show yourself to be of impeccable virtue and filled with royal graces. It should be easy enough—you ever were the most charming of creatures. Queen Mary has an ugly person's fascination with what is beautiful, and you remind her of her aunt and namesake—my mother, the queen of France. You will take whatever opportunity fate presents to pare away Elizabeth's footing at court."

"Is it not dangerous? Elizabeth will hate me for it. Should she become queen—"

"You must make certain she does not become queen. Perhaps Jane was a necessary sacrifice to clear the path for you. Of all my daughters, you would wear the crown with a most becoming grace."

That or lose my head as my sister had done.

"You are squeamish. You blame me, along with your father, for Jane's death. But you are my daughter. In time you will think of the pretty things you would have as queen."

I had noticed them in my early days at court, when Mary had been so certain Jane's life would be spared. Since few ladies-inwaiting would converse with me, I had withdrawn to the queen's chamber, helping her get dressed for the day, selecting jewelry from her coffers.

What would it be like to have all the royal wardrobe at my disposal? The brimming chests of jewels, the damasks and furs against my skin? What would it be like to be queen?

I might have cared. I might have wished for it. I might have, except that Father and Jane were dead and Henry was lost to me. This new betrayal of my lady mother's, this scandalous marriage, would give the courtiers even more to mock me with.

"How can you wish me to chase after the crown after all it cost Jane? Father?"

"If I were the one buried under the stones at St. Peter's, your father would be urging you in the same direction."

"He would not want me in danger! He loved me too well."

"Henry Grey loved power more. He would have risked anything to have a queen of England in his family. Why do you think he joined Wyatt, even knowing that if they were defeated, it would mean Jane's death? He chose to grasp his daughter's chance at the crown. He would seize that chance for you as well. You owe it to him, if you ever loved him."

"You know I did! I do!" I could feel my lady mother spinning her spider's webs around me, manipulating me as she did the threads she pulled through her tambour. Would I be stitched into the pattern she desired for me as well?

"You think on what I have said, Katherine," my mother bade me.

"Will you see Mary before you leave?"

"The queen? I have told you, she has banished me—"

"I meant our Mary."

"Whatever for?"

"She is most distraught. She saw Jane beheaded."

"Perhaps that will teach her to think next time before she does something so reckless, though I doubt it. She is the most vexing little monkey."

"What am I to tell her?"

"You may tell her what you feel best. Or tell her nothing at all. The queen's ladies will have much to say about my marriage. I must go. Sir Adrian waits in the courtyard."

She pinched my cheeks. "You must eat more, Katherine, and take a little air in the gardens. You do not want to lose your beauty. It is your finest asset."

I stiffened as she kissed me, then turned and left me alone. I leaned against the wall, my cheek scraped against a stone.

"Father, I am so sad," I whispered, knowing he could not hear me. I closed my eyes, weary, filled with despair. The world had gone mad. Was there nothing soft or gentle or lovely to bear me up above the darkness where I might breathe again?

The images Mary had cried out in her nightmares crowded into my mind, joining my own imagined scenes of the ax slamming down upon the fragile bumps of the nape of Jane's neck. My sister—once queen—her head rolling across the straw.

Chapter Twenty-three

Kat
17 years old
Summer 1558

I HAVE HEARD PEOPLE SAY THAT SOME SOULS ARE BORN FOR sorrow. I cannot understand why. God would have been kinder had he let Cousin Mary live out her days as a neglected princess cloistered amongst her ladies, slipping from the palace to give alms to the poor, befriending the ill fated or outcast—as she did my little sister. Instead, the queen grew drunk on the happiness that her marriage to Prince Philip seemed to offer. Her simpering smiles and blushes throughout the wedding feasts on that twenty-fifth day of July 1554 made Spaniards smile and Englishmen scowl.

How can I describe the transformation of my royal cousin's joy to sorrow in the years that followed? The alchemy that changed the hope and delight of the queen's early reign to the somber haunting aura of its end? It was as if God had used Philip to light a candle of happiness in Cousin Mary's life-battered heart, then just as it began to glow reached out a divine hand to pinch the wick cold.

Even I grew happy in those first days of her marriage, or as near to it as I could with Jane and Father gone. Although I had my own chamber, in honor of my station as the queen's cousin, I spent much time in the maids' lodgings, giggling and gossiping and spinning dreams of what our lives would be.

My favorite confidante? One who might have been my sister-in-law, had my parents honored the betrothal between my sister and Edward Seymour. Seventeen-year-old Lady Jane Seymour was daughter of the lord protector in King Edward's reign whose head Northumberland had lopped off under false charges of treason. This new Jane understood what it felt like to have the shadow of attainder spread across her family. She knew what it was to lose a father to the ax.

Long after the other maids slept, I would climb into Jane's bed, where we would pull the covers over our heads and whisper. She did not caution me, as my sister Jane would have done, when I spoke of Henry Herbert. Jane Seymour loved romances as dearly as I did.

In the months after the queen's nuptials, even Mary's rift with my mother healed. Her Majesty hurled herself into love with Prince Philip as a boy might throw a bird's nest over a cliff. When she came to think she carried his child, we were forced to watch her poor heart break upon the stones.

Would God I had never seen her exquisite joy that spring, as her husband escorted her to the confinement chamber with us ladies. There, in great pomp and ceremony, she was locked away with her women. It was predicted that sometime in early May she would fill the royal cradle with a Catholic heir. A month after the birth she would exit the chamber in triumph to be churched, and the celebrations planned for the new prince would be the most lavish of her reign. Jane Seymour and I could scarce contain our excitement, planning our new gowns, sifting through our small stores of jewelry.

But we were never to wear our finery. Time swept past the child's anticipated date of arrival, and the midwives and courtiers became restless, Prince Philip even more so. June roses shed their petals. In July the queen insisted the physicians must have figured wrong. By the end of that month we all knew that there would be no child, but the queen would not buckle to that painful truth. She insisted she had felt the babe kick within her.

Late in August, a year after the child was thought to have been conceived, the queen took my little sister's hand and pressed it upon her stomach, asking Mary if she felt the babe too.

Tears stood in my sister's eyes. "Majesty, it is very dark and sad in this confinement chamber," she said. "Do you not think you would feel better in the sunshine?"

I will never forget the heartbreaking day that Queen Mary surrendered all hope, or the glint of triumph in my mother's eyes, masked with sympathy whenever Her Majesty drew near. We ladies returned to court, where I was certain the Lady Elizabeth was equally pleased by the queen's failure to produce an heir to displace her.

Worst of all was the silence. Her Majesty took up her duties without a word about what had gone before, as if the tiny clothes had never been stitched, plans for christenings and festivities to celebrate the child's birth never pored over and delighted in.

Did the queen see the pained patience with which her handsome young husband endured the disappointment and suffered her even more passionate attachment to him? Did she sense his growing resentment that she and the council had hobbled his power in England?

He had intended to add England to the Habsburg Empire, but his reward for wedding a woman much older—a woman whose face was marked by illness and unhappiness—had been to secure the loathing of the English people and the humiliation of being a consort, stripped of any real power. He could not wait to leave our shores for his other kingdoms, to fight Spanish wars, and doubtless to be entertained by other women, younger, prettier, without that pathetic worship the queen betrayed in her eyes.

How many letters did I see the queen pen to her husband after he sailed away, each missive more desperate than the last? My sister grieved for the queen. Philip did not love her, Mary insisted. Why could Her Majesty not see that all her pleading only made matters worse? *Perhaps it is a good thing I never have to worry about some man loving me*, Mary said, peering into a looking glass.

Once I might have said, *You cannot know that for certain*. I would not even have been lying—I would be *hoping* it was true. But the past years had taught me how dangerous hope could be. Loss of it was flaying away Her Majesty's strength one thin slice at a time. If only Philip would return to England, another child would come, she insisted, clinging to that belief with a wild light in her gaze that frightened even those who loved her best.

Her wildness grew more dangerous whenever Elizabeth's name was mentioned. Did the princess guess that the fact that the people would not tolerate Elizabeth's execution saved her from the block—just as their love had once saved this queen from Anne Boleyn?

In the four years following Mary Tudor's marriage, God seemed to have turned His back on the queen. No matter how she groped for heaven's approval, she could not gain it. Crops failed. Rebellions fomented. The reformers threatened her throne, her life.

Suspicion impelled her to fill the corridors with armed guards and heed the militant Catholics by hardening her stand on heretics. The identity of prisoners wending their way to the fires of Smithfield changed. No longer were the condemned limited to the clergy who were "poisoning" innocent minds with their radical ideas. Now simple folk who believed in Martin Luther's teachings were condemned: men, women, and children, even the aged and blind, God forgive Her Majesty.

The March winds of 1557 blew a ship carrying a hundred French-backed rebels into port at Scarborough with their leader, Thomas Stafford, and gave Philip the opening he had sought in the council's defenses. In the face of such an affront, Her Majesty's advisers had no choice but to ally England with the

Habsburgs' imperial cause in war against France. The youths that fluttered about us maids marched off to fight and die on the continent. It was to end in a disaster that would stain Mary Tudor's rule for all eternity. Calais fell—the English crown's last possession on the continent was lost to the French. We thought no worse fate could befall us.

But ill fortune was not finished with us. Crops failed a second time, the people already weakened from hunger. God applied a scythe in the form of the sweating sickness, cleaving bodies from souls by the thousands, then tens of thousands.

It was heaven's judgment against the queen, folk believed. Even the news that Her Majesty was again with child could not stop England from wondering what calamity might befall us next. Would our fate have been different if Jane were still queen? I could not help thinking. If she were here, could she comfort me? Jane accepted sorrow and never turned away from it. She expected little else. Why did four years' worth of grief suddenly gather in my chest? Was it the hopelessness of the queen's cause? The troubles that piled one upon the other until it seemed the world would stay forever dark?

"What ails you, Lady Katherine?" the queen demanded one day as we ladies dressed her. How could I tell her that I could not bear the sadness of watching the wreck of her dearly bought happiness?

"I am sorry to show my distress. I was thinking of my sister Jane."

One of the queen's favorite ladies bustled between us. "It has been over four years since that traitor died! Shame on you for bringing up her name!"

"Jane was my sister for all my life before she was a traitor," my voice cracked. "My father is dead, and my husband—" Why must I still think of Henry that way after all this time? I was foolish to expose my grief before the queen's ladies. Many among them still resented the queen's generosity to me. "I know time has passed, but I cannot help grieving. Everyone I loved has crumbled to dust, and I have nothing solid to anchor to."

Another maid sniffed. "What have you to say to that, Lady Mary? You seem solid enough." She thrust my twelve-year-old sister toward me, but Mary only peered up at me with an understanding that should have cut at my heart.

"You have your lady mother as well," someone said. "She is growing positively stout."

The queen managed to rouse herself in my defense. Or did her own heartbreak find an echo in my misery? "Poor Katherine. You are accustomed to being such a pretty maid. You should have countless admirers, delight in beautiful dresses, and deck yourself in bright jewels here at court. Does your life as one of my maids not please you?"

"She should be grateful!" a lady scolded. "You have taken guardianship of her and coddled her here at court in spite of her family's shame. What is the matter with the girl?"

"I am grateful! I am just . . ."

"Sad." Mary provided the word I could not find. "At Bradgate there is a wall, and the flowers there grow pale and drooping. Kat is a flower, and the sun cannot reach her."

A hint of the cousin who had welcomed us into her court with such forgiveness shone for a moment in Mary Tudor's weary gaze. "I will tell you how we will prevent it," she said, bending to speak to my sister. "We must send Lady Katherine away from the city, somewhere she can drink in the sunshine and get strong breathing fresh country air." She turned to me. "Your grief is real, little cousin. Your father and sister were attainted traitors, and your husband cast you off. Even years after the wound is dealt, it still gives one pain. Yes, I know what it is to be betrayed by those who are meant to love you."

She took her own kerchief and dabbed at my tears. "The question remaining is where to send you. I could send you to join your mother near Bradgate, but that would have too many painful memories for you—such places are haunted when those you love are gone. Too many rooms empty of beloved faces, their voices. Yet your sanctuary cannot be a place where there is so much cheer it will become painful." She paused to consider. "I know. Your friend Jane Seymour has been ill, though it seems not with the sweat. I have been planning to send all the maids away to save them from contagion. I shall send you and Lady Jane by horse-drawn litter to Hanworth Palace in Middlesex. You know the rest of the Seymour family, I recall. Your sister was betrothed to their eldest son Edward." The queen grew pensive. "I have always felt rather sorry for him. Wounds dealt in childhood are difficult to heal."

"Yes, Majesty." My heart had ached when Jane Seymour told the story of her father's downfall at Northumberland's hand. Her brother, then just ten years old, had ridden alone through the night in a desperate attempt to reach Pembroke, to get the earl to rush to their father's aid before Northumberland seized power. But my former father-in-law had betrayed the lord protector as he had betrayed me, playing to the main chance.

Edward Seymour. Jane had called him Ned. She had not loved him but had liked him well. He had always been too solemn for my tastes—not like Henry, with his bold good humor. Those few times I had seen him in the six years since his father's execution, I had avoided him, not wanting to see the marks left by the pain he had suffered at the hands of Northumberland and—I could not keep from thinking—my own father.

The queen's voice broke through my discomfort. "Yes, you should find succor with the Seymours," she continued. "They too went from their state as the most powerful nobles in the country to being nobody in the time it took their father's head to fall."

"Of late Your Majesty has restored much of their former wealth and position," a maid praised.

"It is easy to have empathy for those who suffer so much, though the Seymours' suffering was brought on by

Northumberland, while—it grieves me to say, Katherine—your father's downfall was due to his own wickedness. Still," the queen said, turning back to her ladies, "if anyone will understand our sweet cousin's grief, it is the Seymours." She cupped my cheeks in her hands. "Go to Hanworth, Katherine. Grow well and strong. By the time you return, I will have conceived a prince you will be able to dandle on your knee. Then we shall see about getting a husband for you. Yes, by the time you return, everything will be changed. You cannot imagine how changed everything will be." More prophetic words were never spoken.

How many times in my seventeen years had Tudor cousins altered my fate? Edward's death had taught me the price of ambition, Queen Mary the cost of betrayal and the danger of mercy. I had learned about grief and blame, innocence and guilt, love and hate. But as I alighted from the litter and looked into Ned Seymour's eyes, I could not know that Elizabeth Tudor, the cousin I scorned, would teach me the harshest lessons of all.

Chapter Twenty-four

Kat
Nearly 18 years old
Hanworth Palace, Middlesex
1558

OR AS LONG AS I COULD REMEMBER, I LOVED SPRING, BUT this year the season seemed a mockery. Gloom shrouded my world, and it seemed as if I would never be happy again. As the litter carrying Jane Seymour and me wound through the Middlesex forest toward the old royal palace of Hanworth, the death, hunger, and suspicion that spread across England stalked us like a wolf.

I did what I could to make poor Jane comfortable on our journey, but the lurching of the litter curdled her stomach, and I could see she was trying not to retch. Only when she spoke of seeing her brother again would she manage a weak smile. "My mother says he gathers admiring women as honey does bees. You must guard your heart, Kat."

"There is little danger where I am concerned. I want nothing but peace." *And Henry*, my heart added with a pang. I had little hope of either.

By the time we reached the old palace, I wanted nothing more than a basin of warm water and some clean linen to scrub the dirt of the road from my face. The litter had barely halted in the courtyard before eager servants whisked us to the comfort of our rooms.

I hoped I could follow my friend's example and lie down to

refresh myself. But when I curled up on the bed and closed my eyes, a figure of mist seemed to drift before me. My sister seemed more real than she had at any time since the headsman swung his ax.

"Are you here, Jane?" I asked. "I miss you. I think of you every day. Are you happy?" I could not imagine my solemn sister thus even in heaven. "I understand the sadness in you better now. It weighs so heavy that sometimes I fear I will never smile again."

You are not meant to be sad. Did I hear those soothing words, or did I imagine them? They seemed real, almost alarming, because they were so unexpected. I summoned my maid and had her brush the dust from my gown and arrange my hair to make ready for my introduction to Jane Seymour's family. But they would not be gathering for another two hours. Jane and her mother were closeted away together in private. It was hard to know what to do. I did not wish to return to my rooms, so I chose to step out into the garden.

A breeze rustled my apple-green petticoats, exposing the cloth of silver underskirt beneath. I lifted my nose to breathe deeply. How sweet the air smelled after the stench of the death-clogged city. I meandered along, discovering paths, engaged by exquisitely trimmed topiaries, tempted by the spattering of color here and there where flowers clustered. Squirrels chased through the branches, their bushy tales waving like banners. Birds hopped hither and yon in search of plump insects or stray seeds. Not until I turned onto the most distant and secluded path of all did I stumble across another human wanderer.

Watery sunlight blurred the figure just enough that I had to strain to make out his shape, as he crouched before a large hound, scratching the dog's floppy ears. Broad shoulders almost blotted out the animal's lean form, but I could see the blue velvet of the man's hat and tendrils of black hair feathering his nape. He angled his face just a trifle to one side, and I saw a nose shaped with the notorious hauteur of the beautiful and proud Duchess of Somerset. Ned Seymour. The sight of him reminded me of the wrong my family and their allies had done him.

I started to back away, not wanting to have to speak to him without his sister near, but the hound spied me. With an enthusiastic woof it lunged, knocking its master onto the turf. Ned muttered an oath, then caught sight of me and jumped to his feet with surprising grace. His handsome face reddened, and I sensed he was a man who valued his dignity.

"Down, Achilles," he commanded. The hound that gamboled about me dropped to the ground. Every muscle in the dog's body quivered with the effort it took to obey his master. I kept my attention fixed upon the beast, avoiding meeting Ned's eyes as long as I could.

"I only wanted to be alone for a little while," I stammered. "If you will pardon me, I will find some other place to go."

"I will not pardon you just yet, my lady. As host, I am bound to welcome you to my home." His smile curled, bitter. "I believe you are well acquainted with some former friends of mine. How did you leave the Earl of Pembroke and Henry, Lord Herbert?"

Ned Seymour meant to wound. I lowered my eyes to a clump of gillyflowers. "I am certain you know I have not been in charity with the Herberts these past five years."

"How do you fancy becoming invisible?" Ned asked. "It is a strange sensation, is it not, when people who were once your friends no longer choose to know you?"

He must have been thinking of the numerous times I had avoided him at court, hiding myself in crowds of friends, ducking behind a conveniently placed arras, or retreating to some faraway corner. My cheeks burned. "Perhaps your friends see you but are ashamed of the hurt their families have done you. Perhaps they think you would rather not encounter them." My voice wobbled despite my efforts to keep it steady. "I was glad to be able to tell your sister Jane how sorry I was for your troubles."

Ned's resentment cooled a little. "You have had plenty of your own misfortune since we Seymours fell from royal grace, have you not? I am grateful for your kindness to my sister. She wrote much of you from court."

"Jane talks of you all the time," I said, wondering what my friend might have revealed to him. "She remembers how brave you were, trying to help your father, and she speaks of how determined you are to regain your family's fortunes."

"It is a long climb back from the depths of royal disfavor— more difficult for us simpler folk than for those who are cousin to the queen."

I started to retreat, but Ned stopped me, his hand on my arm. "Forgive me, Lady Katherine. I did not mean to be churlish. You have lost not only your father but your sister as well. I was sorry to hear about Lady Jane. She deserved a kinder fate than to be caught up in the toils of the Dudleys. Northumberland deserved to die for his crimes against her more than for any of the other vile things he did."

"Yes." I recalled Northumberland's cruelty to my sister, her misery.

Ned drew a deep breath. "The duke asked to see me before his execution. Did you know that? He wished to ask my forgiveness for what he did to my father. I pardoned him as best as I could. But my father was a statesman, whose power left him open to such a fate. How do you forgive someone for causing an innocent girl to die such a gruesome death?"

What made me speak? I had kept the queen's silence all this time, but something in Ned's eyes loosened that secret embedded in my heart. "My little sister stole away to the Tower. Mary saw Jane die. She screamed in nightmares for months after. I am her older sister. I should have guessed what she was planning to do. I should have stopped her."

"Is she well enough now?"

"I do not know. Mary has always been difficult to understand. She and I were never close like she and Jane. Most times I try hard *not* to wonder what goes on in her mind. It disturbs me. I do not even know why I am talking about such things with you. I do not run about baring my soul to near strangers. You probably think me a very bad sister."

He gave a soft chuckle. "When I first saw you here among the roses, I was quite sure Achilles had caught a fairy." Suddenly he froze. "Lady Katherine, I fear my dog has damaged your gown." He gestured in the direction of the offense. A smear from a muddy paw marred my petticoat, the skirts disheveled from the dog's enthusiastic greeting.

"I do not mind a little dirt." I bent to stroke the hound's head.

Ned examined me intently. "Most ladies of my acquaintance would be most unhappy at having their gown spoiled."

"My maid is skilled in ridding cloth of such stains. From the time I was small, I was forever haunting the kennels and the stables and the mews, following after my lord father to pet the animals." I would never follow after my father again.

Silence fell between Ned and me, but I could not straighten up to make my escape while tears stood in my eyes.

Ned cleared his throat. Doubtless he had uncovered my secret, despite my efforts to hide behind a fold of the veil attached to the back of my headdress. Yet he did not try to soothe me, only gave me a moment to feel my private sorrow. "If you are fond of the outdoors, Hanworth should please you," he said after a while. "The gardens are pretty, and the stables will be bursting with new foals and calves, and the lambs will be scampering about. Mr. Newdigate takes great care of the grounds." At the mention of that scandal-linked name, I looked at Ned. "You heard that our steward has married my lady mother," he said.

"Your sister Jane spoke of it."

"The rest of court pressed Jane for gossip about the matter as well, I can imagine. It was a juicy morsel, a duchess marrying so far beneath her station. Another shift in fortune we Seymours share with you Greys. How did you manage *your* mother's unfortunate alliance with her master of the horse, three weeks after your father's execution?"

I drew back, and the hardness in his visage softened. "I meant no offense," he rushed to explain. "It must have made your mother's marriage harder for you, coming so soon after you lost your father." There was empathy in his voice and a hint of vulnerability. I was surprised he thought of my pain at all. It forged an unexpected sense of connection between us.

"Tell me, Lady Katherine, do you have any wisdom to share about navigating these rough waters?"

Long ago I might have spun out some fancy tale wherein I was the heroine. Now I was not even tempted to pretty up the truth. "I managed the scandal of my mother's marriage because I had no other choice. Just know that gossip will die down in time and some semblance of normalcy will return." I hesitated for a moment, stroking Achilles' ears. "It is hard when life is so vastly changed. It feels as though I will never get my bearings again. Sometimes I close my eyes and see the swing of the ax and think how frightened Jane must have been. I think how Father must have felt, knowing she was dead, waiting for his own turn upon the block. I miss them every day."

"It has only been four years, a very little time when it comes to healing such wounds. The horror will fade. You will remember happier times. In the end there were so many more of them." Ned's sad smile struck my heart. "Maybe when you feel ready, you could share some of those happy tales with me," he said.

"I barely know you." I could almost hear the argument he would raise. I had already spoken to him of feelings I shared with few, and he had been betrothed to my sister.

"The fact that we know each other so little is why I am the

perfect one for you to confide in. I cannot speak of Father with Jane or Mother—it hurts them. But no harm can come from talking to you of those we've loved and lost, fathers, a sister and friend and you lost a husband." My mind returned to Ned's bitter words about Henry.

Did Ned divine my thoughts? Mary said I kept them printed upon my brow for the whole world to read. His voice sounded, low. "It was cruel for me to mention Henry Herbert. Sometimes my infernal pride impels me to lash out when it is wounded. You are not to blame for the ill doings between our families in the past. Will you forgive me?"

I lowered my lashes. "There is nothing to forgive."

"That is not true, and we both know it. Think about what I have said, my lady, about sharing memories of happier times. I wish to banish some of my own shadows, and it would please me to see you smile."

"I will think on it." I took a few steps away before his voice stopped me, its tone a strange mixture of urgency and reluctance.

"Lady Katherine?"

"Yes?"

"There is one more thing I find I must say to you, though I cannot think it wise."

Something in his face made my knees tremble. "If it is not wise, perhaps you had better not."

He caught my hand as if he feared I would escape him, or that his courage might falter. I looked directly into his eyes and felt myself falling, as I had when I was a girl playing on the stones dotting the brook at Bradgate. The water soaked my skirts, pulling me deeper into the clear, sweet water.

"Henry Herbert is a damn fool," Ned said harshly. "If I loved you, there is nothing—not queen or family or fortune—could make me surrender you."

I turned and left, not guessing that Ned's words would return to haunt us both.

❧ ❧

$\mathcal{D}$ID I TURN CONJURER IN THE WEEKS THAT FOLLOWED, OR WAS Ned Seymour as eager to cross paths with me as I was with him? Often when I thought of Ned, he suddenly appeared, a slight flush on his high cheekbones, his eyes whispering deep magic, his instinctive arrogance worn softer by sorrows he had let no one see until that moment in the garden when we encountered each other.

I had forgotten what real happiness felt like, and recapturing it sweetened my world like the pieces of honeycomb Ned brought to me from Hanworth's beekeep.

We found cozy places beneath the willow trees, Ned and I— wove daisy chains, played at cards or hoodman blind those times Jane accompanied us outside. The country air began to kiss roses back into her fever-wasted cheeks. Or was it something else that made my dearest friend so happy—the thought of the two people she loved best growing close to each other?

We were wandering in a meadow one day, and I had gathered up a lamb in my arms. As the fluffy white babe sucked on my chin, Ned's grin filled his whole face.

"I have not seen Ned smile thus since he was ten years old," Jane confided. "It is your doing, Kat."

I blushed. "He deserves to be happy." Yet there was one at Hanworth who was not pleased by the change in Ned. Hospitable though Anne Seymour was, she regarded me with a cool courtesy that would have troubled me more were it not for her son's warmth.

As Ned and I spent lazy summer days leaning close in conversation, I felt that no one had ever understood my heart so well: the grief, the broken dreams that I tried to piece together so that the rest of my life would not stretch out bleakly.

I understood his moods in turn: the anger that sometimes hardened his mouth, the fierce desire to raise his family's fortunes, and that haunted air of unease when he was remembering how uncertain court life could be. One could lose everything in one cast of the dice. Both our families had done so before.

It was not so strange, then, that Ned's nerves grew tauter, and his gaze more brooding, save for flashes of defiance I sometimes noticed when he looked at me. I had not done anything to offend him—if anything, he sought me out more openly, providing diversions he knew would please me—marchpane shaped into knights and ladies, games of skittles in the sunshine, kittens just toddling out of their nests in the stable. He read to me, poetry and tales of King Arthur. He tempted me with the sweetest oranges, feeding them to me with his own fingers. One day when I had run ahead of Ned and Jane on a woodland path, I found Achilles caught in a poacher's snare. I rushed to his aid, the animal's teeth slashing my hand as I freed it. How shamed Achilles looked at his treatment of me when Ned wrapped the animal in his cloak and carried it to his master of hounds. I helped him fashion a splint and mixed a poultice that the keeper of our hounds had used to help with the healing. When Achilles was freed of the contrivance and bounded off to join the other dogs, Ned's grin shone bright as my own.

It was as if some bond of understanding had spun between Ned and me. I was even so foolhardy as to write to Mary of this connection. *I cannot explain it, but I feel as if I have known Ned forever, yet all the world is new.*

My sister's reply flew back with astonishing speed, its tone biting, as if she had spoken the words instead of scribing them with her awkward hand: *It is no surprise that Edward Seymour wants to know your secrets. Father broke off his betrothal to Jane, and Pembroke got Seymour's father executed. If I were he, I would like very much to steal your love from Henry Herbert. Then I could cast you aside before the whole court and shame you both the way people shamed me.*

I felt so sickened by her missive, I might have stuffed it into the fire, except that Jane rested in a chair nearby and would have questioned me. I tucked the paper beneath the top edge of my stomacher and fled out to the garden to cool my temper and to sift through the emotions Mary had loosed.

Why did she have to ruin the one good thing that had happened to me during these four years? Why make me question the only person who seemed to understand how I felt? Most painful of all, what if Mary was right to warn me?

Could Ned mean me harm? The possibility wrenched at my heart. I remembered the barely veiled mockery I had suffered during the months I first came to serve Queen Mary. I had felt stripped to my shift before the people of court. The prospect of suffering so again—and at Ned's hands—was more than I could bear.

I stumbled toward a rose bower where I loved to hide away. I had barely sat down upon the stone bench to gather my scattered wits when Ned Seymour strode into my retreat, a scowl creasing his noble brow.

I might have thought he followed me, except he appeared so surprised when he realized it was me. "Kat . . . I mean, Lady Katherine," he amended, looking a trifle guilty, a good bit angry and discomfited to see me.

Why? I wondered. Had I caught him concocting some scheme of revenge?

"Ned," I said, bowing so formally, he looked startled. I looked straight into his eyes as if to unravel truth from lie, to discern his true motives for his kindness to me.

"What are you doing here?" He hooked one finger in the collar of his pierced-leather doublet and gave it a tug. His face flushed. His eyes held a spark of anger that only sharpened when he looked at me. My fingers curled tight into my palms, as if to crush my uncertainty. The anger, resentment, the sense of embarrassment I felt emanating from him—were those his true feelings being revealed as Mary suspected?

"I ask you again," Ned pressed me. "What are you doing here? You look as brain-rattled as I feel. What has upset you so?"

"Nothing." My cheeks burned, and I touched the edge of parchment against my bosom. "I mean, it has little to do with you. It is a letter from my sister."

"Little Mary? She is not ill?"

"No. She only vexes me."

Ned's shoulders sagged in some measure of relief. "Sadly, it is a family duty to torment one of its members from time to time. I feared that my lady mother might have spoken to you."

"I have not encountered Her Grace yet today. Why should you fear it?"

"I would not have you caught amidst family unpleasantness. She and I have not seen eye to eye on a certain matter for some time, but we had rather danced around our differences in opinion. Today we cut to its core."

"My own mother and I do not always agree. It is difficult to be at odds with her."

"What is the matter of contention between you?"

I lifted one shoulder, a trifle embarrassed. "My lady mother is a most ambitious woman. She does not feel I have been forward enough in advancing my position at court."

I did not dare be plain about the reason for the war we had waged over the past years—Mother had done all she could to tempt her cousin to make me her heir in place of Elizabeth. I was not doing enough to help—so my mother claimed. But what could I do, save make myself as pleasant to Her Majesty as possible and please her regarding matters in which Lady Elizabeth tried the queen's patience?

The ladies of the bedchamber had often heard the queen say she wished I was her heir. She even spoke to her secretary William Cecil of making it so, but when it came to discussing it with her other ministers, she balked, insisting she would have a son to be heir. It seemed cruel to do as my mother wished and ask Cousin Mary what would happen to England should she be stricken with the sweat and die suddenly as so many had before her. Or to remind Her Majesty that should Elizabeth be crowned, England would lapse from the true faith, and Mary would be responsible for the lost souls of all her subjects. Was not that the same argument Northumberland had used to torture Cousin Edward in his final days?

"Katherine." Ned's voice reached through my musings. "You look so somber and grieved. Do not trouble yourself. This matter is between my mother and me. You must leave it so and promise you will not let it cloud your visit."

"But if you fear my speaking to your mother, your argument must hold something that concerns me. Is she wearied of my company here at Hanworth?"

"No!" Ned exclaimed with such vehemence, I sensed it was a lie. As if he saw the disbelief in my face he flushed. "Well, perhaps . . ." He kicked a clump of grass. "Even if my mother might blame you, it is not your fault."

What had I done to elicit such a reaction from the duchess? "I would not be a burden to your mother," I said, tempted to order my maids to begin packing.

"I am the one she is displeased with." Ned must have sensed my urge to flee. He caught my shoulder, knocking loose the letter from Mary. I grabbed for it, but Ned was swifter. I feared he had seen some of what Mary had written.

"You must not mind Mary," I hastened to say. "She is ever suspicious, and—" I stopped, not knowing how much Ned had truly seen. Perhaps I was exposing my sister's nasty accusations of him for no reason. But another part of me—the part that still ached for that ten-year-old boy who had failed to save his father—needed to know if what my sister said was true. The risk of angering him distressed me, but at least I would be able to find my answer in Ned's face. "Why have you been so kind to me, Ned?"

"You are my sister's friend. My family's guest," he began with a formality far from the natural communion that had graced so many of our conversations. His voice grew taut. "Is it some grave sin—my wanting to see you happy? My mother thinks so, and considering what you say about your sister, so does she."

"Mary thinks you wish to wound the Earl of Pembroke and strike back at my father for sundering your betrothal to our sister Jane."

Ned recoiled. "Your father is dead! Even if I did want revenge, I would hardly take it on you! As for Pembroke, he is not worth a moment of your concern." Ned's eyes narrowed. "Let the earl and his son take care of themselves."

The scorn in Ned's tone startled me, and I sensed layers of enmity lying deeper even than Pembroke's betrayal of Somerset. Enmity directed at Henry, when I believed the two had once been friends. "So you *do* wish the Herberts harm?"

"I do not wish them good fortune, but their fate has nothing to do with you."

"Some would say that it does. I was wife to Pembroke's son. If you were to court me and win my regard, it would be a fitting revenge."

"Do I have to have some dark, twisted motive for the way I feel about you? My own mother thinks I covet your affection because of your royal birth. She fears that I will lose my head for loving so near to the crown. When others learn of my attachment to you, they will think like your sister—that my goal is to humiliate Pembroke and the rest of the Herberts. Let them think the worst of me. I do not care. But you?" His voice broke, and I knew I had wounded him.

"Ned, I am sorry to distress you. I regard you most highly—"

"I love you, Kat." The words seemed torn from him, something painful, something awed. "Do you really think I would hurt you to settle a score with your father?"

I felt as if the ground beneath me vanished, washed away by

the emotions that tumbled through me. Joy and fear, shock and surprise, and the strange sense that I had been waiting my whole life to hear Edward Seymour speak those words to me.

Every part of me quivered with life. In that moment I was more certain than I had ever been of anything in my seventeen years. "I love you." I waited for joy to light his face, for him to gather me into his arms. He only regarded me with an unflinching gaze.

"I did not ask if you loved me." His voice stung me with its stubborn resolve. "Answer my question. Do you believe I would hurt you out of revenge?"

I could not bear the look in his eyes. "I do not *want* to believe it," I said so softly Ned had to bend close to hear. I knew he had, because I felt some thread between us sever. Even if I managed to tie the pieces together, I knew the knot would always be there, reminding us of my failure, his wound. He stepped away. "Ned, I do not wish to hurt you, but my answer is not as simple as it seems. Let us speak more of this!"

"There is nothing to say." His skin seemed to freeze with the iciness that his haughty mother was famous for. "If you believe I would hurt someone I love for such a vile purpose, then whatever love we feel for each other is hopeless. How could you ever trust me?"

I searched for words to wipe away the hard truth in his question. It was as if my little sister popped like some cursed troll inside my head, forming my words: "Can anyone really trust anyone?"

He pressed his knuckles to his chest and rubbed as if to shelter it from another heartbreak. "In that case I will travel to my sister Anne's estate in Northumbria as soon as I am able. I spent time there after our father's death."

So Ned's sister Jane had told me. I could imagine what that visit must have been like, considering who Anne's husband was. I remember the gossip in Father's great hall, how Somerset had attempted to ally himself with the wolfish Dudley faction by marrying his daughter to Ambrose, eldest of his enemy's sons. When Dudley had turned the full fury of his power upon the Seymours, the marriage must have become abominable to Ned.

Being under the guardianship of someone linked to your loved one's death was a special kind of torment. I had learned that serving Queen Mary. That Ned would go to an estate that held memories of such an anguished period in his life to escape me left me chastened.

Only revealing where my doubt had originated might stay him. "You wonder how I could believe you might use me in some scheme. My father loved me. He loved me better than either of my sisters. But if he had survived Queen Mary's wrath, I know he would have made me a pawn to gain the throne in time—even though that ambition had cost Jane her life and might demand the forfeit of my own. If I know this to be true about my father— who should have tried to extend my years as long as possible— is it so difficult to understand why I might wonder about your motives?"

Ned cupped my chin in his hand, ran the pad of his thumb across my lip. "It is not difficult to understand, sweetheart. But it is impossible to mend. Farewell, my Kat."

Three days later he was gone. I hid my tears from the duchess, but the look of relief on her face grated like grit in a wound. I could barely even speak of my loss to Jane, though she tried her best to comfort me. I had grieved over Henry, but this loss was different, as if some part of me—some piece of bone or sinew—were missing. I imagined seeing Ned again, speaking to him, making him understand. But I had seen the resolution in his face, the pride I had wounded, the sense of honor unyielding as stone.

Hanworth seemed to turn from high summer to winter the day Ned rode away. I carried winter inside me. When I received word from court that the danger of the sweat had passed, I was grateful. We maids were ordered to return in all haste to wait upon the queen.

Chapter Twenty-five

Mary
13 years old
October 1558

IT WAS HARD TO STAY SILENT WHEN THE NORNS WERE weaving, spirit ladies shaping even the queen's fate in this darkened chamber where my cousin waited for a child that would never come. Her eyes gleamed wild like wet clay, and her fingers worked feverishly on a tiny gown. She pricked herself with her needle again and again, spotting the fine linen with her blood.

Cousin Mary would have poured out the last drop within her if it would quicken the bulge in her belly. Her ladies, her midwife, as well as her husband, who was far from England, all feared the babe was a chimera conjured by her frantic need. They feared she would cling to the belief that the child was only late, as she did before. Those who loved Queen Mary best cringed because she would have to face the humiliation of leaving her confinement chamber a second time, looking like a misguided fool to the world.

I wished that that was the worst injury fate meant to deal her, but I knew different. I stole up to her while she was dozing in her chair. When no one was looking, I pressed my palm against her belly just as I had done once before.

The doctors and midwife were wrong to think nothing grew inside her. Cousin Mary was growing death.

St. James's Palace
November 1558

The devil did not need to jab at Cousin Mary with hot irons and fiery brands, not when she was so apt at torturing herself. In the time since we ladies reunited at court after the danger of the sweating sickness receded, Her Majesty's condition went from bad to worse. Now, here at her palace of St. James, no one could deny the end was near.

Kat could not bear to see the queen's suffering. My sister ever had a tender heart, but since her summer with the Seymours, the slightest brush with life's roughness has scraped her raw, making her bleed inside. She would not tell me what hurt her. She would not confide in me anything at all. Sometimes she looked as if she almost hated me—for the letter I wrote about Ned Seymour, I would guess. I did not mind so very much. Even when Kat and Lord Hertford were both at court, they barely spoke. I was glad. If the truth about Edward Seymour's motives hurt her now, at least it was a private wound, not the public shame I believed he had in store for her. Kat had borne too much of that already watching the downfall of Jane and our father.

She was reliving that time as she watched courtiers who once fawned at the queen's feet melt away from Mary's presence to swear their loyalty to the banished Elizabeth. How it pained Kat to see allegiances shift yet again. Was there no one in our world who would stand loyal? To a child? To a queen? To a wife? A religion? A cause? Was everyone like grass blades in the wind, blown this way, then another? Willing to sell themselves for royal favor, personal gain, or merely to hold on to wealth, position, their lives?

Cousin Mary groaned, and I watched my sister turn her face away and press her hand to her mouth to keep from retching. The thing inside Cousin Mary had grown teeth and claws that tore at her stomach. Sometimes I watched her swollen belly and feared that the thing would split her open like an overripe peach, exposing all that was rotting.

"Forgive me . . . God forgive me . . . I have failed Holy Mother Church . . ." Her Majesty wept, the sound half drowned out by the priests that droned their prayers all around her. I wished I could make them go away. They reminded her of every sin and failure.

"I must . . . must . . . rally." She clutched her favorite lady's hand so tight that Susan Clarincieux bled where fingernails cut. "Anne Boleyn's bastard must not . . . take throne. Protestant whore . . . destroyed *mi madre*." She grimaced in anguish. "Cannot let . . . enemies win. Elizabeth just like . . . her mother. Black-eyed whore . . . know she whored with Thomas Seymour . . . could never—never prove it. Could have . . . rid of her, like her mother. Why did I not . . . execute her? I do not know why."

I did. The people would not have stood by and let the daughter of their king die. They had saved Mary's life, and now they protected Elizabeth's.

"Majesty, you must not torment yourself," Lady Susan pleaded, her voice hoarse with offering comfort. "It does not matter anymore."

"Of course it matters! She will lead England to hell with her heresy. All those souls. My subjects' souls . . . they will be lost. God . . . hold me . . . accountable . . ."

She let loose a wail that made the small hairs on my arms stand on end. Kat's shoulders quivered, and I knew she was crying. Every lady save Susan buried their tears in their hands. I could not endure it another moment.

I nudged Lady Susan. She looked over, quite hopeful of being relieved, but when she saw it was only me, her face fell. "I would take a turn at my cousin's side," I said softly.

Lady Susan frowned. "I cannot leave her to the ministrations of one so young. And strange."

"Cousin Mary," I said. I reached out to her with my heart, willing her to answer.

"How dare you speak so to Her Majesty!" Clarincieux blustered, but the queen looked at me.

"M-Mary . . . little friend . . . sorry . . . so sorry . . . one more . . . sin. Promise broken. Jane . . . Lady Jane . . . Forgive me, M-Mary . . . ," the queen gasped.

"I do."

"Call my council. Call Cecil. I will tell them . . ."

Did she not know? Many had melted away, riding to Lady Elizabeth, to court her favor. Kat and I had watched them go, remembering how many of the same men had slipped from London's Tower when Jane was queen, riding off to join Mary's cause.

"Drink, cousin. Rest." I pressed a goblet of watered wine to her lips.

"Cannot—cannot. Must save . . . people from damnation. Make your sister queen."

My hand shook. Wine splashed the queen's hand, the liquid thin red. It transformed before my eyes into rivers of blood flooding from Jane's ax-severed neck.

"What did Your Majesty say?" I heard Lady Susan ask. But before she could discern it, I elbowed a ewer from the table. It clattered to the floor, its contents spattering gowns and prayer books. Women and servants flew about to bring the room back to order, the lot of them scolding, calling me clumsy. I did not care. I had won a few precious moments to speak to the queen alone, or as privately as would ever be possible in this life.

The queen's voice rasped like an iron blade dragged through pebbles. "You will see what a fine queen your sister will be, Mary," the queen insisted, oblivious to the confusion around her. "Katherine found the true faith while I guided her. I comfort myself she will keep it once I am gone."

Would she? I pictured my sister at mass, reciting the prayers

Jane had died rather than speak, observing the rituals Jane considered superstitious nonsense, bowing to the Host as if it were alive, honoring the priests Jane saw as corrupt. Had Kat come to believe the Catholic tenets, or was she merely trying to survive, as our mother instructed? In the end, did it matter? One thing Cousin Mary and her husband had accomplished was to cleave England's people into two distinct groups who hated each other with alarming passion.

Horrifying scenes played out in my imagination—God at war in England once again, Reformers and Catholics who had once been friends butchering each other with pike and ax and flame. Making Kat queen during such turmoil would only heat that ocean of hatred to scalding. The people would not care that she was no bastard and so was more fitting to ascend to England's throne. They would not care that she was rightful heir not only by Queen Mary's declaration but by her brother King Edward's devise for succession as well. The country folk, the town folk would demand King Henry's daughter—the child who looked more like His Majesty than any of his others, the beautiful, red-haired young princess who was worlds different from the shriveled, disillusioned woman who had brought a Spaniard to sit upon a consort's throne, the queen who had lost Calais and rekindled Smithfield's terrible flames.

I did not like Cousin Elizabeth, and God knew she recoiled from my deformity. But if Kat took the crown and Elizabeth had to win it from her, I knew Elizabeth would take Kat's head. I had to try to stop it.

"Cousin Mary, I beg you, do not—do not put Kat in danger. Do not force me to gamble another sister."

"Gamble . . . I have wagered much. Your mother . . . Frances . . . she told me long ago to name Katherine."

"But our lady mother does not love me or Kat as you do."

"Mother . . . always love . . . her children." Wistfulness

softened the pain-whitened line of her lips. "If I had children . . . would love them."

I sought a way to comfort her, to draw her mind from the poison that thoughts of Elizabeth released in her. "They are waiting for you in heaven, cousin. Your children." It was not a lie. If heaven were bliss and God were kind, surely he would give Cousin Mary a child to hold.

"Can you not hear them?" I asked her. "Listen. *Tir-a-lira*." I hummed the melody under my breath.

My cousin's eyes widened. "Music . . . sounds like angels."

"Can you see them? Tell me, cousin. Are they pretty?"

"G-golden hair . . . pretty. Not . . . like me. Not . . . like you, little Mary. K-Katherine . . . pretty. Pretty, pretty queen."

Tears burned my eyes. "You must not take her from me. I cannot see her die. I beg you, if you ever loved me at all."

"Poor . . . ugly creature. No husband . . . love you."

Was she speaking of me or of herself? I did not know.

On the seventh day of November a somber delegation from Parliament came to her bedside, reminding me of black crows come to pick a corpse clean. They pressed her to name her successor.

I stood there, feeling Jane's ax hover over us again. I thought of my mother, how angry she would be if Kat were not named queen. I looked at Kat, wondering if she would hate me even more because I had begged the queen not to choose her. I held my breath, wondering if the cousin I loved had the strength to do what I asked of her.

Her Majesty's face contorted in an agony that cut deeper than the disease growing inside her. She locked her eyes on my desperate countenance and forced from her lips the most difficult words she would ever speak: "I name the Lady Elizabeth heir."

Chapter Twenty-six

Kat
Queen Elizabeth's court
1559

HE LAST TIME CORONATION BELLS RANG THROUGH the streets of London and a new queen mounted the English throne, I was the daughter of a traitor and the sister of the girl forced to steal the crown. I was the cast-off bride of a husband I loved and the disgraced child of a duchess who married her master of the horse. My burden of misfortunes grew so weighty during those dark days that I was certain no other season in my life could be more unbearable than that first year Mary Tudor was queen. But I would gladly have traded those early days under the old queen for the far more sprightly court of my cousin Elizabeth.

Queen Mary had not wished to wound my sisters and me, though she did so to gain a husband and keep her crown. Elizabeth cut with a subtler blade, but she left her marks on purpose, making certain they were visible to any courtier with eyes. From the moment I watched the Earls of Pembroke and Arundel gallop through the gates toward Hatfield carrying the ring of state taken from Queen Mary's dead finger, a flood of bitterness welled up inside me. Anne Boleyn's bastard would be queen.

Every scornful word our mother had ever spoken of Elizabeth echoed in my mind, every accusation Queen Mary had ever voiced stirred my discord. Most poisonous of all was the knowledge that Elizabeth had survived Wyatt's rebellion and countless other plots, survived even though the queen bore her a malice she had never borne Jane.

Elizabeth did not deserve such triumph, not when Jane— good, pious Jane—lay buried beneath the stones at St. Peter ad Vincula.

Elizabeth is as sly and cunning as her mother, Her Majesty had often claimed, her lip curled as if she tasted bile. *Never will Elizabeth be queen.*

I had believed her. So had many other courtiers, especially during the turbulent time Jane died. No one had expected Elizabeth Tudor to leave the Tower alive or Robert Dudley either. Yet now the two childhood friends preened like pigs draped in diamonds, making a sickening show of honoring Queen Mary's memory. But all their finery, all the blazing candles, and all the masses said did not cover the stink of Elizabeth's hypocrisy.

Did no one dare tell her how ridiculous it looked when she made a show of mourning her sister? Had she prayed in secret for the queen's death? A terrible sin, that. Treason. Yet if Elizabeth even once asked God to deliver her from captivity or deadly peril, she had committed that transgression.

Somewhere beneath her mask, Elizabeth was gloating. Did that accusation show in my eyes? My sister Mary's? In any of us who had loved the dead queen? Strangely, I think Elizabeth preferred our stark honesty to the cloying interest of those now close to her. At least our opinion of Elizabeth was honest. Sometimes it seemed she trusted us better than those who had contacted her in secret during her years as an imprisoned princess.

I was glad to see the wariness in Elizabeth's eyes. It comforted me to know she carried within her the memory of a Tower cell, that she had silently counted how many steps it would take to walk from that prison, across Tower Green, to mount the steps to the scaffold, cross its straw-strewn expanse, and kneel before the block where Jane had lost her head.

My scheming cousin claimed to have been innocent of any knowledge of the plots mounted on her behalf through the years, but no one could look at her and believe her. She had a gift for intrigue. She invited it, as surely as Jane had shied away from deceit.

Little was simple in Elizabeth's world, where most things were well plotted. But she could not have concealed her reaction to my younger sister even if she had cared to: horror at Mary's crooked back, disgust at her ill-favored face. The queen all but shuddered whenever Mary drew near. But instead of dropping her gaze or attempting to make herself pleasant, Mary confronted the queen in her most irritating fashion, staring at her with that probing gaze that forced people to face the ugliness inside themselves.

Who had first called my sister "Crouchback Mary"? One of the queen's intimates? Who began the sniggering and slights that soon colored all our days? I could not say.

I first felt the sting of Queen Elizabeth's vengence the day she stripped away our position as ladies of the queen's bedchamber. She lowered our station before all the court, made us seem like ill-mannered pups, and banished us as far from her company as possible without causing a stir.

The queen's staunchly Protestant friends would never forgive the Greys for "betraying" our religion in spite of Jane's great sacrifice. When one of them closed the door pointedly in my face, I might have wished with all my heart to go to the country, be quiet someplace, at peace. I might have . . . were it not for the somber, dark-haired man who watched me across every room, his eyes so dark with feeling, it choked any words that I might want to speak.

Ned. As much as I suffered on my own account and Mary's, it was more painful to watch him from a distance, dealing with the rise of the hated Dudley family once again. Robert Dudley was obviously the queen's favorite—she promoted her childhood friend to master of the horse, where he spent every day with her. But the way she looked at him was anything but innocent. She simpered whenever he was near, touched his sleeve or his shoulder with the long white fingers she was so vain of. She hung upon his every word and danced with him with such abandon that no one doubted she loved him.

Many in the court who loathed the ambitious Dudleys whispered that it was lucky Lord Robert had taken a wife in the years before he ever could have imagined he might aspire to become royal consort.

Robert Dudley, who had failed to capture Cousin Mary during that brief, tumultuous time when Jane was queen. His failure had cost Jane her life.

I understood how painful it must be for Ned to see the enemies of his father soar to prominence ahead of his own attempt to regain his family's position in society. But I could not tell him. Even if Ned had been willing to speak to me, I was under the scrutiny of the queen's minions—and I had learned my lesson in humiliation that long-ago day at Queen Mary's coronation when Henry Herbert had snubbed me.

Elizabeth had spies everywhere, watching for the slightest sign of impropriety in her ladies, ready to unleash her famous temper and send anyone of questionable morals back to their country homes.

The tiniest breath of scandal was enough excuse to rid herself of those she disliked. Prim, maidenly, vain, and sly, she disgusted me with her hypocrisy. When my sister Jane had returned from being chief mourner at her beloved dowager queen's funeral, she had told me about Elizabeth.

"Kat, you would not have been able to bear it," she had whispered by the nursery fire one night. "The queen was so fragile, her belly all swollen with child. She and I were walking near the great hall when we stumbled upon Thomas Seymour and Lady Elizabeth with her petticoats caught up and her legs showing." Jane's face had turned as red as a hot fire poker, her eyes filled with shame and horror. "My beloved mistress was poisoned from that moment. It ate inside her, slowly, until when her babe was born, she was almost glad to die."

I could not get that image out of my mind. Kind Dowager Queen Catherine Parr seeing her husband betray her with the girl she had loved like a daughter. Thomas Seymour had brought down his own family with his greed for power as well. Had Ned hated the wastrel uncle who was responsible for the downfall of the father Ned loved?

As the months crawled past—January with the queen's coronation, February with its anniversary of Jane's execution, the spring with crops once again growing and new lambs in the meadows—I wondered if it would have been more merciful for Elizabeth to send Mary and me away: an honest act of enmity, instead of the secretive ones she used to undermine our footing.

By the time another summer came, the tension between my cousin and me grew suffocating, old wounds and slights layered with new ones dealt to her vanity.

One day as we chose partners for the dance at the palace of Nonesuch, the queen noted Robert Dudley staring at me. "Lord Robert, has Lady Katherine broken out in a pox? I vow, you stare at her most strangely."

"Forgive me, Your Grace. I could not help it. I recently saw a portrait of her grandmother, the queen of France. Lady Katherine is very like her."

"Ah, the Tudor Rose," I heard someone behind me say with a wistful admiration. "She was the most beautiful princess in Christendom."

"She was indeed," my mother's friend Bess of Hardwick said. "Lady Katherine is very like her. Even to her nose, with its elegant little dip in the center."

Did I imagine it, or did every eye in the chamber shift from me to the queen's hawkish beak? Was that the spark that ignited the queen's temper? Or was it Robert Dudley's next words?

"The Tudor Rose's beauty was not half as remarkable as the history of her great love," he said. "It is one all mortals might envy."

Elizabeth's features sharpened, her tone a verbal blade. "You would do well to recall that the queen of France shamed herself by wedding a man with no noble blood. My father befriended this commoner, then most generously raised him to a dukedom. How did Charles Brandon repay my father's generosity? His king had trusted him to escort Mary Tudor back to England, but he stole her. Lady Katherine is descended from that thief."

"Majesty, I did not mean to offend you—"

"Brandon was fortunate in my father's mercy. He deserved to lose his head. Now I think on it, he ushered in a tradition with the house of Suffolk. Two of their number have paid fair price for their treachery."

I saw Mary's horror, knew she was reliving the scene at Tower Green all over again. I wanted to strike out at Elizabeth for being so cruel. "Your father's mercy did not extend to everyone," I said. "The Boleyns were not so fortunate." The words slipped out.

Hatred flashed in Elizabeth's eyes. "Enemies can spread lies about even the most upright figures. It is difficult to sort out what is truth. Fortunately, I have my father the king's intellect, as well as his Tudor red hair." She was pointing out those traits to deflect old rumors that she was not King Henry's child. No one who saw their portraits together could doubt that the vengeful king was her father. "As for intellect, it would do me good to match wits with someone who is my equal in such pursuits. Are you a scholar, Lady Katherine?"

She was seeking to trap me in some brash claim that I was.

Then she could humiliate me before all these people. Better to be honest. "I do well enough with my studies, but I am not like my sister Jane."

The queen looked as if she smelled something distasteful. "I remember your sister as far too sour and sober during our time together as children. In fact, she was quite dull. Not the one people sought out when merriment was in the offing, eh, Robert?" she asked, nudging her favorite with one damask-clad elbow.

"Merriment has its dangers, Majesty," I interjected before Dudley could reply. Mary kicked me, but it was too late to take the words back. I did not care. How dare Elizabeth say such things about my sister after the harlot's tricks that the Boleyn bastard had played upon her betters! "Even your old tutor Roger Ascham judged Lady Jane the most learned young woman in England. No one could surpass her."

"If she had lived—but you see, she is dead, while I not only breathe but am queen. Tell me, cousin, who is the more intelligent between us now?"

Dudley chuckled. "Most true, Your Majesty. The lady was not as intelligent as people thought."

"My sister valued her honor and virtue even more than she did her mind. Traits I know the dowager queen Catherine Parr came to cherish when Your Majesty and Lady Jane were both under her guardianship."

Even my blunt sister looked aghast. I could feel every eye in the chamber on me, but my own attention was fixed on the queen. Veins in her temple throbbed under white skin, her cheekbones bloodred. Every member of court knew I was hinting at the old scandal.

"I dislike your tone when speaking to your queen!" Robert Dudley blustered.

"The Greys were ever a vain, arrogant lot," the queen snapped. "One would think the fact that two of your number are shorter by a head would take some of the arrogance out of you, but apparently not. I will take more immediate measures. You will leave court."

"Majesty, I beg you—" my sister began.

"Be quiet, crouchback! You may mourn your sister's leaving with others foolhardy enough to miss her. Think how disappointed the Spanish ambassador will be. He quite worships at your sister's shrine."

It was true. Chapuys had been kind to me, seeking me out to inquire about simple things: how I liked a new court musician, whether I found the latest masque entertaining, if I might enjoy oranges someone had brought from Valencia.

"Ambassador Chapuys knew us from when Cousin Mary was queen," my sister insisted, sensing we were treading on dangerous ground.

"There *are* those who do not share Chapuys's affection for you, Lady Katherine," Her Majesty said. "In truth, some will rejoice to see you gone. Do you not agree, my lord of Pembroke?" The queen turned to the man I loathed. "You will no longer have to endure watching your son make calves' eyes at the lady. What of you, Robert?" she confronted her favorite. "Will you grieve the loss of Lady Katherine's company?"

Dudley swept his hand to his heart in a gesture as grand as a player in a masque. "How could any man notice another woman while you are about, Your Majesty?"

"Not even your own wife," I muttered, but did not finish what I wanted to say: *The fact that a man is wed does not stop Elizabeth from sinking her claws into him.*

Robert Dudley's wife, Amy Robsart, must have felt the grief the dowager queen had. The Dudley marriage had been a love match, one Lord Robert pressed his powerful father to allow. What must it be like for the woman to be banished to the country while rumors swirled about her husband? Even far away, she must know of the man's affair with the queen.

The queen had heard me, and her black eyes burned with fury. "You will learn to curb your tongue! You have been sour since I did not name you lady of the bedchamber. We all must learn to keep our place in the natural order of things."

The natural order of things? God's chain of being: people strung like pearls in their proper place, from the most glittering to the most common. Elizabeth Tudor—a bastard, an adulteress, the daughter of a witch—belonged far down that strand, not at its crown!

"I do not wish to see you again until you have learned humility," the queen said.

I forced myself to curtsy, then backed from the chamber. I had scarce taken three steps down the corridor when I heard awkward footsteps hastening after me and a familiar harsh breathing. My sister was trying to catch up to me.

For a moment I thought of walking faster to escape her, but Mary was stubborn and would not give up so easily. Better to get this conflict between us over.

"What is wrong with you?" Mary gasped as soon as she reached me. "You have been annoying Elizabeth like a child poking a beehive. You'll get no honey that way. You'll only get stung. Now you've kicked the hive over, and the whole swarm is circling around you. It is a good thing the queen is sending you away before you do something even more reckless!"

"You are lecturing me about blunt speech?" I laughed. "That is a change!"

"You are supposed to be the charming sister! You should know that of all the things Elizabeth hates about the Greys, your beauty is the one she will not be able to forgive. She is vain, forever expecting the men to flock around her. But even Robert Dudley follows you with his eyes, while William Herbert sulks about for love of you, and the Spanish ambassador regards you with admiration."

"It is not my fault if they do! I do not charm them on purpose!"

"I believe you."

"I only want to be left alone!" I thought of Ned and all I had lost.

"You will have the chance to prove it. Ned Seymour is coming this way, and if a face tells tales, he is intent on speaking to you."

Something with wings tried to beat its way out of my chest as he drew near for the first time since Hanworth. I allowed myself to look straight into his face.

"Lady Katherine," he said, in that voice so familiar it felt like my own. "I tried so hard not to speak up for you. I knew it could only make things more painful for us both. But after what just happened in the queen's chamber, I could not bear to have you leave court without my telling you how it grieves me to see the way Her Majesty treats you."

"She is lucky to be no more than exiled from court!" Mary said.

I bade her go away. She did so grudgingly, leaving Ned and me alone. I no longer feared Elizabeth's spies. What more could they do to me?

"I will not mind leaving so much," I said. "Court is a painful place for me now."

"You must be missing Queen Mary. Is it difficult to see Elizabeth in her place?"

"Cousin Mary was kind to me. Elizabeth is most decidedly not. It is hard to bear."

"I have found much that is hard to bear of late. Most of all, being apart from one I regard most tenderly." Undisguised longing filled his eyes, no small evidence of vulnerability in one so proud. "I have missed you dreadfully. Cannot count the number of times I have seen an animal's antics or heard some bit of a poem and think of how much pleasure it would bring you. I feel this urge to rush off to find you, to try to make you smile. You smiled quite often at Hanworth. You do not smile nearly enough anymore."

His gentleness pained me more than the queen's cruelty. "My time at Hanworth seems like a dream. I must see the world as it is now. Even Avalon must sink into the mists. My sister Jane always warned me of the danger in thinking that such myths can become real."

"The world would become a very bleak place if there were no more dreams in your eyes, my fairy maid."

Grief caught in my breast. I looked away from him. "Dreams are painful. I do not wish to have them anymore. I came close to making one real, but it hurt so much to lose it."

"Have you lost it?" he asked.

"I am determined to snuff it out, like the embers on a hearth." I tried to smile. "You must not worry about me."

"Katherine, I have spent these many months hating that Queen Elizabeth and her favorites inflict suffering on you, watching you bear it with such courage and grace."

"I am not your responsibility, Ned."

"Worse still was the knowledge that no matter what wounds they dealt you, they could never hurt you as badly as I did that last day at Hanworth. Most of your sister's accusations as to why I courted you were nonsense. But winning you away from the Herberts—in the beginning, perhaps that was a part of my attraction to you."

It hurt me to hear it.

"I was so concerned about the blow dealt to my pride that I did not stop to think how terrible it must be for you to know that your father would cast you into danger if he could. A parent should protect his child. Angry as my mother made me when she tried to forbid my love for you, I knew that her love for me was greater than any hope of wealth or station would ever be. She would rather have me be a simple country nobleman, far from the dangers of court, than be a powerful man in danger."

"I envy you that. Strange, is it not, that even with all of my father's ambitions for us and all of my mother's pride in her royal blood, the only thing I ever hoped for was marriage to a nobleman who loved me. I delighted in the rich gowns and jewels and dancing, but it was like eating too many sweetmeats. In the end I hoped to break my fast with simpler fare."

"Perhaps you might have your wish after all," Ned said as he touched my hand. "I am certainly a nobleman, and I promise you that I love you."

"What of the trust you feared I could never give you?"

"Who in your life has given you reason to trust? Not your father. Not your mother. Certainly not Pembroke or Henry Herbert. I will never forsake you, not if the fate of the whole kingdom should turn on our love."

"You do not know the kind of pressure that can be brought to bear," I said. "Queen Mary did not wish to order Jane's death, but when her hand was forced, she did what she had to do in order to survive. Someday you—for all the love and honor you vow to me this day—might be faced with the same terrible choice. When I think on it, even Henry Herbert was trying to keep the rest of his family safe when he sacrificed me."

Ned stiffened at the mention of that name. "I am made of stronger stuff than Herbert. I love you more than my family—for I would defy my mother's wishes to wed you. I love you more than my pride, because I would wed you in spite of what people said of me. I wish to marry you, Kat."

"Marry me?" I scarce believed that Ned had truly come back to me.

"Yes. Marry you. If you will have me for a husband, I will never forsake you."

"But I am of royal blood. The queen must give permission. I cannot think Elizabeth Tudor would do anything that might secure my happiness."

"Perhaps not now, with such hot words between you. But time will cool her temper. We need only wait and do what we can to prepare an argument that will convince the queen that letting us wed is the wisest course. Let us go to your mother and ask for her aid. Perhaps she can convince the queen that it would be in her best interest to have you far from court and safely wed. I think Her Majesty would be glad to be rid of you. The comparison between her hawkish nose and your sweet one is more than Elizabeth Tudor can bear." Ned smiled and ran his finger down my small retroussé nose. "You have a face so perfect, any artist would wish to paint it. Any woman would envy it, including the queen."

Joy rose up in me. "What the queen should envy me is this: to have Ned Seymour's love."

He smiled—the smile that had haunted my dreams. "All will be well, sweetheart. Go to your lady mother. I will join you there to ask her help. She is a most formidable lady. There is no stone she cannot move if she chooses."

❦ ❦

NEARLY A MONTH LATER I ARRIVED AT BRADGATE, SURPRISED TO find my lady mother sick abed. Pale as she was, she still seemed invincible, as if she could order the earth to spin in whatever direction she pleased. It was unthinkable that she might not recover.

But something new softened her features, as if time had mellowed the hardest edges within her. Was that Adrian Stokes's doing? I wondered, from the warm harbor of my own great love. Had the master of the horse made her happy? It seemed so. I could not begrudge her that. But changed as she was, old habits die hard.

I will never forget the look in her eyes when Ned joined me and we stood before her, the avid gleam of ambition. The slick sweet taste of hope was on her lips, and the cogs of her mind turned like the workings in the Kratzer clock I had seen at Hampton Court, telling not only the time of day but the ebb and flow of the tide on the Thames.

She believed our family's tide was turning as well: a Grey matched with a Seymour would mean royal Tudor blood sweetened by traces of the Plantagenet Edward III that Ned inherited through his mother, Anne.

"You are the obvious heir to the queen," my mother insisted, in the days after Ned left to return to court. "Elizabeth is yet unmarried and has the horror of her mother's death. There has always been something unnatural about her. She cannot wed Dudley, and she will not have anyone else. In fact, it is rumored that when she was eight years old, she informed Lord Robert she would never marry at all."

"No queen can rule alone," I said. "She must marry."

"Even if she does, you might succeed her. Many a treacherous slip lies between the marriage bed and being delivered of a healthy babe, as Queen Mary found. Elizabeth knows this as well. Make yourself pleasing to her. Indulge in no more temper tantrums. Your father always said you would make the perfect queen. Do you remember those times he played with you—placing crowns of daisies on your head and teaching you to walk with your chin held high?"

"It was his favorite game."

"The game is not lost. If ever you loved your father at all, you owe it to him to channel all your effort in that direction."

Did I? Oh, I loved my father—of that there was no doubt. But did that mean I must cast myself into the dangerous currents of court life, scheme as Elizabeth had done, entice allies to my cause, and tempt others and myself with what some would call foolhardy recklessness and others treason? I had been so certain that all I wanted was a simple life, but now I could hear my father's chuckle, feel his rein-callused fingers brushing my curls as he settled yet another flower crown atop my head.

It is a pity you are not my firstborn. You would be far more suited to greatness than Jane. No queen in the world could match you, Katherine—not even your grandmother, beautiful though she was. If ever a girl was molded by God to wear a crown, my darling daughter, it was you.

"Edward Seymour will help you reach your father's goal," my mother insisted. "If you marry an English earl, people will support you even more as heir. He has Plantagenet blood in his veins, no matter how thin it might be. Many fear what befell England when Mary wed a foreign prince—wars we were dragged into, the loss of Calais, the pope thrusting his power back onto English shores."

"Queen Elizabeth could wed an Englishman."

"But she will not. She only has eyes for Robert Dudley, and many hate and mistrust him as much as a foreigner. What is that strange look upon your face?"

"The crown did not bring Queen Mary happiness, nor Jane, nor even my grandmother. She did not find happiness until she wed your father."

"She had done her duty and was known as the French queen until the day she died! You have done nothing as of yet to advance your family. At present just be grateful that your natural inclination bends toward our ultimate goal. The moment I am up from my sickbed, I will go to plead with the queen. I will tell her I could die with my heart at rest if I knew you were safely wed to Lord Hertford. She will grant me my wish. I have swayed queens who had much more reason to hate us. I saved your father from a traitor's death the first time and won back most of our lands and titles. I gained you and Mary places at court."

You could not save Jane. You did not even try, my heart accused, though I would never say so aloud.

"You and Lord Hertford will be wed by next year, I'll be bound. Spring will be a lovely time for the celebration. You ever loved spring, Katherine."

My throat felt strangely tight, surprised and touched as I was that she remembered it of me, but I had set my heart upon an earlier date.

"I would rather marry in October, on Jane's birthday." I wanted to somehow feel that Jane had a share in my happiness.

I was not certain what I expected from my mother—some stinging comment about letting the dead lie quiet, a scolding about the danger of reminding anyone at court about the Grey family's traitorous past.

Instead she turned her face away. I dared not imagine it might be to hide tears. "We could serve sugared almonds and gingerbread among the finer stuff at the banquet," she said. They had been Jane's favorites.

Even now, years later, I close my eyes and imagine the wedding feast that would never be. What might have happened had my mother arisen from her sickbed and sought Elizabeth's favor on our behalf? But come November twenty-first, that formidable lady who had survived so many trials—the deaths of two baby sons, the execution of a daughter, a son-in-law, and her own beloved husband, as well as the stripping away of her fortune—that woman finally faced an adversary who could defeat her. Death.

Ned and I still loved, but our best hope of winning Elizabeth's approval vanished the day we buried my mother.

1560

When Elizabeth summoned me back to court, I could tell that something in the queen had changed. She warred with her advisers as they became more strident, pushing her toward marriage. Her temper grew more capricious with everyone save Robert Dudley and—chillingly, I confess—to me. I found myself swept into the circle of ladies who attended the privy chamber, the queen treating me as if no ill feelings had ever stewed between us. It confused me. Even Mary, fifteen and still banished to the fringes of the queen's attendants, mistrusted my "good fortune."

Did Elizabeth seek me as an ally, or was she merely hoping to give her courtiers some other puzzle to engage their minds instead of keeping track of the time Robert Dudley spent alone with Her Majesty in the queen's privy chamber? I dared ask no one—not even Jane Seymour or my mother's old favorite, Bess of Hardwick, who softened the rough edges of court, though nothing warmed me more than Ned's love.

What did the queen think when she saw how others around the court treated me? With a kind of deference, an expectation . . . yet cautious, as if weighing their possible future against their present safety? The way—I would imagine—they had once regarded Elizabeth herself.

Twice I nearly asked Ned to speak to her himself about our union, but instinct stayed my tongue. If the queen forbade our love, nothing could lift that ban. But if she did not know of it, she could not order us apart.

Chapter Twenty-seven

Mary
Windsor Palace, Berkshire
September 1560

I SHOULD HAVE BEEN GLAD TO SEE KAT AGAIN WHEN THE queen summoned her back to court. I had missed my sister as a shadow must miss a graceful dancer on a cloudy day. Kat was the sun in my world, though she never knew it. That is the way of it between fairies and toads.

I knew she would be angry at my continued warnings about Ned Seymour. But sometimes it seemed as if she hated me. My even more pointedly outcast state suited the queen and most of Her Majesty's ladies-in-waiting fine. Only my mother's old favorite from our days at Bradgate, Bess of Hardwick, tried to soothe me, for Jane's sake. Bess kept a small portrait of my dead sister upon the table beside her bed.

"These rifts between sisters happen," Bess told me. "Your bond will mend in time. Someday you and Lady Katherine will laugh about it, as my sister and I do about our girlish quarrels."

But the chasm between us was less disturbing than the storm I could see gathering behind the queen's brittle smiles. From that frigid January when Kat returned, through spring and summer, I sensed in my bones that Elizabeth Tudor's sweet favor could turn deadly in a moment and extinguish Kat's light forever.

I was not the only one, amid the glitter of palaces and masques and the grandeur of the queen's progress, who smelled danger. William Cecil, whose scholarly wife, Mildred, had written often to Jane, seemed almost maddened by what was afoot. No gold chain of office or sweeping dark robes or bright buckles on his shoes could disguise the queen's secretary's fury whenever he saw Lord Robert Dudley and Her Majesty together.

"Will she risk the destruction of her realm for that gypsy cockerel?" I heard Cecil ask Bess one day, when she had allowed me to pore through some of her books. "By God's holy blood, the queen speaks of securing Dudley a divorce. As for Lord Robert himself, the man is bruiting it about that his wife is ill unto dying. Why then has Amy Dudley been traveling hither and yon this long year? I think he hopes to poison her and convince people she has suffered a natural death!"

I remembered the day in the garden when I heard Father and Northumberland talking of poisoning a boy who looked like King Edward so they could fool people with the corpse. Northumberland had gotten away with feeding the king arsenic when there had been swarms of councilors and courtiers around. How much easier would it be for Robert Dudley to have his poor, cast-off wife poisoned in some distant country house where every servant who waited upon her was loyal to him!

"I wish to God Robert Dudley would die and end England's troubles!" Cecil exclaimed.

"Quiet, William!" Bess looked about her in alarm. "You must not say that aloud, no matter how reasonable your fears that this affair will topple the queen from her throne! You are already in disgrace. Lord Robert knows you are his enemy."

"Would God I could use the ill will I bear him to some practical purpose!"

"They are meeting in secret, you know, the queen and Dudley," Bess said. "She claims his company is her one happiness."

Cecil scoffed. "It is not a queen's duty to seek happiness! It is her duty to look to her kingdom! Can you imagine what chaos will break out if she tries to raise Dudley to the throne?

I have heard from a man in the Spanish ambassador's employ that they are hoping to secure Lady Katherine Grey in marriage to one of the Habsburgs. May God curse the Spanish entourage for their plotting! I think they hope she will be queen one day and they can bring the popish church and Inquisition back to English shores."

I touched my throat. It burned in a line, as if an ax had touched it.

"You have little to fear from them," Bess said. "Lady Katherine is most attached to Lord Hertford."

"I do not care a snap for silly girls in love! The rule of a kingdom is at stake! I would do anything to save it."

In the years that followed I watched William Cecil's face often, trying to peer beneath the web of intelligence and devotion and loyalty to Elizabeth's cause. When news reached court of what had happened at Cumnor Place on September 6, I wondered if he had found a stealthy way to save England and destroy any chance of Elizabeth wedding Dudley. That was the evening servants returned from a day at the fair to find Amy Robsart Dudley lying dead of a broken neck at the bottom of a flight of stairs.

KatBisham Abbey, Berkshire
Late November 1560

The old Bisham Abbey gleamed with candlelight, and the table was weighted with gold plate and sparkling glass. The servants were taking a long time to clear away the remains of the dinner that Elizabeth Hoby and her husband, Sir Thomas, had spread before a chosen few: the Earl of Arundel, who was paying court to my friend Jane; Mildred Cecil, sister to our hostess; Parr of Northampton; Lord Cobham; and—most dear of all—my Ned. His eyes rarely left me, his face displaying his yearning for the kisses that were becoming ever harder to steal amidst the scandal that Amy Dudley's death had created in the court.

Arundel leaned forward, his jowly face showing its age. "I have heard that those servants of Lord Robert's who were banished to the country with Amy were known to say they wished she would die so their master could become king."

Elizabeth Hoby tipped her head. "Is it not odd that every one of them went off to the fair, leaving their mistress alone? With her sick, if the tales are to be believed."

"I do not believe she was ill at all!" Mildred Cecil said. "At least not in body. God knows what the poor lady suffered in her mind and heart with her husband's betrayal the talk of England! It is said Sir Richard Verney sent the whole household to the fair, then ordered one of his men to return and see her dead. They say the servant was then murdered himself to keep him silent."

I thought of the old woman whom Mary claimed had given arsenic to King Edward. Northumberland had had her killed for the same reason.

"Even if Dudley did murder his wife, how will anyone prove it?" Arundel queried. "The queen is quite wild, they say, and has ordered a full investigation. Some even whisper that Her Majesty had a hand in it."

"That is absurd!" Elizabeth Hoby insisted. "All of England would be a-boil with the tale of Amy Dudley's death under such suspicious circumstances. Her Majesty's morals are already in question. She is being scrutinized for dallying with a married man, not for the first time. There was that unsavory affair with Sir Thomas Seymour—the tales were wrenched from Elizabeth's own governess when Kat Ashley was questioned in the Tower."

Mildred Cecil gave a smug nod. "My husband says it will not matter what the inquiry into Amy Dudley's death decides. Whether Lord Robert is judged innocent or guilty, the queen can never marry him now. He will never be king. William says that never has one woman's death been such a salvation for an entire country." She carefully wiped her knife clean upon a piece of manchet bread. I could not take my eyes from the red smear of blood from the roast venison she had cut. Something about her words, so quiet, disturbed me. I could not wait to escape the crowd, find time alone to speak to Ned.

Jane had said marriage was like a glove—you could not tell if it was poisoned until after you had slipped it on. How many wives had died at their husbands' hands? The queen's mother, Anne Boleyn. Young Catherine Howard, who had been wedded to a gross, stinking old man who happened to be king. Now Amy Dudley. Add to their total those wives cast aside, as I had been by the Herberts. Parr of Northampton had done the same, casting aside his first wife and taking another. Perhaps his former bride and I should be grateful we had been merely slighted, not killed.

The company was breaking up. Mildred Cecil was speaking to Ned. "My husband wishes you to attend him as soon as you return to Whitehall," she said. "There is something of great import you must discuss."

"Of course. I have been most grateful for the secretary's friendship, and his support of a—a certain matter close to my heart."

Mildred looked at me for a moment, then flashed away. What I saw in her eyes confused me. Her lips tightened. "You will speak to Mr. Cecil soon, Lord Hertford. This misadventure of Amy Dudley's has changed everything. Nothing is as it was the day before."

That night the woman watched us like one of the ravens at the Tower, hovering near in her black gown with her busy dark eyes. When we tried to slip away to gain a moment alone, she moved with seeming carelessness to block our path.

I did not get to steal the kisses I longed for that night. When my next chance came, Ned was suddenly too much occupied with other things to do more than speak a few abrupt words to me, then duck away on some errand.

A knot of hurt tightened in my chest, growing larger and more tangled as the weeks dragged by. I raked over that night at the Bisham Abbey in my head, trying to think of anything I might have done or said to offend Ned. Or was he merely preoccupied, trying to navigate the turbulent waters roiling about the queen? He had to choose his course carefully, knowing that anywhere amid the shoals of Elizabeth, Dudley, and William Cecil he could wreck his skiff.

In October, when Lord Robert returned to Hampton Court, it was as an innocent man, the inquiry deciding that Amy Dudley had died of "misadventure." It was a way to avoid the label "suicide"—a death that would mean hellfire and burial in unconsecrated ground. Had Dudley's wife flung herself down the stairs? I wondered as the court moved to Westminster Palace. After years of loving her husband, then being abandoned, having no real home or children and no husband in her bed, had the slow torture of imagining him in another woman's arms finally driven Robert Dudley's wife to despair?

I had suffered Ned's indifference for only a matter of weeks, and I was struggling.

I could not confide my distress to his sister—did not want to seem the clinging lover. Besides, Jane was much engaged in deflecting Arundel's attentions. As for my own sister—to admit that Ned was ignoring me was too close to the fate she had warned me of. But when Isabella Markham, one of the ladies who had served the queen longest, came up to Jane and me with a cat's smile, I never expected the blow she would deal.

"Have you heard the latest news of our handsome Lord Hertford? It seems a lady has caught his eye. It is quite a flirtation, so they say."

I thought she was speaking of Ned's attachment to me. I felt my cheeks burn. "I am certain Lord Hertford has his pick of ladies."

"Maybe so." Isabella gave a flutter of her peacock feather fan. "But at present his favor has alighted on Frances Mewtas. What think you of her as a sister-in-law, Lady Jane?"

I saw my friend's face through a haze of anguish and disbelief. Something about Jane's expression gave truth to Isabella's words.

I cast my features as if in marble, forcing the smile to stay on my lips, but my fingers knotted in my skirts.

How strange that Mary drew near and touched me as the other ladies swept away—Isabella to her gossip, Jane to hide the embarrassment so evident in every line of her posture. I looked down at my sister, feeling for all the world as if she were some bad fairy come again to ruin my happiness.

"I am sorry, Kat," she said.

"Do you not wish to say you were right to warn me? You ever wanted to be cleverer than me! Can you never tell when I do not want you?"

I wheeled away from the pain in her face, and the terrible resignation. I should have hastened to my private chambers to weep my heart out alone. Instead I let something new flood through my veins.

Perhaps the time I had spent with Elizabeth Tudor had taught me the power in this fiery emotion. I had never had the courage to say all the things I wished to Henry Herbert. Ned Seymour would not have such a luxury. I stormed off to write him a letter—armed with my anger.

I had Ned's answer the next day. Jane fetched me to the maids' lodgings where we had gossiped beneath the coverlet, shared our secrets in happier times. As she pulled me into the closet where she kept her private things, I was stunned to see Ned pacing, his face haggard, his doublet crumpled, his eyes reddened with misery.

I froze, not sure whether I wished to go forward or back. Jane gave me a little shove into the room and closed the door, leaving Ned and me alone.

He stretched out his hands to me. "I cannot bear it, no matter what harm comes. To have hurt you this way . . ." Grief and regret darkened his face. "When I met with Cecil after the dinner with the Hobys, he forbade me to attach myself to you."

My eyes widened in disbelief. "But that makes no sense. He encouraged our bond . . . when you hinted you had affection for me before."

"That was when he feared Elizabeth would marry Dudley. Now that threat is gone, but the scandal still surrounds the queen. People do not trust her in matters of marriage. Should she choose a foreigner as her sister did, it could throw the country into turmoil. Cecil says that if you and I wed, we would make the government even more unstable."

"That is hardly fair." The injustice stung deep. "Because Elizabeth was foolhardy with Dudley—with another woman's husband—you and I, who have the right to pledge our troth, are to stay apart?"

"That is what Cecil said."

I paced to the window. After a moment I turned toward him again. "Do you want the crown, Ned?"

"I know there are some who think I do, who would argue that any English noble must hope for such power. But I cannot see the benefit in a circle of gold when it threatens to keep me from claiming the thing I want most in the world. Kat, I read your letter a dozen times and knew I should write some cool answer, as Cecil ordered, but there was such iron in your tone, I feared I would lose you forever. Do you remember that first day at Hanworth when you stumbled across Achilles and me in the garden? I told you that Henry Herbert was a fool. If you were mine, nothing would induce me to let you go."

"I remember."

"I am no fool in the way Henry was. But I may prove a greater one once our dice are cast." He closed the space between us, clasped both my hands in his. The warmth of him seeped deep beneath my skin, but all I could imagine was how devastating it would be to lose that touch forever. "Do you love me?" Ned asked.

"I do. But I cannot suffer this uncertainty. Never knowing how the winds will change."

He kissed me, then leaned his brow against mine, both of us breathing harshly. "People claim you are the image of your grandmother, the bold French queen who wed her love without her king's leave. They loved most truly until the day she died. Do you love me that much, Katherine?" Ned asked hoarsely. "Enough to risk Cecil's anger and the queen's wrath? Enough to dare whatever calamity we might face?" I nodded, my answer in my eyes.

"When next Her Majesty leaves the palace, come to my house on Cannon Row. There you will become my wife." Ned reached inside the leather purse dangling at his waist and drew out something sparkling. A pointed diamond ring. I trembled as he slipped it on my finger. "So we are betrothed, this declared before my sister." He gestured to where Jane waited outside the closet door. "Kat, are you afraid sweetheart?" he asked, curving his warm, strong hands over mine once again.

"Yes," I confessed. "But I am more afraid of living without you."

Whitehall Palace
December 1560

Stray flakes of snow drifted across a pewter sky the day the queen and her party left Whitehall for Eltham, lured by the prospect of several good days of hunting before the Yuletide festivities commenced. I struggled to hide my excitement at their departure—suffering "a vile toothache," I dared not dance or laugh aloud with anticipation. No one looked forward to what might be a visit to the tooth drawer's. Few knew that better than the queen, whose teeth were darkened and weak from the fruit suckets she loved so much.

I had claimed my jaw was swollen and begged Her Majesty to leave Lady Jane Seymour behind to keep me company. Elizabeth was happy to be rid of us both. Ned had taken his leave of court the night before, pleading some private business to attend to.

Our ruse might have gone perfectly if Mary had not come into my room bearing a foul-smelling poultice. I had just placed a cluster of almonds in the pouch of my cheek, just as one of my pet squirrels was wont to do at Bradgate.

"I heard you were in pain," Mary said. "Hettie used this to draw the fire out." She extended the poultice to me. I took it and pressed it to my face, knowing it was the quickest way to get her to leave. She looked at me strangely for a moment, and then I realized I had applied the poultice to the wrong side.

"Hettie always made her poultices too hot," I attempted to explain as I slid it to the lump I had created. "I did not want to make the pain worse."

"I see," Mary said.

My face was heating, and I was glad the warm poultice gave me an excuse.

"We have not had a comfortable talk for a very long time," Mary said, looking younger than her nearly sixteen years. "I thought I might stay behind."

"No!" I exclaimed so hastily, my sister winced. "It hurts to talk, and Jane is here."

Mary looked at my friend. The contrast between the two made me ache. Jane, despite the illness that still sometimes plagued her, was willowy and graceful, her eyes twinkling. Though Mary had grown some, and learned to manage her body with more ease, she still stooped, and even her lovely auburn hair was unable to hide the awkward angles of her face. My heart squeezed at the loneliness in Mary.

"You must watch carefully," Mary said. "Do not let the socket grow putrid, Kat."

"I will not. Perhaps the tooth will calm of its own volition and will not have to be drawn after all—I mean, what with this poultice you brought."

Mary's eyes narrowed. "Perhaps."

It shames me now to think how I hastened her away, but as Jane and I slipped from the palace and made our way down the stairs by the orchard, my sister's worried face no longer haunted me. Instead I pictured Ned, waiting to make me his wife.

Down the steps we tripped ever so lightly. Sand from the shore of the river sifted into my slippers as we moved toward the water gate in the direction of Cannon Row. Now and then a ray of sun braved the sky, then disappeared. It was nearly ten in the morning when we reached Cannon Row, and as we hastened up the water gate, a familiar figure hurried toward us.

"I told the gentleman usher to give the servants a day off," Ned explained. "Are you well?"

"In all my twenty years I have never been better."

"Jane, if you would go fetch the priest I found, we will repair to the privy chambers."

Ned led me away while my friend rustled off in a swirl of damask petticoats. The moment the chamber door closed behind us, Ned caught me in his arms and kissed me so fiercely he nearly knocked the gold wire caul from my hair. "It seems a hundred years since we vowed to meet, but it gave me time to secure something worthy of you."

"All I want in the world is right here." I kissed the place where his doublet covered his heart.

Footsteps approached, and we jumped apart, as guilty as a milkmaid and her shepherd lover. Jane entered with a short man of middling years. Black robes and a white collar proclaimed him an evangelical priest, while a fiery auburn beard shone against skin so fair it seemed almost alabaster. I wondered for a moment if he knew how dangerous this ceremony was, or that he might be punished for performing it.

He crossed to the bedchamber window, then turned to face us. Ned held my hand, and we stood before the holy man. He removed a leather-bound volume from his cassock and opened it, revealing the swirling black print of English script. The Book of Common Prayer. It would please my dead sister as she looked down from heaven.

I blinked sudden tears, thinking of my other wedding. Crowds of the most powerful courtiers in the land had been present, my father beaming, proud of my beauty, my mother dreaming of the crown that Northumberland had promised to put on Jane's head.

I remembered Mary behind the pillar, kissing the back of her hand, and Jane looking as if she were Andromeda chained to a rock, waiting for the Kraken to devour her. No Perseus had come to her rescue. No, my family was not present today, but now I would have a new family. A husband and a sister-in-law, a changed life with the Seymours. Soon perhaps I would even have children, pretty babes with Ned's smile and red-gold Tudor curls.

We spoke our vows most faithfully, but when my bridegroom drew a ring from his pocket, all else fled my mind. Five gold links fit together in a puzzle ring, each link engraved with what looked to be a line of a poem.

"I composed the lines myself," Ned said softly, reciting them aloud:

> "As circles five, by art compact, show but one ring in sight,
> So trust unites faithful minds, with knot of secret might,
> Whose force to break but greedy death, no wight possesses
> power
> As time and sequels well shall prove, my ring can say no
> more."

My eyes burned as he slid the ring onto my finger. A knot of secret might . . . that was a perfect way to describe the love we bore each other. Now nothing and no one—not even the queen herself—could break us apart.

Do not tempt fate, I could almost hear Mary say.

Or God. My sister Jane's voice. *No one defeats the grave.*

I stifled the warnings in my mind, felt happiness instead as Jane Seymour slipped the generous sum of ten pounds to the priest and ushered him to the door.

"It is a good thing we maids are always decorating ourselves with new jewelry," my friend said, as she crossed to a table where platters of meats lay spread. "The queen is no more likely to notice your new ring any more than she did your diamond. In any case, she will not guess its meaning." Jane offered me a tender breast of pheasant. "Will you have a taste of this?"

"I have never been less hungry in my life," I said, waving her away.

"For food, at least." Jane gave me a playful shove toward the velvet-draped tester bed that stood across the chamber. "To bed with you then, Katherine Hertford! Make my brother the happiest bridegroom in England. I shall be somewhat at a loss as to what will fill my days henceforth. Your romance has kept me busy passing love notes, arranging trysts, and soothing lovers' hurt feelings."

"You might make a match of your own," Ned teased. "The Earl of Arundel is most enchanted with you."

"I am not enchanted with him! He is an old man and ugly."

"He was not always so. When he was young, he was known to be quite handsome."

"Like your uncle, King Henry." Jane made a sour face. "He did not please poor Catherine Howard any more than Arundel pleases me. No, I will not have a disgusting old man groping me at the banqueting hall before the whole court! Mother told me that when Catherine Howard mounted the scaffold, she said she wished she had been Thomas Culpepper's wife."

A shiver worked down my spine unbidden at the thought of their forbidden love. It had been adultery. She had been a king's wife. Had she loved Culpepper as much as I loved Ned? I wondered, as Jane left the chamber and closed the door, leaving us alone.

"You look troubled, love. What is amiss?"

"I was only thinking how lucky I am."

Ned laughed. "We shall see what you say when we've spent fifty years together and I've lost my looks like poor Arundel."

"I will still think you the most beautiful man in England."

"I pray you will know I am the truest of heart. Come to bed, wife. I am half-mad with wanting you." Ned nearly rent his clothes as he shed them, then threw himself onto the bed and opened his arms wide. I left my own garb in a puddle of fabric on the floor, then cast myself into his embrace. We shared two hours sweeter than any troubadour could spin in the most magical reaches of imagination.

He loved me well in his bedchamber in Cannon Row, and no wife ever loved her husband better.

Chapter Twenty-eight

Mary
16 years old
Greenwich Palace
March 1561

FEBRUARY FLED WITH SLATE-COLORED SKIES THAT ECHOED
the melancholy in the maids' lodgings. Lady Jane
Seymour was sick. Whatever ailment had caused Queen
Mary to send the two girls to Hanworth during her reign was
back. My sister's friend coughed flecks of blood into her kerchief
and her flesh shrank to the bone, until she looked like the death's
head in a painting of hell I once saw. The physician assured us
Lady Jane did not suffer from the sweat or plague, so no one need
fear contagion. But I had lost Kat nonetheless.

My sister divided every moment she was not serving the
queen between the Seymours—coaxing Jane to walk in the
gallery on the arm of the manservant, Mr. Glynne, or stealing off
with Ned Seymour, who was forever underfoot. No one thought
her actions strange. It was likely Jane was dying.

If she did die, would Kat need to talk to me again? Was it
wicked to hope she might? Perhaps it was the same as wishing
Jane Seymour dead, and surely that was a sin. I did not mean to
be selfish. I would pray very hard for Jane to get better if only
Kat would pause long enough in her fussing to tell me what
the strange mix of emotions boiling inside her meant. Maybe
then I could shed the foreboding that had gripped me since
Christmastide.

Kat wheeled between happiness and grief, secretiveness and abandon, wild recklessness and the appearance of bracing herself as if dreading one of our mother's blows. My bones told me that danger stalked Kat now.

The queen's Boleyn eyes darkened whenever Kat drew near her. The new Spanish ambassador, de Quadra, attended Kat with such bowing and scraping that he might as well have stuck Elizabeth with a poisonous arrow. Angering the queen would have been risky at any time, but she and the Privy Council were already at war with each other.

News from the continent had grown more alarming by the week, until not even William Cecil or Bess of Hardwick could hide their frayed nerves. The French thought to wed Mary Queen of Scots to King Philip's son, who would bring the might of the Habsburg Empire to her cause. How could England withstand the Catholic armies of France and the Holy Roman Empire united? everyone at court wondered.

To make matters worse, Robert Dudley was promising the Spanish that if they helped him marry the queen, he would bring an English contingent to a meeting with the pope. Either prospect—Mary of Scots being placed on the English throne or Dudley attending the Council of Trent—threatened to carry England back to Catholic ways. That would lead to Smithfield and faggots piled high. Cecil's enemies would see he was one of the first to burn.

I paced the shadowy palace, feeling ever more the outcast. I do not remember setting out for Jane Seymour's chamber on purpose, but I never could resist picking at a scab, whether on my arm or on my heart. Better to catch sight of Kat for a moment than not see her at all. I was nearing Jane's door when I heard Kat's cry. I did not know what was amiss. I only saw her hasten from the chamber, her eyes red with tears.

"Has Jane died?" I asked in horror, fearing my bad thoughts might have made it so.

Kat's face contorted, and she tried not to sob. "Why do you say such terrible things? Will you not leave me alone?"

"I try to do as you wish, but something is wrong, Kat. I know it. Will you not tell me what it is?"

"Of course something is wrong!" She swiped a red curl from a cheek grown pale. "My dearest friend in the world may be dying, and now Ned is—" She clapped her hand to her brow, knocking her headdress askew. "I do not have time for your fussing, Mary! I must speak to Ned right away. Where could he be?"

A man rose from the shadows, but it was not the Earl of Hertford. The servant, Mr. Glynne, straightened his livery. "I believe his lordship is reading in the gallery."

Kat hurried away. I stared at her back—her petticoats streaming out behind her, wisps of her coppery hair straying from beneath her caul of silver wire and pearls. Would she always be thus, running away from me? Would I always be trying to catch up? Sadness fell heavily on me. I did not have the heart to follow her.

Kat

My legs shook as I raced past walls hung with tapestries, where branches of candles shoved back the shadows, but no matter how hard I pressed myself, I could not outrun the hurt that burned in my breast. How could Ned wound me thus? Was not a husband bound to be truthful with his wife? Was it not right to confide in her the most important events of his days? Why then had his sister been the one to convey such vital news? Why had Ned not told me?

As I entered the gallery, I stumbled on the outstretched paws of one of Dudley's greyhounds. The dog yelped, but I did not even pause to soothe it—testament to how upset I was. I looked around the gallery and found it deserted save for a brace of pages playing at skittles. As I searched further, I marked another occupant. Ned. Garbed in a crimson doublet and black breeches, he sat stiffly in a chair. A book was spread across his lap, but he did not look at it. Instead he looked at a crack in the wall.

I slowed to a more decorous step, not wanting to draw the pages' attention. Ned must have caught sight of some movement. His eyes shifted to me, and in that unguarded instant I knew what Jane had said was true. A secret clouded my husband's eyes.

"Lady Katherine," he said, rising to make me a bow. His formality seemed absurd, considering the many times we had met over the past months, eager, naked. Thoughts of that sweetness and Ned's tender claims of love made it hard to squeeze out the words that could undo my trust forever.

"Is Jane grown worse?" he asked, fear for his sister evident in his expression.

"No," I began, then amended it. "Yes, but what she suffers now is not from the fever. She could not keep your secret any longer." Ned stiffened. "So," I continued, "you are leaving England?"

"It would seem so." Guilt, defensiveness, and that hard Seymour pride inherited from his mother set Ned's mouth in a thin line. "Secretary Cecil is grooming me to advance in the queen's service. He says that a grand tour of Europe's courts is necessary to complete the education of any nobleman who wishes to wield influence. I am to go to Italy and the court of France. The alliances I make there will be useful for the rest of my life."

"You say that as if I would prevent you!" I felt as if he had pressed a raw wound. "Is not my future bound up with yours? Why would you not tell me Cecil's plan?"

"I do not know." Ned avoided my eyes. "I thought it would upset you."

"Being separated from my husband? Of course it upsets me. It is hard enough to sleep alone when I am a wife. Wed these four months, and we have never even spent a night together."

"I would give half my wealth to sleep in your arms, but we must be more cautious than ever. You know what a foul mood the queen is in. She is most vexed with you of late."

"So you are leaving me here to deal with her alone? Even more distressing, you have been deceiving me by not telling me your plans." I waited for him to deny it, to insist that he had only remained silent. He had not spoken a word of untruth, but he spared me that much.

"Nothing is settled for certain," he said. "I did as Cecil wished and applied for the license to travel. Cecil saw that it was granted. That is as far as the matter has gone."

"If you and Cecil have decided this is best, why such secretiveness?" I demanded in a rare flare of temper. "Why the hesitation?"

Ned's cheekbones darkened. "I would not commit to the journey until I ascertained whether . . ." He hesitated. "Whether or not you might be with child."

My breath caught. "I am not! Why would you think . . . I cannot be."

"We have lain together often. You have known pleasure in our coming together. That is the way children are conceived. My babe could be growing in your belly even now."

I swallowed hard, panic snagging my nerves. "The queen would be furious."

"That is why you must tell me how you fare. There are signs only women know."

What he said was true, but the thought of a pregnancy when the queen's temper was so volatile terrified me. I recoiled with an almost unreasonable horror from examining such symptoms. "I do not know what such signs might be! I am thought to be an unmarried maid. I can hardly go marching up to one of the other ladies of the privy chamber and ask how I might know I am with child!"

Ned paled, likely imagining the scene such a query would cause. "There must be a way to find out if your womb has quickened, Kat. I cannot defy Cecil. In truth, I do not want to." His chin rose with that Seymour stubbornness I had seen in both him and his sister. "Can you not see what a grand thing this journey would be for me? I am to be honored at the French court. Think of the powerful connections I will make."

It hurt to see the gleam of excitement in his eyes. Desperation knotted tight as I imagined my worst fears coming true: life without Jane, should she die, and now Ned leaving me, as Henry had.

"Kat, in spite of all the journey's allurements, I will not leave you if you are carrying my child."

No, I thought bitterly. He would stay and resent me, as I resented Mary when she grew too importunate. My pride stirred, and I could not bear to seem a coward before him. "When is Cecil determined to send you?" I forced myself to ask.

"At the end of this month. Surely you will know if there is a babe on the way by then." He cupped his hands about my arms, distressed. "You must tell me what to do, sweetheart," he said, his voice catching. "I do not wish to hurt you."

But hurt pulled me in all the same. It was now my constant companion as I waited upon the queen. It festered inside me during the dark vigil Ned and I kept at Jane's sickbed as we tried to will our breath into her tortured lungs. Our stolen moments together took on a keener edge. We did not speak of the barrier growing between us—neither to Jane nor to each other. But the harder I fought to conceal those wounds from my friend, the deeper Ned's betrayal rooted in my heart. Even that final night when Ned and I knelt beside Jane, each of us holding one of her hands, he seemed beyond my reach.

Death came on wings of moonlight. Jane's last mortal act was to take Ned's hand and press it into mine. "Do not . . . waste the gift you have been given," she whispered. "Not everyone has a chance to love." I wept as she slipped from life into the realm of heaven. She had matched Ned and me from the beginning, been our confidante, our co-conspirator, our dearest friend.

It pained me that my friend had never known what it was like to lie in a lover's arms, to feel souls twine together so deeply that one could not tell where one began and the other ended. But she had been spared pain as well. Jane would never understand my anguish as I waited for that bond to snap.

In the weeks that followed Jane's death, Ned was caught up in the needs of his family, comforting his mother and sisters and brothers and assuring that Jane was accorded all the funereal ceremony befitting a descendant of King Edward III. When they buried her in the same chapel as my mother, my grief doubled.

The final blow fell at the close of March when the court moved to Westminster. Mr. Glynne passed me a note from Ned, bidding me to meet him in the garden. When I got there, Ned looked disheveled.

"Katherine, this cursed indecision is driving me mad! I cannot delay another day. Are you with child or not?"

I stepped back as if he had slapped me, my own agitation unleashed. "How can I tell for certain? It is not fair of you to press me!"

"I do not wish to upset you, but Cecil is most determined I leave. I have never seen him so adamant."

Irritation rose in me. "If Cecil insists, what does it matter what your wife says?"

"It does matter, and you know it! Just tell me you are with child, and I will march up to the secretary and tell him I stay in England."

Could it be that simple? Just say the words, and I could keep Ned with me? Women believed they were pregnant all the time, only to miscarry or discover they had been mistaken. Queen Mary had done so twice. Ned need never know that I had lied. *But you would know,* a voice like my sister Jane's whispered in my head. *That lie would stand between you and your husband for the rest of your lives. Separating of your spirits that way would be worse than being parted from his person for a little while.*

"I cannot tell you one way or the other! I do not know if I carry a child!"

Ned swore. He turned and stalked a few steps away from me. I hated myself for weeping. I heard something rustle— parchment, it sounded like. Then he thrust something into my hands. "I had a will drawn up, naming you as my wife, deeding properties and monies to you and any child we may have."

"I do not want it!"

"This is no time for fits of temper, Katherine. Unfortunate circumstances can occur while crossing the channel or traveling in foreign lands."

"You mean you could die!" The thought of losing Ned broke my heart. "I have not even finished crying over Jane!"

"I miss my sister, also." His grief was naked in his face.

"Then do not leave me."

Ned sounded as if he were calming a restive hound. "I will write you every day, and before long I will return with pretty trinkets for my beautiful wife. That will please you."

There was a time when that might have been true, but my happiness was no longer so easily purchased. He would leave me. A ripple of laughter sounded nearby, but I was too desolate to care.

Ned looked over his shoulder, nervous enough for us both. "Katherine, I must go lest we be discovered, but before I do . . . just know that if—if it turns out that you do carry our child, all you need do is write to me. I will return to you as fast as God's wind in ship's sails can carry me. You will not be alone."

He strained me to him, kissed my lips. "Will you not wish me Godspeed, my love?"

"I cannot think my wishes have any importance at all," I said dully. "I must go and serve the queen." It was true enough. I owed

Elizabeth my duty, as Ned owed William Cecil his. We stole one last night together before he sailed, our coupling strangely silent. There was nothing more to say.

❧❧ ❧❧

MY LOVE SAILED ON A BALMY SATURDAY. I COULD NOT WATCH him go. Adrift in a world without Ned or Jane, I encased the soft girl I had been in a shell that I allowed no one to penetrate. I twisted my marriage ring about my finger, wondering how Ned's "knot of secret might" could have unraveled so soon.

I could not eat, wished only to sleep away the sad hours. So great was the change in me that even the author of my misery noticed it and summoned me to speak with him.

William Cecil drew me into his book-littered privy chamber, the man more somber than I had ever seen him. "Lady Katherine, you seem quite wan of late. I hope you are not missing Lord Hertford overmuch."

I bit the inside of my lip and turned my face away.

"Ah, I see. You do hold him in affection. It is a good thing I have sent him away. Any union between the two of you would be disaster."

What I saw in his face made me tremble. "What disaster could simple love between two loyal subjects cause?"

"My dear child, I do not wish to blight your romance, but more important things than a girl's happiness are at stake. You know of Mary of Scots' treacherous plotting?"

"I do."

"Now Robert Dudley once again has the queen under his thrall. He plots with the Spanish, promising to bring England back into the Catholic fold."

"But he is reformed faith."

"Dudley hungers for a crown and the queen—and I am not certain she can resist his charms. If Her Majesty is foolhardy enough to marry him, she will topple from the throne."

"But the queen has not named anyone her heir."

"Nor will she have the chance to, if these events come to pass. You will be raised to the throne, Lady Katherine. As a good Christian of the reformed faith, you may be the one hope to keep England from civil war."

"But would not Lord Hertford be an asset to the crown? An English earl with Plantagenet blood in his veins?"

"He would be too great an asset. We have many a stormy sea to navigate before the difficulty is settled. The queen would fear that, even without the added complication of Dudley as potential king, her subjects might rise up and topple her crown in your favor." I felt light-headed, as if I were dancing too long in the heat.

Cecil guided me to a chair and helped me sit down. "The prospect of a crown is a great burden, I know. Especially after what happened to your sister," he soothed. "But it is one that destiny has chosen you to bear. That is why I had to send Lord Hertford to the continent. I warned him to keep away from you, but he did not heed my words. Removing the temptation was the only way to keep you—and through you, the whole kingdom—safe. Do you understand?"

"I do," I breathed, my heart sinking. "Why did you not share this with me sooner?"

"As a father, I have discovered that even the most biddable of daughters grows headstrong in matters of the heart. Nothing tempts a woman more than a forbidden love. I confess I feared you might do something rash."

"Marry Lord Hertford," I whispered.

Cecil gave a strained laugh. "Your grandmother, the dowager queen of France, wed Charles Brandon in defiance of rank and of her brother's will."

"But all ended well for them," I soothed myself.

"It would not end so for you. The fate of a kingdom did not turn on your grandmother. It turns upon you."

Late that night I curled up in my bed, my wits frayed with confusion. Had Cecil told Ned his reasons for separating us? Had the secretary spoken of crowns and plotting, religious wars, and the fate of England hanging in the balance?

If Ned had known all that, had he wed me in hopes of sharing the crown Cecil spoke of? Mary's warnings that summer at Hanworth whispered in my head.

No. I could not believe Ned would use me thus. More truthful—I did not want to.

April passed, then May, the spring lambs fattening on the hills. June came, rife with preparations for the queen's progress. Carts were loaded, gowns and jewels packed carefully in chests, their lids peaked so the rain would run off them. I packed as well—my gowns and my jewels and the dread that haunted me night and day.

Come July, I lay in the bath, my linen shift clinging wet to my stomach, my breasts feeling heavy. Was it dropsy, perhaps? Some swelling from jolting across the roads? Was I growing stout as my mother had done when she was most unhappy?

I pressed my palms against my middle to force the swell back to its usual shape. My heart stopped as something strange happened. There, inside me, something—some*one*—kicked me with a force that shattered my world.

A babe—it could only be a babe—was fighting its way to life in my womb.

Chapter Twenty-nine

Kat
Ipswich
August 1561

BRIGHT-GARBED DANCERS WHIRLED ABOUT THE FLOWER-decked hall in the volte, and at their center Lord Robert Dudley tossed the queen high in the air. As his hands gripped Her Majesty's slender waist, I was grateful that my claim of a weak ankle excused me from such pursuits for the present. For if any man touched me thus in a dance, my secret would be betrayed.

When Jane, Mary, and I were children, we made skiffs out of bark at Bradgate. We would choose broad-leaf sails and thread them through with masts of twigs, then set our little crafts adrift to challenge the current. Jane's was painstakingly done, Mary's clumsy because she was youngest. Mine was burdened with flower-blossomed ladies and acorn-helmeted knights, my masts streaming with bright petal pennons. Laden with adornments, it was always first to overbalance or crash against the rocks.

Now I was that fragile vessel, plunging through the foam. The stones thrust out of the water ahead of me, and I knew they would dash me to bits, but I could not change course any more than the flower-people of my childhood could have.

I could not even wail in fear. All I could do was hunch over my writing desk day after day, pen clenched in hand as I scratched out desperate letters:

My dearest husband,
Return to England if you love me. You vowed you would not
leave me to face the queen's wrath alone.

As I watched Her Majesty dance with Dudley, I fought the urge to curve my arm over my belly, to feel the terror and wonder of the life within me pushing its elbows and feet against my womb. I had spent hours alone, my flesh bared as I watched in horrified fascination as the bulge moved, its rump and spine shifting against its prison. Ned's babe and mine. Even with my gift of imagination, I could not pretend it away any longer.

In my letter I pleaded for Ned to return to my side, but I feared he had deserted me. What else could this silence mean? Even had he returned, he could have denied our marriage. His sister, our only witness, lay dead, and I did not even know the name of the priest who wed us. The paper Ned gave me proclaiming me his wife, deeding me property and monies should he die—that paper had vanished. I prayed the queen's spies or some other scheming courtier had not gotten hold of it. I searched people's faces in dread, my nerves raked across a knife's blade. Even if no one else knew yet about my marriage, soon no power in heaven or on earth would be able to shield me from the consequences of my folly.

I finally understood what Jane suffered—the days slipping past in the Tower, her steps toward the block, the space between ax and life dwindling. She had had no way to halt the march of time. I was on a march of my own now and could see no end but disaster.

"My Lady Katherine?"

I stiffened, startled at de Quadra's greeting, his voice heavy with the accents of Spain. "Ambassador," I said with a nod.

"Forgive me, but you do not look altogether well. I hope you are not ill?"

I made a futile attempt to draw in my stomach, then fluffed my petticoats instead. "I am quite well."

"I miss seeing you partnered in the dance. You are quite the most graceful of all the queen's ladies and, might I add, the most beautiful. No wonder the queen does not seek out your company, as she does those who are not so blessed."

There was a time such praise would have pleased me. This time I did not even trouble to reply.

De Quadra cleared his throat. "The queen and her master of the horse dance quite beautifully together, yet so few of your countrymen seem pleased by the display."

"Perhaps the pheasant served at the banquet did not agree with their stomachs." I searched for a more effective way to deflect his probing, wishing he would go away.

"I would say the partner whom the queen has chosen is disagreeable to the company. Robert Dudley has many enemies. My master counts himself among them, despite Dudley's recent efforts to win his favor. Anyone at court must know who champions their cause and who opposes it. You, my lady, have friends among my people. My master remembers your loyalty to his cousin, Queen Mary, when she was upon the throne."

I cast a nervous look at the dancers, but they were still too involved in each other to notice de Quadra's attentions to me. "The late queen was very kind and gracious."

De Quadra stroked his black beard with one hand. "You will forgive me if I submit that this queen is made of far different stuff. Elizabeth Tudor will not easily forgive the fact that your birth is more royal than her own, or that it does not carry the stain of bastardy. There are those who predict her time on the throne is dwindling."

Alarm cut even more sharply through my veins. "It is treason to say so," I told him. "I pray, as all true subjects must, that Her Majesty will live a long, fruitful life."

"With Dudley as a husband?" de Quadra scoffed. "Anyone

may see the passion in Elizabeth Tudor's eyes when she looks at him. Her parents defied the pope and certain hell to consummate their love. How many of your king's own friends and loyal advisers perished in flame or by the headsman's ax to clear the path to their marriage? Is it so hard to imagine, then, that their daughter might risk all to wed a man whom her people hate?" De Quadra's lip curled in derision.

"It is not proper for you to say so."

"I will tell you this, my lady," de Quadra said. "If the queen does not choose him, she will not choose anyone, and if Her Majesty does not marry, she cannot bear a son."

"England needs a prince," I said.

"Indeed, but not one tainted with Dudley blood. England will not have it. The wolves are already dividing into factions, competing for power as they sense the queen may be sinking. They will soon turn on each other. You saw firsthand what such a dangerous climate can lead to."

"It is not kind of you to remind me of circumstances that were so painful."

"I do not wish to pain you. I only wish to reassure you that you will have powerful friends when things grow complicated, as they are bound to do. You have only to say the word, and all the resources at my disposal will be at your service."

To have Spain, with all its power and influence, seeking my favor—how proud my lord father would have been. At that instant my babe kicked, and I wondered what de Quadra would say if he knew I carried the child of my husband—Lord Hertford, whose father had brought the reformed religion to England.

Had not Cecil claimed that Spain hoped for a marriage between the Catholic Scots queen and the Habsburg heir? The tangle made my head ache, my stomach clench with fear.

A black-robed figure came toward us—William Cecil, appearing less than pleased. Had he guessed the tenor of our conversation? Or was he merely determined to let de Quadra know that I belonged to him on this vast chessboard that was court? I did not wish to remain long enough to find out.

"I beg you will forgive me, ambassador," I said. "I find this heat oppressive."

"Go, then. Rest. Your health is very dear to me."

At that moment Cecil drew near us. He stopped and bowed. "Lady Katherine, Ambassador de Quadra, how fare you on this hot August night?"

"Lady Katherine was just preparing to withdraw," de Quadra answered for me. "She is feeling a touch unwell."

"I am not," I said too hastily, terrified Cecil might insist upon sending a physician to examine me. "I find the heat oppressive. That is all."

Suddenly I felt cold to my spine. Someone was watching me. The dance was over, the participants were leaving the floor—all save the queen. She was looking at me as I stood between the two powerful men, suspicion and enmity in her black Boleyn eyes.

What did she see? Plots to steal her throne? Men vying for the favors of a woman who might be her heir? She had been in my position once—she knew how fickle even a seemingly loyal councilor could be.

"Forgive me, gentlemen. I will leave you to argue among yourselves." I curtsied, then fled to my chambers.

I was pacing my small room when I heard a timid knock on my door. Mary slipped in, her face illuminated by the candle she held, her eyes dark with remorse and worry.

"Kat, I have been wishing for a moment to speak to you," she said, crossing to the table where my writing desk lay open. "I need to tell you I am sorry the Seymours are gone."

I stared at her in surprise and anguish. "I do not believe you. You never liked them."

"I *did* wish I could make them disappear." She picked up a wafer of sealing wax that I had stamped with the Grey family unicorn, then torn off when I tossed that letter to Ned aside, determined to phrase something more insistently. Mary rubbed her finger against the hard wax as if by touch she could discover the right words to soothe me. "I thought that if there were no more Seymours at court, you would talk to me, but you do not. If I had real magic, I would make them come back for you."

"Jane is dead, and Ned—Ned is far away in France or Spain."

"I do not care where he is. He does not write you. You send him so many letters and cry over them. It is like Henry Herbert. Do not let him see how deeply he wounds you."

My cheeks burned, and I wondered who else might have noticed my tears. "Mary, do not—"

"Kat, I must say things this time, even if you do not wish to hear them. You are like one of the fairy maids or ladies in the Arthur legends—you are too fine to grieve over any silly man. I cannot bear to see Ned Seymour make you look a fool."

"You wish me to confide in you, yet you call me a fool? You dare bring up Henry Herbert and how I humiliated myself over him?" That long-ago shame seemed as nothing compared to what I faced now.

"I know I am not good at charming people out of their dismals, as you are, or able to unravel any problem, as Jane was. But I am the only sister you have, and I want to help."

She looked so small and tender, strangely young. Mary, who had seemed old and wizened from the time she was a babe. "You cannot help me, Mary," I said, more gently than I had spoken to her in a very long time.

"If I cannot help you, Kat, you must find someone who can."

Wise advice, but who could help me? De Quadra? His mission was to keep diplomatic channels open with the queen. He had claimed that his resources were at my service—if the queen wed Dudley and was in danger of losing her throne. Would William Cecil give me aid? I shrank from exposing my recklessness to him. Besides, he was not in the queen's favor of late, any more than I was.

"Remember Jane's tutor, Dr. Aylmer?" Mary asked.

"I cannot think a tutor can aid me."

"He made the queen quite angry once, demanding that she grant him more preachers. Robert Dudley went to Her Majesty on Dr. Aylmer's behalf."

"Why would Robert Dudley help me? He does not even like me overmuch."

"He likes all the pretty women. Lady Douglas Sheffield and Lettice Knollys. He thinks you are prettier than they are. Even prettier than the queen. I know because he watches you when he thinks no one is looking."

"Oh, Mary, what does that matter?"

"He likes to play the knight, just as much as you like to play the lady that needs to be rescued. Besides, he is still our brother-in-law, even if Jane is dead."

"It is partly his fault that she is." Mary winced and I remembered her incoherent cries in the days after Jane's beheading. How she had blamed herself.

But after a moment Mary seemed to brace herself. "Kat, I am sure Lord Robert can get the queen to excuse anything if he wants to. Think of Amy Dudley with her broken neck. Whatever problem is plaguing you, it cannot be as bad as a murdered wife."

It was true. Robert Dudley had gotten the queen to overlook sins that no one should excuse. Of course, the men sent to examine the situation had called him innocent. Even so, suspicion remained. When the queen's councilors begged her to give him up, she had stood firm, and now she cleaved to Dudley even more tightly than before.

Desperate hope took root in me. I moved toward Mary, wanting to hug her as I might have done when we were small. Mary's eyes widened as if she read my thoughts, her arms lifting a fraction. But at the last moment I quelled my impulse. She would feel the bulge in my belly. I watched the hope in my sister's face fade, and I hated myself for it.

"You came here to help me, Mary, and you did. Now, go to bed."

Mary started back to my desk to put the wax seal down, but I stopped her.

"Why do you not take that seal and store it in your Thief's Coffer? Do you still squirrel things away?"

Her chin raised a trifle with that old defiance, and I remembered all the times I had teased her. "I only keep special things that matter."

"Perhaps you can show your treasures to me sometime. Then I will tell you why your coming here tonight mattered very much to me. I will tell you everything someday. When all is settled and the storm is over."

Mary pressed the hand that held the seal against her heart. I knew the bit of wax had become suddenly precious. "Will you be happy then, Kat?"

"I cannot say," I hedged as I ushered her out the door. I did not even know if I would be alive.

Chapter Thirty

Kat
On progress with the queen
Ipswich
Late August 1561

I HAD NEVER REALIZED THAT BEING PRETTY COULD BE A hazard. But as I scurried along the walls like a frightened mouse, I knew that my gift for capturing people's attention could prove my undoing.

I drew my face deeper into the hood of my cloak, the garment turned inside out to hide the trim of ermine that would announce to anyone who saw me that I was a lady of high station. Counting the doorways studding the wall, I prayed I would find the one I sought. When I saw a gentleman usher wearing the Dudley device of the bear and ragged staff on his livery, I nearly wept in relief. I hastened up to the post he was guarding and spoke low. "I must have an interview with Lord Robert at once. In private, I pray you."

Light from the cresset at the servant's side cast an orange glow across features that suddenly appeared sly, though his lips did not so much as tick up in a smile. "Mistress, it is very late. His lordship is very likely abed."

"My business cannot wait."

"Whom shall I tell Lord Robert calls upon him?"

I almost tried to conceal who I was, but then I realized how futile such subterfuge would be. Whether Robert Dudley helped me or not, the whole court would soon know about this babe.

Seeking a late-night audience with Robert Dudley would not be nearly as perilous as that transgression. "I am Lord Robert's sister-in-law, Lady Katherine Grey."

The servant leaned forward to peer beneath my hood, as if to be certain. Did he wish to satisfy his own curiosity, or did he fear that some enemy had sent an assassin—either to take Dudley's life or to destroy his good name. "Lady Katherine. So I see." A trifle of the tension seemed to drain from the servant's broad shoulders. "I will inform Lord Robert of your request at once and inquire as to his wishes. You may wait in his privy chamber."

With a sweep of one arm, he ushered me into Dudley's quarters, gestured to a seat near the fire. I took it gladly. Yet somehow reaching my destination did not calm me. Rather, my imagination reeled from one disastrous consequence to the next.

What had I been thinking, coming here to enlist Dudley's aid? It was madness.

Too soon an athletic figure strode into the chamber, Lord Dudley dressed in a night robe of crimson brocade, his usually impeccable handsomeness disheveled, his features betraying a measure of alarm.

"Lady Katherine?" he said, a trifle sharply. "You must know the queen would not be amused at this late-night encounter. What business could not keep until a civilized hour, when we could meet as the queen prefers—in the open before the whole court?"

I remembered what Mary had said about Lord Robert watching comely ladies-in-waiting. "Forgive me for disturbing you, but I had no other choice. I am here to ask you, my lord . . ." I had written the words to Ned more times than I could count, but when I tried to speak them, I could not. Once I said the words aloud, I could not take them back. Everything would seem more terrifyingly real.

"*What*, in the name of God? Woman, you slipped into my

chambers in the dead of night, and I could receive a summons from the queen at any moment to discuss some important matter of policy. She would not be pleased to find you here."

"The last thing I wish is to incur Her Majesty's anger. I have come to beg you to use your influence with the queen on my behalf."

Lord Robert rolled his eyes. "Of course. How many times a day does someone come to me with some paltry wish to bring to the queen's attention."

"This is not a paltry matter." I pressed my hands protectively to the bulge concealed by the pleats of my gown. "I am with child."

Dudley stepped back, as if fearing he could somehow catch blame for my condition. "You little fool! I have nothing to do with that."

"I did not claim that you do."

"Who is the father?"

"My husband."

"Have you and Henry Herbert still been meeting all this time? Your marriage was legally annulled."

"No. It is not Lord Herbert I speak of. I wed the true husband to my heart, Edward Seymour, Lord Hertford."

Dudley gaped. "You wed Hertford? When? How?"

"In secret. Last December we slipped away from the palace when the queen was hunting, and a priest wed us at Hertford's house on Cannon Row."

"By God's blood—who knew about this? Did you have witnesses? God help them!"

"Hertford's sister, Lady Jane, was our only witness."

"Lady Jane who is lately dead?"

I nodded. "My lord, I know we have not been close companions since that dreadful time our families suffered in the Tower, but you and I are still brother and sister-in-law. We both lost our fathers and a sister and brother to the ax."

Lord Robert's face stiffened. "You think I owe you for the forfeit they paid?"

Yes, I wanted to say, but checked myself at the last moment, knowing it would serve me ill to anger him further. "I am long past fixing blame, as I pray you are, Lord Robert. I only know we still share a blood tie, and it is for the sake of Jane and Guilford that I hope you might intercede with Her Majesty on my behalf. We did not mean Her Majesty any harm by this marriage. Our only crime is that we loved each other too much to live apart. Lord Robert, you of all people must understand how painful such a separation can be. No one can see you and the queen together without knowing you love her greatly. If Her Majesty came to you and begged you to wed her—even in secret—would you not slip your nuptial ring on her finger, no matter who tried to say you nay?"

Dudley turned, paced away from me. I could sense his thoughts racing.

It gave me the courage to press on. "I promise you that this is a love match. That is all. I am not courting the queen's diplomatic enemies, nor being set up as one who might replace her on the throne."

"Even by that dour-faced clerk old Cecil? No one will believe it. The Spanish have been courting you for years, and now you marry a descendant of Edward III—the son of the man people still call the Good Duke? Any thinking man will believe this marriage is a clever maneuver to gain power. If you bear a son, your standing in the succession would be increased a thousandfold. Your parents would be so pleased."

"My parents are dead, as you well know. Their ambitions have followed them to the grave. I have no wish to follow the path they forced my sister Jane to tread. As for men like Cecil and de Quadra, I cannot help what they think about my claim to the crown. All I want is to make a life with my husband and have God grant safe delivery for my child and me."

"You look so earnest, there are some might even believe you. But the queen?" Dudley emitted scornful laughter. "Ruthless men tried to involve her in far too many plots during her sister Mary's reign for her to dismiss this entanglement of yours lightly. Not when Her Majesty knows that her own Privy Council has been scheming against her—stirring up discord over my wife's tragic accident, trying to break the bond between the queen and me. Perhaps Cecil is planning to use you to further that end, or to mount a coup should his plots against me fail."

I felt sick with fear at Dudley's reaction. Others would see the marriage the same way. "Secretary Cecil sent Lord Hertford to the continent," I insisted. "If there were some plot, would he not have kept Lord Hertford near at hand?"

"It is just another of that dour old fool's tricks to throw me off the scent. He would stoop to anything to get his way. Sometimes I even wonder if he was involved somehow in Amy's death, hoping it would put the queen beyond my reach. Cecil cannot stomach me because he knows I will be no man's pawn. I will do anything in my power to serve my dearest love. My interests are what benefit the queen."

He believed his own words. I pictured Amy Dudley, a lifeless heap lying at the bottom of stone stairs. I feared Dudley would read the thoughts in my eyes, but he was too far gone in his own plotting to see anything but the tool that fate had put in his hands.

"There can be no question that a healthy child with Tudor blood in its veins will complicate things mightily for Her Majesty. If you should bear a son—" Dudley stopped abruptly. He stroked his beard with one rein-toughened hand. I remembered just such a look on his scheming father. "Upon consideration, your situation might work to the queen's advantage after all. She is up to her neck in doomsayers who stoop to scare tactics to weaken those who truly have her best interests at heart. She must wed and produce an heir of her own. Seeing her apparent successor happily married and bursting with life—certainly that will make her see what is best for her: a husband who has loved her from the time she was a cast-off princess with little hope of a crown."

Dudley smiled, then. I shivered. "Lord Robert, the queen loves you above anyone living or dead. If anyone can convince her of the truth in my claims, it is you."

"It is true." His chest puffed up with arrogance that I knew set other courtiers' teeth on edge. "Go now. Return to your chambers. Stay there until Her Majesty sends for you. You had best prepare for a tempest. Even if she forgives you in the end, she will first deal you a generous serving of her father's temper. King Henry demanded the forfeit of people's heads for less."

I touched my throat, felt the leap of my pulse. Life. It was so fragile, so precious. I had wagered my life and my babe's, Ned's life too, upon the skills of Robert Dudley.

Had I been a fool to listen to Mary? I wanted to go and rouse her from her bed. Wanted to spill out the whole story she had been so eager to hear. Was not confession good for the soul? But what would unburdening myself accomplish except to torture her during these excruciating hours that would decide my fate?

I returned to my chamber, sat in a chair by the fire, and listened with every fiber of my being. My breath caught in panic at every sound. Was this how Jane had felt, waiting for her execution? Feeling time slip away from her, unable to catch it, hold it, make it pause? Nine days Jane had been queen, and Robert Dudley had tried to serve her cause. When she had cast fortune's dice with this man and lost, the outcome had been hideous.

Mary

The queen flung things at Lord Robert's head. Every time something crashed or shattered, the other maids jumped. They must have been glad for the heavy closed door between us, but none of them were frightened to their very marrow except me.

I could hear very little of the queen's tirade, but I guessed who she was so angry at. Kat. It must be Kat. I had told her to go to Robert Dudley with her trouble, just as I had sent the warning feather to Princess Mary. Had it been a mistake?

Alarm surged through me anew. No, this time was different. Father was not around to tangle Kat in any of his dangerous plots. Kat was not trying to seize the crown.

Even so, I could not quell my sense of doom.

Lord Robert thrust his head out the door, called to the gentleman usher. "Her Majesty wishes you to gather together a company of her guards. They are to bring Lady Katherine Grey here." The other ladies' cries of surprise fed my terror. "Send word to the water gate that they will be required to escort her ladyship to the Tower."

The Tower? I pressed my hand to my mouth, feeling as if I would retch. I cursed the awkward gait that slowed me as I left the room, my lungs feeling fit to burst. No one tried to stop me.

By the time I reached Kat's chamber, I could barely speak. I staggered in, not even bothering to announce myself. My graceful sister stood with an awkwardness I had never seen. Her face was bleached bone white, but her body made me more terrified than ever. Her arms curled over her stomach as if to shield it, pulling the fabric tight. The bulge beneath it moved. I stared at it, horrified, understanding all too late.

"That is why you wrote to Ned Seymour all those times. The scoundrel! How dare he fill you with his bastard and then run away! I swear, I will find a way to make him pay!"

"Ned is my husband. We were wed last December. Jane Seymour helped us to—" Kat's voice broke. "I know I did not tell you, and it must pain you—"

"I do not care about that now. I do not care about anything save . . . I cannot lose another sister. The queen is sending guards. You must get away from here."

My plea died as I remembered urging Jane to flee on the eve of her wedding. She had told me that there was no place a person of royal blood could hide. My wise, practical sister. Now I was old enough to know she was right. I choked out a sob, helpless. "Oh, Kat! They are going to—" I could not say the words aloud.

Kat reached out one hand. "Mary, stay with me until they come. I am so afraid."

I did not take the hand she offered. Instead, I did something I had never dared to do before. I stretched my stubby arms around her as far as they would go. Kat held on tight.

Too soon the tramp of boots drew near, then stopped outside the chamber door. The oaken panel swung open, revealing the red livery of Her Majesty's guards.

"Lady Katherine Grey, I arrest you in the name of the queen. You are to be conveyed to the Tower, where you shall be questioned at Her Majesty's pleasure."

"No!" I put myself between the men and my sister. "I will not let you take her there!"

"Mary, there is no help for it. You must let me go."

"But the Tower! That is where Jane—"

"I need you to be strong. You must gather my things. My— my dogs and clothes and such. You must bring them to me in the Tower."

"I cannot go to that place again! I am sorry, Kat."

"I understand, sweetheart. Find somebody else to carry out my errands." She gathered me fiercely in her arms, then whispered, "You must find Ned before the queen does. You must warn him."

"He should go to the Tower! This is his fault! If he had come back the first time you wrote him—"

"Do not blame him. Even if he has deserted me, I cannot bear to see him harmed."

"You are too good, Kat. Too kind."

Kat's eyes filled with regret, as if she were counting every time she had snapped at me or shut me out of her thoughts, her life. "Too kind?" she said as she stepped toward the guards. "Oh, Mary. We both know that is not true."

I stayed in Kat's chamber long after the sound of marching soldiers faded to silence. When darkness came, I went to her clothing chest, took out one of the linen shifts that smelled of the dried roses she slipped among her clothes to scent them of summer. A packet of parchment tied in a ribbon tumbled to the floor. Letters. I knew I should tuck them back into their hiding place. I had no right to read them. But the queen's servants might search Kat's chamber, looking for evidence to use against her. What if these held something that might condemn her?

Decided, I took the missives to where a candle burned and unfolded the pieces of parchment one after another. Some of them were gossipy, affectionate letters from Jane Seymour, who shared a bond with my sister that I would never know. Others were love letters from Ned Seymour, written many months ago, the lines filled with passion and dreams, and plans laid for stolen moments together:

Send word with Jane where I dare come to you, my sweetheart, my wife. How precious that word. Wife . . .

Another said:

I tease Jane that she is as caught up in our romance as we are. She delights in knowing all your secrets and all of mine. She says you were the most beautiful bride England ever saw, and I cannot deny it is true.

Near the bottom of the stack, these words:

My love, I fear I am the most vile brother in the world. My sister is suffering so terribly, I fear for her life, but I cannot

help wondering how we will manage when she is gone.
There is no one in the world who loves us as Jane does. No
one who understands our hearts.

"I would have tried," I said aloud, the pain of their rejection cutting through me, "if you had only asked me."

I retrieved Kat's shift where it had fallen on the floor. Tucking the rest of the letters into my stomacher, I curled up on Kat's bed and wrapped the linen folds of the shift around me. I closed my eyes and breathed in the familiar scent of my sister.

Every night after that horrible night they led Kat away, I slept in her bed, as if in some way I could hold on to her there.

❦⸱⸱❦

ONE NIGHT NEAR THE END OF SEPTEMBER THE DOOR OPENED, startling me awake. It took long moments for me to recognize the intruder.

Ned Seymour's aristocratic face was haggard from sleeplessness, his elegant clothes disheveled from his desperate race to reach Kat's side. That famed Seymour pride was nowhere to be seen as he crossed to the bed.

"Love, I did not get your letters. I gained passage on a ship the instant I knew."

"Kat is not here," I said.

Seymour stiffened at the sound of my voice, as discordant as Kat's was lyrical. "Lady Mary? Where is your sister?"

"They have taken her to the Tower."

"God, no!" He staggered—from exhaustion or shock I could not tell. But as he caught hold of the edge of the door for balance, I sensed he was remembering that horrible place as I did. The suffocating walls, the locked gates. Scaffolds and straw to soak up the blood from the headsman's work. He had attended Northumberland's beheading, I knew. Had he gone to his father's execution so the Good Duke would not feel so alone?

"Kat wished me to warn you that the queen knows everything. Her Majesty is furious."

"She will get over it in time, as her father did. She will have to. Not even the queen can thwart the marriage now. Lady Katherine and I were legally wed in the eyes of the church. We will soon have a child. A child." He echoed softly. "It hardly seems possible. When I left, her waist was slender as a willow wand."

"She is considerably broader now and more frightened. It is a perilous thing for any woman to give birth. But to be brought to bed of a child in the Tower? That is no place for my sister to bring forth her babe." The prospect made me sick. Catherine Parr and Queen Jane Seymour had not survived childbed even when they had had the finest care coin could buy.

"When is the babe to arrive?"

"Soon, I think."

"I must be nearby when her time comes." Ned Seymour gave me a weary smile. "I suspect Her Majesty can arrange that. Perhaps she will show mercy on a husband and wife and confine us together."

❧ ❧

INSTEAD THE QUEEN IMPRISONED HIM IN A SEPARATE ROOM within Lieutenant Warner's house—a little way from Kat's cell. The queen insisted they were not husband and wife at all. But even with such vast power, Elizabeth Tudor could not wrest all happiness away from my sister. For in the cold Tower fortress where Jane forfeited her life, Kat gave birth. Even God seemed to give the union His blessing, some dared whisper where the queen could not hear. For how long had it been since England could rejoice in that rarest of all creatures, a hale and hearty boy born of royal Tudor blood?

Chapter Thirty-one

Mary
16 years old
Whitehall Palace
November 1561

I DID NOT MEAN TO BE A COWARD, AND YET I LET THE WEEKS slide past, embracing any excuse to resist returning to the scene of my living horror. Not that I had completely avoided the Tower since Jane's death, but I had endured it with grim resignation. Kat's imprisonment made that impossible.

I eased my guilt by dispatching gifts to my sister—rosy apples and the dogs she loved, coverlets to block the chill of the Tower's dank walls, and a pet monkey that might distract her with its antics. When I noticed a pretty nightingale singing in a gilt cage, I sent that too, though it broke my heart, reminding me sharply of my sister. Was it the sight of that bird that made me conquer my fear? Or had I merely come to the point that I could not stomach my selfishness another day?

Kat's babe was six weeks old when I braced myself to address the queen. I waited until a minstrel had fawned over Her Majesty's skill on the virginal. When Elizabeth—that vain creature—was simpering over a plate of fruit suckets, I pleaded my cause.

"Majesty, I have a boon to ask," I said. "I beg your permission to leave Whitehall tomorrow afternoon to conduct some business of a private nature." I had hoped she would not question me further, but I was not that fortunate.

Her lips tightened in irritation. "What sort of business?"

"I wish to visit my sister."

"I was told you have an aversion to the place ever since you sneaked out from under my sister Mary's nose to make a nuisance of yourself at Lady Jane's execution."

How could she know that? I wondered. Had not Queen Mary, Kat, and I taken a vow of secrecy? Someone at Tower Green must have spied for Elizabeth. Who could that have been? I must have betrayed my unease, for Elizabeth smiled.

"The Lady Katherine has shamed the once-great house of Suffolk. There can be little to celebrate in the birth of a bastard." She looked so prim, I wanted to slap her.

"Many born under the shadow of illegitimacy have risen to make their families and their country proud." I kept my features scrubbed clean of scorn for her, but I could not stay entirely silent. "I *am* glad that little Lord Beauchamp will not have to labor under such an epithet, though. His parents are lawfully wed, as will be proved in time."

"I see no priest brought forth by Hertford! As for Lady Katherine—" An avid gleam came into the queen's eyes—I had seen it often at the bear baiting she adored. "Do you not think it strange that Lady Katherine would marry and not invite her sister to be witness? Lady Katherine told my examiners that you were not privy to the marriage until she was far gone with child. It would seem you are not her confidante."

"That does not mean we do not love each other."

"Do not grow overly fond of each other now. I have no intention of releasing either Lady Katherine or Lord Hertford. There is no marriage. He merely deflowered a royal virgin, like the dog he is. Do you know what the charge is for such a crime? Treason!" She banged her fist against the arm of her chair.

I hesitated to reply until I knew my voice would not shake.

The queen did not wait for my answer. "You have nothing to say to that, do you, Lady Mary? But then, it is not the first time the Greys and the Seymours have been condemned as traitors."

"The ax has claimed victims from all the illustrious houses of England. Even Your Grace was once imprisoned. Think what a show of mercy meant to you then. Allowing me to see my sister will cost you so little."

Elizabeth stood up, affronted. "This affair is costing me peace of mind, what with the rot people are spewing. That I—Elizabeth, queen of England—should follow your sister's example and take a husband myself. I, follow that woman's whorish ways!"

Anger would not get me passage into Kat's cell. "Majesty, I wish only to see my sister, to assure myself that she is well. Childbed is a dangerous thing."

"Yet I swear the whole country is eager to see me sacrificed upon it! Fine. Visit Hertford's little harlot. Ask how she likes her quarters. She will likely be there until her boy is grown a man."

"I pray it is not so."

"Do you pray as Catholic or Protestant, since your family made great show of going to mass when my sister was queen?" Elizabeth had walked that treacherous rope with more subtlety, claiming that she wished to learn Catholic ways, yet managing to avoid ever attending the mass. I had to admire her for her craftiness.

The minstrel returned, his lute restrung, his oiled beard shining. Elizabeth's attention shifted—she had found more pleasurable game to hunt.

"Do not let this sojourn of yours interfere with your duties, Lady Mary," she said, motioning the musician to draw near. "I will not tolerate laxity on your part."

"I should think you would be glad to be rid of me."

"Of you? Yes. But I take pleasure in seeing one of my proud Grey cousins hold the basin that I spit in after I wash my teeth. Now, get out of my sight!"

I bowed, backing from the chamber, hating her as I had never hated her before.

As I crossed Whitehall's courtyard, I crashed into a fortress of muscle and sinew. A black staff of office clattered to the ground. Pain throbbed in my skull, but a giant's hands caught me, then steadied me with a gentle chuckle.

"Forgive a clumsy dolt, my lady. I nearly trampled you." The voice was deeper than any I had ever heard.

"Do not concern yourself. I am used to being overlooked." I used my forearm to nudge my headdress back into place. I had seen the owner of that remarkable voice at the gate at Whitehall at his post as sergeant porter, though we had only shared the vaguest acknowledgments there. Dismissing this encounter, I started on my way.

"Pause for a moment, I beg you," he bade me.

I did as he asked. What business might he have with me? The sergeant porter was responsible for the security of the whole palace and, because of that, for the safety of the queen herself. Turning, I observed the man more carefully. I had always felt small, but he towered above me like some giant from legend. His face was unlike the aristocratic features of the courtiers, seeming hewn with a woodsman's ax. Oaken and strong, he was like one of the Myrmidons lining the road to Bradgate.

"Are you not Lady Mary Grey?" he asked.

The power in his form made me strain to my full height. Pain bored through my back. My hunched shoulder pulled awkwardly, doubtless making me look absurd. I let my spine fall into its accustomed curve. I tried to preserve my dignity by infusing my voice with my mother's haughtiness. I might be twisted in body, but I was royal and as such far better than he.

"I am Lady Mary. What is your name, sir?"

"Thomas Keyes, at your service." He bowed. The shaggy fall of hair across his brow reminded me of the largest dog in the stables, the one boys threw things at when the animal could not reach them.

The strangeness of our sizes made me feel a kinship with this man. "You are as monstrous tall as I am small, Thomas Keyes. You cannot tell me people do not torment you."

"I tower so far above them, I have to strain to catch what they say. I only listen to those I wish to hear." He gave a wry smile as he retrieved his black staff. I did not want to find him charming. "I find myself anxious to listen to you."

"You will get a crick in your neck leaning down so far."

"It is a risk I am willing to take. I have been wishing to speak to you for some time, but you always elude me."

This Thomas Keyes seemed sincere, but his interest in me made no sense. "I cannot imagine what you have to say. People speak to me as seldom as possible these days."

"Perhaps they are afraid of you," he said.

I laughed in surprise. "Afraid of me?"

"You go about with a most forbidding expression on your face. What's more, they fear talking to you would incur the queen's anger. That does not mean they feel no sympathy for your sister and Lord Hertford. Or for you."

"The Greys of Suffolk do not need their pity."

"That empathy will prove your most useful tool in freeing your sister. Even Queen Mary dared not execute one who held the people's hearts. Elizabeth might never have survived, let alone taken the throne, were it not for those who felt sorry for her. Some people still marvel that Queen Mary did not name your sister her heir."

He might have stabbed me with a halberd, his words lanced so deep. How many times had I raked over those last tortured days of Cousin Mary's life in my mind? If I had not interfered, would Kat be queen, beyond Elizabeth's touch? Was I responsible for this calamity that had befallen my sister, just as I had endangered Jane when I sent Cousin Mary the feather in warning?

"My lady, I did not mean to upset you. I only wish you to know that it grieved me to hear of your trouble and that there are others who feel the same. All will be well as soon as the priest who performed the marriage can be found. He must be, with all the effort Lord Hertford has spent."

Edward Seymour still felt like a glass shard in my palm. I told myself it was because he had gotten Kat with child. Deep in my twisted back I knew better—I loathed him because Kat loved him more than me. "Lord Hertford can be no use in the Tower."

"He has given his servant the task. Mr. Glynne is a friend of mine, and he is moving heaven and earth to find the clergyman. Lord Hertford is determined the queen will not be able to label the wee one a bastard for long."

"The queen cannot find the word so objectionable, since she is a bastard herself."

"It is dangerous to say so." Keyes looked around, to reassure himself no passerby could overhear us. "You must be cautious and take heart, my lady. Let public opinion press the queen to let your sister and her husband go. News of the marriage scandal has swept across England—why, I admitted a merchant from Northumbria into Whitehall three days past, and he spoke of the lovers as if they were Guinevere and Lancelot. A woman should be married, he insisted. Katherine Hertford had shown herself a trueborn daughter of royalty, wedding an English nobleman—an honorable one, as serious-minded as his revered father. Would God show Her Majesty such good sense as to follow her example."

Hope unfurled in my heart. "The traveler said that?"

"He is not the only one who thinks so. Be brave. Good will come of this yet."

"Little good has ever come to us Greys by way of our Tudor cousins."

"Babies have a way of softening even the hardest hearts. I know. My wife gave me four wee ones before she died—they are my four treasures, back on my farm in Kent. There will come a time when the queen will no longer be able to resist seeing your sister's babe with her own eyes. Once she does . . . well. I have never met a woman who did not melt at the sight of new life."

I tried to imagine Elizabeth becoming dewy-eyed over a babe, as Cousin Mary had been wont to do. "I do not think this queen has the heart of a woman, any more than I do."

Keyes raised one bushy eyebrow. "I wager a fine blue ribbon that you are wrong."

His teasing made me uncomfortable. Why was he being kind to me? It made no sense.

"You must come and talk to me again, if you will," he said.

"Why? You wish to tell all my secrets to the queen?"

He looked so wounded, I could not doubt him. "No decent man would betray a confidence."

"Men of court do so all the time."

"A few, perhaps. More strive to be honorable, I think."

I stared at him, seeing that he believed it. "Have you banged your head into so many lintels it has addled your brain?" He laughed, a booming, lovely sound. I smiled for the first time since the guards had taken Kat away. "Thomas Keyes, you think too well of the world."

"Lady Mary, you think too ill of it. Hope is the only thing that makes life worth living."

Did Thomas Keyes work some magic? Scrape a hole in the parched soil of my heart and plant a seed there? I only know I felt a greening inside me, tiny fragile tendrils reaching out of my darkness toward his light.

I tried to do as Thomas did, not listen to the whispers from the darkest reaches inside me. In bearing a son, Kat had already done what one king and five queens had failed to do, including the queen's own mother and Elizabeth herself.

Would the babe soften the queen's cold heart, as Thomas said? Or was the birth of little Edward, Lord Beauchamp, a crime Elizabeth Tudor could never forgive?

❧ ❧

IN ALL THE YEARS SINCE JANE'S HEAD FELL ON TOWER GREEN, I had loathed entering the Tower of London's gates. Now, knowing that Kat could not leave the fortress walls, that old horror turned new.

I followed the guard to a heavy door, heard the sharp yap of one of Kat's beloved dogs, then the squall of a babe. It startled me. Why, I did not know, for had I not come to see my sister's son? Yet as the turnkey unlocked her cell, opening the door to give me passage inside, it took all my will to step into the dimly lit room.

It smelled a trifle sour from the leavings of dogs and the babe's soiled breechclouts, and I expected to see my beauty-loving sister fairly pining away. But Kat looked better than I could have dreamed.

She sat upon a threadbare cushion, one hand lifting her breast from her bodice. She barely noticed the flurry at her door, she was so intent on the babe pressed to her nipple.

The squalling stopped, and I heard greedy, sucking noises. Satisfied, Kat looked up to see who had come. She looked pale from lack of fresh air, but there was something powerful about her that heartened me.

"Mary! It is so good to see you! I was afraid you would never come." She stopped, looked awkward. "Not because you were angry with me, but rather, I know this place has memories that still give you nightmares."

"I brought food, some small comforts for you and the babe."

"Your generosity has made such a difference these past weeks. I will send some of this bounty to Ned right away." She looked so delighted, I could not take offense.

"I suppose it would be a sin to let my brother-in-law starve. I still blame him for getting you with child. It was a brainless thing to do."

"You always were the slowest to forgive anyone who slighted Jane or me," she said with a tenderness that made my throat ache. "I imagine you will not be able to stay angry at Ned once you meet your nephew. Come. Draw close."

I concentrated on keeping my eyes stone dry. "I can see him well enough from here."

Kat beckoned me. "You did not come all this way to peep at him from a distance."

I did not tell her I had not come to look at Lord Beauchamp at all. It was Kat I was desperate to see. But I could never resist Kat when she was in this kind of mood—her voice musical and so warm, it drew me as a cheery blaze draws chilblained hands.

Reluctantly, I edged nearer. Did the babe see my movement? He turned his head toward me, the nipple popping out of his mouth. His wizened little face crumpled in a scowl so much like my lady mother's, he surprised a laugh from me. At the sound he set up a howl loud enough to crack mortar.

"That's a Seymour for you," I said. "I suppose I affronted his dignity."

"He is only hungry. Do you not think he looks a bit like Father?" Kat said, fastening the babe's mouth to her breast once more. "I keep imagining how puffed up with pride he would have been, swaggering about, bragging to all his hunting friends. He would have set the master of the horse to training the boy's first pony without delay."

I could not help thinking Father would have been less amused if he had known Mother would marry his horse master.

"What does Hertford think of his son?" I asked, wishing to erase the grief that suddenly shadowed Kat's face.

Her expression altered just as I hoped it would, and she smiled. "My husband says our Edward is almost as beautiful as I am. Or at least that is what George James told me."

"Who is George James?"

"The guard who offered to show the babe to Ned the day after he was born. I cannot tell you what I felt when the door closed behind James and my son. I spent a hellish hour afraid

I would never see little Edward again. But as you see, James returned my treasure to me." She looked up at me, suddenly eager. "Would you like to hold him, Mary?"

"I do not think that would be a good idea." I thrust my hands behind my back as if I feared she would force the infant upon me. "Babes cry when they look at me. I think my face scares them." I changed the subject to distract her. "Kat, I met someone today—spoke with him, really. He is sergeant porter at Whitehall, so I have seen him many times before."

"Thomas Keyes. He and Mr. Glynne are friends. During the months Ned and I were trying to steal away to be together after our marriage, Keyes was quite kind."

"I like him less now than I did a moment ago. Even so, he told me something I must pass on to you. Even the queen dared not execute one who held the people's hearts. There are many who feel sympathy for your cause and Ned's. Keyes says that sympathy will put pressure on the queen to free you. I wish I was as sure."

"The queen will release us in time, Mary. Have no fear. Great Uncle Henry was far more terrible than his bastard daughter could ever be, and he forgave our grandmother."

I did not mention all those, like Thomas More, who suffered the ax instead of receiving the king's forgiveness.

"Ned and I will be showing our little babe the roses and Hanworth come summer. I would stake my life on it."

I edged nearer the small, mewling bundle in Kat's arms. "Perhaps I will try to hold him, but you must rescue him at once if he does not like it."

He did like it. He stared at me with solemn, slate-blue eyes. When next I visited, he grasped my finger. Come December, I brought silver bells to tie about his chubby ankles. He kicked, jingling in delight. Even the Spanish ambassador sent gifts of oranges and spice cakes, asking me to remember him to my sister.

By springtime I would have given my cunning nephew the heart from my chest should he have reached for it. But there was one trinket I would not part with: a sky-blue ribbon that had mysteriously turned up at my door, one end tied to a miniature golden key.

The day I found it, I marched up to the sergeant porter at his post, feeling more out of balance than I ever had in my life. "This is your doing!" I accused. "My sister is still imprisoned. You have not lost or won any wager."

"I did not buy it to meet our wager." His smile melted me inside. "I bought it because it is the exact color of your eyes." I arched my neck until it ached so that I could stare at him.

"Do you know what I think, Thomas Keyes?" I put my hands on my hips.

Thomas's eyes twinkled. "I am sure that you will tell me."

"I think you are mad."

"I am quite sure of it," he said with a grin.

From that time on things began appearing in strange places. Wheaten wreaths and straw braided in intricate heart shapes, a carved wooden lover's knot, and even a polished silver mirror. When I found the last in my sewing box, the other ladies jeered at me.

"Who would give a mirror to a gargoyle like you?" Lettice Knollys sneered. "Perhaps it is like Perseus facing Medusa—the giver hopes to keep you from turning him into stone!"

Stinging, I charged into the room above the water gate where Thomas lived. He looked up from something he was whittling. A unicorn. A gift for one of his children?

"Did you put this mirror in my sewing box?" I demanded, still furious.

"I did. You seemed to like finding my little trinkets."

"Not this! You have made me the jest of the whole maids' lodgings, giving me such a thing before the world. I am ugly. To give me such a thing is cruel."

Thomas flushed. "It was not meant to be cruel. It was meant to be magic."

I snorted in derision.

"It is," Thomas insisted. "If you gaze into this mirror every day, in time you will see how beautiful you look to me."

"I am not beautiful."

"You are to me." Thomas caught my hands in his. His warm lips brushed my ear. "But then, there are people in this very room who will tell you I am quite mad."

I did not want to thrill to his words, his touch, his voice. I would have been an utter fool to believe him. But something astonishing happened when I looked into Thomas's eyes. The Mary reflected back at me was a stranger. She was not ugly. She was not outcast. She had someone smiling back at her as if there were no one in all England he would rather see.

❧ ❧

CHRISTMAS CAME AND WENT, THEN SPRING ARRIVED AND despite the public pressure to release my sister, Kat remained in the Tower. Even so I continued to hope. How could I help it with Thomas Keyes in my life? Every time we courtiers lodged at Whitehall, my joy in its sergeant porter grew until my heart felt like to burst.

He was the dearest friend I had ever had. I did not fool myself that Thomas loved me. I tried not to imagine it, or hope for it. Yet as we stole hours here and there to spend together, I had never felt more alive.

What must it be like for Kat, having known her husband's touch, sworn the vows, cherished him? Then to have that wonder stripped away? How long had it been since their last stolen moment together? I wondered.

I had just set out for the Tower with another parcel of things for them when de Quadra fell into step beside me.

"Lady Mary, I am grateful to find you. I feared I might not catch you before you went to visit your sister."

"Ambassador."

"I have a plaything for the child. Nothing really—just a toy ship from Valencia—not unlike gifts I have sent before." He looked so bland, some instinct in me mistrusted him. But he hastened to soothe my fears. "I am certain there are others now who follow my example and send your sister tokens of their esteem despite risking the queen's displeasure."

He was right. Those who slipped me tiny bonnets they had stitched or embroidered gowns for Kat's quickly growing babe looked nervous, but the more time the lovers passed in the Tower, the more secret allies seemed to espouse their cause. "I have carried some few other gifts to her," I said.

"I am not surprised people regard her so fondly. During her time at court the Lady Katherine was so charming, she won hearts as easily as the wind carries butterflies. You have known her all her life. You must be used to her engendering such devotion."

"I suppose I am." Had I not always watched Kat with that same, almost breathless admiration? Felt as if I sullied her somehow if I touched her with my grubby hand?

"I am keeping you from being on your way. You must hasten, or it will be dark before you can return from your errand. The streets of London are dangerous at night. But then I doubt anyone would realize you are a princess of the blood. In some ways you are fortunate, I think. You will never be a threat the queen will take seriously. I do not mean to be cruel, my lady, but the English would hardly place you upon the throne." De Quadra chuckled. "I think you could marry if you wished and the queen would barely notice. What danger could you prove?"

Was de Quadra right? My heart pounded as I climbed into the litter I had summoned. There, closed in by the curtain, I lifted the little mirror I kept with me always now, hanging on a chain from my girdle. I looked into its depths, remembering a tale Kat had once told of a magic mirror that would show a maid her true beloved on midsummer's eve.

I did not need magic to see Thomas Keyes's face.

Chapter Thirty-two

Kat
21 years old
April 1562

SOMETHING WAS CHANGED IN MY SISTER'S FACE. I COULD see it the moment she entered the door to my modest rooms in Lieutenant Warner's lodgings. Her arms brimmed with parcels. A joy lit her from within. "Have you news from court?" I asked, the chamber seeming less dismal in my eagerness. "Is the queen softening toward Ned and me? Oh, Mary, please say that it is so."

Mary laid her burdens upon the table that had been too scratched for the finer quarters below. The monkey she had given me leaped up and tried to rummage through the bundles. When Mary looked back at me, she seemed a trifle guilty. "The queen remains much as she has been in regard to your cause. I am sorry, Kat."

I turned and went to the grime-streaked window, not wanting her to see how deep my disappointment ran. My fingers brushed the dusty curtains, ruffling the tatters along the hem where my pups had chewed. I had little energy to stop them. "There is nothing for it but to wait," I said. "It only seemed you were happy about something. I suppose it is selfish of me to imagine that it must have to do with me."

Mary's cheeks reddened. "You know there is little I want more than your release."

The way she phrased it gave me pause. "There is something you want more than my freedom?"

"Of course not!" She withdrew a toy from one of her bundles. "But I want things for myself as well." She went to where Beauchamp hung suspended in his iron walker and gave him the plaything. He joyfully crammed the wooden ship into his mouth.

My sister looked so strange all of a sudden. So . . . separate from me. I might have asked her then what things she hoped for. Instead I apologized. "Forgive me. You always seemed so tightly woven into my life and Jane's. Perhaps because you are the youngest."

Or perhaps because of her deformity, a voice in my head whispered. For whatever reason, Mary had seemed to live *through* us somehow, rather than having a life of her own. But maybe that had never been the case at all. Maybe my own selfish perception had merely imagined it so. I suddenly saw the self-absorbed Kat I had been all those years. "Forgive me. I mean to be cheerful, but it grows harder the longer Ned and I are apart. Our boy is six months old, and I have not seen my husband's face for a year now."

"I cannot imagine how hard it must be for you to stay in this place." Mary looked at the moth-eaten tapestries and the green velvet stools that our uncle King Henry had used to put his feet upon. The purple cast cushion was so threadbare, patches of warp and weft showed through. She ran her fingers over the badly worn cloth of a gold chair. "This was in the state chambers when Jane was queen."

"Most of the things in this room are cast-offs from that time. I keep thinking that these prison walls are the only world our son has ever known. He should be tucked up safe in the nursery at Hanworth, sleeping in the Hertford cradle, a flock of servants granting his every whim. I should be lying in Ned's arms every night, able to tell him how much I love him. The only way I can bear it is that I know this separation will end."

"It will, Kat," Mary insisted. "You have been convicted of nothing, nor will you be. The queen does not dare bring you to trial. More people take your side every day."

"That cannot please our cousin. Sometimes my happiness with Ned seems another lifetime. But he sends me letters to hearten me, writes me poems like the one on my ring."

"There is a poem on your ring?"

"I have never shown it to you." The ring caught on my knuckle. I had to twist it to get it free. I shook the intertwined links free, and they fell into a tangled chain. "Read the lines on each separate ring as you put the puzzle back together." I extended it to her.

"I am wretched at handling intricate things. My fingers are clumsy as sausages. You read it to me and put it back together."

I did as she asked and saw her eyes grow misty. Had I taunted her somehow with love she did not hope for? Yet she seemed less wistful than before.

"You must miss Ned very much," she said.

"James is kind. He brings me gifts from Ned. Flowers from vendors, a sketch Ned did of the babe. It is so like little Beauchamp. I know Ned carries the image in his heart."

Mary examined the parchment. "It is a good likeness. Has he seen the babe often?"

"Only once. I write of all the babe's tricks. Ned has missed so much I would share."

"When we were girls, even when we were all living at the same estate, our parents only saw us to give us their blessing in the morning and check progress on our lessons at night."

"I know I sound foolish," I said, reassembling my ring.

"Not foolish, Kat. It is like you to grow so attached to your babe. You spent your life carrying pups and kittens everywhere you went. You were so tender with them and looked so happy. I have never seen anything look more beautiful than you do when you are happy. How I loved to watch you."

I slipped my wedding ring back on and thought of the hurt I had dealt her. "It seems so unfair that you only share our pain. I wish I had told you of those first stolen meetings with Ned and described our first kisses."

Mary squeezed my hand. "It is lovely to imagine, but we both know that if you had told me about you and Seymour, I would have called love nonsense and insisted the affair would end in disaster. I would have ruined everything."

"You would only have been trying to protect me."

"I would have been acting more out of jealousy. Everything always seemed easier for you because you were pretty. The only way to keep myself from hurting was to convince myself that love was so foolish I did not want it."

"Everyone wants to be loved. I wish you could find someone for whom you feel everything I feel for Ned. The emotions . . . they are bigger than you can imagine."

"I have heard they are near the size of a giant." Mary looked as if she were going to laugh. For a moment she seemed about to say something, then changed her mind. "Kat, I really must be leaving now. I have one more errand to accomplish. I wish to get a length of red satin for a petticoat. Do you think it would look comely on me?"

There was a hopeful light in her gaze. My little sister had ever garbed herself plainly—not from seriousness, as Jane had, but to keep from drawing attention to herself.

"Scarlet would be lovely, but are you really going to buy the satin or are you teasing me to avoid speaking of what is painful? You do not have to hide your loneliness."

"I am not lonely," she said.

"I am glad you have made a friend. The queen's maids can be kind when they wish."

"It is not—" Mary stopped, then said, "When I am with the maids, I always miss you. I think about you here. You are not meant to be sad and alone."

"I have a healthy babe. Ned is well, in a chamber just ten feet away from me. The queen cannot keep us apart forever. Sometimes for comfort I read the Greek Testament that Jane left me. She wrote that God's words should teach me to live and to die. Is it not silly? Sometimes I feel I will die if I do not hear Ned's voice."

Suddenly Beauchamp squalled. I rushed to find his tiny finger pinched by a hinged door in the wooden hull. As I freed him, a piece of parchment drifted to the floor. "There, now, my little man." I kissed his bruise. "Tell your aunt Mary we will need to put her gift away until you are older."

"The boat is not from me. The ambassador, de Quadra, sent it."

I covered the parchment with my skirt. "Mary, I am weary. Perhaps you should go."

My sister gave me a hug, then knocked upon the door. The guard opened it. I listened to the turn of the key in the lock, then heard the rise and fall of their voices muffled by the oaken panel.

When silence fell, I retrieved the paper. I buried it among Ned's love notes, then took them to the window, where I read the contraband message.

Do not despair. You have friends who would spirit you away from here—to Spain where they would mount an attack to place you on your rightful throne.

I imagined the risk, what such an attempt could mean were we caught. Ned being led to Tower Hill to face the ax. Me sharing Jane's fate on the green beneath my window. Our little son an orphan, alone in an uncertain world.

Even with the two of us dead, he would be a threat to Elizabeth Tudor. One she could eliminate so easily. Children are fragile, after all. They die every day.

I thrust the note into the fire, but the words stayed branded in my mind. Would someone attempt to free Ned and me? If Elizabeth knew such a plot was afoot, would she not imprison us even longer, in dungeons harder to reach?

I am afraid, Ned, I whispered in my head. *Oh, love, I am so afraid.*

Mary

Never had I been grateful when the cell door closed between Kat and me, but as the guard turned his heavy iron key, I could only feel relief that I had kept my secret locked up as tight.

Guilt nagged, calling me hypocrite. Hadn't I felt hurt that Kat had not shared her love for Ned Seymour with me? Was I not doing the same thing by refusing to tell her I loved Thomas Keyes?

I loved Thomas Keyes. The enormity of it swept over me, flooding me with astonishment and terror. The match was as unlikely as one of the lions in the Tower menagerie uniting with one of the stable cats, but it was real. What could confessing such a passion do but worry Kat even more, when she had enough burdens of her own to bear?

I did not want to hear her words of caution, see her recoil at the idea, or gently say that Thomas was a commoner while I was of royal blood. I did not want to have to justify why a marriage between us might not anger the queen much at all. As de Quadra said, no one could imagine me on the throne. But of all the reasons I did not confide in Kat, there was one that was most pressing of all: I did not want her to ask if Thomas loved me as I did him.

Did he? His eyes lit up when he saw me. His fingers lingered whenever he could find an excuse to touch me. I touched the purse affixed to my girdle. The coins inside the leathern pouch made a metallic sound when they clunked against Thomas's mirror.

The money was to pay for the red petticoat I hoped might unravel the mystery of what Thomas felt for me. Perhaps if I looked well enough, he might dare to ask—

"Lady Mary." Mr. James interrupted my thoughts. I looked into his grandfatherly face. "Your visits do your sister much good."

"I am glad of it. And of your kindness to her and her lord."

"It is unjust to see them kept apart when they are pining for each other. They both insist they were wed. Hertford has written the queen even pleading for her to allow a second ceremony to be held before any witnesses she cared to name. Her Majesty refuses. Hertford is near sick with missing Lady Katherine and the boy. I see your sister grieving for her husband, and I am near brought to tears myself."

"I feel the same."

"Why can't the queen let them watch their little son together and laugh at his antics? He is such a winsome, wee lad. My wife and I are not of their station, I know, but Lady Katherine is so tender, and Hertford craves the tiniest news of her each time I see him. It quite breaks my heart. What harm could there be in allowing them to see each other?"

I looked up at James, every nerve in my body suddenly alert. He had been kind to Kat, and his words hinted that kindness might be stretched farther with the right inducement. My fingers touched the pouch of money at my waist. "It is cruel to keep a family apart. It seems even more so since it is being done to my sister. When we were children, Lady Katherine would ever intervene when someone was cruel to one of the animals. There were so many times she could have been hurt. I remember the stable hands scolding her, even our father reprimanding her, but when some innocent, helpless creature was suffering, she would not be dissuaded. She said she did not care if the animal bit her. It was frightened and helpless and had done nothing to deserve ill treatment. She said that if she turned her back and did nothing to help it, it made her part of the wickedness."

"I did not know Lady Katherine was wise as well as beautiful."

I looked up at Mr. James. "Do you believe as my sister believes?"

"I do. I see enough cruelty in these walls. I do what I can to stop it."

"Would you ease my sister's pain if you could, Mr. James?"

Suddenly he looked worried. "I am a loyal Englishman and servant of the queen."

"As you should be. But would England fall if you left the door to my sister's cell unlocked? She could not escape carrying her babe and all he would need to survive. You would be on guard to make certain of that. Would it be such a terrible thing to allow Hertford to go to her for some small while?"

"I do not know."

I unfastened my purse with trembling fingers, knowing what this gamble could cost me. If word of it reached the queen, I would likely join my sister in these dank walls.

"Mr. James, allowing my sister and her husband to have some brief hours together in their imprisonment harms no one. But it would give great joy to two people who love each other."

"The queen's officers would not see it that way."

"How would they ever know? I beg you, take this purse for your kindness to my sister."

Mr. James eyed it, tempted yet wary. "I am not a man whose conscience can be bought."

"I would not insult you by trying. This purse is a gift freely given. I only ask that you let your conscience guide you. Think of your wife and babes, of my sister and her little son. Think what it must mean to a husband and father cut off from those he loves most. Think what is cruel and what you might do to ease the injustice."

"It is not right to keep them apart," he growled low. "It is not right."

I prayed that he was as brave as Kat had been in Bradgate's stable yard, risking her own safety to spare innocents pain.

Chapter Thirty-three

Kat
Tower of London
May 1562

SOMETHING WAS TROUBLING MR. JAMES. IN THE WEEKS since the arrival of the wooden ship, his kindly smile turned more often to a thoughtful frown, one that darkened those rare times my sister was able to steal away from court. He still carried letters that gave me glimpses into my lord husband's days, but James's nerves seemed to be drawing tighter as if he warred over something in his mind.

I could only imagine what that something might be. Did he know about the secret communication from de Quadra? That the Spanish hoped to spirit me away from English shores? True, I had burned the ambassador's note, but if such plots were being hatched, there would be other missives, other conspirators, other people who might make mistakes that revealed the Spaniard's plans—fearful parties like Courtenay, who had saved his own skin by turning traitor to his companions before the Wyatt rebellion.

Jane had not been involved in Wyatt's plot, but she had lost her head all the same. Could that happen to Ned and to me? The possibility of disaster left me chill as a grave.

Even if no one had yet caught wind of the Spaniards' plot, it was evident that some sort of trouble was brewing. Had James or Lieutenant Warner felt compelled to reveal to the queen's secretary William Cecil or to her spymaster Francis Walsingham that Ned and I were writing to each other? Were those powerful men demanding to read the missives we sent?

I blushed at the thought of cold, calculating eyes poring over every intimate word I had written to my husband. I could only imagine Cecil's disgust. How angry he must have been when he learned of our marriage—it rendered his political maneuverings fruitless, dashed his plans to use me to keep England safe.

It hadn't dashed them entirely, if Mary and de Quadra were to be believed. Many supported Ned and me. But it had made them more difficult—more dangerous—indeed.

Unable to bear the suspense, I decided to address my guard forthrightly. When he entered the chamber to deliver a basket of food and candles from Ned's poet friend Thomas Sackville, I stopped him.

"Mr. James, you seem much worried of late. I hope I have done nothing to add to your list of cares."

He started, and I knew that whatever was disturbing him had to do with me. "You must not concern yourself, my lady. There are parts of my job that I cannot like, but it is not your fault. It is just that you remind me of my own girls. They are not as fine as you, I mean no insult, but there is sweetness in you that they share."

So fatherly was his tone, I could imagine him with his children. It made me wistful. "I hope your daughters know how fortunate they are to have you. You have been so kind to Lord Hertford and me, made this time in the Tower bearable."

He protested, but I held up my hand to silence him. "It is true. You must perform your duty. I know that. But you do so with honor and tender care, giving my family all the dignity you are able to. You are a great friend, and neither Lord Hertford nor I nor our son will ever forget your friendship."

James's face contorted. "I am a coward, or I would do far more."

"What can you do? Can you open prison doors and set us free? Not without forfeiting your own life and crushing your family's fortunes. Besides, you are a loyal man, one of noble spirit. You have taken an oath to the queen. My lord husband is a man of loyalty as well. Do you know how many times he has been interrogated, pressed to recant and say we are not legally wed? They have used every weapon possible against him, and he stands firm."

"You sound surprised by that. I cannot imagine any man worth the name would forsake his wife. Especially if he loved her."

"My first husband did so."

"Pembroke's son, was he not? I remember the gossip. Bad business, that."

"I did not know it was the most fortunate day of my life, the day Pembroke saw that marriage annulled. For if I had not suffered that humiliation and heartbreak, I would never have become Lord Hertford's wife, and we would never have been blessed with our beautiful boy. I live for the day I am able to watch the two of them together in Hanworth's garden, where my lord and I met." I smiled at James, teasing. "You could not arrange that for me, could you, my kind friend? An afternoon in the country? I would return to my cell quite docile afterward."

James tugged at his doublet. "I could not arrange anything so grand," he said. "But I have a feeling you would quite blossom if you had an hour of your husband's company anywhere at all. Even in this very room." Something shifted in James's face. "It is wrong to keep a husband and wife apart from each other. It is against God and nature."

A squawk from the corner made me jump, and I hurried over to where my pet monkey was tormenting the nightingale in its cage. The monkey's little fist was wrapped tight about the bird's wing feather. He had hauled the wing through the bars and was wriggling it to and fro so the sharp beak could not reach him.

"Stop that now, you great bully!" I scolded, maneuvering him closer to the cage to ease the bird's pain while I loosened the monkey's grasp. The frenzied bird pecked my fingers with its beak.

"My lady, you must not!" James cried, coming to my aid. But before he could, the nightingale flapped to the far side of its cage, feathers rumpled, wing dragging, but free of the monkey. Thwarted, the monkey squealed and scampered to the other side of the room.

"Hell-born beast!" James surprised me with his rage. "Look what mischief he has caused. You are bleeding, child."

He fished a kerchchief from a pouch at his waist, dunked the coarse linen in a ewer of water, and dabbed at the wounds. After a moment James looked up to see how I fared. Tears were tracking my cheeks.

"Does it hurt terrible much, my lady? The stupid bird was but panicked. It did not mean you harm. Dry up your tears."

"I do not weep from pain. It is just . . . I was remembering how angry my father would get at times like these. I would get myself kicked or scratched or bitten interfering in fights between the animals at Bradgate. Once he even struck me—there was a pup who was born without a leg. The bitch who had whelped the pup seemed to know Father meant to kill it. She fought and snapped at him until he whipped her to submission. I tried to save the poor mama and got bit for my pains. I could not understand why the pup should be destroyed. I had seen one of the villager's dogs manage after a wolf had torn off its limb. The shepherd had nursed it through, somehow, and the dog got along quite merrily after. I begged Father to let the pup live."

"What happened?"

"He drowned the pup anyway, right in front of my sisters and me."

"That was a harsh thing to do. He should have sent you away."

"Life is made up of cruel necessities, Father said. We had best develop the stomach for it."

"I've no stomach for it," James said. "Not anymore." His grip tightened on my hand. The dabbing kerchief stilled. "My lady, what would you say if I sent up some coppers of hot water for you to bathe with?"

"What?" I pulled free my hand, startled he would speak of something so intimate.

He flushed. "You will have a visitor tonight if I can arrange it, and I know how my wife and girls like to scrub and comb and don their best garb."

My injured hand curled tight around the kerchief, and I did not even feel the tears in my skin opening again. I started to speak but could not squeeze the words out.

"I will not stand by and watch a sneaking little monkey wrench a bird's feathers just because it can," James said. "It is enough that the bird is in the cage and I cannot set it free." He turned and walked out the door.

An hour later he let in one of the lieutenant's scullery maids hauling two steaming coppers of water. I attacked the grime I had lost the will to wash away as time in the Tower dragged on. Then I hastened about, neatening my quarters, wishing all to be perfect when the door to my prison swung open again.

I prayed James's courage would not falter. I prayed I had truly guessed his intention. I kept Beauchamp awake as long as I could. When his head nodded to his chest, heavy as a rose after a rain, I laid him in his bed. I waited, too nervous even to scoop one of the dogs onto my lap, my ears straining to decipher every sound beyond my locked door. The courtyard beneath my window was quiet when I heard the rasp of the key in the lock.

I sprang up from my green velvet stool, knocking it over. The clatter seemed deafening, and I felt terror it would raise an alarm, send those outside scurrying back from whence they had come. But the door swung open.

My parched eyes drank him in. Prison walls had robbed his face of color and made him appear thinner, older. But Ned closed the space between us in three long strides and swept me into his arms.

His mouth came down on mine, and it was as if we had never been apart. He looked down at our boy, tears filling his proud Seymour eyes. He touched our son's curls and kissed him, ever so gently so as not to wake him.

"He is growing so fast," Ned said. "What would you say if I commissioned a limning of the two of you? An image I could keep forever."

"I would love it above all things, Ned."

"All things?" He turned to me, and despite all the suffering Elizabeth Tudor had put us through, I saw a ghost of that wicked smile that had made my heart beat fast every time we had stolen off to make love. "It has been fourteen months since we bedded."

"How much time do we have before James returns?"

"There would not be time enough for me to love you the way I wish if we had eternity," Ned said, scooping me into his arms and drifting me onto the red satin quilt covering my bed. "Now will have to do."

⨾⨾ ⨾⨾

AFTERWARD WE LAY TANGLED TOGETHER, MY HEAD PILLOWED on his bare chest, our palms fitted together, his strong fingers far longer than mine. "How I have missed you," he said. "When will that harridan queen release us?"

I pushed myself upright, scooted around to face him. He grasped my leg where it was near him and kissed my bare ankle. But I stopped him. "I loathe speaking of things that must distress you, but there is something I dared not put into my notes."

Ned released my ankle and sat up, his brow furrowing. "What is it?"

"My sister Mary brought a toy ship for the babe several weeks ago. It was a gift from de Quadra."

"The Spanish ambassador? That was kind of him. But you did not write of it in your letters to me."

"I did not dare. The gift was not meant to be kind. There was a secret compartment in it, a note hidden within."

Worry turned Ned's eyes dark. "Let me read it."

"You cannot. I burned it. It was too dangerous to keep. He said that his master was ready to help us escape, take us to Spain. He said they would launch an army to take the throne from Elizabeth on my behalf."

Ned paled.

"I do not want to take such a chance with your life or my own. In fact, I do not want to be queen at all, Ned," I said in a rush.

He stroked his chin for a long moment, thoughtful. I dreaded what he might be feeling. "Are you certain, sweetheart? It is much to surrender and would mean leaving Elizabeth Tudor in charge of our fates. She has been no friend to you."

"I know, but I almost feel sorry for her, when I put our babe to my breast, feel his mouth suckle fiercely, and see his little limbs growing straight and strong. I bury my nose against the crown of his head all dusted with feathery red-gold hair, and I pity my cousin the queen in her vast bed of state alone. Everyone knows she loves Robert Dudley, but will she ever have the courage to wed him and bed him and lay a son into his arms?"

"She does not deserve your sympathy, Katherine. She spares none for us. Besides, the country would never stomach a marriage between the queen and Dudley. As for de Quadra's offer, England would not deal well with any queen connected to the Spaniards—not after what happened when your other cousin was queen."

"Do you despise me as a coward for not grasping at the throne?"

"Of course I do not despise you," he said, gathering me close. "I just do not know what the future might hold. God's blood, what a tangle! Most of England believes we married as part of a plot to secure the succession on your behalf, but when it comes down to the mark, all either of us really wants is to be left in peace with each other and our babe. Can you not imagine our little fellow at the pond at Hanworth feeding crumbs to the ducks? Or on his first pony? A fine, strapping animal."

"A gentle one to begin with."

Ned smiled. "A gentle one, then. I have written the queen so many times, telling her we mean her no harm. She does not believe me."

"If she could hear us now, she would have more reason to hate us than ever. We have what she will never know—love that runs deeper than ambition or rank. Have we not just proved it to each other? Vowing to choose our love above any throne."

A soft knock on the door made Ned kiss me one last time, then garb himself. I wrapped myself in my nightgown, and we crossed to Beauchamp's cradle, staring at his red-gold curls upon his bolster. We held hands tight until James opened the door.

Did he see the desperation in our faces at the prospect of parting? It felt as if my heart were being wrenched from my chest.

"Do not grieve overmuch, my lady," James reassured me as Ned released my hand. "I will bring him back to you on the morrow."

I did not fight my tears. "Thank you, oh, my dear, dear friend. Thank you."

The next night James was as good as his word. Ned came to me again, loved me again, marveled over our little son. I could not believe our good fortune. In the end it would have been wise not to believe it. On the third night Ned came to my door. I heard him, his voice, so familiar, so precious, so heartbroken when the heavy panel remained locked between us.

"I love you, Katherine," he told me through the door. "Never doubt I love you."

Should I have been angry that James had lost his courage, or grateful he had given us the chance to say goodbye through the wooden panel? I could not blame him, no matter how I longed for Ned's touch. He had all to lose and nothing to gain by what he had done.

The jailer would not even speak of it. He brought Mr. Hilliard, the artist Ned hired to paint little Beauchamp and me. He praised the sweet miniature when it was finished and carried it to Ned with a note I had written. In fact James went about his duties as if the two nights Ned and I shared had never happened.

His secret might have been safe, but for one small detail.

Ned's seed planted itself in my womb yet again. This time I knew the signs when they came. I wrote to my husband, my love, feeling joy that I was carrying his child. But I awaited his reply as nervously as I might a summons from the queen.

The queen . . . she would be furious. Would Ned be angry as well, knowing the trouble this might bring to our cause?

I could scarce breathe as I opened his note of reply. I laughed, I cried, as I read of his elation. Another babe to be born of our love? How could he do anything but rejoice? But we must keep our secret between us, Ned cautioned. The efforts to acquit us could come to fruition in the coming months. The queen was bound to be furious over the child, and that could delay our freedom. Anyone else who knew of the babe could face Elizabeth's wrath as well.

Ned understood how guilty I felt about not telling Mary about our wedding, but in this matter he was right. Much as I loathed hurting her again, it would be better if my sister could face the queen honestly and say she knew nothing of my pregnancy.

I shuddered inwardly, imagining the force of my red-haired cousin's rage.

As if he read my fears, Ned wrote to soothe me:

You must not worry overmuch about the queen. This babe will only help our case before the people and the parliament. Perhaps I have not yet been able to find the priest who wed us before Beauchamp was born, but we both declared ourselves married before the Archbishop of Canterbury when we were interrogated after our arrest. No thinking person can declare this babe a bastard. Not even a queen.

I pressed my hands to my belly. Surely Ned was right. Perhaps this tiny life would be the key that would finally open our prison door.

Chapter Thirty-four

Mary
Hampton Court
October 1562

O Y OLD NURSE, HETTIE APPLEYARD, WARNED ME that curses are like starveling kinsfolk—their ghosts return to torment those wicked enough to send them on their way. Perhaps that was why the queen suffered in her sickroom. Her bitter loathing and jealousy of my beautiful sister attacked her within.

Or perhaps it was but chance that Elizabeth Tudor was dying, or so her doctors said. Smallpox racked that vain woman's body with seven days of fever. No pustules blistered—the dread disease turned inward, eating away at her strength.

Hampton Court seethed with panic, facing the prospect of war. The queen, selfish fool, had insisted that she alone be the center of England's universe. She would brook no rival for her courtiers' attention, refusing even to name an heir. How many times had I heard her advisers beg her to do so in the years since she had become queen? I could not say.

In the months leading up to this disaster, the argument over the succession had become all the more fierce. The council argued madly, factions trying to outmaneuver one another, while my sister languished in the Tower because of the queen's spite. Some, like Cecil, championed Kat's claim, but others wished to put Mary Stuart, the Scots queen, on England's throne. A smaller number put forth the Earl of Huntingdon or the Countess of Lennox. The queen had dismissed them each in turn, but her impending death left little time for strategy to sort it out. When Elizabeth drew her last breath, chaos would reign. I wondered if some part of her hoped for just that result—for if she could not hold the scepter, no one should.

I paced outside the privy chamber with the others keeping vigil and wondered what we Greys could hope for when Elizabeth died. Might Kat be released from the Tower, where she had been imprisoned these fourteen months, even if she did not gain the throne? Or would she be in more danger than ever, the other claimants eager to steal not only the crown but her life? A bloody purge almost always obliterated those who could contest the right of a new monarch.

What was happening behind the closed doors to the queen's sickroom? I wondered. The missive I had received from Thomas four days past quelled my usual impulse to slip in, unnoticed, and eavesdrop upon what transpired there.

You must have a care, my dear. I could not bear to lose my sweet friend.

His sentiments were more precious to me than I could say. I thought of the hours we had spent talking and laughing in the gardens and in his rooms above the water gate at Whitehall and was glad that the queen disliked me. Let her favorites risk catching the pox, closed up with Elizabeth in that fetid room. Thomas Keyes was eager to keep me safe.

Even so, I lingered near enough to the privy chamber to watch the comings and goings of those who visited the queen and to hear what they said. When the door swung open, the queen's council exited in a flurry, Cecil in the lead. His black robes flapped around skinny ankles, his face so pale beneath his black cap that the three warts on his nose stood out like blots of ink.

"We must have been witless to make such a promise to the queen, Cecil," the Earl of Pembroke complained as I eased myself closer. "Declare Robert Dudley the lord protector of England? How can Her Majesty command such a thing?"

My eyes widened. Was that why I had seen Dudley in the presence chamber an hour ago with that strange mixture of grief and elation on his face? He had approached the throne, stroked it as if it were his lover. Had he always loved it more than Elizabeth herself?

"Can you imagine that popinjay strutting about making a muck of things!" Norfolk raged. "It is not to be borne."

"It will not be," Cecil said, as I pretended to warm myself near the hearth.

"You promised the queen you would see her wishes carried out," Pembroke accused. "Hellfire, we all promised her!"

"Let the woman go to her maker believing she has made Dudley a king in all but name. I have no intention of honoring that promise. Do any of you?"

A murmur rose from the other councilors, agreeing with him.

"Then who will you have take the throne? Mary Stuart?"

"A Catholic who might as well be French as well as Scots? No. There is an obscure edict from the time of Edward III that I will use against her—an English monarch must be born on English soil."

"Will you support Huntingdon, then? The Countess of Lennox?"

"Lady Katherine Grey is the wisest choice," Cecil said in that low, persuasive voice. "She is of royal blood, is already wed to an Englishman of noble family, and she has produced a son. The future succession would already be secured."

"You would have another woman rule?" someone scoffed.

"One who has a husband to guide her in making decisions," Cecil said.

"Better if we could avoid the woman altogether," someone suggested. "We might make her son king and declare a regent. Then we could mold the boy as we wished."

I thought of Cousin Edward. How small he had seemed—a spindly, pale doll, helpless at the mercy of Northumberland. The devil duke had maneuvered him into ordering the execution of one uncle, then a second. When the boy-king was coughing up bits of blackened lung and death would have been a blessed relief, Northumberland had fed him arsenic to postpone death long enough to put evil plots in place.

I thought of my nephew, who loved to cuddle sweetly against Kat's breast. Protectiveness reared up in me as fierce as any lion. No boy-king had ever found happiness or safety in his crown. Kat knew that as well as I.

My sister, there in her Tower prison, had been almost luminous when last I visited her, at peace for the first time since our sister Jane had died. "Ned came to my rooms, Mary, for two precious, precious nights," she told me. "Ned and I spoke, we loved, we made a vow. We do not wish for any crown. We only wish to retreat to one of his small manor houses, to live there in peace with our child."

These powerful men would not allow Kat peace, I knew with sick certainty. Not if Elizabeth died. I hastened to the chapel to do what I never believed I would. I prayed for a miracle—for my hated cousin to live.

It was a prayer God granted, and one I would live to regret come New Year. Misfortune seemed to boil like a witch's cauldron, each calamity more distressing than the last. France exploded into civil war. Catholics under Mary Stuart's uncle the Duc de Guise slaughtered Protestants in the streets of Paris.

The queen lost flesh, as she ever did when stress beset her, and her gowns hung on her frame, her cheeks gaunt. Fear—I could smell it on her. She must be imagining the worst—the cauldron boiling over onto English soil, sweeping her away.

She could not even guess from which direction the deadly flow might come. From the northern Scottish wilds, backed by the treacherous French de Guises? From the Spanish, who seemed to be scheming with the pope himself? Or from inside her own council as they pressured her to wed and battered her with demands to secure the succession, insisting that if she had no child of her own, Robert Dudley was not an acceptable choice?

As the tumult built, I never expected to be pulled into the center of that maelstrom or suffer its fury. Near midnight on the happiest day of my life, just as the January winds began to howl, the queen had me summoned.

Whitehall Palace
January 1563

The rooms over the water gate glowed with candlelight, and the bits of holly and ivy sent to Thomas by his children gleamed green and lustrous. He folded his big frame into a chair that looked small, dwarfed as it was by his long legs and arms. I smiled, leaning against his knee as he spread a linen shirt across his lap and showed me the small stitches, with a pride that touched my heart.

"Cecily, my eldest girl, sewed it with Margaret trying to grab the needle at every turn. They are but six and two."

"The stitches are crooked. Would you like me to reset them?"

Thomas gave a gasp bordering on horror. "Never touch them! I would not change a single one."

I wished the words back. "I do not mean to be critical, Thomas. It is just that when I was Cecily's age, my nurse would have made me tear such work out and begin again until it was perfect." I made a wry face. "My father would never have worn anything that was not the finest."

"I think this the finest shirt a man will ever wear. It was no small task for those little hands to stitch. She might have made a knight's pavilion with the same amount of work as she put into a shirt for her giant of a father."

I fingered the hem, my throat feeling tight. I wondered if Cecily Keyes knew how lucky a daughter she was. "Do your children look like you, or do they favor your wife?"

How I envied the woman who had been wed to Thomas Keyes.

"Margaret is like me, Cecily fair like her mother. The boys, Tamkin and Roger, are a mixture of both."

"Do they miss their mother?"

"She has been dead since Margaret was born, but Cecily remembers her, and Roger, perhaps. Tamkin was barely toddling himself."

I could not help but ask, "Do you miss her, Thomas?"

"I used to miss her very much. Got used to it really, like shoes that are too tight or door lintels that are too low. It hurt, but I expected the pain."

"Was she pretty?"

Thomas's finger hooked beneath my chin and gently forced me to look up at him. "Why does it matter when all I want to see now is you?" He ran his thumb over my cheekbone. "I love you, my little elf, more than all the fairies in the world."

His words struck me as lightning strikes a tree, splitting the last hard trunk and revealing the soft white within. "You love me?"

"I do, and if you were not so far beyond my reach, I would have you for my wife. But a commoner cannot hope to wed a Tudor, no matter how much he loves her."

"He can if the Tudor says yes! In fact, a commoner should obey a princess of the blood if she commands him, should he not?"

"What are you saying?" Thomas asked. I knew what it felt

like to hardly dare to hope for something—did he feel that way now?

"I am saying that I love you. That I will marry you. That you will take me to your farm and let me meet your children."

Joy flared in his gaze, but he dampened it with gentle regret. "That course would not be wise. Look what the queen has done to your sister and her husband. The queen would hardly give permission for us to wed."

"It is different with Ned and Kat. They are both noble, both perfect in heritage and body. We are not. You, my beautiful commoner, and me—a dwarf with a twisted back. No, Elizabeth would have nothing to fear from us." I laughed and held my arms up to him. He stood and swept me up high over his head. I near could touch the ceiling.

"Thomas, do you want to know something strange?"

"What, my heart?"

"I am glad I was born this way. We can be happy, and it will be a threat to no throne."

Thomas kissed me. "It is true," he said. "Our love can harm no one at all." He stopped for a moment, thinking.

"What is it?" I asked.

"We cannot be wed right away. I must dispatch workers to make the farm ready for you. The children must be prepared, and then there is the queen."

"I thought we agreed she will have no reason to thwart us."

"Royalty does not always need a reason. Let the queen herself find a husband. Then she will be more kindly disposed toward us."

"She has not taken a husband yet. I am not sure she ever will. I do not want to wait."

Thomas smiled. "Neither do I, but it will only make the wedding night sweeter. Let me do what I can to shield you, Mary. It is a husband's most important duty."

"And a sergeant porter's," I said wryly. "Keep the palace

safe, keep the peace, quell any disturbance, and keep the rabble outside the gates. Only this time you are the rabble, sir, and my gates are willingly and most entirely flung open to welcome you."

"Things will grow better between your sister and the queen as well."

"You cannot still believe that."

"It grows wearying to hold a grudge overlong. It is a burden the queen will want to put down."

"I rather think the queen will decorate it with pearls and cloth of gold and wear it as a headdress," I joked. "She does not easily forgive, and she never forgets."

"Have faith, Mary. All will end well if we are patient."

"I hate patience," I said. "I want you now!"

He laughed and kissed me and teased me until I had lingered there as long as I dared, the two of us spinning dreams and making plans.

When at last I returned to the maids' quarters, a guard was waiting for me. The other maids looked fearful, as if I were to be carried to hell. "You are to wait upon Her Majesty the Queen at once."

Foreboding washed over me. Had the queen discovered my love for Thomas Keyes? Or had something befallen my sister at the Tower? "The Lady Katherine. Is she well?"

He would not answer. I followed him to where the queen awaited.

I had seen the queen angry. I had seen the queen spiteful. I had seen the queen cunning and subtle and brave. But she had never looked more overwrought than she did now—not even during the reign of Cousin Mary, when Elizabeth was one stroke of a pen away from execution.

Fear, fury, and an air of being betrayed swabbed hot spots of color on her ice-white cheekbones, which were sharpened almost to blades, she was so thin. Her eyes frightened me most of all—the black depths frantic and dangerous, like those of a cornered beast. What had made her feel so hunted? What did it have to do with me?

I curtsied deep, longer than I needed to, grateful to blot out that royal visage that boded so ill. But the brief moment it gave me to think dredged up a memory that chilled me. Mary Tudor in those wild, desperate hours before she died, when she realized her most hated enemy would triumph. I had begged her not to make my sister queen.

Elizabeth's shrill voice made my body prickle with sweat. "Groveling in the dirt will not save you this time or your traitorous whore of a sister! Get up and face me. You will answer my questions here and now, or I will send you to the Tower and hand you over to Master Topcliffe and his rack!"

It was an empty threat, and we both knew it. No noblewoman had ever been tortured, and Kat and I were of blood royal. "I am willing to answer any question you ask, Majesty. I have no secrets to tell worthy of such harsh methods of extraction."

"Liar! Do you mean to tell me you know nothing of your sister's plotting? She has been communicating with the Spanish these past two years. That fiend de Quadra has been sending things to her in the Tower."

"Nothing of value," I protested. "Some oranges, playthings for the baby. Many people send my sister what few comforts they are able, to make her stay less harsh."

"Harsh? Is she in a cold cell as I was? No. She is in the lieutenant's own house, with more comforts than she deserves at her disposal. As for these 'people' you speak of who interfere in the queen's justice, perhaps I should have them hunted like the rats they are! See what they have to say about the plot being raised against me."

"Your Majesty, you say there is a plot—I cannot believe my sister would be part of such a thing. She is so enamored of her babe, she would never risk leaving him motherless. I have heard her say so herself. She wants nothing more than to retire to one of her husband's smaller manors and live in obscurity."

"She told you that, did she? Well, she might have shared that information with Ambassador de Quadra. He and his master hope to put her on the throne."

My heart plunged to my toes. I felt as if my knees might give way. "Majesty, I do not believe my sister would have anything to do with such a plan. She is an Englishwoman through and through. She saw the grief the Spaniards brought into Queen Mary's reign."

"I say she does know! She is sneaking and false enough for anything! I will not brook such interference in my kingdom from anyone—not de Quadra, not the pope or the emperor, and certainly not from a nasty piece like your sister. She dares to defy me? I will teach her a lesson she will never forget!"

Terror filled me, and I remembered the metallic stench of blood soaking into straw as Jane's head fell. I pleaded for my sister's life.

"Majesty, Lady Katherine can no more help what people say about her than you could prevent such talk during your sister's reign. There are so many enemies to speak against her, and she can say nothing in her own defense. I beg you to remember Thomas Wyatt—he rebelled against the queen, but that did not mean you were party to his scheme. I swear on my life she is innocent."

Was she? The question dug its barbs into my mind. I remembered times I had caught Kat trying on the queen's jewelry. I thought of her petulance, saying it was a waste for Jane to be queen. I thought of how many times our father had told her what a fine monarch she would be. She was Ned Seymour's wife now, and I had always believed Seymour hungered for a crown.

"Innocent?" The queen paced the room, near rending one of her gossamer sleeves when it snagged on a chair. "You dare claim her innocent after what she has done?"

"You have told me what others have done, perhaps in her name. She has done nothing."

"Is she not imprisoned for the crime of licentious behavior with the Earl of Hertford? Did she not bear him a bastard son? That is proof of her rebellious temper, is it not?"

"They do have a child," I said carefully, knowing it would be too dangerous to argue that they were wed. God alone knew what such defiance on my part would drive the queen to do. I thought of what Thomas had said about babes healing rifts between people. Sucking in a steadying breath I said, "The little Viscount Beauchamp is a beautiful, strong boy, Your Majesty, with red hair and the look of a Tudor about him."

Had I cast a burning brand into black powder, I could not have caused such an explosion. The queen grabbed me by the shoulders and shook me until my teeth rattled. "How dare you mock me, you grotesque little toad!"

"Majesty, I did not mean any harm."

"I suppose your sister did not mean any harm either when she used her prison as a harlot's lair!"

Oh, God! The queen knew of the two nights Kat and Ned had stolen together! I had caused this fresh disaster by bribing her guard.

"Soon all England will know how they defied me! Those two smug traitors! They will make me a laughingstock when this new bastard is born."

I went limp in Elizabeth's grasp. She released me, and I stumbled back, staring.

"Kat is with child?"

"Do not try to tell me you did not know it!"

I fought tears of shock, felt again the sting of betrayal that Kat had kept another secret from me. Why? It could only have been to protect me. "I did not know," I said, and knew the truth must show in my eyes. "Majesty, they do not wish to harm you. They wish only to be left alone to raise their son."

"Perhaps Beauchamp will be an orphan! Perhaps I will see to it and appoint a guardian capable of breaking that wicked Grey family pride!"

I imagined the cruelty she could inflict on a helpless child. I fell to my knees. "Majesty, I beg you to hear some small plea on their behalf. I ask for their lives in exchange for a service I have done you."

"What could you possibly have done for me?"

"When your sister, Queen Mary, lay near to death, she had not yet named an heir."

The queen kicked over a stool that held her work basket, spilling embroidery silks across the floor. "An heir, an heir—I am sick to death of hearing about heirs!"

"Everyone knew the queen did not wish to give the throne to you, Majesty. You must have known it also."

"I was next in line according to my father's will!"

"You were reformed faith and the queen knew it, and she could not forgive you for the grief caused her mother. We all heard her say most decidedly that you would never follow her onto the throne. Have you never wondered what changed her mind?"

I could see my question had pricked at the queen.

I rushed on. "Queen Mary was ready to declare my sister her heir, to name Katherine in your place. I begged her not to."

"You expect me to believe that? You little fool!"

"My favorite sister died in the attempt to wrest the crown from the rightful heir. I could not lose another sister. I beg you, Majesty, to show mercy because I helped your cause. Do not take the life of the sister I was trying to save."

The queen stared at me with a loathing even deeper and a rage even fiercer. "You are trying to say that I owe my crown to you? A little nothing troll? It is not true! It is not true! Damn you, Mary Grey, and all your house! And damn your sister and her brats! I will make certain of one thing, I can tell you! There will be no more Hertford bastards! Your sister does not tell you her great news? Well, I will let you carry my message to her."

"Majesty."

"Go to the Tower—you need not think to find the soft guards that minded her before. The lieutenant who oversaw her imprisonment thus far is in a cell of his own. As for the other workers, they are under arrest as well."

I thought of Mr. James's kind face. Regret stung.

"Go to your sister and give her a message from me. She had better get accustomed to being lonely, for I vow by my father's majesty that your sister will never see her paramour again."

Tower of London
January 14, 1563

Kat clasped her son in her arms, the bump where her unborn babe grew making her look like an embattled mother in the paintings Father had seized from an abbey. At fifteen months old, Beauchamp was eager and bright and the light in my sister's life. "Mary, what is that strange smile for?"

"You look like one of the paintings Father took from an abbey—one of the Israelite women protecting her son from Herod's soldiers. You are quite a fierce mother, Kat, and a good one. I was wondering where you learned it."

"It just happened when the midwife laid him in my arms. I feel as if I could fight lions to protect him. I can bear almost anything, as long as I know that he is safe. I am sorry I did not tell you about the new babe."

"Do not waste any regret on that. I know you wanted to. You were right to fear the queen's reaction. She is angrier than I have ever seen her."

Kat nibbled at her bottom lip and nodded. "They have

hauled Ned to the Star Chamber and interrogated him. Fined him fifteen thousand pounds for deflowering a kinswoman of the queen, for getting me pregnant this second time, and for breaking his imprisonment by visiting my chamber."

"The fine is a grim one."

"What else can they do to us? I have heard that people in the streets are on our side. They say it is wrong to keep a husband and wife apart. They believe we are married in God's eyes and in the law. I have even heard John Foxe has written a Book of Martyrs that has Jane's story in it, and that has also roused opinion in our favor. Still, the tale of Jane hurts me when I read it. Jane was not a saint, Mary. She was our sister."

I reached out and squeezed Kat's hand.

"I know I am not nearly as good a sister to you as she was, but I wanted to be," Kat said.

I wanted to drive some of the sadness from Kat's eyes, knowing how much more sorrow might be coming her way. I thought of Thomas's way of teasing me and said: "You are my very favorite sister in the world."

Kat shook her head. "Jane was both of our favorites, and—" But suddenly she stopped. I knew she understood why my mouth had crooked in a grin. "I am your favorite *in the world,*" she said. "Jane is in heaven. Mary, you made a jest!" She looked as if I had just achieved some great feat of magic.

"It seems Jane is always destined to be the best among us. You remember Roger Ascham, the queen's childhood tutor? He wrote a book called *The Schoolmaster* where he recorded an account of how he once found Jane reading Boccaccio, saying she was grateful for such harsh parents because it made her love learning. And Sir Thomas Challoner wrote an elegy declaring that Jane's learning was superior to all." This time my smile turned fierce. "That did not sit well with the queen. But I think Her Majesty had better become accustomed to vexation. I have news of my own to share with you."

"Please let it be something happy. I am thirsting for a drop of sunshine."

"This is the happiest news of my life, Kat. I am to be married myself."

Beauchamp squirmed, and this time she set him free. He toddled over to his wooden ship. "Married? To whom?"

I refused to be hurt by the surprise on her face. "Do you remember the sergeant porter at Whitehall? Thomas Keyes?"

"He is as tall as a tree. How could anyone forget him?"

"He is also the kindest, most amusing and tender man I have ever known. He loves me." The wonder of it still astonished me.

"Mary that is—that is wonderful, of course, but I cannot believe the queen approves."

"The queen does not know."

"You are not planning to wed him against her wishes?" Kat asked in horror.

"As you married Ned?"

"That was different! She was not already enraged at our family as she is now."

"She has always hated us, but then it is only fair. We were taught to despise her from the time we were in the cradle. Kat, you must not worry overmuch. The reason the queen hates you and Ned so much is that you are more worthy of the throne than she is and she knows it. The circumstance with Thomas and me is different. We cannot ascend to the throne. It would be ridiculous to think we could. Not that the queen is incapable of being ridiculous. Sometimes when she is in a rage, I think a dousing with an ewer of cold water would do Her Majesty good."

"Mary, you must be careful. It is miserable and painful and frightening, being imprisoned at Her Majesty's whim. Being separated from one you love."

"A more terrible fate would be never to have the one you love at all."

Kat stilled for a moment, then surrendered to that truth. "You are right, of course," she confessed.

"Kat, there is one more thing the queen bade me tell you, though I hate to burden you with such a threat. She plans to keep you and Ned apart. I do not believe she can—not with so many people flocking to your side of the quarrel."

Kat swallowed hard. "I have my little boy, and I know Ned is nearby. I can feel him, Mary, even though walls separate us. He breathes the same air, sees the sky from his window just as I do. The guards who bring me things speak to him, perhaps touch him. It is enough for now."

I rose to leave.

"Be happy, Mary. You always had so much love to give, and most of the time I was too stupid to take it." She rose and hugged me tight. I could feel the bulge of the coming babe against me. I did not know it was the last time I would see my pretty, loving Kat alive.

Chapter Thirty-five

Kat
23 years old
August 1563

ONFIRES SMEARED LIVING FLAME UPON THE NIGHT sky. Bells rang, while people cowered in their houses, waiting for death to call. That dark summer the plague sacked London like a robber prince, its plunder near a thousand dead in a week's time.

I did what I could to keep my boys safe—my darling Beauchamp and Thomas, who was only six months old, so small and helpless, it struck me through with dread—but what could even the most devoted mother do to protect her children from such a terrible foe?

I heard the queen herself was barricaded in Windsor, away from the contagion. She had a gallows built upon the road to prevent anyone who might carry the illness near her. As weeks passed, I began to wonder if she was hoping for the plague to breach the Tower walls, if secretly she might hope Ned, our babes, and I would die.

When news came that we were to be taken from the city, I rejoiced. But when I heard the queen's terms, they struck, cold in my belly.

"You are to be sent to Ingatestone with Lord Thomas, Lady Katherine," my jailer informed me. "The Earl of Hertford and Viscount Beauchamp will go to Hanworth."

I grasped the edge of the chair, the cloth of gold tearing under my grip. "Can we not all go to Hanworth? Her Majesty cannot mean to take my little boy so far away from me."

"There is no mistaking the queen's orders."

"My child and I have never been parted. He will be so afraid."

"Would you rather he remain here in London?" the man asked coldly, always conscious of the fate of the last guards who dared to show us sympathy. "Once this transfer of custody is accomplished, you will not be allowed contact with anyone, not the Earl of Hertford or the Lady Mary Grey."

I felt as if the queen were closing me off from light and air. My knees quaked. "Surely Her Majesty will allow me to hear how my boy fares?" I begged. "She was separated from her own mother as a child. She will let me write to him."

"You are not in a position to question Her Majesty's orders. We set out in an hour's time. Do what you can to prepare the viscount and say goodbye."

Did my wee fellow understand that something dire was coming to pass? Did he sense my heart breaking, though I tried with all my might to hide it? He twined around me like ivy, as if he were trying to melt into me, fuse with me so we could never be forced apart.

I will never forget the feel of my son's sturdy little body being pulled from my arms. How hard I tried not to weep and frighten him even more. "You must be brave, sweeting," I said, "and take good care of your lord father. You will play in the prettiest garden I have ever seen, and have a pony and friends to play with."

He was so small, so much his father's son. He did not wail, though I knew he wanted to. "You and Tom Tom come to see my pony."

"I would like that more than anything. We shall pray for that every night. Until then, you must tell your secrets to this little fellow." I pressed his favorite puppy into his arms. "He will help you save them up until we are together again."

The jailer started to walk away. Beauchamp's lip quivered. "Tomorrow, lady mother?" He asked over the man's shoulder. "Together tomorrow?"

"Not tomorrow, but soon I hope." Panic gripped me, a ripping away deep in my chest. "Mr. Dalton, you must tell my husband that the boy kicks his covers off. He must tuck the quilts around him tight and check them during the night. Also, his shoes are growing too small. I wanted to order larger ones, but I feared whoever made them might bring the plague."

"They will be staying with the Duchess of Somerset. I am sure she will know what to do with the child." *But she cannot be his mother,* I thought. *She can never be his mother.*

The jailer walked through the door with my little son and closed it. The last thing I saw was his eyes peering back at me.

Before the morning was out, Thomas and I left our Tower room as well. We were bundled into a litter scattered with pomander balls to ward off the plague as we wound through the embattled city. Not until we were beyond London's walls did I dare peek out from behind the curtains, show little Thomas his first sight of forest and meadow and unbroken blue skies.

It felt so strange to be in the world again, beyond the fortress walls after two long years. It was all too big, too open, too unfamiliar. I felt that sensation I had had as a child when I dreamed of falling.

I was falling. Falling away from everything I knew. Away from Ned and little Beauchamp. Away from London and my rooms and the noises of the Tower courtyard beneath my window.

After we reached the more modest quarters at Ingatestone, I tried to be brave. But as time dragged on, I could not eat, wanted only to sleep. For when I slept I could dream I held my older son in my arms. Was I a terrible mother to prefer those dreams to caring for the son I had left? Much as I loved Thomas, he could not fill the gaping hole that losing Beauchamp had torn in my heart.

That void widened as my son turned two years old without me. It grew vaster every night I could not feel Ned near me or touch Beauchamp's velvety cheek. I could not even write to them of my love.

I spent hours writing pleading letters to anyone who might help us, to Robert Dudley, to Cecil, all to no avail. As one year fled and then another with no sign of the queen granting us a reprieve, I feared I might never see my husband and son again.

Dread and loneliness hammered at my nerves. I was breaking inside, pieces of my spirit falling away one by one. Desperate, I tried to catch hold of my strength, my will—for Thomas, for Beauchamp, for Ned. But I could not put myself together again.

Chapter Thirty-six

Mary
20 years old
Whitehall Palace
July 16, 1565

OW LONG CAN ONE WAIT FOR JOY BEFORE IT CRUMBLES like the dried petals of a flower, all the beauty sucked away? For two years Thomas and I loved. He drew me into his circle of warmth, friends he had made with his loyalty and kindness, people smaller and often weaker drawn to my steadfast sergeant porter as one clings to an oaken mast during a storm.

I bloomed under his tender care. I learned that beneath even the nastiest bullying by the other maids lay fear. Who could they trust? Each other? They grappled for a handhold in a world of shifting sand, where others were desperate enough or greedy enough to make even their best friends fall.

That was what Elizabeth faced as well, queen as she was. Even Robert Dudley valued her crown more than her love, while she tried to use him to further her own ends. The court watched in outrage as Her Majesty made him Earl of Leicester, openly planning to send him to Scotland to wed their troublesome queen. Elizabeth's intent was to have a loyal Englishman on the Scottish throne. But even that sacrifice was to no avail. Mary Stuart wed one of the queen's other subjects instead, eloping with Henry Darnley, the Countess of Lennox's comely fool of a son. A pretty, petty boy whose

Catholic parents had once stirred rebellion in Yorkshire.

I confess to feeling some pleasure in the discomfiture of my cousin, this woman who ruled our world. She still could not mold it to her liking, stir love where there was none, nor crush love where it flourished.

She could clutch her power, she could rage, and she could pretend to be worshipped by legions of courtiers. But she would never know the richness I knew, the calm, the peace, the *home* I found in Thomas Keyes's arms.

By July of the year of Our Lord 1565, Thomas and I both knew we could wait another year, another five, another ten, and little would change. Elizabeth Tudor could never trust love, so she must loathe it. No wonder she hated my sister so.

But surely she could not feel the same bitterness toward Thomas and me, we reasoned. She could scorn our love openly, laugh at it with her favorites, and mock us easily if she chose. I did not mind. I would have Thomas as my husband until death parted us. She would be alone.

So it was that, come July, Thomas put everything in place for our union. The queen and her favorites were off to another wedding at Durham House, and I was left behind. Strange to think that my opportunity to seize happiness hinged upon Her Majesty going to a wedding at the very place where our fatherhad hurled Kat and Jane into Northumberland's web,my sisters more sacrifices in some bloody myth than brides.

How I missed them. How I wanted them with me to share my joy that night.

I hesitated a moment, peering up at the stars.

"What is it, sweetheart?" Thomas asked. "That is a pensive look on your dear face. We might still call the wedding off if you are having second thoughts."

"No, Thomas. Nothing like it. I was just thinking about my sisters."

"It is cruel of the queen to ban you from even writing to the Lady Katherine or from visiting your nephews."

"I have not heard from Kat since last I saw her in the Tower. But I was reminded of another time, long ago. The wedding the queen is attending is at Durham House, where Jane wed Guilford Dudley."

"I see."

"Jane was so unhappy, Thomas. Beaten until she agreed to the match. Only now do I understand how she must have suffered taking those vows."

"Lady Katherine was married the same night, was she not? To Pembroke's son?"

"Kat loved him. It is so easy for Kat to love. But he deserted her when the seas grew rough. Of all she has endured with Ned Seymour, one thing is certain. He has stood firm in his love for her. Sometimes I fear it will not be enough, that Kat will wither to nothing without him and their older boy."

"She has not seen them since they left the Tower?"

"No. Beauchamp is nearly four years old now, and he does not even have his father to care for him anymore. The queen discovered that Ned was trying to get clerics on the continent to judge the marriage legal, and she grew so angry she sent Ned away from Hanworth into the care of Sir John Mason, a man who loathes him."

"Poor, lonely little Viscount Beauchamp," Thomas said.

I fingered the blue ribbon I had used to trim my wedding gown. "It is painful to be separated from the little fellow, I know. But it troubles me when I hear how unhappy she is. Why can Kat not be content with the child she has left?" I looked to Thomas, confident he could unravel such matters of the heart.

He brushed a tendril of hair from my cheek. "Babes are as different from each other as sisters are, Mary. Each fits a special place like"—he paused, then smiled—"like a key fits a lock. Only one person can open that room in your heart. Think of spring, when all the rooms are open to the fresh air—how sweet it is to breathe. Your sister has always lived in a heart with doors flung wide. The queen has shut her in a tiny room, and she cannot help but long for what she has lost."

I looked up at him—this man who would be my husband—and felt blessed to the depths of my soul. "Thomas," I said softly, "do you know how wise you are? I have spent my whole life shut in a tiny room, allowing even my sisters only glimpses inside. You opened me up, so wide that I could never go back to that dark and solitary place now that I have known love. Poor Kat. To have all the love in the world and have so much of it taken away. It must be like losing the sun. As for Jane—she never had love at all."

"She had you and Kat and her books."

"I will love you enough to make up for what she never had. I will make certain that Jane can look down from heaven and see it. When we have a little girl someday, I will give her the poppet Jane made for me, and I will tell our daughter how much I loved my sister."

"You will never have to tell that daughter how much I love you, my elf. She will see it in my eyes."

We started on our way again. The windows in Thomas's rooms, high above the water gate, shone golden as our hopes and dreams. Behind those glittering panes our future was waiting.

Thomas paused at the foot of the stairs. He lifted me up to kiss me, his mouth soft and warm, his beard tickling my cheek. "I love you, Mary Grey," he said.

"I would rather be Mary Keyes." I reached my arms around his neck.

"So you shall be, my own, my wife. The priest awaits within."

He did, a short man with graying hair. He performed his office there among a cluster of friends Thomas had gathered, determined we would not risk what had befallen Kat and Ned, a single witness dying. I felt beautiful the moment Thomas slid his tiny gold ring onto my finger. I *was* beautiful. I saw it in my husband's eyes.

❧ ❧

ᕼOW DID I EVEN KNOW, TWO WEEKS LATER, THAT MY SECRET marriage had been revealed? No one had told me. I felt it—a crackling in the air—as I knew in childhood when lightning would strike a barn or thatched roof or a tree.

That devil who had twisted my back must have whispered: *Listen to the guard marching nearer, Mary Keyes. This time they come for you . . .*

Strange, I was not as afraid as I should have been. Deadly calm descended over me as I went to the maids' lodgings. I crossed to my chest, opened it. Sifting through petticoats and bodices and shifts, I found the one thing I possessed that mattered: the Thief's Coffer. I pulled it from its hiding place and opened it. Touched its precious store. Jane's wedding glove and my poppet with its mismatched eyes. The iridescent feather that Cousin Mary had returned to me when she promised to spare Jane's life. The disk of sealing wax with a unicorn pressed into it, taken from one of Kat's letters to Ned. A red-gold curl I had clipped from their first Tower-born babe. The blue ribbon I had used to trim my wedding gown and—most precious of all—Thomas's mirror, the mirror in which I saw that love could make me beautiful. I cradled the Thief's Coffer against my breast.

The guard marched nearer, and I remembered something Jane once said: *Sinners must carry with them the burden of all the wrong they have done.* This coffer held my heavy store.

I squared my shoulders and straightened as tall as I was able. Pain wrenched my back, but I did not flinch. I faced my captors like a princess of royal blood. I faced them prouder still that I was Thomas Keyes's wife. The door swung wide, and the scarlet livery of the guards filled my sight. The captain entered, but I did not wait to hear what he said.

"What is to be done with my husband?" I demanded.

The man froze in surprise. "Better to ask what is to happen to you, my lady."

I gave him the fierce look I had seen my mother level at people so often.

The captain answered my question. "Mr. Keyes's breach of trust is a terrible one. As sergeant porter, he was charged with the security of the whole castle. His betrayal of the queen is even greater than yours."

"He betrayed no one. He only loved me, married me. That will not make Whitehall's defenses fall. The queen should be grateful to him for giving her an excuse to banish me from court. She has always hated me. Let the two of us go to Mr. Keyes's farm, as her sister Queen Mary allowed my mother and her horse master to retreat from court."

The captain wiped his brow. "It is not for you to decide. The queen has given me orders that Mr. Keyes is to be taken to the Fleet Prison."

Horror spilled through me. The Fleet was notorious for its pestilence and filth. "It is a death sentence!" I charged. "The queen would have been more merciful to deal him a blow with an ax."

"True enough," the guard said, looking miserable. He knew Thomas, I realized, respected him. But he was hiding something. An even darker secret lay behind his eyes.

"There is more," I said, bracing against yet another blow. "You will tell me."

"My lady, I cannot think Mr. Keyes would want you to know."

"You will tell me!"

The captain's Adam's apple bobbed in his throat. "I fear in some ways your husband's fate will be even worse than death," he said, his voice strangely gentle. "Once I deliver him to the Fleet, Mr. Keyes is to be placed in the smallest cell the jailer can find."

I do not know how I stayed on my feet. I wanted to crumple to the floor. I wanted to wail and shriek and claw out Elizabeth Tudor's vicious black eyes.

I wanted Thomas. To tell him I was sorry. To tell him I loved him. To beg him not to die. Or was that crueler still? Four years Kat had been a captive at the queen's command. I thought of Thomas, his long limbs used to striding across the courtyard, always outside in the sun and wind and rain.

Elizabeth would crush the life from him in a room so small he could not stand, he could not stretch out his legs and arms. She would crush him in that tiny cell because her own heart was so small.

"Lady Mary, you are to go to the Tower," the captain said.

I should have felt terror, but I had none left to spare for myself. My sisters had been there before me, and I had spent a lifetime being closed in by walls. Until Thomas Keyes had flung my heart open wide.

Chapter Thirty-seven

Mary
23 years old
Suffolk House, London
February 1568

THERE ARE MANY KINDS OF PRISONS. WE GREY SISTERS knew. Jane had been locked in the Tower for six months. Who guessed her bloody end might have been the more merciful? Kat had spent seven years without freedom—the only time she had seen the world beyond was when she was shifted between five different prisons. I had been a captive in three. My time in the Tower had been the darkest, that place where I could sense Jane's very bones beneath the ground. When the queen moved me to households far from London, I was grateful to shed the Tower's yellow stone walls, but I carried the guilt with me.

Most recently the queen had moved me to Suffolk House, the home of my grandfather Brandon's third wife—the far younger woman he had wed after beautiful Mary Tudor died. Sometimes I think it was an act of spite on Elizabeth's part to burden the dowager duchess with my care. Fiery and opinionated, my step-grandmother had had her own sorrows— her two beautiful sons, who had been King Edward's friends, had died of the sweating sickness within one hour of each other. She kept their tennis rackets, their garments, even the rings they used to practice tilting—all the treasures of boyhood preserved with tender care.

I admit that Suffolk House was beautiful. But houses—even the finest—were only another cell when their walls kept you from the ones you love.

Was it so unreasonable for Kat and me to imagine we would be granted happiness in our marriages despite their rocky beginnings? Our grandparents had defied a king to wed. They were forgiven, allowed to love and spend their lives free in country air. Who could have predicted that Kat and I would not be so lucky? My Thomas and her Ned remained the queen's captives. When it came to our family, this queen was as vengeful as she was vain.

I spent my hours of captivity writing to Kat and to Thomas of my love for them or to the queen and all her councilors pleading for mercy. Much as it pained me to do so, I begged Thomas to get our marriage annulled so he might be freed. But just as having too few witnesses at her wedding had proved my sister's undoing, our party of friends in the rooms above the water gate proved ours. With so many people privy to our vows, no bishop could find reason to break those ties.

But there are some bonds no one can ever break. Even queens grow to be prisoners in their own royal skins. Though I could not walk free, I gathered the news in the houses where I was held captive as I always had—by listening to those around me speak of what was happening in the world beyond.

Elizabeth Tudor walled herself in with bricks made of her own caution and the fear that had been embedded in her when a swordsman from Calais struck off her mother's head. Mary of Scots was a prisoner of another kind: her jail was fashioned of the ungoverned passions that she had learned when she was the overindulged darling of the French court.

This reckless, selfish woman was what Elizabeth preferred to consider for her heir instead of Kat with her great love for her husband and her beautiful healthy sons? What a pair of fools the two queens had become.

I marked their destruction with interest. What else had I to do?

Henry, Lord Darnley was murdered—and then the Queen of Scots married the man who most believed had killed her husband. Angry Scots lords imprisoned Mary Stuart and crowned her three-year-old son in her place. In England, Elizabeth watched events unfolding, maddened by the impudence of Stuart's rebellious subjects. Elizabeth could see danger in what transpired in Scotland. She feared for her own life.

Bess of Hardwick confided that the queen gathered all the keys to the doors that led to her chambers. She hid them all save one. It grieved Bess that Elizabeth was so afraid. Not I. Let Her Majesty sleep with fear—it was the bedfellow she deserved.

We Greys had many flaws, but we were not afraid. We were born of rebellious blood, determined to seize love despite the cost. It was a toss of the dice, just as Father and the devil duke had wagered three maids for a crown that long-ago day when I spied upon them from behind the tapestry. I wondered how our game of chance would end.

I could not rule out the possibility that the queen might release Thomas. One of Thomas's friends had told me that she might be moved to mercy by his current plight. The new jailer put in charge of him was so vile that any sane person would be revolted by his actions. The man had taken away the slings Thomas used to kill birds he could cook over his little fire. The guard had forced Thomas to eat rotted meat, even dropping Thomas's food into a vat of poison used to treat dogs with mange, then feeding it to him, nearly killing him.

But when Sir Owen Hopton, my sister's current keeper, arrived at Suffolk House the second week of February, all the light in the world seemed to dim. I had dreaded his arrival as rumors of my sister's failing health grew more alarming. Now he held his plumed hat in hands knotted with ropy veins, his kind face dragged down with sadness. He blinked tears from his rheumy eyes. "Lady Mary, it grieves me to tell you that your sister—"

I held up one hand. "You need not say it. I know that my sister is gone." Why did I stop him? Words could not make my loss more real. Kat—dead. How could all that warmth go suddenly cold? If Jane were here, I knew what she would say—that Kat had gone to a better place. We should rejoice for her, not mourn. But I was not Jane. I wanted Kat here. Alive. Gathering flowers and caressing her babes and dreaming of the day she would kiss her husband again. What would little Thomas do without her? And Beauchamp—could either of Kat's sons guess how much they had lost? Would they ever know what a remarkable woman their mother had grown to be over the past twenty-seven years?

I remembered Kat, all her varied faces over time. Kat being scooped up by our father, her small face glowing as he called her "my beauty." Kat dirt-smudged and determined, trying to save one of her stray animals. Kat jealous over Jane's wedding garb but delighting in her own handsome, love-struck young husband. Kat changing after Jane's death and Father's death and Henry Herbert's betrayal. Wounds that had startled the sister who we all were certain was "the luckiest girl in the world."

But those very wounds may have helped Kat leave the confines of her fairy-kissed world and venture forth into a deeper, truer love for Ned Seymour. They may have made her the tender, fierce-loving mother that had awed me, humbled me. Made me so painfully proud of her.

"The queen must be pleased," I said bitterly. Hopton looked uncomfortable. "When did it happen?" I asked. It. My sister's death.

"The twenty-seventh of January."

"No one told me."

"The winter roads were vile, and there were others must be notified before you."

"Perhaps the queen did not think it mattered when I was

told, since she would not allow me to see to my sister's burial."

"We laid her to rest at Cockfield Chapel. The queen gave her a funeral befitting her royal blood. It cost a thousand pounds."

"How generous of Her Majesty. Too bad that generosity did not stretch to allowing my sister to see her elder son and her husband while she lived."

Hopton flinched. "My lady, please know that I did all I could to save your sister. She ate but little. Her heart was filled with such sorrow, she had no hope she would ever see her husband and son again. I think she willed herself to die."

"No!"

He started at my fierce denial.

"No," I repeated, softer this time.

"My lady, I was there. I know what I saw."

"Believe what you choose, sir. I know my sister. Kat would never willingly leave her sons." She would fight. Fight as she had for the life of the pup my father drowned so long ago. Someday I would make certain Beauchamp and Thomas knew that. And Ned. Poor Ned had been separated from Kat and Thomas, then later sent from Hanworth and little Beauchamp because he would not stop trying to prove his marriage valid. He had risked everything for his wife and sons, and Elizabeth had not even allowed him the comfort of telling Kat goodbye. He must be shattered by Kat's death. Was he even now imagining those last moments she was without him?

I blinked back tears and forced myself to ask the question for which both Ned Seymour and I would need the answer: "Was Lady Katherine in any pain?"

"No. She gathered her most treasured belongings to give away, then wrote two letters and asked me to deliver them where she directed."

"Did she write to me?" I could not say how desperately I wanted something to hold on to, some last words, some tangible bit of Kat, now that she was gone.

"No, my lady. She did not have the strength to compose a letter to you. Only to the queen, begging Her Majesty to have mercy on her husband and children, and of course she wrote to Lord Hertford."

"Of course." It was only right.

"Never have I seen a man more brokenhearted than Lord Hertford was when I gave him the news. She sent him three rings—a pointed diamond that was her betrothal ring, a wedding band that was a puzzle ring circled around with the verse he'd written for her, and one last ring she'd had engraved for him just before she died. It read: *While I lived, thine*."

My throat felt too tight to speak. Hopton looked at me, his love for Kat evident in his face.

"My lady, to have a wedding and betrothal ring . . . Lady Katherine must have wed Lord Hertford in truth. She would not lie about such a thing when she knew she would soon face God."

"No. She would not lie."

"My lord Hertford kissed the rings, and he swore by his love for her that he would not rest until the world knew that she was in truth his wife and that their sons were legitimate in the eyes of God and the church."

I could not imagine how Ned would find the priest now. Had he not been seeking the man with every resource available to him these many years? More likely the question would never be resolved, and Kat's little boys would forever bear the name bastard. Thoughts of Kat's sons stirred a new worry inside me.

"What happened to Lady Katherine's son after she died? Lord Thomas was in your charge as well."

"A more woebegone babe you have never seen. Poor lad. I was directed to take him to the earl's mother, the Duchess of Somerset, once my errand to Lord Hertford was done."

I imagined the nephew I had never seen. "Lord Thomas was only six months old when the Hertfords left the Tower. He knew no other family except my sister."

"He was quite afraid, I am sad to say. I would have been hard pressed to leave him at Hanworth were it not for his brother."

"Viscount Beauchamp?" That bright, happy little boy—what had these harsh years done to him? "Tell me of Beauchamp, Sir Owen, I beg you. What is he like?"

"Like sunshine he is—pretty and charming. There is not a soul who could resist him. When the duchess told him the lad was his lost little brother, Beauchamp took Lord Thomas's hand and said, 'Do not cry, and you shall have a cunning wee kitten.'"

"Just like his mother," I said, thinking of a time when Kat had accidentally tripped me and tried to distract me from my scrape the same way. "The boys will have to take care of each other now, with their father forbidden to see them."

"Lady Mary, I have one more office to perform for my Lady Katherine. She sent a gift to you."

My breath caught in surprise and a mixture of relief and gratitude that Kat had remembered me. Hopton drew a cloth-wrapped bundle from the pouch at his waist. He handed it to me. Slowly I unwrapped it. A gold-wire caul set with seed pearls shone bright against my palms.

"Lady Katherine bade me tell you she wore this headdress for her wedding to Lord Hertford. She wished you to have something from that day and said that she was sorry you were not there to share it."

I took the caul in my hands and ran my fingers over the delicate gold web. "Tangled threads made beautiful," I said, imagining the headdress on Kat's glorious hair. The pearls gleamed, as lustrous as her girlish dreams.

"My lady, I am very sorry for what happened to your sister. She was a kind and lovely lady. We were all most fond of her."

I could not doubt him. I had seen the same expression so many times when someone spoke of my sister. "No one could help loving Kat," I said, "except the queen."

Now Elizabeth had won her long battle with my sister. Kat

lay dead, no more a threat to the Tudor throne. Jane had been gone these many years. I was the only sister left.

May 1573

A wintry December sun streaked through the mullioned glass windows that morning in 1569 when I received the most welcome news of my life. Thomas Keyes—my husband—was free. I was still a prisoner of the crown and could not go to him. I could not see him. The queen forbade it, despite Thomas's pleas that we be allowed to live as man and wife. But I could cling to joy as Thomas had taught me, knowing my gentle love was in Kent with his children. A few brief years he knew peace. At least I prayed it was so. For in September 1572 Lord Cobham came to deliver dire news.

My husband—that giant of a man, strong as any oak, kind and healing as spring rain—had died, his body broken by his long, harsh captivity.

I hugged myself tight, trying to remember what it had felt like in Thomas's arms, trying to reconcile myself to the fact that those too-brief memories were all I would ever have of Thomas Keyes. I could not breathe, imagining a world without him in it.

Had he thought of me when he lay dying? Did he blame me for his ruin? Or had he thought of me with the love and longing forever lodged in my own heart?

I closed my eyes to hide my tears from Lord Cobham. Had I killed Thomas Keyes, surely as I had been party to my sisters' deaths? Was I doomed to damn everyone I dared love?

The dowager duchess stared down at the letter that informed me of Thomas's passing. I saw the glob of pressed red wax bearing the royal seal. "You are free, Mary," the older woman said.

"Free?" I echoed. That word had little meaning without Thomas in the world. What use was freedom?

"Where will you go?" she asked. "To Bradgate? I imagine your stepfather would make room for you there."

I hesitated, uncertain, thinking of that palace of my childhood where the Myrmidons stood guard and the brook once laughed between its banks at three wayward sisters. I had heard that the steward had pollarded the tops of the oaks leading up the drive, reminding all who saw them of my sister Jane's execution: the beheading of an innocent. But Bradgate belonged to Adrian Stokes now, and to my sisters' ghosts.

If I could not bear to go to Bradgate, where was I to retreat to? I nibbled at my bottom lip. I had no parents, no sisters, no husband. Kat's sons were with the Seymours. They had no need of me. Besides, even if the Seymours welcomed me—which was not assured—my presence could only remind the queen of the link between our families and delay whatever mercy she might extend to the boys and Ned now that Kat was dead.

But two days later when a legacy arrived for me, I knew where I must go.

Father could not hold a pen to write you himself,

Cecily Keyes had written,

but he wished to send you this.

I clutched the bundle of linen that Thomas had sent me— the shirt his daughter had made for him that long ago Christmas day. I pressed the folds to my face, breathed in the lingering scent that was Thomas Keyes's alone.

Father wanted you to know he loved you very much. He said you were a most formidable lady and wise and funny and kind.

"I do not feel like I am any of those things, Thomas," I whispered aloud.

It is very sad here without him,

the girl finished.

Roger is angry all the time, and Tamkin cries when he thinks no one can hear him. Margaret will not speak at all anymore.

I stared at the script, so carefully formed by what must be Cecily's hand. I handed the note to the dowager duchess. "You asked where I was going to go now I am free," I said as she read it. "I am going to the first real home I have ever had. I am going to Thomas's farm, where I can mother his children."

The dowager duchess stared at me, alarmed. "You cannot mean that! A farm hovel is not a home! You have had the best of homes all your life! Lived in palaces! This Keyes was a commoner, imprisoned all these years. His property must have fallen to ruin."

"All the more reason for me to go, since his troubles came from wedding me."

"He made his own choice. A foolhardy one, but his own nonetheless. This is a stupid course you are choosing—rushing off to a place you have never seen. What do you expect to do once you are in Kent? You know nothing about the workings of a farm."

Her objections to my plans only strengthened my determination to carry them out. "Thomas must have had a steward of some kind tending the place in his absence. What he does not know, the children can teach me."

"You are a stranger to those children. Besides, what do you know of mothering?"

It was true, I thought with a deep surge of fear. What did I know of mothering? I had wanted children as desperately as my cousin Mary had, one more yearning that we shared. But I had had little hope of realizing that dream until Thomas.

My own mother was such a hard woman. I remembered her raging at the three of us: *Why did God not grant me sons? Daughters are worth little enough. And you, Mary—you are good for nothing at all!*

You were wrong, Mother. That simple certainty poured through me like warm honey. *Wrong about all of us and especially about me.* I smiled. *I will go to Kent and love my husband's children enough for both mother and father. I will tell them what a miracle Thomas Keyes was in my life.*

"Mary!" the dowager duchess snapped. "You did not answer me! What do you know about how to be a mother?"

I looked up at her, at all her ladies-in-waiting gaping at us from across the room. I did not care who else I might have to confront. "I know how to love. Thomas Keyes taught me that that is enough."

Kent
June 1573

No one warned me that being a mother breaks your heart as well as heals it, but I welcomed the pain. It showed me I was alive when so many I loved lay dead, beyond feeling this strange brew of fear and hope and frustration and delight.

It was a slow business, winning the children's trust—each one wary in their own way. They watched me, some with Thomas's eyes, some with those of that other woman he once loved. I envy her—his bed, his babes, the exhausting days and worrisome nights when it seemed the crops might fail or the stone fences needed shoring up. What would it have been like to lie in Thomas's strong arms, my head pillowed on his chest, listening to the rumble of his deep voice as he calmed my fears?

I wished I could calm his children's anxiety half as well. *In time, sweetheart,* I could almost hear him say. *You cannot rush the heart.* Then Kat's voice, her hand outstretched to a nest of motherless kittens: *Stay very still or you will scare them. Let the babes come to you.*

But as patient as I had been in three months at the farm, Thomas's children and I seemed no closer to understanding one another. Cecily, at sixteen years old, had been grateful for the help with household chores too heavy for her thin shoulders, but she treated me as if I were still a guest. Roger insisted they could manage on their own, and stomped about the property, trying to fill Thomas's boots. Tamkin was the nearest to accepting me, the gangly, sweet-faced boy so like his father. At times I could even coax him to smile. Margaret pained me more than all the rest. The girl seemed far younger than her eleven years, but she had never known a mother's love and had reason to fear a world that had imprisoned her father. She spoke only to Tamkin, whispering in his ear.

But today I hoped to change that. After a springtime of hard work, they had earned a day to set their cares aside. I promised an outing like the ones Thomas described—taking a basket of food to a meadow by the stream where they could catch trout.

It would have been perfect, if only God had cooperated with my plan. Instead He sent rumbling thunder and rain thudding onto the cottage's thatched roof.

"The whole day is ruined," Roger complained as we gathered for breakfast, the boy looking so disappointed it surprised me. "We might as well go clean out the barn."

Bracing myself, I climbed onto the high stool Thomas had had a carpenter make sometime during our courtship, so when I finally was able to go to the farm, I could sit comfortably at the table. His gesture touched me, as it always did. That simple kindness proved he had imagined a future for us.

As I settled into my place, I saw a bright splash of color beside my plate, a wreath of flowers woven by a child's hand.

"How beautiful!" I gasped.

"Father said you were a princess," Tamkin said. "A princess should have a crown. I wish it was the finest in all the world."

"It is." I thought of crowns of gold and the terrible price they had cost my sisters. "I will keep it forever."

Tamkin beamed.

"Do not tell him you will keep it," Roger said. "People do not keep silly things forever."

"I keep things I treasure."

"A flower crown?" Cecily asked, disbelieving. "It will get dry and crumble all away."

"I will still keep it. I have a special place where I keep the things I love most."

"May I see it?" Tamkin leaned forward, eager.

"Why would you want to?" Roger asked. "There is nothing any good to see anyway. Not if she's putting things like this in it." Roger flicked the crown, and a shower of petals drifted to the table.

An idea struck me. "Perhaps you could all decide for yourself if my little store has anything good in it. At least it will while away the time on this rainy day."

I went to my room and retrieved the Thief's Coffer. I brought it to the table.

Cecily gasped at the finely wrought surface. Roger brushed dust from its edge with a bit of a sneer, while Tamkin hovered over it as if I were about to reveal all the mysteries of the Orient. Even Margaret seemed interested, though as always, she hung back, biting her fingernails. With great ceremony I opened the coffer's lid.

Roger eyed my hoard in contempt. "What is special about that tangle of stuff?"

"Everything in this box has a story connected to it. I have saved them up since I was younger than Margaret is now."

"The stories cannot be very interesting," Roger said as Tamkin reached out to touch the iridescent feather. "It is not as if you have knights in there or dragons."

"There are stories of queens and kings and the Tower of London. Stories of love and of sorrow and of strength. There are stories about your father tucked in here too."

"Will you tell us Father's stories?" Cecily asked.

I felt in the depths of the coffer until I found the hard, smooth oval of Thomas's true love mirror. "Your father gave me this when—"

I had barely begun when Roger snatched the feather from beneath Tamkin's hand. "Tell about this. Where did this come from?"

I chose my words carefully, hoping to pique their interest. "It came from the garden in Bradgate Hall. I tried to trade it to Queen Mary for my sister Jane's life."

"A feather?" Roger scoffed. He and Tamkin began to scuffle.

"Me first! I was the one who had it first!"

"She did not finish telling about the mirror," Cecily complained, trying to elbow her brothers out of her way. At that instant I noticed Margaret in the noisome crowd. She looked so small, so lost, forgotten, as I had so often been. Gently but firmly I brushed the other children away.

"Margaret, you are the only one not shoving. I will let you choose something from my box, and I will tell its story first." For a moment I expected her to shake her head and back away, unwilling to be part of the game. But the little girl crept forward, eyes big.

"Lady Mary, you must not let Margaret go first!" Roger insisted. "She is littlest."

"I was the youngest in my family, too," I said, in the soft way

Kat might have spoken to her sons. "It is hard to be the small one, is it not, Margaret?"

Margaret nodded and edged a little closer. I pretended not to notice, not wanting to startle her. "Choose something, and I will tell you a story," I urged.

Margaret leaned against me as she carefully examined my treasures—the first time she had willingly drawn so close to me. After long minutes her attention fixed on a rag-stuffed figure from the chest. She did not speak—she only pointed to the poppet Jane had sewn for me on the eve of her wedding to Guilford Dudley.

"My sister Jane gave me this one day when I was very worried," I began.

"Jane should have been the one who was worried. She got her head cut off," Roger said. He gave a grunt of pain as Cecily kicked him in the leg.

"You must not say that! Father would not like it."

Tamkin piped up. "Margaret worries all the time."

"Only since Father died." Cecily stroked her sister's hair. I remembered times when Jane and Kat tried to do the same thing to me. Why had I not allowed myself the magic of that touch? They might be vexed with me, might wish to be left alone, but when I grew sad or scared of hurt, they had wanted to offer comfort.

"Perhaps Margaret is lonely. I know I was much of the time. Jennet helped me feel safe even when Jane was in a Tower cell and the world was falling apart, when rebel armies were at London's gates and I could hear explosions in the distance. Jennet even carried my sister's last wish to me when she was beyond my reach in a world where I could not follow."

"What wish was that?" Cecily asked.

"That she wanted me to be happy," I said, touching Jennet's red-stitched smile.

Tamkin frowned. "I think Jennet is bored living in that

coffer," he said. "You are a lady and have no time to pay proper attention to her. Maybe Margaret could tend her."

Even as he said the words, I felt a frisson of panic and wanted to thrust the poppet behind my back as I had when my mother threatened to take her away. But Margaret's eyes grew wide.

Thomas's daughter looked as if she did not believe I would give Jennet to her. I squeezed the familiar soft cloth body one last time, then gently laid Jennet in Margaret's arms. The little girl cuddled it to her breast.

Tamkin was right, I knew in that instant. Jennet had looked abandoned, lifeless in the coffer. In Margaret's arms she was precious again. What if my coffer did not preserve treasures, as I thought, but trapped them in a kind of shell, cut off from light and life?

Perhaps it was time to let go of the things I had hoarded like a dragon in one of the legends Kat loved. Not the objects, really—Kat's wedding caul, Thomas's mirror, all the little stolen pearls I snipped from ladies' gowns—but the guilt I saved with them and the hurt that made me feel ugly and small.

I let each child choose something for their own. Cecily fastened Thomas's mirror to her silver girdle. Tamkin thrust the feather jauntily in his cap. Roger would not choose anything yet, but I promised him he might later if it pleased him.

I spun stories through that long afternoon until my voice grew hoarse and it was time to start evening chores. As I went to put my coffer away, Margaret stole up, Tamkin at her side.

"She wants to give you something for your box. I told her you would not want it."

The little girl crept forward and held out her hand, displaying a rumpled square of cloth.

"It is the first thing Margaret ever sewed," Tamkin said. "She wanted to fill up the space where Jennet used to be."

I looked into Margaret's face, those wide, solemn eyes, perhaps a little less sad now with Jennet in her arms.

"It is a fine idea, Margaret," I said as I accepted her treasure. "Now that Jennet has you to love her, my coffer has room for other things. Like Tamkin's flower crown and your first stitching. Maybe Cecily would let me have a lock of her hair, and perhaps one day Roger might give me one of those glossy chestnuts he is forever polishing on his sleeve."

"Why did you start to save things?" Tamkin asked. "Roger says you must be crooked in your head."

"As crooked in my head as I am in my back?" I chuckled when Tamkin flushed.

"Roger said that, not me!" he protested.

"The day I began gathering things in my coffer, Jane and Kat were busy with some game I was too young to play. I could not keep up even though I kept begging them to wait for me. Kat lost a ribbon, and I kept it because she would not wait for me."

"Sometimes Cecily will not wait for me." A tiny voice. One I had never heard. Margaret.

"I know it makes you sad," I said, "but she cannot help it. That is just the way of things with sisters." I knew that now.

I closed my eyes, picturing the three of us on a bright summer's day at Bradgate. Before Jane was queen, before Kat loved Ned, before we were all swept into futures charted by our royal blood. Even then I knew Kat and Jane were destined to set out on their journeys before me.

"Tamkin, you asked why I started to save my treasures. It was because I feared what would happen when my sisters left me behind. I thought they would take their love with them."

"Did they?" Margaret asked, slipping her hand into mine.

"No. They left it right here," I said, pressing Margaret's hand to my heart. "Now Jane and Kat will be waiting for me. When I join them, my coffer will be full of brighter things. It will make a precious store to show my sisters when next we meet."

I closed my eyes, and suddenly I was in the meadow at Bradgate again with my sisters. Their presence washed over me, so real I could almost touch them. Kat's imagination painted the scene with hope bright as rainbows. Jane's certainty about what was true poured strength into my vision. I ran toward them— pain and grief and guilt and betrayal falling away.

A rhyme spun through my head unbidden:

What have I to wager? Three maids for a crown.
I send them in turn, each to London Town.

So they had—our lord father and lady mother. First Jane, then Kat. Would they have wagered me as well if they had lived long enough? No doubt. But I had wagered my own life in London with Thomas Keyes. Our father would claim that all three of his daughters lost their wager. I know better. Jane won the courage to stand up for herself. Kat won a true and noble man and a pair of sons to lavish with all the tenderness in her heart. I won something precious as well, the knowledge that I could be loved and give love in return. And that I could survive in spite of all I had lost. Those victories my sisters and I won were richer crowns than our parents could imagine, treasures no one could ever take from us. They would be ours—mine and Jane's and Kat's—even after crowns of gold crumbled away.

Edward Seymour kept his promise to Katherine Grey. Forty-eight years after their secret wedding, he found the priest who performed the secret ceremony at Cannon Row. King James did not remove the stain of illegitimacy from their sons because he did not want them to become threats to his own crown. He did, however, make it possible for them to inherit the Hertford titles. Ned died at eighty-two and was buried at Salisbury Cathedral. Their sons had Katherine disinterred and buried with her husband, the two lovers reunited at last. Their love did prove "a knot of secret might," just as in the poem Edward Seymour had engraved on Katherine's wedding ring.

One of the most exciting things about writing historical fiction is the fact that you get to have your characters experience historical events, not with the "bird's-eye overview" of the modern historian, but from the very personal perspective of someone living at the time. Much as I admire many of Elizabeth I's achievements, she—like all of us—had a dark side as well as the bright Gloriana who defeated the Spanish Armada, a feat that has made her an icon more than a flesh-and-blood woman. This triumph was in her future as my story takes place. The Elizabeth that I write about is one with an uncertain future—her crown and even her survival were in jeopardy. Her animosity toward the Grey sisters is a historical fact, and her cruel treatment of Mary and Thomas Keyes was not her finest moment. Her treatment of Katherine and Edward is easier to understand as they could have posed a real threat to her crown. But evidence points to the fact that their union was indeed a love match, one whose resolution is sure to touch the heart.

The Nine Day Queen is based on historical events, but in the end it is a work of fiction. I have sometimes shifted things for the sake of the story. For example, Mary Grey was not in the chamber when Jane was told she was queen. Jane did, however, lie unconscious on the floor as I portrayed, and no one—not even her parents—came to her aid. As to the Duke and Duchess of Suffolk, Henry and Frances Grey, there is some debate now as to whether they were as ruthless and hardhearted with their daughters as was popularly thought because of the scene described by Roger Ascham in *The Schoolmaster*. My portrayal of them is based on Ascham's account and the historical fact that after Queen Mary gained the throne, Jane's mother pleaded for her own life and property and for her husband's. She did not mention Jane.

For the liberties I have taken, I beg your indulgence. This is the story of three royal Tudor sisters who all felt the force of a queen's wrath. As princesses of the blood, they paid a terrible price for their ancestry. In the end each sister decided to live life on her own terms—Jane, refusing to sacrifice her faith for her survival; Katherine, embracing love without the permission of a queen who could not give her own heart; and Mary, seizing her own brief happiness with a man who had not only a giant's body but also a heart equally large.

The historical fact is that Mary was not allowed to raise Thomas Keyes's children, though she became very close to one of his daughters. But it seemed to me important to bring full circle the bond of sisters—hence the final chapter. As I often told my daughter when she was a little girl, being a real princess wasn't all about tiaras and fairy godmothers that make dresses turn from pink to blue. The strength and resilience of women during the Renaissance is a triumph of the spirit worth exploring.

ACKNOWLEDGMENTS

The Nine Day Queen was written during a time when my world was falling apart, then opening up anew. I would never have made it through without the love and support of my family and friends. First, I am grateful to my daughter, Kate Bautch, who has been the light of my life from the day she was born. Ever since she and her husband, Kevin, laid my grandson, Sam, in my arms, I knew she could finally understand just how precious she is to me. Thank you all three for being my North Star above stormy seas. As for Grandma—what can I say? She taught you to cheat at cards, Kate, let you stay up all night and watch Liza Minnelli in *Stepping Out*. She listened to opera because that was your passion. You were two party girls at your overnights, and she was so thrilled with the woman you've become.

To my niece and nephew, Drake and Rianna Ostrom, whose tenderness with Mom while she battled cancer and Alzheimer's disease still touches my heart. You changed pajamas, made coffee, helped steady her halting steps, and brightened up hospital rooms with your nightly visits. In the end, you made her smile when no one else could. I hope you know how much your grandma loved you.

To my dad, Warren Ostrom, who put his artistic career on hold to take care of Mom. I know how hard it was for you and how much it cost your own health. I'm so proud of your exhibits in museums. I know you miss Mom, but she's smiling in heaven.

To my brother, David, who never missed a day visiting

Mom. You delighted her with your mischief from the time you were a baby, and you grew into a man she was so proud of. The greatest gift Mom left all of us was making us more aware than ever of how precious family is.

To the women who keep me sane: Susan Coppula, Maureen Dittmar, Stephanie Wilson, Trudy Watson, Gina Hinrichs, and Sheila Burns. You helped me navigate the uncharted waters of divorce and moving to my own place, and you supported me through my mom's illness. Thanks for giving me a safe place to vent, to cry, just to be me. I'll never forget how you threw together the most beautiful baptismal open house ever at my place the day after Mom's funeral. After weeks of sitting by Mom's bedside and the chaos of funeral plans, I left a house in disorder but returned after Sam's baptism to a complete gift of love. You are amazing and generous, and each one of you is a blessing in my life.

To my agent, Andrea Cirillo, and my editor, Heather Lazare, who gave me an imaginary world I could lose myself in when my world got too real. Thank you for the moral support and for helping make my Grey sisters shine.

To the Divas—Eileen Dreyer, Karyn Witmer-Gow, and Tami Hoag—my long-distance lifelines who hauled me to Ireland when I was listing a hundred reasons I should stay home. You may have saved my life. (But then, you already knew that.)

To Bob Bradley, whose heart never ceases to amaze. Thank you for helping care for my mom as tenderly as you cared for your own the year before. Thank you for bringing peace and love into a time that was filled with turmoil.

To everyone at the Moline Public Library, especially the staff at Dewey's Copper Café, Robert, Salma, Gonzalo, Catherine, and Ashley. You offered me caffeine and friendship and made me laugh. Hugs to all of you.

And last, to a future bright with possibility.

1. All three sisters were used as pawns by their parents. How would you have felt if you had been in their positions? What kind of effect does that have on a child? Do you feel that powerful parents today still use their children to promote their own status? Can you think of any examples?

2. Jane Grey and Mary Tudor were resolute in refusing to change their religion, even when their adherence might cost them their lives. In contrast, Elizabeth Tudor, Katherine Grey, and Mary Grey took a more pragmatic view, willing to accede to whoever was in power at the time. When King Henry VIII broke with the Catholic Church, he set in motion a religious upheaval that would divide England long after the end of his daughter Elizabeth's reign. As monarchs shifted between varying degrees of Protestantism and Catholicism, lives of courtiers and simple people depended on taking an oath adhering to the religion of the party in power. How would you have navigated those treacherous waters if your family had been in danger?

3. Kat and Mary must have felt conflicted, serving the woman who had had their sister executed. Is it possible to love someone yet hate the actions they take? How do you think little Mary survived the terrible time from Jane's arrest through the aftermath of Jane's execution? What do you think it cost Queen Mary when she realized she had killed her cousin for a man who could never love her? Can you think of examples in your own life

where you've had to hide your true feelings—of revenge, hatred, or contempt—in the interest of self-preservation?

4. Katherine went from being the cherished beauty of the family to being an outcast, a self-centered girl to a woman, wife, and mother capable of great sacrifice. How were the hardships she suffered necessary for her transformation? How different would she have been if all had gone well with Henry Herbert?

5. Katherine and Mary Grey were not unique in risking Elizabeth Tudor's formidable temper by marrying in secret without the queen's permission. Many of Queen Elizabeth's ladies-in-waiting and favored gentlemen, including Robert Dudley and, later, the Earl of Essex, faced the queen's wrath in just that way. What were the dangers and benefits of such unions, from the queen's point of view, and from the view of the Grey sisters? If you were faced with such a choice, how much would you risk for love?

6. What kind of a queen do you think Kat would have made if Mary Tudor had done as she threatened and named her as her successor instead of Elizabeth? How might Kat have fared if she had faced the threat of the Spanish Armada?

7. During the Renaissance, a woman's main function was to produce heirs for her husband. This was even more important in families of royal blood. Pregnancy figures largely in *The Nine Day Queen*. Twice Mary Tudor believed she was pregnant: she went into confinement and had to emerge without producing the desperately needed heir to the throne. How do you think the kingdom responded when the queen did not produce an heir? What would you have thought if you'd been a subject? Katherine could not tell Ned whether she was pregnant until she could feel the baby moving inside her. Imagine what it was like for women before they could confirm they were with child.

8. Mary's Thief's Coffer held treasures that reminded her of people she loved. If you had a Thief's Coffer, what might you put inside it? What makes something worth saving? Was she wise, at the end of the story, to let some of her treasures go in order to make room for new things? Are there memories and old talismans that you would be better off releasing?

9. *The Nine Day Queen* is the story of three very different sisters, how they grew and changed, each one dealing with her heritage and the ambitions of those around them in different ways. Which sister do you identify with most? How do the struggles between them relate to family bonds that exist today?